GODLESS COUNTRY

ALARIC HUNT

MINOTAUR BOOKS

A Thomas Dunne Book

NEW YORK

A THOMAS DUNNE BOOK FOR MINOTAUR BOOKS.
An imprint of St. Martin's Publishing Group.

GODLESS COUNTRY. Copyright © 2015 by Alaric Hunt. All rights reserved. Printed in the United States of America. For information, address St. Martin's Press, 175 Fifth Avenue, New York, N.Y. 10010.

www.thomasdunnebooks.com
www.minotaurbooks.com

Library of Congress Cataloging-in-Publication Data

Hunt, Alaric.
    Godless country : a mystery / Alaric Hunt. —First edition.
        p. cm.
    "A Thomas Dunne Book."
    ISBN 978-1-250-06753-1 (hardcover)
    ISBN 978-1-4668-7588-3 (e-book)
    I. Title.
    PS3608.U569G63 2015
    813'.6—dc23

                                        2015017026

Minotaur books may be purchased for educational, business, or promotional use. For information on bulk purchases, please contact the Macmillan Corporate and Premium Sales Department at 1-800-221-7945, extension 5442, or write to specialmarkets@macmillan.com.

First Edition: August 2015

10 9 8 7 6 5 4 3 2 1

For Dark Beauty

GODLESS COUNTRY

There is no one righteous, not even one;
    there is no one who understands;
    there is no one who seeks God.
All have turned away,
    they have together become worthless;
there is no one who does good, not even one.
Their throats are open graves;
    their tongues practice deceit.
The poison of vipers is on their lips.
Their mouths are full of cursing and bitterness.
Their feet are swift to shed blood;
    ruin and misery mark their ways,
and the way of peace they do not know.
There is no fear of God before their eyes.

                               —Romans 3:10–18

CHAPTER ONE

If anyone had asked, Rachel Vasquez would have been forced to admit the stupidity of getting drunk and picking up college boys; good Puerto Rican girls in the city didn't cruise. So she dodged the question before it was asked.

Since she worked for a private detective in midtown Manhattan, traffic, long drives, and stakeouts cluttered her days and nights. Encouraged by some mumbled excuses, her parents chalked overnight absences from their Lower East Side tenement apartment to her busy schedule. Her loco overprotective brothers Miguel and Indio had already stolen all her school years of adolescent exploration, but her job placed her suddenly outside their grasp. They would never catch her at Skinny's, the white dive she prowled on the edge of the Lower East Side.

After September had become October, and then a wild Halloween screamed past, Vasquez realized she cruised out of defiance. Each day, she made the motions of living, but at night her fists clenched and she wanted payback.

So sometimes after work she slid into soft, faded blue jeans, a too tight T-shirt, and running boots from the bundle she kept at the office. In the bathroom before she left, she checked the beads threaded onto the damaged lock of her long black hair, cut short by a knife-slash the previous August; the dark wooden beads melded the loose lock, tucking it above her ear. She always added a small feather to the beads before she went drinking. She crowned herself with a Yankees cap tilted with an East Side twist, then prowled.

The bouncers at Skinny's always passed her with a shrug after eyeing her fake ID, and the dark interior was perfect for her. The speakers blared Pantera instead of Pitbull; dancers swayed and ground. The white boys liked skinny girls—easy for her, a young woman with no curves, to catch eyes. In the drunken darkness, Vasquez took the chances she had left. She always found someone willing to take her home, no matter what her face looked like. All too often the boy she chose clung to her like a prize, bruising her mouth with eager kisses; faint marks from possessive hands lingered afterward like fingerprints on her shoulders and calves. Alongside a few stiff drinks, boys were enough to lift her outside the box of herself. The fierce sex scalded away her memory. While she could taste their sweat on her lips, Vasquez was happy. Late at night she knew the truth: Any hope of more had ended when her face was destroyed.

That Thursday night started like any other. A teeming mass of young people filled the narrow space edged by the wooden bar at Skinny's. Slashing guitar riffs alternated with shouted vocals. Rows of bottles glowed behind the bartender. Vasquez killed a rum and Coke while she threaded the crowd. She brushed away unwanted hands, then paused at the far end of the bar to wave her empty glass at the bartender. While she waited, she began to vibrate with the music, swimming on the dark undercurrent of the rum.

Vasquez found a boy named Steve Hartford, with broad shoulders and a mop of curls that looked in the darkness like honey swirled in chocolate. She caught her second rum and Coke without taking her eyes off him. She paused along the way for sips of her drink and angled glances, then slid as close as his shadow. His hair was as soft as fur and clung to her fingers like rings.

At Skinny's a smile substituted for hello when the music blared. Hartford had bright eyes and a startled grin with a few slanted teeth. He was unclaimed. He rested his hands on her shoulders while they danced, and traced the lines on her palm with a fingertip as they shouted in breaks between songs. Steve was young, cute, and earnestly drunk—exactly how Vasquez liked her boys. She tugged him through the crowd. By the time he entered the pool of light around the door, he realized she wanted to leave.

They stopped at Hy Ly's on Pearl for dim sum and jokes. The night was cold and clear. A student at Fordham, Steve had a tiny fifth-floor walkup in the Heights. After the cab rides and the rushing cold air on the sidewalks, the apartment seemed warm and cozy. He played jazz on his radio, they had a nightcap, and then they explored his bed. Afterward, Vasquez settled into a blissful, rum-soaked sleep.

In the small hours Vasquez wanted slow, sleepy kisses, followed by a face-to-face wound in sheets. Steve Hartford had other ideas; his golden curls were the angelic disguise of a demon. He tried to turn their drunken hookup into a kinky interlude. Vasquez snapped wide awake when she heard the rattle of handcuffs. The sound opened a wormhole to the fight in August that had almost left her dead; she threw a punch without asking questions. A few more punches and a bite broke up the date.

Vasquez wasn't an innocent to bad endings for overnight adventures. On previous occasions, she called a girlfriend to bail her from messes. Isadora's anxious looks reminded her that her friend knew her brothers, a loco mess she should tiptoe to avoid, and held a mixture of guilt; Isadora invited her out onto the limb of cruising. Downstairs in the cold vestibule of the Washington Heights walkup, Vasquez sobered enough to realize she didn't want to be second-guessed.

A fistfight with a hookup was a bigger mess than usual, carrying a couple of complications. Vasquez hadn't brought a jacket. With drunken hindsight, she realized a mid-November night needed a jacket, even though baggage made catching a boy harder. On top of that, she was broke, after splurging her pocket money on a two cab fares, Chinese food, and a bottle of Bacardi Golden Reserve for the nightcap. She needed a ride. The subway stopped well short of her parents' Henry Street tenement, not to mention the dashes for mid-town transfers.

Reluctantly, Vasquez called Tommy Johnson, a boy who worked for NYPD Investigative Services. He was a small-town kid from Ohio, transplanted to the city with some guidance from her boss, Clayton Guthrie. The boy was oafishly cute, with a lingering case of small-town helpfulness that brought him to the hospital repeatedly to see her while she recovered, in August, from having her face rearranged with the butt of an empty pistol, a condition never completely cor-rected despite surgery. Working for Clayton Guthrie included mo-ments of insanity mixed into the pedestrian yawns. The killer was insane; Tommy Johnson was a yawn.

"I'm cold," Vasquez suggested on the phone, once Johnson seemed awake enough to understand. She repeated the address, and then while she waited she took off her running boots for long enough to put on her socks. She considered marching back up the stairs to demand her underwear, but decided Steve Hartford deserved a trophy to go with the punches. She did have the bottle of Bacardi. She settled on the bottom step, hugging her knees for warmth, and drifted on the downward slope of the rum.

Johnson materialized at the door, peering through the glass. He rattled the knob. Vasquez rose unsteadily to let him inside; her legs cried asleep with an insistent prickling. He wore a dark, heavy pea-coat, and held a lighter jacket by its collar.

Johnson brushed by Vasquez. Worry lines on his face morphed into an angry scowl as he studied her. He caught her arm and shook her.

"What're you doing, Rachel?" he demanded.

"What?" she asked, tugging to free her arm. He didn't let go. His grip was as sure as a slugger's grasp on a baseball bat. Sitting at her bedside in the hospital, he'd never seemed large. In the small vestibule he was huge. Vasquez barely came up to his shoulder; he was even bigger than Indio, her middle brother. His anger startled her.

"Look at you!" Johnson whispered fiercely. He dropped the jacket, and plucked at the tag jutting from the neck of her T-shirt. In a hurry, she had pulled it on inside-out and backward.

Vasquez shrugged. "So?" She tugged to free her arm again. Even drunk, she wasn't going to blurt out the apology bouncing between her ears, not for Tommy Johnson. "Let me go."

"That's it?" he demanded. "The time I spent worrying about you, trying not to rush you when you were hurt—holding your hand when you wanted someone to talk—" He shook her, like jabs of punctuation forceful enough to rattle her teeth. "You needed me to get you *drunk*? I can't drink!"

"Let go!" Vasquez fired a sloppy jab, but Johnson pushed her to arm's length and she couldn't reach him. She aimed a kick, but he hoisted her into the air with an effortless jerk. Her foot grazed him harmlessly. The big man was pissed, and she was helpless.

"Tommy!" she yelped.

He lowered her to her feet, and his scowl softened into sadness. "I'm sorry," he said. "Really, I'm sorry." He shrugged his peacoat from his shoulders and wrapped it quickly around her. The warm coat swallowed her almost to her ankles. He slipped into the jacket he had dropped.

Johnson had a recently acquired rust-eaten classic Challenger and some unfulfilled plans for restoration. Some of the original red paint was visible. The old car's throaty engine provided the only conversation during the drive downtown, then rattled like firecrackers when Johnson peeled out after dropping her off on Henry Street.

Vasquez kept his peacoat without a twinge of guilt. In her closet, she had a growing collection of clothes adopted from her boys— jackets, ties, and oversized shirts. She never gave them a second thought. She stripped to sleep, then dragged Johnson's peacoat to her bed. It was as wide as a blanket, and it smelled like *pernil y pastele*, exactly what Mamì cooked on holidays. Vasquez smiled as she drifted to sleep beneath it.

———

Since then, the Thursday night misadventure demanded Vasquez's attention at offhand moments, another item on a list of things that she thought about when she should be doing something else. That wasn't what she wanted. She liked her job as a private detective, at least when she was holding her paycheck or firing her pistols at the range. Her thoughts wandered when they wanted, then returned unexpectedly to leave her holding the bag.

On Monday morning, her boss received a phone call from George Livingston asking him to protect a woman from a stalker. The detectives drove down to Ruger's, a Twenty-fifth Street art gallery, for an interview, but Vasquez couldn't focus. She could see that Stephanie Morgan was scared; the heiress's fear interrupted the symphony of aesthetic in the art gallery like a repetitive discord of screaming. Vasquez drifted, sparing puzzled glances for the bright paintings surrounding them. A clerestory topped the gallery's soaring quadrangle of light cream walls, and a handful of freestanding dividers broke the space into bays and a court. A few silent customers paid the mismatched detectives the sort of inattention due ballboys at the U.S. Open.

"I really do hate bothering anyone with this," Stephanie Morgan said in a hushed voice. She darted glances at the customers, and sighed unhappily when she noticed a clerk watching them with a pinched face of disdain. "I expect I'm probably making too much of nothing."

"Stephanie, a stalker is a serious matter." Morgan's husband, Peter Ludlow, briefly wrapped her slender shoulders with a protective arm. She answered him with an anxious smile.

Clayton Guthrie nodded in agreement. "That sort of thing can build up from a slow beginning," the little detective said, shaping the brim of his brown fedora with his hands as he spoke.

The customers in the gallery carried their coats and wraps over their arms, revealing patterned dresses and sharp-edged Italian suits—except for one hipster in a Nehru jacket pointedly examining a framed street scene assembled from bold colors like a pane of stained glass. By stepping away from the detectives, the Morgans could've blended with the sparse crowd. Ludlow, a tall lean man with a too-even tan, wore a navy suit and a crisp red tie. He gestured with the practiced care of a courtroom lawyer. Stephanie Morgan's creamy skin and honey-blond hair glowed against an umber silk sheath dress. A gold link belt tightened the dark silk around her slender waist.

The detectives looked like AA members searching for a meeting at the wrong address. Guthrie's rumpled navy suit needed some dry-cleaning and replacement buttons, and maybe a dye job to match colors with his sun-bleached brown fedora. The little old man's grizzled fade had more shine than his shoes. Despite that, the clerk's disdain was squarely aimed at Rachel Vasquez; a trail of scuffs led across the shiny white tile floor, directly from the entrance toward her dusty jungle boots, like fingers of accusation. The young Puerto Rican detective wore a yellow windbreaker, a tilted Yankees cap, paint-stained blue jeans, and an angry scowl that didn't disguise sharp-featured good looks.

"George Livingston mentioned that a guy was following you," Guthrie said, "but he didn't spend time on details. What I need is for you to explain what's happening. Start at the beginning, and I'll put it together from that."

The heiress sighed. "I'm sorry. I suppose this might take some time, but I can't leave right now. I need to meet some of these people."

The little detective glanced around the gallery. "Someone's coming?"

"I'm afraid so. Several, in fact. We're having an opening for Werner's new paintings, but I suppose that's less important at the moment."

"Tell him about the festival, Stephanie," Ludlow said.

She nodded unhappily. "That's where this started. I thought I'd only had a New York moment." She sighed, and crossed her arms with a shiver. "I follow the trends in art. Being current, is, well, current. I've been told that I shouldn't apologize for packaging charity with art. I'm an artist—not a talent, I'm too representational . . ."

Ludlow took her hand for a brief squeeze, and smiled gently.

"I'm sorry," Morgan repeated. "I really do know I'm babbling. I must be reminding myself why it's so necessary that I do what I do."

Guthrie nodded. Vasquez watched him wait through the moments of silence, reminded of something the little detective told her before. "Sometimes you gotta let them talk. If you ask questions, a witness works on answering. If they're talking, maybe they say something you didn't know to ask about." She watched Ludlow attend carefully to his wife's mood, and flashed alongside it an image of the casual insult of indifference from a boy at Skinny's, too far drunk to care.

"A great deal of the DUMBO festival features sculpture," Morgan said, and smiled. "Some buyers prefer a good price by the pound. My primary interest is painting, but when so many serious artists open their studios, I can't be finicky. I visit, listen, take notes . . .

"The new park is changing the feel of the festival, I think. More of the traffic is ordinary. I mean, they don't come specifically for the festival. They happen to be caught in the whirlpool, and maybe decide to take a look out of curiosity. A few years ago, I never saw anyone at DUMBO who wasn't connected with art: artists or dealers, critics, buyers, suppliers, advertisers, scholars and students. Now, the festival has a holiday feel." Morgan blushed. "This year I had a few glasses of wine while I visited. There are vendors right on the street, if you can imagine.

"At the beginning of October I visited Prudel's studio. He's sculpting lions in marble, and he has some young men there with him making wrought-iron vines and foliage. The old man is full of ideas. He's very rude to these young men, but it's funny. Afterward, I sat outside for a while. The morning wasn't chilly. I scanned my notes, looked out across the river, and thought about lions. All completely ordinary."

She paused, uncrossing her arms to reach up with one hand as if to check her upswept golden hair, then stopped. "I had my hair down, in a loose tail." She shuddered. "That's how he caught my attention. He ran his fingers through my hair. For a moment, I thought Peter was surprising me.

"*He* seemed startled when I turned and saw him," she said. "I don't know . . . maybe he thought no one could see him, a sort of invisible crazy man. I ran away. I was definitely more startled than he was. I ran away, and he stayed. From that morning, I mostly remember that he seemed ugly and large, massively oversized like a statue. I kept my notebook, because I was holding it in my hand, but I left everything else. I ran all the way down to the park, then spent a few minutes recovering my courage, and I realized I couldn't even call the police. My phone was in my bag. I walked back carefully, looking for him, and outside Prudel's studio it was as if nothing had happened."

Morgan shrugged. "My bag was gone. As the day went on, I convinced myself that that was all that had happened. I'd had a New York moment: an encounter with a strange person.

"Several days passed before I saw him again," she continued, frowning anxiously. "Outside City Hall, the restaurant in TriBeCa. That was only a moment, and he disappeared before I could point him out to Peter. Seeing him from across the street, I realized how large he truly was. Even stooped over he seemed as large as two or three ordinary men."

Guthrie grunted. The little detective eyed Peter Ludlow, an ordinary man larger than both detectives. Vasquez and Guthrie each stood five and half feet, and weighed less than a hundred and fifty pounds. Stephanie Morgan shook her head.

"No, much larger—twice Peter's size." She sighed. "He wasn't outside after we ate, but for a few days after that, I saw him irregularly, always employing a vanishing act before I could show him to anyone."

"Then I did see him," Ludlow said.

"Peter finally saw him across from our town house. He noticed immediately that the man was carrying a camera. I must've always been so frightened that I couldn't notice."

"That did give you an idea, though," her husband offered.

"I carried the camera on my phone ready in my hand until I caught him," she said. She pulled her phone from her clutch, and browsed the archive for a photo. Her face twisted with distaste and fear, studying the photo for a moment before she handed it to the detectives.

The stalker looked startled, caught with his own unaimed camera in his hand. His broad, pasty face was striped with dark slashes from bushy eyebrows above dark, hollow eyes and an overgrown mustache above brown teeth; a misshapen lump bulged from one side of his towering forehead. A brickred muffler collared his thick throat. He wore a black greatcoat and heavy boots. Half-hidden by his body, a blue United States mailbox on a pedestal didn't reach his waist.

Guthrie let out a hiss of surprise, and Vasquez said, "That's walking around in the city?"

Stephanie Morgan nodded unhappily. "I took the picture before he began leaving the roses in my Saab. I keep the car in a garage. Somehow he found the car. He unlocks it, leaves a yellow rose on the driver's seat, and relocks it."

"He's done that four times," Ludlow interjected.

"You showed the picture to the police?" Guthrie asked.

"I did. I can't prove he left the roses. They said that might be trespass, but he isn't communicating with me. He can't be charged with stalking unless he does something overt."

"After the felony, they mean," Ludlow said. "They're worthless."

"Peter, please don't be angry—" She stopped when her husband deflated with an angry sigh. "When I went to the police station, I discovered that the man really hasn't committed a provable crime. They were very nice about being unable to help me . . . Then, as I was leaving, a detective spoke with me. Mr. Walls recommended that a private investigator might be able to gather evidence that could *prove* stalking."

"That was the precinct on East Fifty-first?"

Morgan nodded.

"The One-Seven. Walls is an old guy that never took the exam for sergeant. I'm afraid he's right. Stalking is a crime, but it ain't something the police can solve. It's a crime for a prosecutor to use after something else happens."

"I said that from the beginning," Ludlow said. "Stephanie, I can call someone to warn him away—"

"Peter, you mustn't." Morgan's glance was sharper than her tone.

The tall man deflated again, but quickly smiled at Guthrie. "Perhaps that's something Mr. Guthrie would be prepared to do," he said.

Guthrie studied Ludlow, noting his unscarred face and manicured hands, then shrugged. "This world ain't as simple as it used to be, Mr. Ludlow. Having a look at that man's picture don't convince me he's dull. I won't be warning him. I'm gonna trap him like a rat. You ought not to do anything yourself you wouldn't want to see on YouTube, right?"

Stephanie Morgan sighed. "Thank you, Mr. Guthrie," she said. "I see that we've been sent to a capable man."

The little detective nodded. "George Livingston said to take care of you," he said. The Whitneys and Morgans shared social and business connections that disappeared into the past of the city. H. P. Whitridge was the family fixer for the Whitneys; he paid Guthrie a hefty retainer and kept his pocket full of expense money. Livingston was his hatchetman.

"I'm gonna start this by putting a man in your pocket around the clock. That rat won't get near enough to touch you again. I'll look around to see what else I can do. I'll need a copy of that picture, and some addresses, door keys, that sort of thing. Are you gonna be here for a while?"

"Werner's opening won't end until four o'clock," she said.

"I'll have a man here before then," Guthrie said. He stepped away, and took a picture of Stephanie Morgan with his phone. "He'll recognize you."

CHAPTER TWO

"That rat's three hundred, maybe four hundred pounds," Guthrie said as he started his old blue Ford.

He glanced at Vasquez, in the passenger seat, before he pulled out onto West Twenty-fourth Street. Traffic was light. Distantly, the Empire State Building held aloft a gray lid of clouds above the city.

"We're gonna need a nose tackle to deal with him," Guthrie said.

He glanced at Vasquez again, and she repeated her silence. He shrugged, pulled his phone, and dialed. He turned on the speaker, then clipped the phone to the dashboard. The little detective used a speaker for his calls, saving himself from repeating conversations to Vasquez.

"Hello?" a heavy voice demanded, as Guthrie worked his way into the right-hand lane of Eighth Avenue. Vasquez watched bundled pedestrians hurry along in the chilly November mid-morning.

"Avram! This's Clayton Guthrie," the little detective said.

"You're still alive? I thought I read something in the paper—"

"Very funny. I think that was the other guy."

"You could be right."

Guthrie punctuated the silence with another glance at Vasquez. She was still staring from the passenger window. "I need you to do some bodyguard work for me," the little detective said.

"I'm retired. You should know that. Did you know I have great-grandchildren? One of those is almost ready for a bar mitzvah."

"You owe me, Avram. I don't care if you're a hundred and twenty. I'm not gonna forget."

"You had to go there," the heavy voice said. "All right, already. You're still up there near Macy's, that same old place? I'm near there now."

"Sure."

"But since you mention it, I hear from a distance that Miriam's still not happy with you."

The name caught at Vasquez's ear, but she didn't move. Miriam Weitz had worked for Guthrie until the previous November, quitting before the little detective appeared at Vasquez's door with a job offer. Her name filled the operative box in hundreds of laconic reports in the little detective's files. The dry twist of her words translated into unintended humor.

"So? That don't change nothing."

"I said already that I was coming," the heavy voice growled.

"All right, I hear you. I'm headed that way now."

The little detective's office was on Thirty-fourth Street. He turned into an impromptu parade of subway crowds knotting around some street-carts selling hot food. Guthrie glanced at Vasquez again, who was busy staring from the passenger window. She pretended to not notice.

"Rachel, I'm keeping in mind that you cash the checks, and don't seem to mind the raise."

The young Puerto Rican woman didn't flinch. Her nose was almost pressed to the window glass. She didn't expect to be fired, no matter what Papì said. "I would fire you," he said, again and again. "I guess your boss isn't much of a man, after all. You're late again. For what he's paying you, you should run to reach work on time."

"Cashing the checks means you want the job," the little detective said. "But now I got work to do, and I won't have a spare hand to carry you around like a piece of luggage. You understand?"

"I got you, *viejo*," she muttered.

Guthrie's face knotted with a scowl, but then he let out a breath and concentrated on the traffic. Vasquez relaxed as if a heavy hand had lifted from her neck. Guthrie owed her, but the little man had a heart to match his face—a brick.

He hired her fresh from high school in May, and before the summer ended, took a case that led to a killer. The little detective solved the puzzle, but after the showdown, Vasquez spent the second half of August recuperating in the hospital. That killer, Gagneau, shattered her face.

Somehow, she'd lasted to the middle of November. Cold whipped into the city to replace the searing heat of summer, but she still thought a lot about Gagneau. Flurries of pistol shots broke her dreams, becoming her heartbeat when she realized she was awake, but the gleam of Gagneau's knife was what she always remembered.

During the daytime, Guthrie made her study surveillance tapes, sift résumés, write reports, and wire up electronics. When she left work, she only wanted to forget—even if that was pretending—that among other things, she had killed a man before her nineteenth birthday.

Her own failure hurt worst. Every shot she fired at Gagneau when it counted had missed. Each time the gunfire replayed in her mind, she spent a handful of minutes staring blankly, usually at her desktop blotter, then drew a heavy breath to ask Guthrie why he still wanted her to work for him—but then she would let the breath out in silence. Asking was pointless. The little old man kept a reply ready for any tough questions he wanted to dodge: "You're a smart girl, Rachel. You'll figure it out."

Guthrie parked his blue Ford a half block down the street from the office. A frosted-glass panel filled the office door on the third floor, with CLAYTON GUTHRIE, DETECTIVE AGENCY painted on the glass in simple gold lettering. Two windows lit one end of the rectangular office, and two dark wooden doors opened on the other end—a bathroom and a storage room. Dark wooden wainscoting circled the walls. Two desks, two mismatched couches, a low table, and some filing cabinets cluttered a space too small for two people to avoid seeing each other except by hiding in the bathroom.

The little detective settled behind his desk with a cup of coffee left over from the morning. He transferred Morgan's addresses and itinerary to his desktop computer, then searched for some maps to examine her town house. Vasquez made fresh coffee, after checking the view from the office windows and pausing for a break in her desk chair.

Guthrie muttered some semiaudible remarks ending with "garden," then said, "We have a few things going for us. Morgan's got no kids. Kids make bodyguard-work complicated. Then, they have a town house—"

The office door clattered open and a large man slid through, shutting the door smoothly as he entered. He had short, dark hair, a hatchet nose, and a stern expression. A charcoal suitcoat hung from his broad shoulders like a slack flag. He paused after closing the door to rest a hand heavily on the back of the oxblood leather couch that blocked the door from the center of the office.

"That's a lot of stairs, Guthrie," he rumbled.

The little detective frowned when he looked at the large man. "I should've come to see you, Avram," he said. "It's been a few years, right? How's your health?"

The large man shrugged, studying Vasquez intently as he walked gingerly around the couch. Some of the red began to drain from his face. The leather couch creaked when he settled. "I lost some weight. Now my feet don't hurt as much."

Guthrie grunted. "Abraham Swabe, this's Rachel Vasquez, my new operative." He paused to turn to Vasquez before continuing, "You might be calling him Avram if he decides he likes you." After another look at the big old man, he finished, "I'm having some regret about calling you like that. Are you up for this?"

"I still got some moves. Did you see the door when I came in? A leaf would be jealous." He coughed into his handkerchief. "I'm not gonna kid you. I'm fading. I want to do this, though. I want to clear everything up, you know?"

After a long pause, Guthrie said, "Let me show you the rat." He printed pictures and handed them to the big old man. "The blonde is the client. The rat wants to be her friend—he keeps giving her yellow roses."

"I was that size when my Ruth was alive," Swabe muttered. "He looks like a dozen Cossacks. You need me. You have that part right."

"Okay, then there's an itinerary for Morgan."

"I'm just keeping her safe, right?"

"Sure. Trapping the rat's a separate operation."

"You and—" Swabe glanced at Vasquez, who was pushing paper clips on her blotter like a football coach.

The little detective shrugged. "The whole operation is in three parts," he said. "I need you to do the security while she's active. I'll have some guys to cover her at home. I'm running the surveillance after I look around at the situation. Her town house is over in Turtle Bay, at the end of Fifty-second Street. The laws are tricky, but at minimum I have to catch some trespass."

The two older men watched Vasquez study paper clips while Guthrie spoke. The detective scowled briefly, then continued, "Most important is hunting the rat. He's nesting in Brooklyn."

"Really? Didn't you catch this job today?"

"Sure. But he has to be in Brooklyn. He chanced across the client one morning in DUMBO, at the beginning of October. He ended up with her purse. Two weeks later, he was following her around. So the rat fell in love with her purse, but he chanced on her in DUMBO."

"That's thin. Maybe he happened to be there."

"In DUMBO? The Brooklyn-Queens cuts across there—"

"And there's no such thing as coincidence. I know." Swabe's voice descended to an angry, gravelly rumble.

Guthrie sighed. "Old man, one thing we can't change is the past." He watched Vasquez for a long moment, hidden beneath her Yankees cap, while she added a row of alternating red and yellow thumbtacks to her army of paper clips. He finished his coffee and set down his cup. "Okay, Rachel, I've had enough of the crap."

"I'm listening, *viejo*," she said, and rearranged a thumbtack.

"You're not listening good enough!"

Vasquez looked up at him, startled.

"Go with Avram. Watch what he does, listen to him, and do whatever he tells you." He walked back around his desk. "I got things to do."

Traffic sounds from Thirty-fourth Street underlined the frosty silence in the office while Vasquez checked her pistols before she left her desk. She carried two semiautomatic Smith & Wesson Chief's Specials in kidney holsters: a .40-caliber loaded with blue plastic bullets to discourage trouble, and a .45-caliber loaded with wadcutters to end it. Swabe watched her careful ritual with the pistols and seemed satisfied.

Following Swabe slowly down the stairs, pausing at every landing, Vasquez lost the edge from her anger. The big old man needed to pace himself. On the street, a line of step vans loading clothes was gapped around a white Dodge Ram pickup with a plumbing decal. Swabe lumbered into the street to reach the driver's seat, and unlocked the door for Vasquez as he settled at the wheel.

Swabe drove down to Twenty-fifth Street on Seventh Avenue. The ride to the art gallery crawled through traffic, but he wasn't talkative. Vasquez's curiosity stirred when they reached the gallery. Swabe walked through, scanning every corner, then settled by the entrance to watch. He nodded to Stephanie Morgan when she noticed him for the first time, then waited as quietly as a piece of sculpture.

"I think I have this figured out," Vasquez said. "You stand and watch like the Secret Service."

"That's right. A perfect job for a big dumb Jew."

"So," she said, and stared blankly at him for a moment. "When you give the okay, I'm back with Guthrie?"

"I feel I got to say that he and I have a disagreement that goes back a few years. Maybe you caught some of that by accident. But I didn't get that idea from what he said—clearing you with my okay, right?"

Vasquez let out a hiss of breath, and rotated her Yankees cap like an irritated shortstop. She took a few quick steps away, then turned back. Her black ponytail whirled around her neck.

"I make sure this schmuck doesn't get to her," Swabe said. He squared his charcoal suitcoat, gripping the lapels in big fists, and scowled. "See?"

"*Entiendo*," Vasquez muttered. "I'm not gonna do that."

"That's right."

"What're you gonna do if he's waiting outside?"

Swabe shrugged.

"So I should go out and spot for him?"

"I guess there is a reason you're working for Guthrie." A slight smile tinted his blocky face.

Vasquez drew a breath, trying to ignore the punch of embarrassment in her gut. The old bodyguard's smile revealed a glimpse of the boxtop picture belonging to the jumbled, unassembled puzzle of things necessary to protect Stephanie Morgan. Across the gallery, a handful of buyers surrounded Morgan, enthralled by her gestures and assessments of the paintings on the walls. The young Puerto Rican detective cut Peter Ludlow from the crowd and got the location of Morgan's Saab. Then she brushed past Swabe on her way out.

The traffic on Twenty-fifth Street looked like the last bit of bathwater draining from a tub, splashed by fresh cold from a tap that wouldn't quite close. Tawny brick buildings dropped cold shade onto the street. Vasquez paced the block. A scattering of well-heeled New Yorkers moved with the unruffled composure of unwary pigeons. The street was peaceful. Vasquez peered into alleyways and doors, pausing briefly at big windows to scan the darkness for a glimpse of watching shapes. She caught her own reflection. Above the street, fire escapes, billboard ledges, and water towers hung like empty nests. Vasquez patrolled. After a few minutes, she was satisfied.

On the next block, the parking garage looked like a chocolate and cream torte, with dark layers made from the shapes of cars. Traffic slid and gathered in obedience to the lights. Vasquez studied the hurrying customers with hands crammed in their pockets or full of bags.

The attendant shrugged and waved her into the hollow belly of the building. The crank and whoosh of cars filled the garage with a reek of exhaust that lingered into the silences.

Before Vasquez found the Saab, the shadows moving in the dim interior of the garage spooked her. She checked her pistols. Every few steps, she turned to look down each row of cars and watch for movement. She began checking car windows, to see if anyone was hiding.

"*Estoy loca,*" she muttered.

The four-door Saab was black and blocky, a long shape built as solidly as a tank. Vasquez stooped to look beneath it before she approached. She used a penlight to study the seats and floorboards. A raincoat and umbrella waited on the backseat. A slender tube of plastic sat propped in the driver's seat. Vasquez cursed and pulled her phone.

"You ain't been gone an hour," Guthrie answered curtly.

"*Viejo*, we got a problem." She studied the plastic tube with her light.

"Okay, fill me in."

"There's a rose on the seat of Morgan's Saab."

The little detective cursed.

"It's *red.*"

CHAPTER THREE

A call from Guthrie woke Vasquez early the next morning. She rolled to her feet and dressed by the dim cast of the streetlights outside her bedroom window. The bedroom was little more than a closet, her privilege for being the only daughter, and the youngest child after three sons. A dresser and single bed left an arm's length of space to sit at the window and walk to the door. Her brothers had shared a larger single bedroom when they were younger, but now mostly weren't home at night. Roberto, the eldest, lived in Connecticut and visited the city on holidays. Her middle brothers, Indio and Miguel, spent most of their time on the street making trouble, then dodging being caught for it.

"No more late nights, *hija*?" Mamì asked, pouring Vasquez a cup of coffee as she tried to slink from the apartment. "Mornings again?"

"We got to go to Brooklyn before rush hour," Vasquez said. She considered the coffee, with her yellow windbreaker wrapped around her gunbelt held like a shield against Mamì's questions. She sighed, and sat down at the kitchen table. The laces of her jungle boots were still untied. While Vasquez sipped coffee and tugged at her laces, sausages hissed and spit in the skillet on the stove.

"You could have some eggs," Mamì said. She swept a loose, curling lock of her dark hair behind her shoulder, and frustration showed in the angle of her shoulders. Her dark face turned serious as she paused against the counter in the dim kitchen.

"Mornings are better," she said, after watching her daughter for a moment. "I like it better when you go to work on time."

"I work at night, too," Vasquez said. The lie darkened her pale face.

Mamì smiled gently. "*Hija*, your boss doesn't pour rum in your coffee."

Vasquez emptied her mug and eyed the door.

"I worry, *hija*. First your brothers, now—"

"You're worried enough that you haven't said anything until now?"

Mamì smiled again, her teeth a quick bright crescent in her dark face. "I can't say I'm not glad my daughter came alive. *Something* should be better than hiding in your bedroom night after night. You did that while you were in school. You were too serious."

Vasquez stared. Her mother was short; she had cinnamon skin and dark wavy hair like many island girls. Her tiny brown hands stayed busy. Rachel's pale skin came from her father, but the sharp prettiness came from her mother, with black eyebrows angled like raven's wings and a rosebud lip. Mamì was still a dark-eyed beauty after fifty years. She tightened her old brown bathrobe after scattering sausage with the edge of her spatula.

"Not one single boyfriend," Mamì said. "I worried then, too. A girl shouldn't lock her heart away."

Vasquez's brothers, while she was in school, beat up every boy that even looked at her. That was something her mother didn't know. She never had a boyfriend because her middle brothers were loco bangers. The wallpaper in the kitchen had been bright peppermint, then, but now it was faded with years of scrubbing. Vasquez shook her head.

"But with this drinking, now," Mamì said. "*Hija*—"

"Don't worry, Mamì."

Another sad smile lit her brown face. "You know something I don't, *hija*, that I shouldn't worry?"

Vasquez clenched her teeth. Rum unlocked the courage she needed to talk to a boy, but she couldn't say that. She swept up her windbreaker and gunbelt from the table and fled.

Guthrie waited in front of the tenement on Henry Street, drooped over the steering wheel of his old blue Ford. He flicked a glance at Vasquez when she climbed into the passenger seat with her pistols tucked under her arm like a football. He drove over to Williamsburg, calling ahead to warn Swabe. The big bodyguard was waiting on the street in front of his brownstone off Lee Avenue, oblivious to the cold morning. The little detective parked his Ford in the middle of the quiet street, and they climbed out. The wind from the East River cut sharply.

"I could've took the train," Swabe said. "So some schmuck slashed my tires." The old bodyguard shook his head.

"I want to see it."

"Am I sensing a bigger picture here?" Swabe asked. He pointed at his white Ram, squatting on flat sidewalls three spaces down.

The little detective walked down and took pictures with his phone. Vasquez huddled in her yellow windbreaker with her arms crossed. He finished with pictures, then took long looks up and down the quiet street.

"Guthrie, I think you've been working too hard."

"Are you sure?" Guthrie asked.

The old bodyguard shrugged.

"I want you to stay in a hotel, say the Marriott on Lexington," Guthrie said. "I'll get the tab."

"What am I going to do about this?" Swabe jerked a thumb at the Ram, then at his brownstone.

"I think you're supposed to air your den out every so often, anyway. There's a law for that, right? I'll get somebody out here for your truck."

"I should've took the train," he muttered. "I could've missed your mouth."

"This's serious. This rat is sharp."

"And somehow he found his way to Williamsburg and slashed my tires? This is another Otto Skorzeny? Should my arm be burning?"

"Will you or won't you?" The little detective glared. "I ain't slept. I been up all night watching that kid prowl the town house. Work with me."

The old bodyguard answered with a defeated sigh. He disappeared into the brownstone. Vasquez climbed back into the Ford and snuggled up to the heater. Guthrie paced in the empty street, studying the neighboring brownstones, some with lights glimmering in the windows. He frowned. Swabe came out with a case, rumbling instructions to a sleepy-looking bearded man in the doorway before he came down.

"You know, I'm glad Stephanie Morgan is easy to get along with," the bodyguard said, after he wedged his case in the backseat of the Ford. "I couldn't stand an ache in my other ear right now."

"Houseguest?" Guthrie asked.

"An overnight guest in the shtiebel. He don't talk half what you do."

Guthrie scowled and concentrated on driving.

"She has a nice house. Not like mine. She must've had someone come to match the colors for her. I smiled just being inside." Swabe paused, peering at the detectives.

"She can draw. I saw a few things hanging up in there that she did. She said they weren't much, but I liked them. Look." He thumbed his wallet open, and slid a postcard of the Fifty-ninth Street Bridge over the seat. Vasquez glanced at it. "That took her about ten minutes."

Vasquez scowled and looked again. "She painted this in ten minutes?"

"Some kind of chalk and a ballpoint. I swear." Swabe retrieved the postcard with an impossibly long arm, without sitting forward in the seat of the Ford. He tucked it carefully into his wallet.

"Don't slobber on her," Guthrie muttered.

When the detectives dropped Swabe at the Marriott on Lexington, Guthrie peeled a dozen fifties from the roll of cash in his pocket, and handed the money to the old bodyguard. He ignored Swabe's dirty look when he suggested choosing a car at the concierge's desk when he picked up his keys; the arrangements were already made. Guthrie shrugged away his unvoiced accusations. The detectives drove over to Turtle Bay as the sky brightened.

"That old man is a spider," Todd Royal muttered. The young black man stood looking up, a knit cap tugged low around his face. A down jacket padded his narrow shoulders. A crescent of gold showed between his lips as he gaped.

Guthrie was hanging grimly from some Italianate trim on the third story of Morgan's town house, positioning a camera to watch East Fifty-second Street toward First Avenue. Still hanging, he used his palmtop to check the resulting view, then prodded the camera again. Leaned against the old blue Ford on the street below, Royal and Vasquez had coffee and doughnuts. The high-powered breakfast had more kick than the weak sunlight firing the distant tips of the big buildings in midtown as dawn broke.

After Guthrie inched back through the third-floor window, Vasquez asked, "See anything last night?"

Royal shrugged. "Bunch of drunks went back and forth from that apartment building." He pointed at a dark, glassy tower. "Had to be some party." He strode down Fifty-second Street for another circuit before Guthrie came from the town house.

Morgan's town house was on the end of Fifty-second Street between Sutton and Beekman, surrounded by luxury towers and foreign missions. The town house had a yard wrapped in enough wrought iron to pass for a garden—a holdout from the neighborhood destruction caused by the East Side Highway—with three entrances, an alley access, and a basement apartment occupied by a niece. Iron-skirted trees, cars, and stoops punctuated the streetside hardscape, while the alley was a nightmare of loading docks, nooks, underground entrances, and decorative flourishes.

Swabe arrived in a taxi to take the handoff while the little detective stood on the curb finishing the doughnuts. The sky brightened. The detectives drove back down to Brooklyn, whipping past the clotted inbound traffic on the LIE to turn into DUMBO after they crossed the bridge.

Big plans for development remained on the drawing boards. Silent factories and quiet lots were leavened with small businesses and loft apartments. Guthrie caught the paperboy for a long conversation of unchewed monosyllables, and hustled the businessmen when they snapped their doors open. Hardened Yankee suspicion dissolved each time the little detective flashed a picture of the stalker and asked, "Can you help me find my pet rat?"

A long, cold morning spent showing a picture of the gigantic, ape-like stalker produced two pages of notes on Guthrie's pad. The detectives polled foot traffic on the sidewalks and carried doughnuts around to the construction sites, paused to mark rough maps, and eventually concluded that the stalker could have a dirty white van, either a GMC or a Ford. Where he slept or parked, they had no clue.

"We could've done worse," Guthrie said when they paused for lunch at a kosher deli in the Heights. Vasquez didn't comment. She was chilled to the bone and glad the sun was warming the bricks.

After lunch, the little detective threw the car keys to Vasquez. When he climbed back into the Ford, he clutched his knees and rested his cheek on the dash. He admitted needing some sleep. He had watched Royal on the overnight prowl. He pointed Vasquez through turns to the precinct house, in a rebuilt boardinghouse dating from the Heights' slummy nadir.

The desk sergeant broke from a doze when the detectives walked into the precinct house. One old lady sat on the waiting bench with a patent-leather purse clamped between her knees. Soft telephone conversations floated from open office doors. Guthrie peered across the desk at the sergeant.

"Good afternoon," he said, rubbing his red eyes.

"You got a complaint?" The sergeant's tag read: BULLENS. He glanced at Vasquez, flashed interest, then settled back tiredly.

"Sure," Guthrie said. "More like a problem I think lives around here, but wandered up into the city. I got a license, and I ran across him on the Upper East Side." Vasquez doodled on the high desktop with a fingertip.

"No kidding," the sergeant said. "Let me see something."

Guthrie handed over his license. "This rat is a monster. He probably has complaints from scaring kids on nights besides Halloween." He slid the stalker's picture across the desk. "Ever seen him?"

Sergeant Bullens laughed. "Oh, yeah. That mope. Oh, yeah. What's he done this time?" He handed the license back and lifted the picture.

"He's stalking," the little detective said, breaking into a smile. "My client lives on East Fifty-second. If you got particulars—"

"Stalking, that's a problem." The sergeant's voice flattened. "I want this mope for anything, even pissing against a wall, but stalking?"

"He's taking pictures of my client."

"Yeah, well, that's perfect, but that's going nowhere with this mope."

Guthrie sighed. "I maybe got some trespass, too, but he's covered his tracks so far."

"Roses, right?" The sergeant shook his head. "The mope is Duane Parson. Mostly we get complaints about intimidation, but it ain't a crime to be that big. My problem is the thing with Alice Powell.

"You've seen the mope up close?" the sergeant asked.

Guthrie shook his head.

"He's huge. But we didn't know that when it started. Alice Powell came in to complain. She was underage, so her parents came with her. She's a real pretty black girl, and she was about to graduate from school. The mope started with taking pictures—that caught attention, this gigantic white man, ugly as sin, strutting in a black neighborhood—and moved right on to leaving roses. Parson never left a note or made a call. He just stared and took pictures. So Alice Powell came in to complain.

"We picked up some gossip on the street while we were looking around. A handful of uniforms, three detectives . . . you've seen the mope. Who doesn't get a little scared looking at that? So it seems like some locals from the neighborhood encouraged Parson to desist. That went like shouting threats at the traffic on the LIE, and then rough stuff backfired. So we heard. The mope isn't somebody to play with.

"Once we had the complaint, we left the uniforms to observe, got a warrant on the observation, and arrested him. Parson isn't normal. Ordinary handcuffs won't fit his wrists. Then he didn't even make it to the Brooklyn House. We had to kick him from the precinct with a warning. The mope is a professional photographer for an outfit in the city. Oh, yeah, what a smile." Sergeant Bullens held measuring hands out to arm's length.

"We couldn't do nothing! That mope, well, you should've seen him. We didn't get measurements, but he ducks door frames. We put him in the cell while we checked his information, we took his belt, his shoes, the ordinary business. The nasty mope don't wear socks. He's got opposable thumbs on his feet, like a gorilla. I kid you not. Then he talks like a lawyer out of that mouth. Oh, yeah." Some uniformed officers that had collected to listen when the sergeant grew loud shook their heads.

"I don't like where this is going," Guthrie said.

Sergeant Bullens shrugged. "We had to kick him."

"What happened?"

"What happened? Nothing. We were lucky. The mope went right back with the camera. That little black girl was scared to death. A pretty girl like that shouldn't never wish to be ugly, but that's what she said. I won't ever forget that. She has beautiful hair, all fluffy in a big black cloud. Beautiful."

Sergeant Bullens frowned. "We were lucky. She went away to college somewhere across the country. That was the end of it, except I have this lingering problem with the mope. Stalking?" He snapped his fingers. "Like that."

Duane Parson lacked particulars beyond a white GMC van and an address in Brownsville. The sergeant provided the license number and address as a courtesy, written on a scrap of paper and pushed across the desktop while he whistled softly and looked pointedly the other way. Guthrie collected the slip, and then the detectives walked back out to the quiet street.

"Something felt off about this from the beginning," Guthrie said. "Trespass with no theft or communication could go on forever—it's a misdemeanor." He signaled for the keys before they reached the Ford. "I'll drive. You do a background on Parson and put a report together for me. I don't want to look at a screen right now. We're going to the office to get the rest of the cameras. East Fifty-second Street is gonna be a peepshow when I finish."

Vasquez's palmtop was a custom rearrangement designed by a Korean geek named Fat-Fat; it contained a suite of electronic skeleton keys that opened database doors across the country. Those keys, the search engines, and some careful thought always dynamited a geyser of information from the Web, but Duane Parson was a dry hole. The license plate from the GMC, the name, and the address provided three points of entry that led nowhere, instead of an endless cascade needing to be sifted for useful hits.

Duane Parson was born in Scottsdale, Arizona, in 1956, then vanished. He had no military service and no criminal record. He appeared in New York in 1996 with a vehicle registration and driver's license, then disappeared again in 1998. He reappeared in New York with another registration and license in 2008. The Brownsville address was an SRO. Parson filed taxes seven times—usually without paying—split into two sequences bundled behind the vehicle registrations in New York. His W-2s from MAGNUM were smaller than a schoolteacher's salary, but that professional connection deadended at an unscratchable firewall.

By the time Guthrie paused at the office on Thirty-fourth Street to collect cameras, Vasquez decided that Duane Parson was a fiction. Guthrie was deliberately secretive; he paid cash and dodged entanglements, but the data-miners still spit lists of his preferences. On Duane Parson, she found nothing. She made puzzles from his name, tried misspellings, and cross-checked dates, but still ended with electronic emptiness. She had sifted enough résumés to conclude she had the wrong information.

Vasquez bundled her electronic clippings and typed a report on her dossier for Parson. Guthrie muttered along the way about crosstown traffic. After that, she directed some bored glances at the street, then researched Alice Powell. Her high school record reminded Vasquez of her own school years of imprisonment—perfect grades from a studious, dutiful girl born exactly nineteen days before Vasquez. This was her Papì's changeling daughter who was willing to go to college. She chose the University of Washington, accepted a complete scholarship, and left Brooklyn. Once she began tracking the girl in Seattle, Vasquez began cursing in Spanish. She ignored Guthrie's questions while she checked more sources.

"Damn it, what is it?"

"Alice Powell was murdered."

CHAPTER FOUR

"*Viejo*, I'm not gonna know what I'm doing," Vasquez protested.

"Avram said you got it—stand there like the Secret Service."

"*Eres estúpido*," she muttered.

"*Usted es estúpido.* I'm the boss, remember?" Guthrie didn't mind if she used informal address; the jab was only a reminder. "Our number one priority is keeping the rat from biting our client. It's a change of plan for tonight—don't worry."

Morgan's evening itinerary included a banquet for the Art Commission, where Abraham Swabe would look like a battleship in a fish tank. She didn't want to spend the evening frightening donors with her bodyguard. The commission needed their checks. She remembered Vasquez from the interview at the art gallery, and offered assistance blending her with the upscale party crowd so that she could stand in for Swabe.

Vasquez shook her head. "I don't like dresses."

The little detective laughed.

Traffic whizzed on Fifth Avenue after Guthrie dropped Vasquez in front of Henri Bendel. A procession of well-dressed shoppers marched on the sidewalk, handcuffed with shopping bags. They threw sharp, acquisitive glances at the offerings in Henri Bendel's windows, neatly sidestepping Vasquez, who looked like a recent escapee from a thrift store. The young Puerto Rican woman's yellow windbreaker repelled the Burberry-clad shoppers like a warning light.

A clerk hurried from the store. "You must be freezing!" he exclaimed, winding a measuring tape around his neck like a muffler. His short, dark hair was brushed up into a cockscomb. A dark vest and slacks made him a trim wedge topped with a white buttondown on broad shoulders.

Vasquez didn't notice the cold wind sweeping the avenue until he mentioned it. She shrugged. She was three hot cups into a Frappuccino overdose. The clerk rubbed his arms, then caught her elbow and tugged her inside with the bossy assurance of an older sibling.

"You have to be Rachel Vasquez," he said.

After the busy street, the warm air inside Henri Bendel tasted like new clothes, a smell sweeter than opium to a deal-addicted shopper. Fascinated customers wandered along racks of cotton, wool, and silk like bees gently dusting for pollen. With a glance and a bored sigh, the clerk whisked Vasquez to the back stairs.

"I'm Samuel," he said, pausing on a landing to grin. "The girls are going to faint. Stephanie promised a pretty package, but you are incredible."

Before Vasquez could wedge in an insult, Samuel hurried up the remaining stairs, yanking her arm. He flung open a dark walnut door at the top. Bright light poured down the staircase. Racks of clothing lined a long loft with a steeply pitched back wall. A tall triple mirror waited on a stage hung with lights. A cutting table, a pair of sewing machines, and some bins covered the end wall, overlooked by one narrow window with a view of rooftops, water towers, and a slice of Fifth Avenue.

Samuel tugged Vasquez through the door, clicked it shut, then swaggered into the loft's walkway. "Bonnie! Gail! The Morgan package has arrived!" he exclaimed.

Two women looked up from the tables. Gail wore her dirty blond hair piled in a twist above a rounded face that was a guilty reflection of too many hasty doughnut breakfasts. Dark eyebrows, electric-blue eyes, and a neatly upturned nose sharpened with a measuring look as she studied Vasquez. Bonnie was younger, a slender, dark-eyed brunette in her twenties; she pricked her finger on a needle and tumbled from her chair, then blushed as she scrambled from the floor.

"Don't worry, she sews better than she sits a chair," Samuel said. He mounted the low, mirrored stage. "Come on up here. We need to see you in the lights."

"I'm supposed to get clothes for a dinner party," Vasquez offered, peering at the far, dark end of the loft, as if someone might be hiding there.

The fashionistas exchanged startled looks. "Do you suppose she ever smiles?" Gail asked.

"With those eyebrows, why would she?" Bonnie murmured.

Vasquez scowled. "Clothes? Fifteen minutes?"

"That probably works on the boys," Samuel said, wagging a finger, "but you get nowhere with me. This is going to take some time." He pointed incredulously at her clothes. "Seriously, you dressed out of a Dumpster this morning, and your manners—ew!"

"We have some work to do," Gail said, and sighed. "Coffee?"

"This is ridiculous," Vasquez said.

"You have *no* idea," Samuel said.

Bonnie, the dark-haired seamstress, watched while Samuel and Gail stripped the Puerto Rican detective. Her gunbelt terrified the fashionistas the way a coiled snake paralyzed birds, but it was forgotten after being banished to a corner. Vasquez rescued her keys, wallet, and knife before her paint-stained blue jeans were tossed aside like trash, and she stood startled in the harsh light. Guthrie's little folding knife fit snugly in the crease of her hand, a talisman of invisibility to shield her against their unfamiliar world.

Guthrie had given her the knife at the end of August, when she returned to the office on Thirty-fourth Street after leaving the hospital. Midtown's traffic bounced like peppers in a smoking skillet, the burning afterimage of a fiery summer. The little detective tossed a five-gallon bucket beside her desk, jolting Vasquez from a daze.

"Hand me that bucket, Rachel," he commanded.

With a sour look, she rolled her chair, retrieved the bucket, and rolled again to hand it over. The white vinyl read DILL PICKLES, and other assorted information in blocky green lettering.

Guthrie flourished the bucket like a charlatan preparing a trick, then dipped two fingers into his trouser pocket. The knife's blade clicked open, and he locked eyes with Vasquez as he pressed the blade against the lip of the bucket. The vinyl parted with a weary sigh. He pressed it against the floor and it opened to the bottom. He closed the knife with a single finger and a soft click, then handed her the slaughtered bucket.

"That's what puts men apart from animals, Rachel," he said. "We carry our teeth in our hands. That's my fault. You needed teeth at Twin Oaks, but I didn't give you any."

Vasquez felt her heart accelerate, but she didn't say anything. At Twin Oaks, they'd captured Marc Gagneau at the end of his string of killings. Vasquez narrowly escaped being his last victim.

The little detective pulled a red square of hard plastic from his pocket. A slot in the plastic admitted the knife blade, and a tug freed it. He demonstrated the sharpener a few times. "This blade should cut anything," he said softly. "It has a good firm lock. I rarely want anything larger."

The words flew past her, and Guthrie frowned at her incomprehension. "Stand up," he commanded. He gripped her shoulder while he tucked the knife into the compact pocket of her blue jeans. "That's a good place to keep it."

The folded knife was always warm when it came from her pocket, like a piece of herself. The smell of the steel as she sharpened it was better than a pinch of salt on fries. After a handful of minutes spent standing in her underwear on the lighted stage, Vasquez was cold. She exploded, interrupting another round of measurement mixed with argument about colors and patterns. Gail meekly provided a floral-patterned kimono. Samuel studied the effect and smiled.

"I don't think so," Gail said. "Too *Kill Bill*."

"Only if she keeps standing *that* way," Samuel said.

"We have two hours, and you want to teach her demure?"

He shrugged, smiling with patent falseness.

A half hour scrubbed away her impatience. When clerks rushed up the stairs, Samuel fired strident warnings that bordered on insult. He was the gatekeeper and master of ceremonies. Bonnie produced dresses, and Gail conjured accessories. Vasquez slid into clothes, endured appraisal, and sullenly stripped when Samuel's head began to shake. She recognized an ordered economy to their motions during arguments about season and time, but that ended each time her guns clashed with an ensemble. Bonnie suggested responses to questions, and gave instructions on refusing a drink or plate. Samuel coached sitting, standing, and walking, then threw his hands up when Vasquez flunked every impossible test.

"I won't be held responsible," he muttered repeatedly, glaring when Gail and Bonnie hid smiles.

By the time Samuel mocked up a demonstration of a fancy table with plastic tableware, Vasquez had relaxed. Wearing heeled shoes, a red gown, and a swatch of undyed cotton for a bib, she laughed when one of Gail's quiet barbs drew a scream from Samuel. All three fashionistas stared openmouthed.

"That's just not fair," Bonnie said.

"Don't be jealous, girl," Samuel said. "She can't help it."

Frowning in sudden puzzlement, Vasquez jabbed a forefinger around the table. "All three of you are crazy."

Gail sniffed. "You're from Mars. It's the only explanation."

"Not Mars. The Lower East Side."

The fashionistas laughed, and toasted their bottles of flavored water. Considering the two-hour deadline, they had produced success. Vasquez didn't move like a model, but they weren't afraid she would punch someone for helping with her wrap. She could manage heels, but they gave her snappy black flats, a long, wide camel skirt, and a fitted cream silk top. They opened a long golden Prada clutch-purse at each end and resewed it to secure her holsters; she could draw a pistol by reaching into the clutch. A long golden cape and beret finished the ensemble, and left her arms unhindered.

Their smug satisfaction surprised Vasquez. The fashionistas pointed her at the mirrors, but she didn't recognize the reflection. That slim brunette with a worldly air belonged in the realm of the mirror, where the fashionistas surrounded her with glowing smiles. Their smiles died after a long moment. Their world, like the mirror, needed a hard frame to protect it. That hard frame was Guthrie, and that was her. Vasquez turned away; nothing she wore, not jewelry or silk or upswept hair, nothing would straighten her crooked face.

"Don't worry, Mrs. Morgan said to dress you," Samuel said softly when Vasquez discovered that her blue jeans had been replaced with Joe's. A maroon buttondown with silver snaps, a string tie and turquiose thunderbird clasp, buffed black lambskin boots, a long sleeved black bolero, and a plain black felt cowboy hat were beneath the jeans in the Bendel bag.

"Well, you can't keep my kimono," Gail said.

Vasquez scowled.

"You can have your dirty stuff back," Samuel said. "But only if you try these on." His tone was adamant. "*This* look is *you*."

"Technically, I guess maybe it's just a little bit illegal," Guthrie admitted. He shrugged, pinching air between a thumb and forefinger, and clutching his coffee in the other hand.

Vasquez was startled enough that she didn't laugh. Clayton Guthrie usually fell short in explanations. Keeping other people up-to-date on his intentions rarely appeared on his list of priorities. If she drove past Forty-seventh Street, he would pour a complaint into her ear about needing to stop at Edison's for a Reuben. Clients received the same treatment. The little detective would ask for the key to their house, then take a picture and make a copy. The next day, they might walk through their own door while Guthrie stood sorting their mail and jotting down return addresses. Vasquez had decided that he kept secrets because he was afraid they would hurt; she had seen that come true.

After she left Henri Bendel, Vasquez took a taxi to East Fifty-second Street. Guthrie worked on in the dim light, wearing a dark blue coverall with a tool belt, and a cap instead of his fedora. A white Toyota king cab with double ladder racks had replaced the Ford. He propped ladders against the streetlights, and checked the view toward the East River. If he liked the view, he opened the access, borrowed some electrical power, and installed a digital camera that linked to a server in Brooklyn. Once she found him, Vasquez stood at the bottom of his ladder for about ten minutes. Bitter wind rushed along the street, but he clung without moving.

"That took a while," she said when he dismounted the ladder.

"I forgot what I was doing," he said. He watched a string of limousines roar past. "Those were Ukrainians?"

Vasquez shrugged.

"They're thick over here. Ukrainians, Polacks, Argentines, all kinds. *They* got cameras. I ain't had any success getting them to let me take a look."

"Are you serious?" Vasquez studied him. The little detective's ears glowed red. "*Viejo*, you've been out here for hours. Maybe you should sit in the truck and drink some coffee."

His face darkened with suspicion. "Ain't you supposed to be dressed for a party?"

Vasquez took the handoff from Swabe, and an earful of instructions, at the Fifty-second Street town house. Stephanie Morgan helped her play dress-up, adding some jewelry and makeup. The heiress wore her blond hair swept up with a few hanging curls, and a draped navy gown accented with a silver clutch and jewelry. She soothed the young woman with some softly murmured compliments and the aura of ease she had with her own beauty. Peter Ludlow wore navy flannel and a wide red tie with subdued silver stripes. He played chauffeur for the

Saab, preoccupied and quiet in the driver's seat. Brisk chill leaked through the windows of the car while they drove to the Four Seasons.

The lobby of the Four Seasons Hotel swirled with people. Vasquez held her golden clutch in her left hand, and kept Morgan within reach of her right—Swabe's first and last instruction: monitor the client with your gun hand. Shield first and shoot second. The crowd made her edgy—too fast, too many, and most of all too close. She found little consolation in the knowledge that Parson would be as obvious as a rolling rack of cold beef in the crowd of well-heeled socialites.

Morgan and Ludlow greeted everyone they knew, performing a stream of handshakes, air kisses, and brief conversations. Vasquez tried to smile and remember her lines; Samuel's sighs of exasperation lingered like a tonic. A tall, red-faced, middle-aged man almost earned a sudden kick from Vasquez when he rushed by to exchange a whisper, laugh, and rough handshake with Peter Ludlow.

"Peter, I am *glad* to see you," he said. "I need you here—my tongue is in a knot." His Tom Ford suit swelled around his belly like a tent held up by narrow shoulders.

Ludlow nodded, but his shoulders drooped under a martyr's load. "You've met Stephanie," he said, forcing a smile. "You remember C.C., don't you? Charles Congdon, one of my partners from my old firm."

The elevator ride relieved Vasquez, surrounding them like an armored vault after the open lobby, but Congdon crowded the small space with a booming voice better suited to a Mount Vernon barbecue than polite chitchat. After patting her husband's shoulder, Stephanie Morgan buttered up the man as easily as warm bread.

"I am *so* lucky," Congdon said. "The mayor is here, but you know that. I hear this is really your Art Commission . . . not that I have an ear in the right places."

The elevator opened onto a broad concourse with a dense burgundy carpet and plain walls. A sign-in table waited for the commission banquet. Blooms of people mingled, waited, and milled through open doors on the concourse. Morgan strode toward the sign-in, and

Ludlow took a single step to block Congdon from following on her heels. Vasquez stayed with the heiress.

Three commissioners, two old white men in charcoal flannel and a young black woman wearing a red gown that showed one dark shoulder, waited at the table with a newspaper photographer. Parson ducked under the door frame of the double doorway in the emerald-papered wall to the left of the table and walked out, trailing a pair of excited young men in uniform vests. The stalker looked like a jetliner dropping across the East River toward La Guardia.

"*That's* the guy you were talking about?" Congdon's question boomed in the concourse.

Vasquez slid her hand into her golden clutch, gripped her Chief's Special, and whirled around Morgan to block the black-coated giant. She felt like a gnat, staring up at him, but rammed an elbow into his stomach. The giant was as hard as a boulder. His eyes narrowed when he glanced down at her, but he stopped after she matched his sidestep and elbowed him again.

Parson rummaged in the pocket of his black greatcoat and pulled out a camera. Stephanie Morgan saw him when she looked up from the sign-in, preparing to greet the commissioners. Up close, the stalker smelled like mothballs, and the massive lump on his forehead twisted his face off center until his mouth was a diagonal slash. Wild hair from his mustache sprawled around his face like a cat's whiskers. Vasquez planted her feet and pressed.

The stalker aimed his camera above Vasquez's beret and snapped pictures. Vasquez struggled with the Special; her wrist creaked from squeezing the pistol. She wanted to shoot him; she could see him, hammered by the bullets, feel the whipcrack of the shots along her arm. If he touches her, I shoot him, she thought—poor consolation. Glancing over her shoulder, she saw fear twisting Stephanie Morgan's face. She jabbed with her elbow again.

The stalker's fashion show stretched seconds into an eternity. Morgan hurried down the hallway and stepped through the door of the banquet room while Vasquez stood her ground. Parson laughed softly, snapping more pictures of the gawking crowd. Bellhops thickened into a screen around the giant stalker. Peter Ludlow watched grimly, surrounded by darting glances and a buzz of conversation.

Once Morgan vanished, Parson glared down at Vasquez. He aimed his camera at her face and took a handful of pictures, then nodded. She floated on hot anger, but backed away, still blocking his path to the banquet room. The giant brushed bellhops from his path as he pocketed his camera.

"This is public property," he growled as he drifted toward the elevator. The choppy conversation around the sign-in swelled to a crescendo as the bellhops goaded him into the elevator.

Vasquez waited at the banquet-room door to see the elevator descend, filmed with the sweat of relieved anger, and shot glances into the crowded room. Monitor the entrances, the old bodyguard had said. If the client stays still for more than a few minutes, know where all the doors lead. A handful of doors on the far end of the banquet room made her anxious. The elevator light ticked down, and she hurried to check the doors: bathrooms and service doors to the kitchen.

Peter Ludlow offered a thumbs-up when the young detective approached the couple at their table. Morgan was shocked but not broken. "Miss Vasquez, I am impressed," Ludlow said. He unfolded from his chair and glanced at the door.

"I'm fine with Rachel here," Morgan said. "Maybe you could stop C.C. from making quite so many enemies."

Vasquez and Morgan surrendered their wraps to a checker, and waited at the table. Morgan drank wine and explained the Art Commission's work on the city's landscaping and parks—a subject dull enough to slow a racing heartbeat. They watched Ludlow rescue several conversations by hooking C.C. for walkaround handshakes and hellos. The contrast between the cavalier and the stooge was worth a few quiet laughs.

The newspaper photographer attended a slow stream of dignitaries visiting the table. After the commissioners, the mayor sat for several minutes. "Next year, this is you," he said softly while he held

Morgan's fingers. The guests were a mixture of artists and financiers; Morgan knew which checkbooks would open and which artists had talent. The commission, all appointees, needed both.

The meal washed away Vasquez's anxiety. She settled against the wall nearby and Ludlow returned to his wife's side. Congdon was banished to a distant corner. Waiters shuttled with drinks, appetizers, plates, and messages; the service doors fluttered like the blades of a fan. Conversation waxed during the courses, and waned for the speeches. An octogenarian in a dark suit delivered the keynote with a pause to praise Stephanie Morgan's eye for statuary.

Morgan had admitted a specialty in painting, but drew praise for a lesser skill. Her humility glowed in the room full of stuffed shirts congratulating themselves for some cosmetic surgery on the dirty city. Vasquez smiled in the darkness. Sometimes her job was worth the effort.

CHAPTER FIVE

Early the next morning, Vasquez found Guthrie idling along Henry Street below her parent's tenement in his old blue Ford. He mumbled complaints while he drove uptown from the Lower East Side. Fog from the East River rolled along the streets.

The night prowler, Todd Royal, recorded verbal reports during his rounds, without knowing that Guthrie spent the night watching the town house through binoculars. A United Nations mixer concluded with a Third World after-party into the small hours. Limousine drag races accompanied a world-music singing contest. Royal's recorded mockery of the privileged excess left Guthrie wondering if the young man missed something quiet beneath the glittery surface.

Quiet gathered in the car after he drained his complaints. Murray Hill warmed up slowly, like a sleepy jogger. Streetlights lit the interior of the Ford, followed by passages of darkness between the casts of light. The little detective sighed.

"Damn, I should've turned back there. I'm tired. I need some sleep."

"Why'd you watch Royal last night? You can't be that worried about him. Nobody broke in the town house, right?" Vasquez rummaged for another apple danish.

Guthrie studied a storefront as the Ford rolled past, with the air of a man who hadn't heard. His hands tightened on the steering wheel.

"No," he answered. "Yes. Who cares? I *tried* to sleep. I got a room at the hotel, just in case. I couldn't sleep. When I laid down, the world moved too fast. So I watched with the binoculars. Then I'm tired. Once I stretch out on the mattress, I'm on a racetrack. So I reach for the binoculars." He pounded the steering wheel as they crossed Forty-sixth Street. "Damn it, I got to turn around. We're gonna end up in Harlem."

"We're not going to Morgan's?" Vasquez asked.

"The office. I thought—" He crisscrossed blocks until he hit Forty-second Street crosstown. A burst of pedestrians scattered from Grand Central into the seats of taxis loitering in the canyons. Guthrie was sleepwalking, but the city was awake.

"Alice Powell is your lead, Rachel. That's on you this morning." The little detective paused to search his desk drawer. "You carried on after the summer like you couldn't hear me tell you to take some classes. You can't even bother to crack the books on the shelf back there." He jabbed a thumb at the supply closet.

"So you think Duane Parson killed her? Prove it. I'm going to see what he did on Fifty-second Street last night. You've got as long as it takes me to scan the video."

A Brooklyn server networked Guthrie's cameras; he could scan from any connected device. The setup transformed cheap cellphones and digital cameras into Big Brother's smiling eyes. Scanning for a rat on video required a footprint—at least one recognizable image—to backtrack using a map of the video layout and time markers. Fog, darkness, and an oversupply of captured footage were his enemies. The little detective quartered his monitor to show four video feeds—

beginning with cameras posted at Morgan's town house—and accelerated the footage. He settled with a tall cup of coffee and stared.

Vasquez drummed her desktop blotter with ink pens as she stared at her computer, but the little detective didn't offer suggestions. She circled around his challenge before admitting to herself that she usually followed his instructions. She was an operative, not a detective. A computer search for Alice Powell revealed her death, then came to a sudden stop.

Fat-Fat's tool kit located a credit card, supplied by her parents, that Powell used for trivial purchases. Itemized bills outlined a daily schedule that Vasquez pinpointed with dots of red Magic Marker on a map of Seattle printed from GoogleEarth. Powell's odyssey of coffee, pizza, books, and cosmetics ended four days before her body surfaced at a roadside dump.

A parallel search for Parson uncovered only one good result: his electronic invisibility eliminated any electronic alibi. Vasquez dug a hole of failure. Every query about Parson returned hitless. Her searches led from nothing to nothing. Guthrie broke her frustration at mid-morning with a racket of cursing.

"The rat got me again!"

At various times the previous night, some of Guthrie's cameras stopped transmitting. Others shifted to show a piece of dark sky, pavement, or the side of a building instead of some useful view of Fifty-second Street. Beginning at 2:00 A.M., a majority of the cameras winked out or drifted. One camera at the town house shot an eight-second clip of Parson at 5:42 A.M.—but without the network a single video print couldn't prove a pattern.

The little detective assigned his nonfunctional cameras to Parson using paranoid logic, a remix of the mess Vasquez found when she wanted Parson's absence from New York City to prove his presence in Seattle—but Guthrie didn't hesitate to blame the stalker. He snatched his fedora and overcoat, marched from the office, and quickly returned.

"Come on, Rachel, you're driving," he said.

Guthrie kept his work truck in a Hell's Kitchen garage tended by a skinny old man named Daniel. The old man wore baggy blue cotton work pants strapped to his waist with rope, and several T-shirts and thermal tops grimy enough to have slowly accumulated since summer without any ever being subtracted for washing. His blue eyes held a crinkle of smile. He polished his nut-brown hands and the dome of his bald skull with a red rag that passed from pocket to pocket like a bad magic trick. The old man worked up a coughing fit while he loaded ladders on the truck, and Guthrie slipped him a folded fifty-dollar bill.

Spates of traffic and mumbled cursing punctuated the crosstown drive on Fifty-second Street. Past Madison Avenue, Guthrie began offering driving instructions: "Pull over here!" "Slow down!" "No! That one over there!" "Change lanes!" The little detective craned his neck to point binoculars at the streetlights, and shuffled his palmtop from lap to dashboard as he found and checked cameras. Off-kilter cameras forced stops to deploy his ladder.

A dull gray sky covered the cold hardscape. Vasquez practiced her rude gestures on the stream of taxi drivers, couriers, and hungry pedestrians. A cop stopped while Guthrie was upstairs, sniffed around the truck, and crossed his arms while he waited for an explanation. The little detective climbed down. He traded his cellphone back and forth with the cop for a conversation with the 17th Precinct watch commander: all clear.

The cop shrugged. "You could move it along faster," he growled.

"I knew it wasn't no pigeons. I think the rat shot my cameras with a paint gun," Guthrie said, watching the cop glide into traffic. The surveillance cameras in the parking garage on Twenty-fifth Street had been blinded with paint before Vasquez discovered the red rose in Morgan's Saab. "I feel about like Ducky Elsworth about that. I know *why* he would want to do it, but I can't figure how he found them in the first place."

With navigational aid from the little detective, Vasquez drove Fifty-second Street. Each time he went up the ladder, she opened her palmtop for some work. Seattle PD recovered Powell's body from the forested outskirts of the metro area, courtesy of a jogger exercising his dogs. Newspaper headlines unlocked two puzzles. They begged for identification of the badly beaten body, and screamed suspicions about a predator hunting the city. Silent kidnaps in Seattle ended with a dump after a few days. The city expected more victims.

"He killed her, *viejo*," Vasquez said to the little man while he warmed his hands at the dashboard vent. "Look at her hair."

Powell's fluffy hair filled the screen of Vasquez's palmtop. The young black woman had a model's cheekbones, coffee-dark skin, neat round ears, and a cloud of ringlets. "It's the hair," she insisted. "He touched Morgan's hair."

Guthrie sighed. "That's what you got? We'll dig at it a little. Would you remember this is about Morgan, though?" He rubbed at his red ears with his heated palms.

Early on while working for Clayton Guthrie, Vasquez learned that he was an expert liar. He drew from a bottomless well of earnest lies when he pried out answers. Clients weren't immune. He caught a faithless wife by delivering flowers; she blushed with pleasure instead of blanking with shock. Signal victories closed case files and earned a sharklike grin.

His weakness sprang from lacking official authority. When he squeezed, NYPD surrendered information, but that needed time. Some of his sources originated with H. P. Whitridge, the city aristocrat paying his retainer and daily expenses, but others were echoes from an eventful life, spent many places besides clodhopping in West Virginia.

The little detective's newest trick, created by the Korean geek in Brooklyn, transformed his phone into a chameleon. The application unlocked a prepunched hatch in the city government's firewall, letting him make calls and send e-mails from official lines. The digital handshake provided instant authenticity.

Impersonating Eric Landry, a Major Case detective, Guthrie connected to the task force squadroom in Seattle. He bluffed through the introductions while scanning IRS records on Joe Wentworth, the detective on the phone. The Seattle detective was a year from retirement, and bored with desk duty.

Guthrie started with simple bait. "I'm passing along an inquiry from Powell's family."

"You don't say?" Wentworth said. "I think we'll crack it eventually. Our kids went to school, too."

"So you got a suspect?"

"The invisible man did it. You haven't had a snatcher work the East Coast, not like this one. He wants high-class girls. Powell must've thought she was walking away from that, coming to nice, quiet Washington."

"Isn't that the point? How is it you guys haven't pinpointed this skel yet? He has to stand out, out there, like a barber pole."

"Unsub, that's what professionals call them. Can you pronounce that?"

"Help me." The little detective put his feet up on his desk.

"Well, I don't know any good bedtime stories for grieving parents. That's tough. I'm not going to miss that part of the job. You know, one time I told a little homemaker about her daughter, it was like I vanished. She turned right to my partner, Kozue, and started a fresh conversation with him. She started right over at hello without wondering how we got into her living room. Kozue gave it to her again, and then she walked into the kitchen and started lunch. She couldn't see either one of us. I'm serious."

"You called a doctor?"

"A priest." Wentworth paused to shout abuse at someone in his squadroom. "Would you believe—Powell caught it bad. Our skel is what they call forensically aware. I love these college kids, and the feds. He's careful and he's learning."

"Yeah?"

"Our ME is ready for sick leave. The feds say the skel's taunting us. Usually, I say that's crap, but he's exposing the bodies that would be safer to bury. He keeps adding tricks to his repertoire."

"He ain't doing the same thing again and again?"

"I told you: the East Coast ain't seen this. We have Hollywood perps—they think bigger. The feds figure his moment comes during the kidnap. Everything else is gravy, a forensic disguise. Powell is the end result. Our ME can't decide which was worse, the sodomy, the rape, or that she screamed until her throat bled. That started a few vics back, adding sodomy, and maybe using an object—like using his junk wasn't enough to do the damage he wanted and so he found something bigger. Or he figured to track over his junk. That's what our ME thought. Maybe he thinks we'll use dickprint analysis."

"You don't figure he's smarter than that?"

"It's the smart ones that do the dumbest shit."

"In the paperwork, we noticed Powell was beat bad. That's COD?"

"Massive blunt force. That was the theme on both ends of Powell. I'm sensing something. Are you leading for something?"

Vasquez left her desk and walked to the office window while Guthrie paused. The sound of the speakerphone filled the office. She couldn't walk away from it, but she wanted some distance from the dark insensitivity the old cop used to block his discomfort.

"Yes and no," Guthrie replied. "Your vics out there were manual strangulation, right?"

"The fed said forensic disguise."

Guthrie cleared his throat.

"Come out with it, will you? I'm retiring next June."

"I got a square peg. Powell had a complaint in Brooklyn. Did she stay in Seattle long enough to pick up your guy and bring him to boil? You sound like he ain't opportunistic."

Paper fluttered, and a drawer slammed shut. "Let me get your name again," Wentworth demanded.

"No, you want Brooklyn," Guthrie said. "I'm just being nosy."

"A smart guy?"

The little detective disconnected the rest. Even a liar like Guthrie could only play for so long. His eyes burned like hot flints in a face of brick. Vasquez kept quiet, unwilling to add I-told-you-so to the little old man's anger. Guthrie's hard side emerged during trouble, otherwise being no more visible than the dark side of the moon.

H. P. Whitridge paid him to sit waiting empty-handed in the city, because when trouble turned up, the aristocrat wanted him on hand to deal with it.

Vasquez looked down on Thirty-fourth Street. A crowd of shoppers paraded the sidewalk going to and from Macy's, down past Seventh Avenue, all fluffy like sheep in their winter coats. Vasquez wondered if Alice Powell shopped at Macy's the year before: they might have stood at a counter together, counting change to buy gloves for their brothers or a handkerchief for their fathers. The shoppers marched on unconcerned. The gray sky above Manhattan didn't look like grimy death to them. They were busy with the holiday.

Vasquez turned away from the window. Time had come for business.

CHAPTER SIX

"Todd wasn't bleeding much, not to start with," Guthrie said, tugging at the brim of his brown fedora. Early morning darkness mixed with artificial light left him ghostlike, with dark-circled eyes.

Vasquez turned onto First Avenue. Taxis and ambulances slid alongside them beneath the glowing windows of Bellevue Hospital. She drank from a Styrofoam cup of coffee nestled in the console. Abraham Swabe filled the bench backseat of the old Ford, while the two detectives had room enough to rattle around in the front.

"Wasserman would've done this different," Guthrie said.

"That schmuck would be sliding from the back of a dumptruck. I loved the old man, but sometimes—" Swabe watched a knot of people surround a newstand on the avenue. More softly, he continued, "Who misses one more?"

Guthrie nodded. "He used to say that when he cleaned the Luger. That always gave me a chill."

Swabe sighed. "I should have never—"

Guthrie shrugged. The old men shared silence.

Vasquez finished her coffee with slow sips, pausing at a light. On summertime breaks from school, she spent days with Papì at the old social clubs in El Barrio. Faded pictures of baseball players and singers stared down from the walls at the old men crowding the domino tables. Their conversations edged around old-man secrets, sharp with machismo like the quiet peacefulness of a cooling gun. The annoyance of exclusion returned like an insistent fly.

"What happened?" she demanded.

Guthrie shrugged. "Quick version: that's a damn smart rat," he said. "Last night, I couldn't sleep. I went back to the hotel and watched the town house. Early on, people hustled along Fifty-second Street, and the traffic died. Todd chattered on his rounds, same as he did the night before. All around the city, heads are dropping onto pillows, but I can't catch a wink.

"I tried a trip to the bed. That worked better than coffee. I took the laptop and watched *on* the balcony while I watched *from* the balcony. Morgan is getting her money's worth. By then, one of the cameras was out."

"The schmuck did it?"

"He killed nine cameras last night, but missed four."

Swabe nodded.

"I tested twenty-two cameras filming Fifty-second Street yesterday afternoon. This rat's real trouble, Avram. Help me figure what his move is, will you?"

The old bodyguard gripped the back of the seat until it creaked. "What's he going to do?"

"Maybe he kidnaps her," Vasquez said. "Maybe he rapes her. Maybe he beats her to death and drops her body beside the road."

Swabe sat quietly in the backseat. First Avenue's lights slid by outside the old blue Ford's windows. Vasquez grimly recounted the slim pamphlet of Alice Powell's final summer, bookended by Brooklyn and Seattle. She detailed dead ends and blind alleys in the stalker's threadbare identity, finishing with a list of maybes. After rattling for a minute, she noticed Guthrie's unconcern.

"Now would be the time to suggest what I'm missing, *viejo*."

The little detective sighed. "First, our job is to keep the rat from biting our client. That's easy to forget," he said. "Stephanie Morgan has surgery today, whether she wants it or not. Avram, you get her there. She's getting an implant to track her in case she gets lost, so we can find her damn quick." He fished a slip of paper from his suit pocket and handed it across the seat, with the address of a veterinarian who would install a GPS locator.

The avenue passed in eerie quiet alongside the conversation. Vasquez caught glimpses of the East River through breaks in the hardscape. "Okay, but I still don't know what I'm missing," she muttered.

"Take it easy on the kid, Guthrie," Swabe said.

The little man scowled at the dashboard. "Rachel, you went looking for Duane Parson," he said. "That's after you pointed out he doesn't really exist in New York. What made you think you would find him in Seattle?"

Vasquez's stomach crashed. She had failed the test—then asked for the answer. Guthrie had ignored her questions, evidently hoping she would see the obvious connection.

"Look, that's police work," he continued, his voice softening. "We punted them that football yesterday. Our job is what the police *can't* do—protect Stephanie Morgan. You're seeing to go about it by collaring the rat for the Powell murder in Seattle. I'm not saying *no* to that—"

"Then what the hell are you saying?" Vasquez pounded the steering wheel.

Swabe patted her shoulder. "Hey, that could break, you know?"

"Okay, Rachel. Two things. The rat is so big he can't hide. He has to stick out in a report—he's three hundred pounds, easy, jumping up on ledges and what else? The rat needs to eat, he needs money. Once we find these things, his footprints might jump out. Second, you dropped the connection to MAGNUM when it wouldn't open. That computer turns your head in the direction of what it shows you—if *it* can't see something, *you* can't see it. So he created the identity to work for MAGNUM. That doesn't make the connection useless."

Vasquez took it on the chin quietly, grasping desperately at the implications. The stalker was invisible because she'd looked for a false identity he created. Guthrie's tirade splashed a light onto the hand above the puppet show.

"Anyway, the rat killed a camera before I thought to check the video feeds the first time," Guthrie said. "I sat on the balcony and watched."

"You put some of your cameras watching your other cameras?" Swabe sounded hopeful.

The little man shook his head. The United Nations loomed up on their right, pressed against the river by Tudor City and the other big apartment buildings. Traffic trickled from the tunnel and bridge.

"I felt like I was watching a video game. I have GPS on the cameras, pinging on a map. I can tap the feeds by hitting them with the mouse. I sat watching my cameras fall like dominoes down Fifty-second Street. Todd prowled around the town house. I spent some time looking through the binoculars.

"I should've warned Todd, but the rat did this same thing the night before. Likewise he didn't get every camera. I got to remember to see Fat about that. How did he find the cameras, and why did he miss some of them?"

"You didn't warn the kid?"

"I didn't want to tip him off that I was watching him."

"Guthrie, that's lousy." Swabe paused. "I admit being puzzled—that kid has more tattoos than a rap star, a mouthful of gold teeth, and no ears for instructions. You hired him why?"

"Todd's got some issues. He lost his mother and his brother this summer. His head ain't wrapped around it yet. But I know for a fact he'll shoot, not stand there looking with a blank face like he forgot he's carrying a pistol."

Swabe nodded acceptance. Courage compensated for many sins. "That's *lousier*. You have faith in him, then don't warn him?"

The little detective shrugged. "I warned him later. The rat circled the town house. I shot video that plays like a Three Stooges bit, around that wrought-iron fence and through the alley, hoping to catch him shooting the cameras attached to the sides of the town house. That's private property. That could be a good destruction charge. I didn't want Todd to spook him."

"You thought that up afterward, didn't you?"

"Do you want me to tell the story?" Guthrie sharpened the demand with a glance over the seat. "The rat disappeared. He went missing for a quarter hour. I catalogued the cameras and kept an eye on the town house. I meant to wait until this morning to scan the video for proof he shot the town house cameras. He killed two of those cameras, but I missed that with the binoculars. I swear it seemed he knew I was on the balcony. He sure had Todd's pattern.

"So then I see the dogs—a pair of Rottweilers—pouncing along Fifty-second. They looked like a couple of kittens with a ball of yarn. I thought they got away from a walker, then I noticed the laser dots whirling on the sidewalk. Todd walked around the corner and the lasers leaped onto him.

"That's when I warned him. I broke into his channel with a warning about the dogs. The Rotts raced down the sidewalk. Todd froze. I mean, it's dark. The dogs are dark. He could've looked the wrong way, I don't know. Then he bolted for the alley once the Rotts hit him. I don't want to listen to that again. He's afraid of dogs."

"So how is he?" Swabe asked.

"The Rotts tried to rip his legs off. He climbed a fire escape in the alley. They got his shoes, his pants pockets, like that. They didn't eat much of him. He'll still have a family."

Vasquez spit a mouthful of relieved laughter.

"I called panic on Morgan's security, but the rat was long gone."

"He was testing the system?" Swabe asked.

The little detective pulled his palmtop and keyed a video clip: Morgan's town house glowed blocky and gray in the streetlights. A white van rolled to a stop on Fifty-second Street. Duane Parson spun from the driver's door and rushed the town house. A running leap from the sidewalk carried him up the Italianate façade like a ladder. He dangled from a third-story window ledge by one hand, spent sixty seconds using a tool from his coat pocket, then dropped, rushed to the van, and pulled away.

"This makes me believe he slashed my tires," Swabe said.

"Later, we look at what he did."

After they dropped Swabe at Morgan's town house, the detectives returned to search DUMBO riding a garbage truck, wrapped in secondhand brown coveralls and surplus boots. The driver and the loaders on the truck recognized Parson by his picture. They cracked rough jokes about the dirty giant, who lived beyond a hole in the wall at the end of a grimy alley piercing a block of old factories and machine shops.

"Straggles out scratching his ass every time we go in there," Brulie, a tall stiff-backed loader said.

Guthrie paid out a palmful of fifties to get a ride on the truck. Vasquez spotted from the cab, and he rode on the back. He wanted to go in and plant a camera. DUMBO was smaller than a hangnail on the fat hand of Brooklyn, but loading the truck burned slowly through the day. Condos full of hipsters laced the old industrial blocks, providing a mix of fresh paint, sharp edges, and neat trim that looked like overdone flowers in an industrial graveyard.

The garbage truck's purr boomed inside the high walls of the alley that tunneled into a cold, lightless mix of docks, lots, and narrow traverses. A grim dock overlooked the final turnaround, where a white GMC van blocked an arm-width break in the buildings. Guthrie scuttled up and down a pipe to plant his camera while the driver hoisted the Dumpster.

When the Dumpster hammered the ground, Vasquez saw Parson's huge head floating above the roof of the GMC. He rubbed at his eyes, then smoothed his bristly hair. The shoulders of his black greatcoat and the red splash of the muffler winked above the van.

The back of the white GMC ground slowly away from the opening. Parson pushed out into the loading lot like a bull. He stretched again, then took two steps and opened the driver's door. While he lifted a bottle to drink, the garbage truck pulled away.

"Should I have mentioned he does that?" Brulie asked, hanging on the back of the truck beside the little detective.

Shadows reached along Fifty-second Street, brushing lingering sunshine from the hardscape. The town houses and apartments glowed like frosted cakes in a baker's window. Vasquez wanted a shower after the grimy day sifting DUMBO's garbage, but Guthrie refused to stop. He was burning brains for fuel. He fell repeatedly still in the old Ford's passenger seat, shrinking beneath his brown fedora until his head lifted with a cautious jerk. At Morgan's town house, he creaked into motion.

Guthrie studied the third-floor window frame from the sidewalk with a video camera until three neatly dressed old ladies gathered to watch. Then he fetched a small toolbox from the Ford, and Vasquez followed him into the town house. The detectives had wadded their brown coveralls into a laundry bag, but Stephanie Morgan's housekeeper wrinkled her nose at the aura of their earlier operation. He marched from room to room, filming window frames, then came to the third-floor studio.

An empty easel with a stool, a broad tilted drawing table, and two tall locked cabinets facing the windows surrounded an empty rolling table. Sketches of the city decorated the cream walls. Guthrie filmed the window frame through the glass, then gestured for Vasquez to aim the camera. He opened the window and yanked a small stud from the frame with needle-nose pliers.

Vasquez shot a close-up, then asked, "What is it?"

"Looks like a camera," he said. "I can't figure the power source. I found three more on the walk-through—"

Peter Ludlow strode into the studio. "Forget cameras, Mr. Guthrie," he said, reddening. "Tell me what you've discovered about the stalker." He shrugged from a trench coat and tossed it onto the drawing table.

Careful ink sketches of Central Park scattered. Following her husband, Stephanie Morgan came in and quietly gathered the papers.

Guthrie glanced at Ludlow, pocketed the camera stud, then stowed his pliers and locked his toolbox. Morgan's housekeeper slipped into the studio and said, "He went inside your bedroom." Her angry expression turned to startlement when Swabe appeared behind her, sealing the door with his bulk. The old bodyguard glowed with worry.

"You've spent five days investigating," Ludlow said. "I want a report. I could already conclude that I compounded a mistake, by hiring you on another man's recommendation. Your background is messy, Mr. Guthrie."

The little detective considered, watching Stephanie Morgan tuck more sketches of the East Side Highway into a portfolio. "You didn't hire me," he said. "I don't work for you."

A flare of anger left Ludlow speechless. He clamped a hand over his mouth and glared at the dirty, rumpled detective. Guthrie was indifferent.

"Mrs. Morgan, I'm sorry about the tracker," he said.

"That hurt!" she exclaimed, rubbing gingerly at the back of her head.

"After last night, I want the precaution," he said. "I'm not positive, but this man looks dangerous. He orchestrated an attack on one of my operatives last night."

Peter Ludlow smiled as he listened. He opened the jacket of his navy wool suit and pulled out a pen and notebook.

"What's the call sign on the tracker?" Guthrie asked.

"Steffie 209," Swabe answered.

"Once this wraps up, you can have it removed," Guthrie said. "I'm going to harden the night-prowl, Mrs. Morgan. I still don't think it's necessary to put a man inside the house, but I'll have a handful of armed guards outside every night. Avram will hand off with them when he works or leaves."

"Have you any idea, yet, who the stalker is?" Ludlow interjected.

"Avram will still be your day guard," Guthrie said. "Just don't stray away from him." He frowned at Ludlow.

"I have another dinner this Sunday," Morgan said. "Could Rachel accompany me again?"

The little detective nodded.

"Have you discovered anything about the stalker?" Ludlow demanded.

Morgan shifted a look between the detective and her husband, sighed, and said, "I think this is a fair question, Mr. Guthrie."

The little man nodded, then rubbed at his bruised eyes. "Right now, he's using the name Duane Parson. He has a press credential for the camera. He unleashed attack dogs on my operative last night and planted something in this window." He pointed. "I suspect he may be involved in a kidnap-and-murder earlier this year."

"Kidnap?" Morgan echoed softly. Her fingertips brushed gently at her blond chignon.

Ludlow scribbled briefly, then asked, "An address?"

"An SRO in Brownsville," Guthrie said. "He has a white GMC van. That's not much use."

"Aren't the police looking for him?" Morgan asked.

"Rachel connected him to that murder," Guthrie said. "That's unofficial."

The tall lawyer shrugged and pocketed his notebook. "As you say," he said, before lifting his trench coat from the drawing table. He sniffed, and scanned the studio with a puzzled look. "What's that smell?"

The housekeeper pointed at the detectives. "He went inside your bedroom," she repeated, in a hurt tone.

Swabe slid through the doorway. Ludlow strode out with an exasperated sigh. The housekeeper followed quickly, before the old bodyguard could move again. Stephanie Morgan gathered sketches of Washington Square from the drawing table and closed them into her portfolio.

"You are doing what you can, Mr. Guthrie?" she asked softly.

The little detective glanced at Swabe. "Sure," he said. "He won't get to you." He lifted the toolbox, frowned, walked out, then reappeared at the door a moment later. "Would you show me the way out? I might've mislaid it while I was looking at windows."

Swabe caught Vasquez by the sleeve before she could leave. He held her for a moment while the footsteps and voices disappeared. Wearing a black trench coat and a worried expression, he looked like an undercover superhero.

"Tell your boss she's scared," Swabe said. "On the way back in the car, she was shaking like a little bird that was thinking about flying away."

Vasquez shook her head. "She should be scared."

"No," he rumbled. "She was scared *before* Guthrie mentioned the kidnap. Peter won an argument, something they've been fighting about before."

"What?"

He shrugged. "Couples use their own language, kid. Think how your parents can talk around you. Like that. I just know he won." He turned away and disappeared through the doorway, leaving the studio full of light.

Vasquez felt misplaced in the neat room, and wished Stephanie Morgan could've folded her into the portfolio with her ink fragments of the city. She trailed Swabe through the perfect rooms, painted cream and soft green, accented with emerald, turquoise, and ultramarine. Padded cushions alternated with strict, linear woodwork. The window frames drew searching glances, but Vasquez didn't see the cameras Guthrie found.

Nightmare images flickered jaggedly into the pastel dream. Vasquez wondered if Parson had seen her when his sleepy gaze drifted across the garbage truck's windshield. Morgan was under siege by a fairy-tale ogre, without a steel-clad prince to protect her.

Downstairs, Guthrie waited on the street in his old blue Ford. The little man kept life simple. He looked as solid as blowing smoke, but wore his fedora jammed firmly on his head. Vasquez climbed into the passenger seat. She wanted to go home, but in her imagination only empty rooms waited. They echoed old gunfire when she slept.

CHAPTER SEVEN

Guthrie hired three armed operatives to prowl the circuit around the town house and garden, then added a pair of off-duty NYPD officers to sit and watch. The little detective scooped Vasquez from Henry Street early in the morning, then they returned to the town house. Fifty-second Street was quiet and empty; the FDR leaned against the East River like a lazy fence.

The detectives took the handoff from the NYPD officers, who sat parked overnight pretending to eat pizza on a brief stop. The cops couldn't moonlight, but if they just happened to be nearby when something happened, the city expected them to do their duty. Del Rio and Hanson knew Guthrie from a previous operation in Queens.

"We had pedestrians all night," Del Rio said.

"Lot of apartments around here," Hanson added.

The little detective shrugged a reply.

"One thing, though," Del Rio said.

"What's that?"

"A red Pontiac. I took the plate," Del Rio continued, handing over a slip of paper. "Looked like a gunship full of skels, so help me, but what corner they're cruising this side of First Avenue I couldn't tell you. I thought they parked down the street a few times, and they did some standing. I don't know."

"I got it," Guthrie said.

"They didn't do all that while I was eating my pizza, right?"

"No, I got you."

After Swabe arrived to take over Morgan's detail, Vasquez drove to Brooklyn with Guthrie wilted in the passenger seat of the old Ford. Morning traffic vacuumed them across the Williamsburg Bridge. Vasquez fought through the crush in the streets to reach the Heights. Guthrie planned to lurk by DUMBO, tracking the intermittent feed from his camera, and search Parson's hole when he left.

While they waited, the little detective scratched together a map of the block. Google showed a wall blocking the dark opening, but the city's power-service plan revealed an easement left over from early Twentieth-century industry. Old drawings showed an internal hub, heavy with reinforced concrete and iron doors. A circle of commercial redevelopments and a load of condomiums buried the easement.

The previous day's collection of black-and-white stills—the camera snapped a picture each ten minutes—revealed two gaps. The white GMC disappeared between noon and dusk, returned for two hours, then disappeared again until the small hours. Parson kept late hours. Time creaked by like glacial ice while the detectives waited for him to wake and leave.

Vasquez drifted through her notes and reports on Parson, and even tried making lists on paper to change the way she handled the material, but nothing broke the deadlock of ideas. She dredged the Uniform-Crime database without much hope—suspect size wasn't mentioned—and trolled through endless reports on stalkings, all detailing harmless, retarded Peeping Toms and bitter estranged husbands. She drooped back into the seat before lunch, tired of searching for a crime to pin on Guthrie's pet rat.

"That's it!" she said, and slapped the steering wheel.

Guthrie emerged from beneath his fedora with a scowl.

"I already know *what* he did. He killed Alice Powell. *How* he did it might connect someplace else, say Arizona? I need that autopsy and crime-scene report. Gagneau left clues all over his killings . . ." Vasquez stopped, and glared at the little detective. His sharklike smile made his ghostly face resemble a skull.

"*That's* my girl," he said. He pulled his palmtop from his coat pocket, and scanned for the latest picture. "The rat's gone from his nest. Let's go."

The detectives drove into DUMBO in a hurry and parked in a surface lot. The tangled industrial enclave towered above the lot and the dark warehouse beyond it. On his map, Guthrie had found an arcade in one of the commercial developments that pierced through to an interior lot, providing foot access to a point far along the alley. They walked. Three delivery trucks and a taxi passed on the quiet street. An old man tapped along on a cane, window-shopping in the sunshine. The access door to the alley at the end of the arcade was locked. Guthrie glanced around, then picked the lock.

Beyond the door, the smell of old machine oil and dusty bricks replaced fresh paint and construction. Walking briskly, the detectives threaded the alley, a damp slash between the high stone buildings. Two turns led them to the dead-end loading dock. Guthrie glanced up at his camera. Vasquez walked forward and looked through the easement.

Massive iron piping surrounded a diamond-shaped concrete slab. Tiers of pipework protruded into the space on trusses. Catwalks serviced rows of rust-thickened valves. A slow funeral march of groans and cries reverbrated from the pipes. Four service corridors branched into darkness, like tunnels hidden on a jungle floor. Guthrie cursed softly.

"Try your headset," he said. "We need to split up." He pulled his earpiece from his suit-coat pocket, and tucked it into his ear.

Vasquez fitted her earpiece and heard a tinny signal. A narrow bar of light flared her yellow windbreaker as she walked among the pipes. "Maybe," she said.

Guthrie stalked the perimeter of the concrete diamond, winding among the pipework. Once he made a circuit, he walked back to the far corridor and pointed. "I'll take this one. Take that one on your left." He pointed again, then disappeared into the darkness.

Vasquez peered down the corridor through a crowd of pipes divided by a double layer of rusting catwalks. She lit her penlight. Shadows deepened around the pool of light. The first door was an iron hatch sealed with wads of rusted weld. Another narrow hatch waited above the first catwalk; the second catwalk glimmered and disappeared in light and shadow. She saw no stairs.

The old iron groaned while several minutes passed. Vasquez searched. Her corridor dead-ended with an overhead ceiling some-where above the looming catwalks. After the first few doors, her palms were red-brown with rust. Some doors led to dark concrete boxes, their floors scarred with drag marks and corroded bolts. Others hid pitch-dark shafts that stank of rust, oil, and rancid water. Vasquez doused her light and paused each time the pipes reached a crescendo. She listened intently to the racket with her eyes closed. When she reached the dead end, a dull boom sounded—heavy iron on concrete.

"—got some—here—" Guthrie announced, with static for punc-tuation.

The young Puerto Rican detective retraced her steps. "*Viejo*, say that again. You broke up."

Static replied. She doused her light, hurrying toward the concrete diamond. Light filtering down from the narrow opening between the buildings made that seem like a forest glade. She rushed into the open, then stopped to consider which way the turns had pointed her.

"*Viejo!*"

"I got the rat bastard," Guthrie said, static-free. For the first time in days, his voice sounded energetic instead of flat.

Vasquez turned right and strode across the diamond. As she reached the opening of the service corridor, a dark shape loomed. Par-son stepped from among the pipes.

"Do you think he can hear you?" Parson asked, his voice almost inaudible as a pipe groaned. "Would it matter?" He grasped pipes on each side, spanning ten feet, and penned Vasquez within his reach. His blocky head tilted above his spread black greatcoat like a loose stone balanced on a walking wall. His bushy mustache stretched above a satisfied smile.

Vasquez stepped back. Parson shifted forward. In two steps she found the dirty wall, but couldn't escape his reach.

"Shout for him again," he suggested. "That was lovely." He smiled. "The whites of your eyes are lovely."

Vasquez choked, flattening against the wall; Parson *wanted* her to scream—Alice Powell had screamed. Vasquez almost begged for Guthrie, riding the bolt of fear wrung from her like a carelessly twisted rag. Her fingers dipped into her compact pocket. The steel of her knife glowed against her fingertips with the heat of her body.

The giant stalker released one of the pipes. His hand floated forward, disembodied by the black cloth of his coat, and he caught gently at Vasquez's black ponytail. His brow smoothed with contentment while his fingertips slid, tugging softly, until her hair ended and fell from his grasp. He smiled.

For Vasquez, the ritual of knife-sharpening was the easy part. Her red plastic sharpener held two slivers of white ceramic, perfectly angled to hone a knife's edge to a razor. The whickering sound and heartbeat rhythm laid a backbeat for her song about the knife: "This will cut through bone." She thought about Gagneau's knife and the fatal glitter as he tugged it from his belt. She sharpened her knife every day; that kept the steel sharper than tears.

Pulling the knife was the hard part. Men were lucky. Men breathed knives. Guthrie opened his with a casual thumbnail flick. Miguel and Indio carried butterfly knives, like the Russian gangster Guthrie shot to death in the office on Thirty-fourth Street. Vasquez envied their ease. Her custom Schrade had a brass forefinger lock, to close it without needing to switch grips, and a brass lip added to the back of its blade to assist Guthrie's flick. She practiced.

For a month or so she practiced every day. Working kept her from spending the solid hours she had spent practicing the pistol, and Guthrie didn't stand with a stopwatch and bark commands. The little man had taught her the pistol, and that spread comfort across it that lacked with the knife. Two fingers in the pocket and press with the fingertips to pull the knife; thumb-flick the blade lip and finger-press the handle into her palm to open the blade. This should've been like snapping her fingers, but she lacked some essential rhythm.

Parson sniffed his fingertips, closing his eyes for a moment. The great block of his head, weighted by the lump on his huge forehead, drifted like a stone ready to fall. His dirty brown teeth clamped shut, and his eyes popped open with a sneer. "Alberto VO5? That's fine for a schoolgirl," he said, "but you deserve something very much better."

Vasquez pulled her knife and opened it with a click. "Don't touch me," she said.

"Oh," Parson said. He eased back. "You really shouldn't have that."

Hurried footsteps rang on a catwalk down the service corridor, and then Guthrie dropped to the concrete floor. He landed in a crouch and extended his revolver. The little man caught at his breath. Parson took a second step back.

"*This* is public property," Parson said, and gestured at the concrete diamond. "Behind the doors—that's private. I would press charges, if I thought it necessary." He smiled, and took a third step, carrying him well away from Vasquez. "You don't need to threaten me with a pistol. I'm unarmed."

The little detective stood and walked forward with the revolver leveled. "Keep moving," he said. "Don't have me decide that'll be easier."

Parson grinned. "Lovely," he said, then turned and walked across the diamond.

The little detective holstered his revolver, and gestured for Vasquez to stay quiet. He indicated his ear and eye, then made a circle in the air with his forefinger. He was angry, but not enough to say more where they might be recorded. The anger kept him energetic for the walk back out to the Ford. Parson had made them when they rode the garbage truck, then drawn them easily into a snare.

CHAPTER EIGHT

The detectives cooled on the drive away from DUMBO. Streetlight pauses spread silence on the ashy coals of anger. Daylight smoothed away the unwanted memory of Brooklyn's industrial guts. The day was young but they were worn out. Vasquez skirted along the edge of Prospect Park and stopped at a package store. Guthrie bought two glowing liters of Norwegian vodka. Wind sweeping across the park made the old Ford groan and shiver while they passed. Vasquez turned on Ocean, floated in the traffic, and escaped to find a lot on a side street.

The detectives walked back to Barney Miller's; the electronics store didn't have a parking lot. Two bays divided the cool, dark interior of the store. On the right, a double handful of aging hippies browsed dusty bins of old record albums, while a phonograph blared a wordless, bouncing jam by Phish. A skinny black man with a drooping goatee lounged against a wall of shelves full of wire, conduit, amps, and neatly racked tools. He watched the hippies glumly, while they vibrated to the music and gathered vinyl records, calling excitedly to share discoveries. On the left, a dusty pharmacy sat as motionless as an empty discotheque. The music washed through it without leaving a mark. Long shelves held old, unwanted medicine, jumbled together with repaired electronics and boxes of files. Bright droplights hung above the pharmacy cage, like floodlights on an empty stage. Bitter smoke oozed among the lights.

An opening in the wire cage admitted the detectives to an electronics sanctum sanctorum. Fat-Fat, a gigantic Korean wearing a black jogging suit, presided at a wide worktable covered with tools and components. Shelves crowded with monitors and scopes dripped black and colored cables that gathered like water into twisting drainpipes, seeking electricity and connectivity. The Korean seemed as sad and quiet as Abraham Swabe, perched on a stool, resting his heavy shoulders on folded arms the size of an ordinary man's legs.

"Yo, Guth, I can't take it," Fat-Fat said. His dark eyes wandered over the detectives, and he sighed heavily when he saw the vodka bottles, without otherwise moving.

"I thought you liked winter weather," the little detective said.

"Winter? Man, this *noise*." He glared, and aimed his chin at the shelves concealing the other half of the store. "Them freaks been jamming the Grateful Dead for a *week*."

"That's Phish, not the Dead."

"How can you old guys tell that shit apart?" The big Korean frowned.

"That kind of skill needs a connoisseur. If you had years—"

Fat-Fat held up his hands, fingers spread like stop signs. "I remember why you're here. I'll skip the lesson on why old people think they're cool. What happens is that the cameras wave flags at passing cars. That's how your guy found them—he went fishing for the signals." He grinned. "That's how he missed them, too. Those lash-ups don't stream. If they weren't transmitting while he was in range, he missed them. He used a scanner to pull in the cell band. That's not cool. Do you need me to speculate why he does that?"

The little detective shrugged. "Could be pulling fraud, right? Then maybe he saw me moving and wondered what I was doing. I think this rat puts two and two together faster than most." He pulled the gray stud he removed from Stephanie Morgan's studio window from his pants pocket, and dropped it on Fat-Fat's worktable. "I would rather you speculate on what this is."

Fat-Fat frowned. His eyes lingered on Guthrie as he lifted the stud from the table. He rolled his stool and tugged a magnifying lamp into position. He peered at the stud.

"*Looks* like a camera. Very exclusive stuff. That's a lens, and an infrared port on this side. Maybe it talks." He rolled his stool, retrieved a keyboard, and placed it on the table. His huge hands flurried on the keys, and screens came to life around them on the shelves.

"Exclusive?"

"Hard to come by," Fat-Fat said. "The cameras I lash up for you are low-end. Something task-specific could maybe be this small, if I shopped it tight."

"This rat has a lot of gear in his nest," Guthrie said, glancing around. "Looks like this."

The Korean shrugged. "Maybe. I don't figure the power on something that small. Nothing's visible." The computer chimed. "Damn thing talks Java. I'll run the picks and see what's there."

"So it's got power?" Vasquez asked.

The Korean nodded. "Let me try something," he muttered. "That case . . ." He pulled a remote from a drawer under the table, checked the label, and keyed it. The lights in the electronic store died; a moment's silence from the music was broken by outraged voices. Only a dim glow from one small computer monitor marred the absolute darkness.

"Fat!" a harsh voice demanded.

"I *got* it, boss, *relax*," the Korean boomed. His grin glowed faintly in light reflected from the monitor. "How sweet it is—that's it, silence and victory." The lights returned, accompanied by a rush of music and cheers. "Crazy freaks."

"Well?" Guthrie asked.

"It's solar—it just died in the dark. That's seriously exclusive." He studied the monitor, and typed a flurry on his keyboard. "Directory access. The software's typical stuff, it rolled over with a level-two pick, let's see—" More typing. "Takes still photos when triggered by a motion sensor, but needs a recharge time. The resolution's low, caps

at nine or ten images. Probably dumps into something more elaborate nearby, or a driveby. Your guy has a van and goes fishing . . .
end of story."

The little detective sighed. "He installed a few of these. How's this:
the camera watches a room, telling you when people come in, and how
long they stay. About right?"

The Korean nodded. He plucked up the bottles of vodka from the
table, and slid them into a big bottom drawer at the worktable. "It's
reusable. You could use that thing." He grinned and tossed the stud
to Guthrie.

"I got something else," Guthrie said. "I shot some video this
morning. Can you clean it up?" He pulled a palm recorder from his
suit pocket and handed it to the big Korean.

Fat-Fat nodded, extracted the disk from the recorder, loaded it into
his own system, and cycled software. Celebratory laughter and cheering
during a lull in the blaring music twisted his wide face with a scowl.

"When you're wondering if your sanity is worth it," Guthrie said.

"I know," the Korean said. "Find something tall and jump off. I do
that, right? Then I wake up the next morning tangled with some little
blonde."

"Stop wearing the parachute."

Fat-Fat grinned. The big Korean was a dedicated BASE-jumper;
he worked to save money for taking trips that ended in falls. He typed
some commands on his keyboard, and parsed menus with flicks of a
mouse. Monitors lit on the shelves with a sauntering view of a service
corridor at the pump station in DUMBO. Speakers hissed beneath
the sound of quiet footsteps on concrete.

"Ooo, shit! Movietime!" The Korean pushed the volume; pipework
groaned an eerie melody over the hiss, padded by footstep drumbeats. He pulled menus and tweaked filters. The hiss flattened.

Minutes slid by as the recording played. Iron doors and pipes
loomed and veered, with some close attention to scuffs on dirty concrete. Footsteps rattled steadily. A barely audible voice caught Fat-Fat's
ear, for replay and amplification: a brief complaint, in Spanish, about a
rusty door.

"That's Vasquez," Fat-Fat said. "Where's she at?"

"Another corridor," Guthrie replied. "The recorder caught my headset."

"Man, I love digital," Fat-Fat murmured.

More footsteps accompanied a floating examination of overhead ironwork. Along a colonnade of groaning pipes, a narrow catwalk granted access to more iron doors. The video focused, with an on-record grunt from Guthrie; two abrasions on the rusty iron glowed beside untouched oxidation.

"I got some clear tracks here on the catwalk," Guthrie announced on the recording. Darkness swallowed the image, but sound remained: muttered laughter, scuffling boots, and the rush of breath. Footsteps rang on an iron walkway, and the catwalk appeared suddenly in a slow pan.

Vasquez slowly reached around her waist and gripped her Special. The pistol felt reassuringly solid, while she watched Guthrie find an obvious trail. Parson climbed into parking garages and up to window ledges; why hadn't she looked up?

On video, the hinges of the nearest iron door showed steady usage, even in the dim light. The door opened with only a faint creak. Pedestals and grooved compartments in a long, narrow concrete room suggested absent machinery and provided a row of deep niches that substituted for rooms. Bright lights radiated in some, while others were dim or even shadowy.

Vasquez's hand burned, too tight on her pistolgrip. She pulled her hand from her jacket but couldn't relax her fists. Her stomach warned her that Parson was coming from the darkness.

The video lurched forward, stabbing into each niche: a naked mattress, and a pile of crumpled clothes instead of a dresser; a stack of massive water bottles and two tables crowded with canned food; a workbench lined neatly with tools, scopes, and computers; dimly lit galleries papered with images around low pedestals; and a bright gallery frosted with pictures surrounding a low pedestal that held a black leather purse.

The pictures featured Stephanie Morgan, a slow pan of video that seemed like a striptease or endless trips along a catwalk. The heiress walked, sat, ate, taught, drove, talked, smiled, frowned, sulked, and even slept. Guthrie's exclamation, and another slow pan of Parson's shrine came to a jerky halt, then rushed back to the door. The video somersaulted and coiled.

"What'd I miss?" Fat-Fat jabbed with his mouse for a rewind. "I could brighten some of this." Pausing in a darkened gallery, he brightened and contrasted. Some of the larger pictures sharpened. "Your guy likes *Kaleidoscope*, Guth. Look." He tagged some pictures with his fingertip. "Those two were covers."

"Kaleidoscope?"

"Man, you're wired. You can't be missing that. It's better than *Gawker*," the big Korean said. "You're not serious! *Kaleidoscope* is a Webzine, images from the city . . ."

"I'll look into it," the little detective said. "Covers?"

"Right there. It's a monthly freeze-frame. Your guy's an aficionado—the word you were looking for earlier for the freaks." He tapped the video into slow motion, studied the registers, and grunted. "Some audio here." He filtered.

"Do you think he can hear you?" Parson asked, his voice disembodied on the video. "Would it matter?"

"Screw that," Vasquez muttered. The big Korean glanced at her.

"That's you and who?" Fat-Fat asked. He studied the registers again and replayed. "Something else." He applied a filter and amplified. The video ran again; while it somersaulted, a hiss of low static resolved: "Did it *again*, you stupid little man."

Running boots sounded like drumming thunder, crescendoed on the iron catwalk, and then slammed into concrete. Harsh voices blared, but Parson's voice sounded silky and conversational. Fat-Fat refiltered the exchange, and glanced at the detectives after they listened.

"You want to clip the end, Guth?" he asked.

"Better keep it," the little detective said softly. "I'm pretty sure he has his own copy." His gaze wandered into the darkness beyond the monitors.

Fat-Fat took a long look at the little detective while he stood un-moving. "Old man, you're a wreck. I don't look that bad after I blast an ounce. What's going on?"

"What?" Guthrie shook his head. "Nothing. I was thinking. I need something else." He pulled a scrap of paper from a pocket. "Your tool kit drew a blank on this place earlier this week."

Fat-Fat unfolded the slip. "MAGNUM?"

"Rachel tried to raid them Wednesday. I raked them through the IRS. This's a big photojournalism outfit right in the city. We want into their archive."

"You know I like challenges," he answered. "I'll send a pick along, folded in an e-mail."

"Soon?"

A brief chorus of howls accompanied the beginning of a jam by the Grateful Dead. Fat-Fat winced. "Soon," he said.

The detectives left the big Korean working. While Vasquez drove the old Ford back into the city, Guthrie had a long telephone conver-sation with George Livingston about the material they had collected on Parson. The accumulation of pictures was disturbing but not ille-gal, except for the pictures where the heiress lay sleeping. Paired with the secretly installed cameras, they had a case for invasion of privacy—a civil complaint.

Livingston remained doubtful. Direct danger from Parson was unproven, even if the connection to Powell's murder in Seattle could remove him completely. Vasquez suggested that Powell had operated under a similar idea: avoiding instead of confronting the danger. Powell wound up dead. The conversation turned chilly like the November day—gray, overcast, and without promise.

"So protect her," Livingston finished. "He's a known threat. Protect her and keep digging. A civil complaint will only warn him of what you know. I wouldn't walk into a courtroom with that strategy."

"This ain't a courtroom," Vasquez muttered.

"What's that?" Livingston asked.

"Nothing," Guthrie said. "We're on it."

CHAPTER NINE

The detectives drove up to Turtle Bay through hissing traffic. Lines of cars jammed together for the tunnel and the bridge as the city emptied. After they passed the UN, they began circling the blocks. Morgan was coming crosstown from NYU to stop at the town house briefly and collect her husband before going out for dinner. Swabe detailed a quiet day over the phone.

An e-mail arrived from Fat-Fat with the *Kaleidoscope* address and a lock pick for MAGNUM. An old-school firewall protected the archive, too simple for the slick lock picks needed elsewhere. While Vasquez prowled Fifty-second and Fifty-third Streets at the East River, Guthrie scanned on his palmtop. The Webzine featured visual content—sharp mosaic collages, and contrasts like late-night lightning. The current cover showed a handful of dark-skinned girls wearing pigtails and frocks, circled beneath a Harlem stoop playing jacks with a miniature Tompkins Square Park. They swept up cars, students, and jacks alike with a bounce of the ball.

Parson surfaced as a contributor and editor at *Kaleidoscope*. The stalker's name produced an additional rush of images from MAG-

NUM'S archive. After a few minutes, the little detective sighed, staring at a picture from Hue, Vietnam.

"Maybe after Swabe hands off tonight, you could take a look at this," Guthrie said. Vasquez glanced at him with a frown. He shrugged. "My hands ain't broke, but my eyes are swimming. And this rat took pictures in Vietnam. I don't know how that adds up. But I'm going to that hotel and try to sleep. I ain't *slept*."

"I got it, *viejo*," she said. She slid a smooth turn onto First Avenue and worked her horn at a taxi driver, with a gesture added to explain that yellow cars didn't own the right-hand lane. Guthrie stared through the front glass, with his palmtop drooping onto the car seat like the wilted flower forgotten by a jilted lover. His eyes drifted without focus.

When she turned onto Fifty-fourth Street, he swayed against the passenger door and laughed softly. "I was asleep!" he claimed, with excitement softer than finger-clapping.

Vasquez shook her head. "No way," she said. "Your eyes were open the whole time. Then we only went half a block—" She turned to look from the window and quietly cursed the taxi driver beside the Ford, a Jamaican with dreaded hair bulging a green knit cap, to avoid seeing Guthrie wiping away the tears that rushed suddenly down his pale face. She pounded the steering wheel to cover his stifled sniffles.

"I got to get back on Fifty-second," she said. Black limousines with dark windows slouched along fouling traffic like two-bit gangsters in need of attention. Taxi drivers supplied salutes and trumpet blasts for the parade. She turned on Sutton; the southbound lanes sailed past the oncoming jam seeking the bridge. Fifty-second Street yawned briefly as they passed.

"Damn it, there he is!" The little detective pointed.

Vasquez rolled past helplessly, unable to turn onto Fifty-second Street; the one-way street emptied onto Sutton. She slowed, since the white GMC was coming toward them, but the delay didn't let the stalker catch up. He whipped into a service alley on the south side of Fifty-second close enough to watch Morgan's town house, but tucked out of sight. Vasquez muttered a curse, and gunned the Ford for Fifty-first Street.

"I don't think he saw us," Guthrie said.

Vasquez shrugged.

"Stay on this side of him, on the north side of Fifty-second, so we can watch him while he watches the town house, right?"

"I got you," she said. The block passed in slow motion. Knots of coated pedestrians huddled against the chilly breeze, idly fishing with their eyes into the river of passing traffic. Horns screamed on First Avenue. Fifty-second Street seemed like a quiet boulevard by comparison.

"Go ahead and park," Guthrie said, after Vasquez picked a spot along the curb that allowed a slim view of the nose of Parson's GMC. "I figure he's got twenty minutes before that Italian guy comes out from that sign shop and starts kicking the side of the van to move him along."

"More than I'm gonna have before I get a ticket," Vasquez said.

"Standing's just gonna get an air ticket with it," he said.

Street noise replaced the engine; traffic's whoosh wove with still-ness, hisses of wind stroking the old Ford's body, and distant clangor from the avenue. Guthrie aimed a camera, hoping to catch Parson squashing the Italian. The detectives watched Parson drink repeat-edly from a bottle.

"What do you think he's drinking, there?" Guthrie asked.

"*Viejo*, you're desperate."

He shrugged. "Better men have fallen for less."

Stephanie Morgan cruised by in her Saab, surrounded by a flotilla of taxis. Swabe crowded the big backseat, looking presidential with a beautiful blond chauffeur. She parked on the other side of the town house, stopping to dress for dinner and collect her husband. Pedestri-ans floated along beneath the slender young trees spaced on the sidewalk. Parson didn't move.

The traffic lights cycled a few times, sluicing the street with traf-fic to thicken the getaway turns from First Avenue. Wind rippled on the Ford's body. The old blue car shivered with a chill. A rimmed red

Pontiac with shaded glass swam like a shark among the cars rolling past, then veered to a sudden stop, halfway into the south lane a few dozen feet past Parson's white GMC. A handful of masked men wearing trench coats slid from flung-wide doors and leveled pistols. The traffic froze. The men poured gunshots into the GMC tucked into the narrow alley, then whirled and disappeared into the Pontiac.

"Shit!" Guthrie hissed. He pushed open the passenger door and stepped into the street as the Pontiac roared through open space before startled drivers raced to flee. He dashed across Fifty-second Street just in front of an eight-limousine motorcade with miniature Venezuelan flags flapping above their headlights. The diplomats barged haphazardly along both lanes with horns blaring.

The little detective drew his revolver as he dashed up the sidewalk to the service alley. A stunned old woman stood above her fallen pocketbook while a small gray dog ran yapping to wind its leash around her motionless ankles. Others scuttled away from the alley, but others hurried out for a glimpse of the drama. The white GMC sagged in the alley like a staggered boxer, with a stitchery of holes across the windshield and numerous winking gleams of fresh punctures in the faded paint on its nose.

Guthrie dodged his eyes above the dashboard for a glance. The driver's seat was empty. He slid into the alley, cracked the driver's door open, examined the seat, and checked the rear compartment. Fractured glass glittered on the carpet like lost diamonds. The rear doors were closed. He saw no blood.

"He ain't here!" he barked, a wasted complaint. The revolver hung loose in his hand. He slid it back into his shoulder holster.

"What'd they park there for, anyway?" the Italian demanded, stopping at the corner of the building. "What a mess. I got a delivery coming." He craned his neck as Guthrie brushed past. "They dead?" He deflated. "Man, are they dealing out of my alley?"

Across Fifty-second Street, Vasquez stood on the curb beside the Ford. The motorcade bullied its way farther down the street, while the sidewalks knotted with postshooting commentators. Guthrie jabbed a thumb over his shoulder at the van, then shrugged, palms up. Then more gunshots hammered, down the street. Car horns squealed.

The little detective rose to tiptoes, but traffic and sidewalk crowds blocked his view. He drew his revolver and ran toward the town house. Vasquez glanced at the traffic, scowled, and slammed the door of the Ford. She turned and ran down Fifty-second Street. The little detective had a lead, on the other side of the street, but she closed it quickly while he labored.

She caught up with the tail of the Venezuelan motorcade, crawling along at gawker-idle, and cat-footed through a scattering of people; shock froze their frightened expressions but churned their legs. Vasquez broke through a crust of hardened gawkers to the stretch of sidewalk in front of Morgan's town house.

Sprawled bodies slowed the young Puerto Rican to a walk. Lakes of blood drained from Morgan, Ludlow, and Swabe, and poured into the curbside gutter. Stephanie Morgan's housekeeper stood silently in the open door while the Venezuelans passed like a cortege. Elsewhere, horns blared and a siren sprang to life, but a hush surrounded the dead.

Guthrie jogged tiredly across the street, stopped in the gutter and sighed. He holstered his revolver again, wearing the bitter look of a man with a hammer who needed to turn a screw—wrong tool, wrong time, wrong place—again.

"Go on get the car, Rachel," he said softly. He knelt and traced his fingers through the damp sand in the gutter.

Vasquez scowled. "How'd he do this, *viejo*?" she demanded.

Guthrie walked to where Swabe lay dead, making a dark hump on the concrete. The little detective stepped gingerly around his blood, knelt and brushed Swabe's dark hair away from his ears. The big Jew looked young, without his cares. Guthrie gently dusted his thumb and fingers above Swabe's body, sprinkling sand.

"Don't argue with me, old man," he said softly. "I got him."

Vasquez knelt beside the little detective. "What?"

Sirens crept closer. Guthrie stood and tugged Vasquez to her feet. "We got to go, Rachel," he said.

She snatched her arm from his hand, and pointed at Morgan's body. Her blue velvet gown was dark with blood. "How'd he do this?"

Guthrie shook his head. "He didn't."

NYPD rushed the murder scene as the detectives walked away. Guthrie wasn't in a mood for questions on the cold November night. He had lost his client. Eyewitnesses gathered on the sidewalk. Vasquez glared at them when they rolled past on Fifty-second Street, while uniformed cops secured the scene. Guthrie kept quiet. He pulled the brim of his fedora low to keep the housekeeper from recognizing him.

The detectives drove back to the office, a long struggle through crosstown traffic at the worst time of day. Vasquez felt alone behind the wheel, while traffic rushed around them. Gunshots echoed, again and again, in her mind, remixing until she couldn't remember which rattle was first, last, or long ago. Every time she noticed the traffic, she was under fire from taxi horns, or catching glares from the corner of her eye that disappeared when she turned to look. The little detective gestured silently, conducting some disobedient orchestra of thoughts.

Vasquez ground her teeth and tried to ignore him. Along the way to Thirty-fourth Street, she left behind, bit by bit, the reasons for her anger, and finished the drive staring at the reflection of her red-rimmed eyes in the rearview mirror, after she tapped it to keep from seeing the traffic chasing her.

The office was quiet. They wrote reports, and Guthrie burned CDs of surveillance footage. After pizza and beer, the killing faded. The little detective drove Vasquez home to Henry Street in quiet that seemed late.

CHAPTER TEN

The next morning was Sunday, but the sound of Mamì's voice jerked Vasquez from sleep. The sky through her unshaded window showed gray morning light.

"I don't want to go to church," she moaned.

Mamì sighed. "I know, *hija*," she said softly. "But you're going to work." She crossed her arms, tugging at the sleeves of her brown robe. That meant: *You will.*

Vasquez huddled beneath her blanket a moment longer, then tossed it when she heard the sound of the old Ford's horn blowing on Henry Street below her parents' stoop. A familiar note of annoyed insistence tinted the clangor. A few times in September, she let Guthrie blow until the neighbors walked down in ratty bathrobes and surrounded the old blue car. The little detective ignored complaints. The neighbors switched their efforts to the door of her parents' apartment, and that drove her from bed.

She shuffled her thoughts like a losing hand of solitaire while she tugged on her blue jeans. Getting out of bed made no sense. The morning was cold, and Stephanie Morgan was dead, but Guthrie's horn insisted. Vasquez marched, giving Mamì a glum look as she slid by the kitchen on her way out.

Once they reached the office on Thirty-fourth Street, the little detective marshaled all of the preliminary work and operations reports on the Morgan case to prepare a final report. He fell silent and still for handfuls of minutes while he worked, with sheaves of notes forgotten in his hand or a cup of coffee paused before a sip. Vasquez watched him. At some point, he seemed certain to spit out a string of parts, grind to a halt, billow smoke, and then explode. He admitted passing another night without sleep.

A late-morning phone call from Mike Inglewood, a detective from NYPD's Major Case squad, interrupted his disjointed efforts. Guthrie's operation at the Morgan town house was noted with the watch commander at the 19th Precinct. This placed the private detectives on a list of potential witnesses. Ame Hernandez caught lead on the case at the 19th Precinct, and drew Rocky Devlin as his partner from Manhattan South Homicide. They wanted a quick break to keep the brass at One Police Plaza from reassigning the case to some prima donnas from Major Case—a jab worth a rough laugh from Inglewood.

"That's good, Mike," the little detective said finally. "I would've volunteered for an interview sooner or later."

Inglewood's laughter came through the phone like a dog barking. "I like that, Guthrie," he said. "My point is more that you should unvolunteer your services past the interview. Stay out of the way. It's not gonna be helpful if you get your nose in this. We don't need reminding that your client was important."

"NYPD's offering after-the-fact special service?"

"Do you gotta go there?"

"All right, sorry, that was a cheap shot," Guthrie muttered.

"Okay. We're good, then?"

"Sure."

After the telephone conversation, the little detective sat at his desk chair for a few minutes with his brogans kicked up on the blotter. He watched the gray limestone buildings across the street through the office window. He shuffled to life and handed Vasquez a business card for his lawyers, and told her to dummy up if the NYPD detectives tried to corner her.

Guthrie planned to be forthcoming, without appreciating a suggestion to keep his nose back. He didn't know the detectives assigned to the case, but he doubted before he trusted. He figured they would lack proper motivation. They spent some time roughing the outline of the final operation report before the NYPD detectives showed at the frosted-glass office door.

Ame Hernandez was a tall, dark-skinned Dominican with fluffy curls atop a fade. His thick eyebrows were nicked with old scars. He held himself upright, determined to get every advantage out of his six feet and change, but rawboned leanness kept him from having any real size. He wore a black wool coat, calfskin gloves, and blue suede Paul Smith derbies.

The detective from Manhattan South, Rocky Devlin, had an off-kilter face from a bullet wound. Thinning black hair above a receding hairline showed off his pale skull. Wraparound sunglasses and a trench coat made him seem old. Both men walked around the office for a careful look. Devlin paused at the windows, looking out.

"What's this private gig pay?" Hernandez asked. His gaze drifted to Vasquez, and he slid his left hand into his coat pocket.

"The retainers can go high," Guthrie said. "You can imagine, with a Morgan, right? They own a bank. I think I have some good stuff for you."

"You have a Morgan retainer?" Hernandez glanced around the office. "I bet you meet them at lunch. Right?" A disdainful look at the brown faux-fur couch suggested the detective wouldn't risk dirtying his coat.

"What can I say?" Guthrie said. "My uncle gave me the couch."

"Well, you can't choose your family," Hernandez said, and shrugged.

The office door banged open without a knock. Miriam Weitz, a slim young woman with dark cropped hair, rushed inside then lurched to a sudden stop when she saw the NYPD detectives. She carried a motorcycle helmet in one hand and a newspaper in the other. Black leather made her look like a soldier. She threw the newspaper over the back of the leather couch, onto the coffee table, and scowled.

"You work here?" Hernandez demanded.

"No," Weitz replied. She added another scowl, and a glance at Guthrie.

"Try coming back later," Hernandez said. "Police business."

Weitz glanced at the newspaper, then bolted from the office.

"I can see Macy's! Right here," Devlin said after the door slammed. His grin disappeared like a collapsing bridge as he turned away from the window. "Stephanie Morgan hired you to bag a Peeping Tom?"

"Sure," Guthrie replied. Vasquez recognized a curt edge to his voice that often signaled an angry outburst. The little detective's gaze dropped briefly to the newspaper half scattered on the coffee table.

"Mrs. Morgan gave some pictures to the One-Nine. Turns out that's a serial stalker named Duane Parson, right?"

"Sure."

"That's what gave you the idea to get Morgan a bodyguard?"

"Seeing the picture brought the bodyguard, right at the beginning. I didn't wait for background."

Hernandez nodded. "A Morgan retainer. You did find that Brooklyn stalking?"

"Sure. That jumped out."

"Find anything specific on him?" Hernandez's question oozed out with a double side of nonchalance.

"Sure. He didn't do it."

Both police detectives studied him. Hernandez said, "Some people give you high marks. You've had your name in lights."

"*Then* you miss the obvious," Devlin added. "This was Parson."

"I see a gleaming needle in his future," Hernandez said.

Guthrie nodded. "He has a white GMC van," he said, "that got shot to pieces on Fifty-second Street last night. Did you get a look at it?"

Hernandez calculated with a frown. "We have an unrelated shots-fired."

"I got there while pieces were still rolling away. The shooters missed him—"

"There was no van," Devlin interjected.

Guthrie laughed. "I bet that Italian had it towed."

"Eyewitnesses want a *big* shooter." Hernandez glanced at Vasquez.

The little detective grinned. Vasquez recognized the maliciously overjoyed look he had when he saw a big laugh coming at someone else's expense. They had reviewed their surveillance footage from the night before. One camera on the Morgan town house caught the shooting perfectly.

The lead car in the Venezuelan motorcade edged along, teasing a white Toyota with the possibility of changing lanes. A double dozen pedestrians dotted the sidewalk, facing west toward the oncoming traffic as a man in a black knit cap pointed vigorously and supplied some silent urging. One tall man standing against the iron skirting of a slender tree glanced back toward the camera. A muffler wrapped the bottom half of his face, with the ends tucked neatly into a long black coat. Dark glasses and a blocky fur hat masked the rest of his face.

The Venezuelan motorcade slid forward like a tired avalanche. Abraham Swabe pushed out onto the stoop of Morgan's town house. He filled the recess in the florid Italianate doorway, looking grimly both ways on the street like a man studying heavy traffic, then strode down the steps. Stephanie Morgan and Peter Ludlow hurried out impatiently. Two people hustled past on the sidewalk, cutting through the milling gawkers.

Morgan's Saab waited curbside, a few dozen feet west of the door. Swabe led the way, cranking his head as he strode, sweeping the sidewalk with his scowl. Morgan walked right behind him, neatly within his outline on camera. The tall man at the slender tree turned and pushed his coat open like a parting curtain. His brown hands emerged with a cutdown Kalashnikov.

An old, silent gangster movie followed. The gunman rushed forward. Billows of smoke marked his shots. Swabe swept his hand behind him, found Morgan, and brushed her neatly into the gutter. Then he sidestepped and pulled a long, gleaming pistol.

After startled reaction takes, some bystanders dove for the gutter, and the rest scattered. One dashed into the street and rebounded silently onto his ass after broadsiding a Venezuelan limousine. Peter Ludlow bolted for the door of the town house. The tall gunman hammered Swabe with shots. Swabe corkscrewed as he fired his pistol, missed, and fell heavily.

Stephanie Morgan sprang from the gutter and dashed for the town house. The gunman shot Ludlow before he reached the door; he rammed the corner of the ornate doorway, then rolled back down the stairs. Morgan caught his arm and lifted valiantly. Bullets flung them both against the stone railing. The tall gunman ran beneath the camera and disappeared. The Venezuelan limousines bumped along, drifting in startlement.

"Duane Parson—and I doubt that's his name—didn't shoot Stephanie Morgan," Guthrie said. "Save your time."

Hernandez nodded in consideration. "You got nothing on Parson?"

"That's a blind alley. You're gonna catch up to yourself on your way back out."

Vasquez laughed and Hernandez's face darkened. "You got jokes?"

"I know things."

The interview turned hostile, but Guthrie stood no chance of being arrested for anything but nuisance. The NYPD detectives plainly had a heads-up about the Seattle murder, but didn't mention that to the private detectives. They wanted Parson for the Morgan murder before Seattle could fit him for Powell. The competition turned their heads. With crafty insolence, the little detective pushed them toward Parson by pulling at the right moments, and sent them out the door with the unheeded suggestion that Peter Ludlow was the intended target of the murder.

"*Viejo*, they're gonna be pissed later," Vasquez said, after the office door rattled shut behind Rocky Devlin.

The little detective grinned.

The office door banged open again and Weitz rushed inside. She dropped her helmet on the oxblood couch and marched past the corner of Guthrie's desk. The little detective sprang to his feet to face her. The smile faded from his pale face.

Weitz pointed at the newspaper on the coffee table. "What happened?" she demanded.

"He was guarding Stephanie Morgan," Guthrie answered softly.

"He was seventy-four!"

"And still better than two men half his age."

Weitz's green eyes lit. "*That's* the truth!"

The little detective sighed.

She poked a finger into his chest. "We have to find the schmutz that did this—"

He gave up a step, then firmed, cutting her short. "*We're* not doing anything. I got this. You can't work on this. Not like this. Look at you."

"Clay, I knew somewhere there was a soft spot in your head. This schmutz killed my grandfather—*to start*—now you think I'm sitting down like some pisherkeh? I would rather be a *Muslim*—"

"Mireleh!"

"Don't you call me that, you coldhearted prick!" Eyes shining, Weitz stepped forward and rapped Guthrie on the chin with a left jab. His teeth clicked together and he staggered a half-step. He brushed aside the right cross that followed, and gripped the sleeve of her leather jacket. He wheezed a curse after a punch to the ribs, but tangled her left arm with a clinch.

"Let go!"

Vasquez watched, wide-eyed. The little detective smothered Weitz with his grip; he twisted her jacket and pressed her against his desk. Her curses sank in volume without losing their venomous edge. She needed her breath. Guthrie pulled her into an embrace that looked more like a headlock. Her curses drifted into an incoherent snarl of anger.

After staring at Vasquez long enough to catch her eye, he jabbed at the door with his eyes and chin. His bleak scowl said the rest: Get out. She took the keys to the Ford and went.

CHAPTER ELEVEN

The old blue Ford waited on Henry Street overnight, a reminder of the little detective's silence. Guthrie didn't call. Vasquez didn't want to think about it. She drank, and floated on the cosy warmth of rum, looking from her window and watching the bleak sky turn dark. She dodged her parents when she crept to the bathroom and visited the refrigerator. The night fit snug on the shelf beside forgettable nights on the bookcases of September, October, and November. Her memory vanished in the darkness.

Guthrie called in the morning with instructions to meet him on Lexington Avenue. Predictably, Vasquez ran late and fought the rush traffic in midtown. Grand Central Terminal bubbled like a backed-up drain. On the edge of the swirl at Forty-fifth Street, Davis Polk and Wardwell filled an office on Lexington, overshadowed by the MetLife Building straddling Park Avenue.

Rows of brooding founder portraits stared across the law firm's polished marble lobby. The firm didn't advertise, but they furnished with pure money. Deep wool carpets and Louis XVIII trim framed the painting and statuary. Vasquez felt dirty by comparison.

A power-suited blond functionary introduced herself as Maria, and led the detectives to a waiting room away from the perfect lobby. Maria had coltish legs, a perfect heart-shaped face, and a polished demeanor that fit the office. She tossed disgusted looks at Vasquez while pretending to listen to her earpiece as they waited.

Wearing a soot-smeared yellow windbreaker and grubby jeans, Vasquez thought about the equestrienne outfit the fashionistas at Henri Bendel chose for her, and wondered if that would wipe the smug disdain from the tall blonde's face. Guthrie looked like a brick wrapped in burlap, but red-rimmed eyes and an anger-stamped face discouraged even silent comments.

A tall white-haired man in a gray wool suit strode into the waiting room. He nodded at the coltish assistant and she departed, with a last sharp stare at Vasquez.

"Mr. Guthrie, I cannot say that I am glad to meet you," the tall man said. His grip had the bone-saw firmness of an orthopedic surgeon; for Vasquez, he extended his upturned fingertips and a smile. "I'm William Sinclair, the senior estate partner with Davis."

"This's Rachel Vasquez, my operative," Guthrie said.

The lawyer paused, frowned over a question, then left it unasked. "I offered to meet you," he said. "I hoped to trade questions for questions. When your contact came through to our managing partner, some immediate suggestions were made. You . . ."

Guthrie took the offered opening. "I reached out through George Livingston for a look at Peter Ludlow," he said. "He was killed two days ago."

The lawyer nodded, but his face hardened.

"I was asked to trap a rat, but I decided yesterday that I was watching the wrong rat." Guthrie flapped his brown fedora against his trouser leg. "I'd like to talk with anyone who worked with Ludlow. And see whatever he worked on. I'm free to sign a confidentiality arrangement."

The lawyer nodded, then led them through the office, conjuring and banishing lawyers, clerks, and administrators that all bent to diligent work when they saw him. Along the way, he instructed an assistant through his headset, producing an out-of-synch tour where audio didn't match video. Time was valuable.

A warren of offices, libraries, and conference rooms awaited them upstairs. The carpet silenced every footfall, but telephones murmured. In the open reception area, the coltish blond assistant laid confidentiality agreements on a polished mahogany table. The detectives signed.

Sinclair led them to Peter Ludlow's office, on the upper leg of the capital *H* formed by the corridors. A sequestered library and conference room formed the guardian doors of the cul-de-sac. The lawyer whisked the door closed after the detectives entered. The office window peered across at the MetLife Building.

"You feel Ludlow's death is connected to his work at Davis?"

Guthrie shrugged. "I'm gathering background."

"So you don't subscribe to the theory held by the police?"

He shrugged again. "I had an interview yesterday morning. They're running in the wrong direction. They disregarded my advice, or they would be here right now."

Sinclair frowned. "Peter was assigned to R.J. Reynolds, some typical corporate litigation about product infringement. Does this sound—"

"Did something turn up recently?"

"I doubt it. Corporate litigation is glacial." The lawyer walked to the window and looked down. "Peter was a mistake. I wish Stephanie had never met him. After their marriage we were forced to fit him in here, despite his cunning nature."

"You knew him well?" Guthrie asked. He settled behind the desk, and began opening drawers. He pointed at the cabinets and bookshelves, frowning at Vasquez. Her hands slid from her jacket pockets and she rummaged busily.

Sinclair settled in the windowsill. "I'm afraid I did," he said. "Stephanie was promising. He was beneath her, but the knight-errant will always catch the eye of the princess."

"But he was a lawyer?"

"Of course. And gifted, in his way. He practiced criminal defense before he came to Davis, another sly man of representation and misrepresentation. They connected through one of his clients—a street artist slash purveyor. He pursued her. That will always be a family weakness: Morgan heiresses are desirable."

Guthrie nodded. He plucked a worn leather journal from the big bottom drawer of the desk, tucked beneath the expanding files. Vasquez shifted law books on the shelves, peering into each dark gap before returning them.

"Stephanie Morgan was beautiful," Guthrie said. His eyes flicked up at Sinclair as he cast the bait.

"Indeed," the lawyer murmured. His face smoothed pensively. "Then came Peter." A scowl drifted across his brow. "Now a double disaster."

Guthrie opened the journal and scanned the pages. Vasquez rearranged a cabinet crowded with liquor bottles, glasses, and cutlery. They rang like background music in a cheap diner.

"Stephanie was so gifted," the lawyer said. "She had a stalker? Stephanie had a *thousand* stalkers. We hoped that she would satisfy her charitable impulses in her youth, fulfill her need to teach, and then be ready for true community service—politics. Why not the Senate? Why not higher?"

"Except for Peter?" Guthrie asked. He pried aside a book wedged in the back of the desk's top drawer, slid in his fingers, and pulled out an automatic pistol. "I thought I smelled oil," he muttered softly. He lifted the pistol, sniffed, and then dropped it into his coat pocket.

"Peter Ludlow was a plebeian millstone," Sinclair said. "He was unworthy. *Now*, I cannot say which is worse: that he needed to survive her to save her patrimony, or that she wasted herself on him. The Morgans placed many eggs in her basket."

"She was a first-generation trust?" Guthrie asked.

Sinclair nodded.

On the desk blotter, neat handwritten notes outlined days of calls, meetings, conferences, and appointments. The little detective drew out a notebook and jotted names. "Mr. Sinclair, do you have someone here with the initials C.C.?" he asked. "Everything else is a complete name."

The lawyer walked around the desk and looked. "We have over seven hundred lawyers," he said. "Add numerous other employees . . ."

Vasquez came to the desk. "Where?" she asked.

Guthrie pointed at some notations on the blotter.

"Charles Congdon," she said, tapping a date. "He showed at the commission dinner."

The little detective nodded. He added times and dates to his notes. Sinclair ordered interviews with Davis employees from Guthrie's list; others were corporate executives or opposing counsel. The little detective handled the face-to-face while Vasquez tracked Ludlow on the Net. Sinclair provided his corporate password, but she switched to electronic keys for the wealth of information outside the law firm.

Vasquez traced Ludlow's cell phone through a bank payment to the provider, who surrendered his number with the Internet equivalent of "I really shouldn't . . ." She pried open his call log and scraped it into a file for later consumption. Maria presided over Guthrie's string of interviews with sour disapproval but perfect efficiency; time was valuable. The tall blonde appeared and disappeared with quiet magic. She brought a tray of coffee and sandwiches at lunchtime. Vasquez discovered some sly pleasure in overlooking her.

Early in the afternoon, the detectives dropped from the office. The perfect lobby exhaled them onto Lexington Avenue with a breath of leather, antique wood, and old paper while the cold hardscape cycled relentlessly through tricks, like a circus without a ringmaster.

"Did I miss something?" Vasquez asked as they walked toward the garage.

Without turning, Guthrie asked, "What?"

"The lawyer seemed real familiar with Stephanie Morgan," she said. "You don't seem caught on that."

"I caught it," he said. "Maybe he had motive, or some of those men had motive, but that's one of those things that waits until last to open. This situation is ugly enough without starting at the bottom of the toilet. Then there's simpler answers."

She frowned. "He pushed you hard toward Ludlow."

"I don't like that, either," the little detective said. "But why hitch a zebra with a mule right by? I got a throw-down in my pocket—a pocket-sized 9mm with no serial. Is that a plant *and* a push?" He shrugged.

"These old families in the city stay with the same lawyers for generations. Sinclair works estates. He worked there before Stephanie Morgan was born. A man like that has a strong professional interest in the outcome."

Guthrie paused to glance up at the gray sky. Vasquez stopped to let him catch the step. The crowd churned around them with muttered curses.

"The Morgans are a powerful family," he continued. "Stephanie was twenty-nine. I expect they thought to have another forty or fifty years out of her before the money rolled over."

Guthrie sighed, examining Vasquez's blank look. "Okay, the law lets a trust skip taxes for a generation. Ain't no such critter as a perpetual trust. The money has to change hands. Sinclair let on that the Morgans put a lot on Stephanie, and now the generation ended early. Ludlow would've kept the trust alive. They died without children. There's a lot of Morgan money floating in the air right now."

Vasquez walked a few steps, then said, "So it's gonna hurt."

"Sure. Paying taxes is an unexpected slap in the face." The little detective pulled the leather-bound journal from his pocket, and slapped it against his leg a few times before thrusting it at Vasquez. "All right, you get to figure this out."

The detectives waited on the sidewalk outside the garage as the valet ran for the Ford. Guthrie eyed Vasquez and shook his head. "You ain't wearing that to Avram's funeral," he said. "We'll stop at your place on the way to Williamsburg."

The young detective glanced down at herself. Blue jeans, jungle boots, a black T-shirt, her Yankees cap, and the yellow windbreaker fit the hardscape around her. She noted some grimy patches on the seams of her jeans where she wiped her hands, and shrugged. Guthrie had on a clean suit, but he still looked like a dusty brick. The old Ford lurched from the garage, and he waved her to the driver's seat.

Beginning on Saturday afernoon, deliveries had walked up the stairs of the Henry Street tenement to Vasquez's door. Stephanie Morgan tapped some machinery into motion that continued after she was shot to death on Saturday night, meant to prepare Vasquez for a dinner engagement on the Sunday that never came, and whatever more the heiress anticipated through the holidays. The deliverymen shrugged as they took signatures; the packages were paid.

The packages kicked Vasquez in the pit of her stomach. Her closet and the space beneath her bed bulged with a designer rummage sale in bags and boxes. Cosmetics, accessories, shampoo, and carefully marked instructions from Samuel, Gail, and Bonnie filled a crate. Fruit baskets, candy, and flowers collected from every delivery lingered in corners and on tabletops.

Vasquez fumbled beneath her bed, snatched loose the bag from her visit to Henri Bendel, and dumped it on her bed. Once she slid into the bolero and donned the black felt hat, Guthrie nodded. With the hat, even the grimy jeans and boots were acceptable.

An army of mourners, dark in frock coats and beards, waited at the cemetery in Williamsburg. An old man with a gray beard covering the front of his black coat and vest intercepted Guthrie before he could reach the center of the crowd. They argued. Vasquez couldn't understand the Yiddish. The bearded man was taller, his gestures more dramatic from the extent of his reach, but Guthrie's eyes burned in deeper hollows; the man's words fell on shoulders hunched with the solidity of an ancient stump. Their voices curled into soft thunder. The old man turned away sadly, the victor, and the detectives drew back to watch from a distance.

Bare dark trees rose above the crowd. Markers and monuments lined the neat, manicured lawns within frames of black asphalt. The silent mourners parted for Swabe's casket, swayed during the pauses, then sighed at the mausoleum. Vasquez felt lost in the crowd, stretching far to each side and thickly to the gate.

Walking away beside the little detective, she said, "That's some family."

He shook his head. "Avram was an orphan from the camps. He didn't have no family except his children. And he had us."

"Who are they, then?" she asked.

"Jews. They ain't gonna forget." Guthrie strode along quietly for a few steps. "That was his son that I argued with. He didn't want Miriam to see me. She might've wanted to fight at the funeral. She's angry."

Vasquez wanted to ask him why he hadn't settled that on Sunday, but the words died in her mouth. Miriam Weitz worked for Guthrie before he hired Vasquez, and she had concluded that Guthrie hired her because Weitz quit.

That thought hung from slim evidence. For a handful of months, the little detective's acquaintances asked about Weitz when they noticed Vasquez. Weitz didn't stand out on inspection—green eyes, a pretty face, slim and young, with cropped hair and an attitude. The similarity suggested that the little detective needed interchangeable sidekicks.

"*That's* why he didn't fire me," she muttered.

CHAPTER TWELVE

The next morning, the little detective looked worse than Vasquez felt. He held himself upright by clinging to the steering wheel of the Ford. He studied her as she struggled to pull on her windbreaker as she sat in the passenger seat. Headlights from the sparse traffic splashed in passing across the rain-speckled glass.

"Take that trench coat on the backseat," he said. "It's turned too cold for them little jackets."

Vasquez abandoned the windbreaker sullenly. A bag of doughnuts and coffee waited with the coat on the backseat. She pulled the coat across her lap. "Where're we going?" she asked.

"The Bronx. We ain't done running down Ludlow."

"What for?"

Guthrie flicked a glance her way. The Ford hissed along on wet pavement. He turned onto Clinton Street. The city opened before them like a crowd lining a parade. "You remember that H. P. Whitridge pays my retainer? He knew Morgan since she was a girl. He wants the killer found. Since NYPD assigned some half-wits, I'll make sure of it myself."

Vasquez grunted. "What's in the Bronx?"

"More lawyers," he answered. "Harper Congdon and Lynch. They're about to receive a visit from a curious man."

The detectives dropped down onto the rain-curtained Bronx from Macombs Dam Bridge. The law offices were tucked among the mismatched architecture off the Concourse, tightly wedged between the gutter of Jerome and eight lanes going nowhere. The courthouse and jail were chunky outcrops standing above all the litter beaten flat by rain. Traffic spurted along.

Guthrie parked in a shallow lot across the street from the offices. An undersized bare metal sign with black lettering marked the door. Heavy grilled bars protected the windows. A checkerboard of unswept debris decorated the lot fronting the offices, while a stream of tired men, collars up against the rain, splashed through puddles on the sidewalk as they hurried past. The detectives watched.

"I doubt that's the only entrance," Guthrie said.

The rain slowed to a drizzle. Traffic thickened. A handful of Spanish men lingered against a storefront beside the office, cupping cigarettes, studying the traffic, and trading conversation.

"You watch here," Guthrie said. He tapped his earpiece to test the signal and slid his brown fedora onto his head. "I'm gonna have a walk."

The little detective disappeared down the sidewalk. The office windows stayed dark. Vasquez decided that the men under the storefront were Mexicans, small and gaunt with drooping mustaches. Faded bills around them offered groceries at discount. She pulled her palmtop and tapped some notes on Ludlow, glancing up occasionally.

Gusts of rain swept up the street. Vasquez shook her head when Guthrie griped. She raked Ludlow through the Net, beginning with accounts he shared with Morgan. Their last purchase sent a chill through her guts: a hundred and twelve thousand dollars at Henri Bendel. The clothing purchase was lumped among eight-hundred-dollar dinners and seven-dollar coffees, but the couple steadily pegged at a quarter million dollars each month.

Ludlow's income at Davis Polk and Wardwell covered about half of their expenses, but the midtown partnership had begun after the marriage. During the years with his old firm in the Bronx, Ludlow rarely quartered his new income. Sinclair's suspicion beat like a dull, heavy bassline beneath the background check.

Idly trolling through the case notes, Vasquez pinned the red Pontiac on Ludlow with a transposition. The Pontiac was registered to Myster Reed, a twenty-six-year-old black male residing at 2134 173rd Street in the Bronx. Ludlow made repeated phone calls, on his cell, to a phone owned by Aaron Reed, residing at 3412 173rd Street in the Bronx. Reed's cellphone was active, and the log included attempted calls to Ludlow shortly after the Fifty-second Street shootings.

Digging deeper for Reed, she found that Myster owned a sheet of petty convictions for simple possession topped by ABHAN and DUI. A lone distribution charge was null prossed. Guthrie listened to Vasquez's outline of the car and calls. "That'll be the crack that sends all them poor dumb bastards to jail," he said. "I wonder how it went wrong."

"They missed Parson," Vasquez said.

"Not that. Who decided to quiet Ludlow?" The little detective muttered a curse. "I found another parking lot in the alley around here. I'm being kind. This's a wide puddle where some people have parked cars."

"*Viejo*, this's *the Bronx*."

Soft laughter rattled Vasquez's earpiece. "You have some feelings about that. I got a piece of dry asphalt here to stand on, but I'm having to share it with some garbage cans. I took down some plates."

The Puerto Rican detective watched the street and waited while he came out. Thinning clouds and a rising sun brightened the tops of the buildings. Late traffic still surged without hinting at the coming lull of mid-morning. Indexing the law firm was a typical Guthrie operation, built around his idea that anything could be taken apart and examined as easily as a lawn mower. In business, money goes in and out; people handle it; some product changes hands. Harper Congdon and Lynch were destined to fill a poster on the wall of the office at Thirty-fourth Street, neatly described with names, dates, addresses, and figures.

The reductive process distilled people to a few letters, photos, numbers, and lines of relationship, but Vasquez felt criminal lawyers deserved a neat box. When the system gripped her brothers, Indio and Miguel, criminal lawyers served the process. Indio called them all "Mr. Smith": interchangeable and useless. After his last four-month assault stretch at Rikers Island, his first laugh came from Miguel's suggestion that maybe Mr. Smith could fix the clogged toilet in the apartment above them. "No way! Mr. Smith can't do *nothing*!" Her brothers rolled on the carpeted floor and howled like puppies until they cried.

Guthrie walked into the parking lot and rapped on the passenger window of the Ford. He jerked a thumb at the office entrance across the street and turned away, hunching his shoulders against the drizzle. Vasquez followed him, dodging traffic and fans of spray.

Unshielded fluorescent bulbs lit a small, overheated lobby. Three cheap wooden doors and a cutout reception window faced two steel-framed industrial couches wrapped in greasy teal upholstery. A coffee table offered a thick layer of old magazines. A slender Bengali woman rose and looked through the cutout.

"I can offer you assistance?" she asked. Her mouth sharpened with a habitual frown. A severe ponytail and a high-collared jacket erased the remainder of her beauty.

Guthrie handed her a card and examined her office while he asked to see any of the firm's partners. A laptop and a landline straddled her desk blotter. Cheap green steel filing cabinets separated two more cheap wooden doors.

She eyed Guthrie's card, then roadblocked with excuses and incomprehension. The little detective offered her a job and drew a blank stare. She turned cooperative after he explained that Peter Ludlow was dead, and he had information that could be useful to her bosses.

"Mr. Harper has not arrived," she said.

"How about Charles Congdon?" Guthrie asked.

She grimaced dismissively but nodded.

Congdon's office was midway along a hallway lined with offices. Flakes of old paint dotted the thin carpet in the hall. Filing boxes were stacked haphazardly between the closed doorways.

A gap in the cheap plastic shoe molding beside Congdon's office door exposed a zigzag line of dried ochre epoxy. The office held a crowd of government surplus furniture and more stacks of filing boxes. A sleek chrome computer dominated the desktop.

The lawyer sighed as he shifted boxes from the chairs in front of his desk. "I apologize for being behind the computer revolution," he said. "I'm creating our firm's first database—a little insurance, I call it." He sank into his chair with a grateful sigh.

"Hiring some help could carry you along," Guthrie said.

The lawyer nodded. "In legal matters, confidentiality can be more important. Can you tell me what happened?"

"A single gunman shot them," Guthrie said.

"Stephanie had trouble with that stalker. I saw him at the commission dinner. I saw then how large he was. Peter told me, but imagination doesn't suffice—" The lawyer frowned. "I'm afraid I'm forming an impression that you believe the stalker didn't kill them." He shifted his attention to Vasquez. "You weren't there?"

"The dinner was a one-time," she said. "Swabe doesn't do—didn't do much with mixed company." Vasquez stopped; watching the silent video of the shooting had forced her memory to supply the sound of the gunshots. That rhythm didn't match. Her heart accelerated, and her face twisted with a scowl.

"Abraham Swabe was the daytime bodyguard," Guthrie said.

"He died," Congdon said, unnecessarily. "Don't the police believe Stephanie's stalker was the killer?" He opened his desk drawer and extracted a mangled paper clip. His fingers shaped the wire absently while he studied Guthrie.

"Right now they're looking that way," Guthrie said. He shrugged. "Would Peter reach out to his old firm for help on that situation with his wife?"

Congdon stiffened, pinching flat the circle forming in the paper clip. "I doubt anyone here is qualified to wrestle that monster I saw at the Four Seasons," he said. "You were the specialist Peter brought in to deal with the problem."

The lawyer frowned, and before Guthrie could ask another question, he continued, "I'm sorry. I'm speculating. Let me be direct. Peter didn't ask me for help."

"That's fair," Guthrie said.

"You knew Peter for a very long time," Vasquez said. "How long is a very long time?"

The lawyer sighed, and a smile lit his face. "After he took the bar examination, we knocked heads over a clerkship for a superior court judge," he said. "That was almost fifteen years ago, in Philadelphia. The antagonism pushed us together. We were taking the same steps at the same time, and quickly became allies. Peter had sharp judgment and a ready phrase; he won over the people I usually lost."

"A rival?"

"Rivals make good partners. And we weren't rivals outside the law. Peter spent his evenings with young ladies, while I preferred my books. I wrote, he presented. Finally, we partnered with Harper as part of our intention to relocate to New York."

Vasquez watched him drift for a moment. The entries in Ludlow's journal were devoted to women. "He didn't write?" she asked.

"He did, but he had no ambition for a judgeship. That was mine."

"Who won the clerkship?"

Congdon smiled. "I did. Peter was sharper, more presentable, but also younger. We wanted the clerkship for the same reason—to meet others—but being older, I had already met some of those others. I was given their faith, from experience, whereas he had only brilliance to impress them."

"So you met Harper in Philadelphia, too?" Guthrie asked.

"No. He was practicing in the city already, without even an associate. We formed an equal partnership."

"I suppose you can provide a list of people here Peter worked with?"

"Donald Harper, of course. Ed Pratt associated after Peter left, when we reorganized. Pamela Lynch was associated before Peter left."

The little detective scribbled in his notebook. "Do you know Myster Reed?" he asked, glancing up.

The ruined paper clip shot from Congdon's fingers, tumbled across the desktop, and Vasquez flicked it aside like a goalie sweeping a slow wrister. "Sorry," he said. "That slipped away from me."

The little detective finished writing names in his notebook. "Myster Reed, a young black man with a little difficulty making legal distinctions. You might know him? Maybe as a former client—or a current client?"

"I'm afraid a client relationship—past or present—would be confidential."

"I ain't a cop," Guthrie said. "The names of your clients ain't confidential, though. A trip to the courthouse settles who represented him, and when. Do you want to save me the trouble?"

"I should save your trouble, but gain my own? Ethical dilemmas aren't my specialty, Mr. Guthrie."

The little detective shrugged. He pulled his palmtop from his coat pocket. Congdon watched silently as he searched a list of license plates from behind the office. Vasquez tossed him the ruined paper clip.

"Siva Despati drives that green Taurus out back," Guthrie said. "This's a long time from the 1970s. Things appear at the touch of a button. How about Myster Reed?"

Congdon sighed. He opened files on the sleek chrome desktop. "Reed has been a client," he said. "Pamela Lynch did his courtroom appearances."

After some reading, he continued, "She was an associate at his first appearance. Peter was still with us."

"That's fair," Guthrie said. "Did Peter reach out to him?"

Congdon reddened. "I wouldn't know."

"Don't want to know?"

"Mr. Guthrie, I've tried to help you—"

"He's dead. There's a snake out in the grass somewhere."

"I've tried to help you."

The little detective nodded. "I reckon I'll talk to these other people, then."

CHAPTER THIRTEEN

The detectives spent the morning gathering negative answers in the downtown stretch of the Bronx. The rain-drenched Concourse played and replayed the same off-key song by traffic over their efforts until it sounded flat.

Donald Harper, a tall man with dark eyes and a pencil mustache, pointed their questions back to Congdon. "Peter Ludlow—pardon any suggestion about the dead—didn't have much use for us after he jumped to Manhattan. This is a no-frills criminal practice. He didn't do his pro bono work here. Peter and C.C. were a team," he said. "They split courtroom presence and sharp writing. We made a good firm while it lasted." Harper dressed with Italian sharpness, brightly out of place on the grimy street.

After a third unsuccessful visit to the law offices of Harper Congdon searching for Pamela Lynch, the detectives switched tracks. Lynch's cellphone swallowed messages, so Guthrie scratched into her background while they ate an early lunch. Lynch was scheduled for a Criminal Court appearance, but her phone log dead-ended at 9 P.M.

on the previous night. The little detective decided to drive up to Mount Vernon for a face-to-face visit.

The silence outside the city was deafening. Mount Vernon unrolled like a weekday trip to a small-town museum and stopped on Lynch's suburban street. Storm doors gleamed from painted porches, sunken driveways tunneled into understory garages, and dogs were forbidden to bark. A neatly restored Karmen Ghia filled Lynch's driveway; her Quattro brooded in the dark silence of the garage.

Guthrie strode back out to the sidewalk after peering into the garage, looked up and down the street, then tugged off his fedora and scrubbed at his eyes with his suit-coat sleeve. Vasquez slammed the door of the car. The street smothered the sound.

"Her car is here," Guthrie said. "Maybe the classic is her boyfriend, and they're recuperating from a date."

She nodded. "Do we wait or come back?"

"I ain't drove up here for a rain check," he said. He turned and walked up the steps, across the narrow yard, and onto the porch.

"*Viejo*, you really think she'll be so overjoyed to be pulled from bed that she'll answer questions?"

Her suggestion stiffened his back, but he yanked open the storm door and knocked. He tried the bell, then knocked again. He studied the view of the foyer through the marbled glass. He rang the bell and knocked again, then paused to scan the street. He studied the nearby houses carefully. Vasquez watched him. In the city, a muchacho studying hard on a door meant burglary. A sick feeling gathered in her stomach. Guthrie strode from the porch, then disappeared around the side of the house.

"*Coño mierda*," she muttered. After a glance at the quiet street, she followed him.

The houses were separated by a waist-high hurricane fence twined with withered ivy, narrow strips of grass, and a path of large square paving stones. Dark windows stared across the narrow space. A square of grass edged by more hurricane formed the backyard, with a rusty, overgrown swing set idle in the middle. The back porch was screened. The neighboring yards were empty. As Vasquez came around, Guthrie opened the screen door and stepped onto the porch.

The Puerto Rican detective hurried to join him on the porch. He peered through the windows of the kitchen. He pulled a handkerchief from his pocket and tried the back door; it opened.

"What are you doing?" Vasquez hissed.

"It's broken," he said softly, and pointed. Long splinters of molding and jamb showed startling brightness of raw wood under neat, dark paint. He pushed and slipped inside. "Don't touch anything."

"*En serio?*" she muttered.

The quiet inside was broken by a heater's tired sigh. A small, dark kitchen smelled of old cooking and withered strings of herbs, peppers, and garlic. Two empty cabernet bottles and a meal's worth of unwashed dishes waited in the sink. A dim open hallway suggested the living room and foyer, while closed doors looked like a pantry and cellar.

Vasquez's sick feeling peaked. The empty house felt wrong. Something about the smell of the kitchen made her queasy. Guthrie checked the doors in the kitchen, using his handkerchief to turn the knobs. The sound of the old heater amplified when he opened the cellar door, and shrank when he sealed it.

Guthrie walked down the hallway. Vasquez followed hesitantly. The dining and living rooms opened without doors onto the hallway. Old shag carpet kept their shoes quiet. At the bottom of the bare wooden stairs, the detectives paused, finding a butcher-shop aroma with a side order of sewer. Framed photographs lined the staircase—Pamela Lynch smiling, with parents and boyfriends, clinging to the rail of a sailboat, ribbon-wrapped for confirmation, along the Battery, stern-faced in courtrooms—all alive, while the smell said dead.

The little detective found Lynch in the master bedroom, half wrapped in dark satin covers, in flagrante with a hairy-chested jock. The bedroom was a playground; padded cuffs adorned the bedposts and upright mirrors were tucked against the walls. Thick curtains shielded the windows. Lynch's slender blond body seemed unmarred by the bullet holes, but blood didn't suit her complexion. Her lover still clutched possessively at her hips in a lingering half embrace, his chest and ribs pocked with holes. A ragged flap of scalp drooped from his misshapen head; part of his skull was missing. The cream and gold walls across the bed from the doorway held a darkened crimson abstract composition.

"I reckon the shooter stood about here," Guthrie said, pausing a few feet inside the door. He pulled a camera from his coat pocket and snapped pictures. "See any bullet casings?"

Vasquez shook her head. She pulled her cellphone from her pocket, but before she could dial, the little detective stepped to the doorway and caught her hand.

"What're you doing?"

"Nine-one-one."

He shook his head.

"This's for the cops, Guthrie," she said. "We could screw this up."

"We ain't calling this in," he said softly. "They'll come on it soon enough."

Vasquez pocketed her phone and stepped back from the bedroom doorway. Guthrie aimed his camera at the scene. The strobing flash cut time and darkness into slices while she considered. After being scraped down to raw nerves by sleepless nights, the little detective lacked restraint. She didn't want to second-guess him; he could unmask a killer while the police ran in circles. He had found Gagneau, a killer who didn't exist. The flashes from his camera opened a door to the other shooting. Lynch's lover clung to her, but Peter Ludlow had fled. Stephanie Morgan had tried to lift him when he fell.

"He was a *cobarde*," Vasquez said.

"Who?"

"Peter Ludlow. He ran and left her in the street."

Guthrie took another picture, then considered. "It ain't about him, now is it?"

The Puerto Rican detective looked in on the bedroom, at scattered clothing and rumpled sheets. Hollowed stubs of scented candle sat on the nightstands like beseeching hands. The motionless bodies weren't resting. Death stole the sleep that should have followed their silken pleasure. An unopened bottle of wine waited beside blood-splashed glasses on the nightstand.

Vasquez didn't know which was more important: letting the little detective stop the killer, or saving him from himself. So she waited and watched.

Guthrie stared silently across the parking lot on River Avenue, through the passenger window of the old blue Ford. Gray clouds boiled overhead, rushing west in the failing afternoon. Light rain fell on the car. Streetlights burned in the false twilight. Vasquez sighed, but the little man waited with his anger hidden by a years-high wall of habitual patience. People filtered among the cars parked in the lot.

On the drive back into the Bronx, the little man had played fill-in-the-blanks with Harper Congdon. Two dead lawyers equaled a jackpot, and Myster Reed connected them like handcuffs. Reed had called Peter Ludlow before the Fifty-second Street shootings, and called every other lawyer in the Bronx law firm afterward.

Guthrie erupted with curses while he studied the length of numerous cellphone conversations. Harper spoke with Reed for seven minutes on one occasion, and Congdon spoke for eleven minutes on his first. The little detective wondered if they billed quarter hours. He found Congdon's Infiniti by examining credit-card payments to the lot on River Avenue. Then he settled to watch. Congdon would come for his car before he drove home to Yonkers.

Cars shifted around the detectives like windblown litter. Vasquez ran for sandwiches. Rain lulled and gathered. After darkness filled the sky beneath the clouds, Charles Congdon hurried into the parking lot beneath a black umbrella. A handful of wet, dispirited youngsters from the Jackson projects watched him from a storefront overhang but didn't move. Congdon settled into his Infiniti.

"Follow him," the little detective said.

Vasquez started the Ford and followed, expecting him to take the Concourse or Jerome north, but he turned for Macombs Dam. Traffic swept them quickly across the Harlem River. Congdon turned north on St. Nicholas. The lawyer never noticed them. He turned on 174th Street and parked in a narrow lot. The detectives drifted a dozen spaces down the street and parked. Guthrie cracked the door and watched the lawyer walk up into a brownstone.

"Would you look at that," he said.

"You knew he was stopping in the city?" Vasquez asked.

Guthrie shook his head. "I gotta say it makes this easier."

"How's that? Now we're gonna wait a while, *then* drive into Westchester. This'll be all night."

"We ain't gotta follow him. I'll talk to him when he comes out of Kiki's. One of the girls will have him buttered up by then." A grin slid onto his face. "That's a Dominican brothel. There's working girls in every room of that brownstone."

Lucky breaks came with the job—bad and good. Guthrie took advantage. The detectives drove back around the block and parked. They waited, drinking cold coffee from Styrofoam and rooting disinterestedly in an old grab bag. An assortment of men visited the brownstone. Congdon's party ended after fifty-five minutes. The tall lawyer barged from the door of the brownstone. Light and music billowed out onto the dark street beside him. He shouldered his black umbrella like a rifle, paused for a long look up at the sky, and marched toward the parking lot.

"Get your pistol out," the little detective said. He switched the dome light off, then cracked his door.

"What?" Vasquez was incredulous.

He scowled. "In case the Dominicans have an objection. Do you mind?" He slid from the car.

The Infiniti chirped, then purred to life as Congdon strode into the lot, blissfully unaware of Guthrie. The little detective caught his wrist before he could open the car door. The umbrella spun under the next car.

"I don't appreciate being jerked around," Guthrie said.

"What do you mean?" Congdon snatched at his arm, but couldn't escape. "Let go of me!"

"Keep your fool voice down," Guthrie snarled. He twisted Congdon's wrist and shoved him against the door of the Infiniti.

"I'll call the police," Congdon said.

"From outside a whorehouse in Washington Heights." Guthrie shook his head. "You lied to me. You're mixed up with Reed. You let me run on that wild-goose chase into Westchester—which might save your life—but you're gonna talk."

Congdon glanced around for help, but found only Vasquez and an Asian man wearing thick-framed glasses, gawking openly as he stumbled toward Kiki's. "I don't know what you're talking about."

The little detective snatched Congdon's coat sleeve and yanked. He kicked the tall lawyer in the belly when he stumbled forward. He slapped the lawyer's ear, caught a handful of his hair, and mushed his face into the driver's glass of the Infiniti. Congdon squealed. Guthrie clamped his arm to keep him from turning, and twisted his hair. Congdon screamed. Guthrie let him go, planted his feet, and kicked the lawyer in the ass. He tumbled to the ground.

"*Viejo!*"

"Quiet, will you!" Guthrie said, glancing at Vasquez.

Congdon curled into a tornadoproof ball and stuttered out pleas.

"I ain't playing," Guthrie said. "Neither are these other people. Pamela Lynch is dead. I know Myster Reed called you." He nudged the lawyer with his foot. "Get up."

Congdon climbed shakily to his feet. "Pamela Lynch?"

"So your ears do work. Good. I need to know who Reed is crewed up with. That's first. Five kids jumped from his Pontiac on Fifty-second Street and shot hell out of a white van. They rolled off. I need them."

"I don't know their names—"

Guthrie grabbed the lawyer's coat sleeve again. "I've had enough of no—"

"Reed called me!"

"Tell me about it," Guthrie said.

A tall, dark-skinned Dominican kid strolled into the lot with his hands crammed into his pockets, and sidled up to listen and watch.

Congdon's dignity reassembled as he talked, cutting glances at the Dominican. He brushed sand from his coat, mopped his face with a handkerchief, and smoothed his hair. Along the way he recounted his conversation with Reed, also known as Ready, a street lieutenant in Tremont. Despite his firm language, the lawyer's voice vibrated with distaste and fear.

The gangster was hired on to discourage the nuisance stalking Ludlow's wife. The coincidence of Ludlow's murder encouraged him to consider legal implications. Congdon provided typical legal advice—come forward as a witness—but Reed refused. The gangster called other lawyers at the firm, heard the same advice, and tried Congdon again.

Newspaper accounts of the Fifty-second Street shooting didn't mention any other gunfire, but it was a nonstop media event that left the gangster swimming in paranoid suspicion. Congdon made some discreet inquiries, and found no warrants or BOLOs for Myster Reed or Andre Sanders, another member of the Tremont set previously represented by Harper Congdon. A follow-up call didn't calm the gangster.

"He thinks NYPD would gull him with the newspaper and television," Congdon finished. "Maybe he left the city. He's worried enough."

"Maybe he's gulling you," Guthrie snapped. "Lynch is dead. He knew her. Ludlow is dead. He knew him. Would he want them dead?"

"For what!"

The little detective glared.

"*No mas.*" The Dominican kid drew himself upright.

"I guess that's your business, right now," Guthrie said. He slid a card into the lawyer's coat pocket. "Call me when you remember something. I could be easier to deal with than gangsters who want you dead."

Congdon frowned as the little detective turned away. Rain fell softly. The detectives climbed into the old Ford and pulled out before the lawyer settled into his Infiniti. Guthrie turned on Broadway, ignoring a stream of glances from Vasquez.

"We could eat before I drive you downtown," he said. "That should miss some traffic."

The Puerto Rican detective snorted. "Why not? It could give you some time to explain that back there."

"The lawyer? So I roughed him up. He talked, didn't he? I should've kicked him some more and screw the side action, when he decided to shut up again."

She laughed. "*Viejo*, maybe you should see a doctor."

He shrugged, then checked the rearview. The stream of oncoming headlights threw speckled slices of shadow along the roof of the car. He turned on 158th Street to eat at a Dominican place in Hamilton Heights. Industrial fluorescents, hot food, and beer slowly relit the detectives.

"There's no darker curse upon a boy in West Virginia than a stupid dog," Guthrie said. "You can't have however many you want, or change them like pairs of pants. A boy can grow up with one dog, starting from a fat-bellied puppy when he turned ten."

"In general?" Vasquez spooned a bite of fried banana.

"I wish. I'm speaking from experience. I had a bloodhound. That's a droopy brown dog with long ears and black flanks. As a rule, they ain't bright, or overly cooperative except when they're inclined—and generally they ain't." He paused for a long drink of beer.

"Anyway, Thunder was full bloodhound. I know, who names a dog Thunder? I was ten, with some funny ideas how a dog should sound, baying deep in a hollow. I had plenty of uncles thought something of how I ended up with a full bloodhound, little as I was. A walker, they said.

"Thunder was plain stupid. I should've called him Pony, or Whiparound, for how easy raccoons rode his back, and how he danced while they were aboard. I knew before that how stupid he was, but didn't want to admit it.

"When Thunder was little more than a handful, my mother's husband would take after him with a roll of newspaper when I let him in the house. A sideboard in the front room had a gap underneath high enough for him to get under and hide. Then he would mope and poke his nose out." Guthrie mimed crossed paws under a dog's muzzle.

"Well, he crept in the house again a few months after." The little man grinned. "A bloodhound can get your size, full grown, a hundred-something pounds easy. Out came the newspaper, and Thunder ran for the front room. His head could still fit beneath the sideboard, but there wasn't room for the rest. My mother's husband lit into his hind end. Thunder never lost his determination to get under the sideboard. I hauled him out by his tail after my mother got tired of laughing." The little detective mimed pulling on a rope.

"You're *lying*," Vasquez said.

"Anyway, I hope Congdon is smarter than that dog. He talked, but then he ran for the sideboard. We'll see if he turns around before he gets too big a dose of the newspaper."

Vasquez paused. She finished her beer, and looked through the window at the dark street faint behind reflected light. Guthrie studied her face. He sighed.

"This's a dirty business," he said. "It won't always wash off after. Maybe he told us everything if I talked long enough to convince him—or maybe he walked away, figuring he didn't need to listen to me. What men like him don't know won't usually hurt them. They built this world to protect themselves. Then other times, the lights burn out and darkness is in charge. Will Congdon be alive this time tomorrow?"

Three men at the counter spoke softly in Spanish. The sound of traffic seemed distant. Vasquez stared across the table at the little detective.

"This's a dirty business," Guthrie repeated. "This ain't like sorting money in a bank or filling out forms. There's always light to see by in that world. Here, sometimes we have to make a move in the dark."

CHAPTER FOURTEEN

The next morning, Guthrie picked Vasquez up early at her parents' Henry Street tenement. He shivered like a man with the chills, muttering incoherent strings of curses that transmuted back and forth to prayers. He tottered drunkenly on the walk up to the office on Thirty-fourth Street after driving uptown.

"I got to sleep," he said. "No matter what, I got to sleep." He searched in his desk drawers until he found an old bottle of prescription painkillers.

"Look, I'm gonna stay here at the office. I got a hammock I can hang in the back. You take the car. Come back and check on me tomorrow morning. If I'm sleeping, *leave me alone!*" A palmful of pills disappeared, slapped to his open mouth. He lapsed into silence with his eyes clamped shut. Dark bruises filling his eyesockets made his face resemble a skull.

The office filled with a deadly hush. Vasquez watched the little detective from some towering distance outside herself. She plucked the car keys from the desk and slid them into her pocket without a word. Too often she felt forced, gripped and held while he stood at her shoulder as she worked, waiting for her to screw up, then not bothering with an explanation afterward. The grip was gone. Vasquez knew she had screwed up when Gagneau smashed her face. Guthrie saved her because he wanted her for something. Released, she floated for a moment, then turned away. The office door sealed behind her with a hiss and click.

Vasquez drove down to Chinatown and found cars bustling like hungry piglets, looking for sweet pork and spicy duck beneath signs crowded with good luck symbols, then circled the big buildings aimlessly until traffic thinned into the pulse of a dying giant. She turned east after twilight. On Orchard Street, she slid into an empty parking place, locked her pistols into the Ford's armored lockout, stripped off her trench coat, and walked down the street to Skinny's. Crunching guitar riffs vibrated faintly into the street.

The bouncer awarded her a startled thumbs-up after he recognized her. The flat black cowboy hat and black bolero carried her from street to sharp. The narrow dance floor in the dive held a crowd grinding roughly to Lamb of God, while the huddled tables along the wall bounced in unison. Vasquez took a rum and Coke at the bar and searched the crowd of kids blowing off steam on the night before Thanksgiving.

Vasquez's first visit to Skinny's was a tag-team roll with Isadora, her friend from school. Not too long before that, she had been trapped in the hospital waiting for her teeth to stop hurting. Isadora studied her face while visiting at Henry Street, crammed together in her tiny bedroom, and said, "You need to get laid."

Isadora was irrepressible, her one friend from school that was never intimidated by Vasquez's loco brothers. Irrepressible had sometimes equaled foolhardy, and Isadora's exploits had provided Vasquez with a substitute for her own straitjacketed life. After August, they started something new. Vasquez's pistols were on the table; trades were even.

On that first night, Vasquez gave her Yankees cap an extra twist for courage. Every eye was on her—not true, but that was how it felt. Isadora stuck her nose up and walked past the bouncer. Isadora slapped the bartop until drinks arrived. The eyes were on Isadora; her friend had nut-brown *jíbara* skin, chocolate eyes, long wavy hair, and thick legs. She plied advice and pep talks for a week before Vasquez tried a prowl—and only after they found Skinny's, a white dive her brothers would never visit.

"You gotta own the place, *chica*," Isadora said. "It's about you. A muchacho's gonna put on his show for whoever, so you pick the one you want. Don't wait on the one who wants you to come over, see? Pick the one *you* want."

Fueled by alcohol and terror, Vasquez slid an arm around the neck of a blond grad student with a neat mustache and shoulders like a boxer. He tried out a handful of tardy lines while she circled, searching for the side of him that felt best to lean against. Isadora rolled her eyes. "*Ya me lo imaginaba,*" she said, ruffling the boy's golden hair.

Loud music and rum substituted for conversation. Vasquez hypnotized the boy with her gestures, fed him with kisses, and then pulled him from the bar when Isadora came along with a rawboned man with a square dark beard and streaming hair. They split up. Vasquez's boy shared an apartment in the Village, but for the night they had the space to themselves. He could do more with his hips than use them for a place to hang his jeans. The buzz lasted for days. Isadora teased, but Vasquez was hooked. She prowled the dive on Orchard Street until the bouncers sighed like she was a kid sister.

Returning after weeks, Vasquez expected to be eager, not frustrated. The music had all the melody of thunder, and the black hat had no tilt or twist. She edged along the dancing crowd, pushing hands aside when they tried to grasp her, and looked for a missing face. The smiles were mockery. She didn't know the joke. She found the corner, her favorite turnaround. A second rum and Coke made her sweat. She wedged against the wall beside the telephone and stared out.

Isadora came to Skinny's a second time, for Halloween, wearing painted cat whiskers and a fingertip of pink on the tip of her nose. Vasquez wore a spotted bandanna and a black eye patch. The white boys played wild, dark music. Lights and rushing sound whirled with the electric energy of a carnival, but the costumes were minimal. T-shirts, jeans, and dark glasses still served for most, though once the drunkenness peaked, some men stripped to the waist and wore their beards on their chests.

The cat whiskers made Isadora glow. Early in the evening she acquired two interchangeable admirers: tall, dark haired, and as lean and long handed as basketball players. During songs, one danced with Isadora; during breaks, one teased her hair, whispered, and tugged at the belt loops of her blue jeans. Half the evening passed before Vasquez realized two men were trading places. One had dark eyes, the other blue.

Drunk and happy, Isadora flirted with both. By late in the evening, guitar riffs signaled their exchanges and Isadora could almost turn from one to the other. Vasquez watched, revolving slowly around the boy she had captured. The first flame of her astonishment brightened with fuel from her imagination and stole her voice. The party rushed around her, but she only waited. Finally, Isadora clasped one man's hand. She signaled for Vasquez and rushed the door. The other man followed.

"Hey, what's the hurry?" Blue-eyes asked. He whirled Isadora in the crook of his arm on the sidewalk outside Skinny's. A rush of drumbeats scattered through the open door. Vasquez came out with her boy behind the dark-eyed man.

"You know, baby, it's that time of night," Isadora said. "The moon is full and it's time to howl."

He laughed, unrolling her from his arm with another spin. Isadora floated into the other man's waiting arms, with one hand still extended and her fingers twined. The tall men swept her into a double embrace. Guitar crunched along over hissing vocals.

"Little pepper, you can't do this without both of us," he said. "You know you need two pieces of white bread for a sandwich."

With four hands on her, Isadora trembled like a leaf. "*Easy, muchacho!*" she cried, sparing a startled glance for Vasquez. Both men molded to her, transforming her struggles into caresses.

"We're gonna make you purr until you pass out, little pepper," Blue-eyes said.

Isadora snatched her hand free and raked her teeth across a chest. The man flinched. She bolted two steps, then turned to face them. "You're crazy!" she cried. "What you think you're doing?"

"C'mon, pepper," Dark-eyes said. "You've been grinding on me all night."

"Dancing!"

"For real? How many times did you slide your hand in my pocket?"

Isadora reddened. "So now you get to walk out with me? I didn't ask you out here, muchacho."

"You kiss me," Blue-eyes said, "then you turn around and kiss my partner? We were looking, but you cast yourself in the role, little pepper. *Now* it's a switch up. You ain't gone cold. You don't want your little white girlfriend to see you get down? Ditch her!"

Isadora shot a glance at Vasquez. *"Escuchas?"* she asked.

Vasquez pitched into the argument, but her boy took the other side. They exchanged insults: pricktease, asshole, bitch, flake. As a drunken chorus gathered to watch, the bouncers broke up the escalation on the sidewalk. Suggestions for cold showers and dildos provided the send-off, finished by a curtain call of threats to call the police. The onlookers scattered with drunken grumbles.

"Blancos estupidos," Isadora said. "Puerto Rican girls will do anything, right? We're hot, right? *Blancos estupidos!"*

Ten strides later, looking vainly for a taxi on the empty street, she said, "I know, I know. But it was good. I mean I didn't realize they wanted to go to bed together, like some little private porno, to watch while—" She grinned. "They were so *bad*. I couldn't help myself. Did you see, I swear, Rachel, he was like *that*." Isadora held out a measurement with her hands.

"Chica, you're crazy."

They walked some more, beginning to shiver in the chilly night. "I am so drunk," Isadora said. "You know, you can't let it get to you. That happens. It wasn't that they were white, you know. Don't take it like that. I know one of them made a crack—"

"I get it," Vasquez said. "They're boys."

"We weren't exactly in some high-class joint."

"That wouldn't matter," Vasquez said. "I never told you about the games they played at Columbia. There's a place up there—"

Vasquez traced out a story of college sexcapades Guthrie uncovered during an operation that summer. The fraternity boys and sorority girls played games at a bar in Morningside, complete with cameras and spin-the-bottle hookups. She lightened the Halloween mess with the story while they walked down Rivington hoping for a taxi.

In sober darkness the next morning, Vasquez reconsidered. The college kids at Columbia traded sexual favors with a willing air. Isadora's admirers took some thought for drunken advantage, and picked the girl that didn't fit the collection. One more drink, or without Vasquez to support her, and Isadora might've collected an unwanted story. The white boys tried to corner the solo Spanish girl.

Vasquez didn't say it, but a thought lingered: Skinny's was safe for her for more reasons than her brothers would never come through the door. Her pale skin blended with the crowd. The other angle was uglier; her brothers protected her so fiercely on the Lower East Side because *she* didn't fit the collection.

Drinking while she prowled settled Vasquez. A buzz made lingering hands an invitation instead of an insult, and unlocked unexpected words. Isadora swam those waters easily, but Vasquez felt like a novice except when she was drinking.

Standing beside the telephone, Vasquez tried twisting the flat black hat. She was disconnected. She hadn't been back to Skinny's since Guthrie took the Morgan case. Now it seemed like a small, noisy box full of drunks and blaring, tuneless sound. She didn't see a single boy on the floor that made her want a kiss. The rum burned in her belly without lifting her.

The bouncer loomed suddenly, walling off Vasquez's view of the bar. He was a little smaller than a door, with short black hair, a hawk-like nose, and wire-rimmed glasses. "Maybe this isn't your night," he said, timing his words into some Slipknot pauses.

Vasquez nodded. The bouncer peeled her from the wall and led the way to the door. She followed. Outside, he offered to call a taxi, but she shrugged. The windy night stripped the rum's heat. After the walk down the street, she felt sober before she climbed into Guthrie's Ford. She drove home. Her parents' apartment held unexpected late-night quiet, with a note on the refrigerator suggesting some leftover *rellenos*.

She ate, floating on the smell of the *pernil* in the oven. The night sloped downhill, pausing while she polished the kitchen counters, emptied the sink, and showered, then wandered to bed.

Tommy Johnson's jacket waited, hanging from the headpost of her old twin bed. Streetlights glowed through the window, and the tan jacket hovered like a ghost. Vasquez dropped onto the bed and wished she still had his peacoat. That had been as large as a blanket, with a collar that snuggled neatly around her ears but left a space to breathe. Her blanket wasn't heavy enough, and lacked a silk lining that fit like a second skin. The tan jacket was only good for a pillow.

Mamì was cooking supper the night Tommy Johnson came to take his coat. Vasquez answered the door, then paused when she saw him looming above her. A few more inches would let the door frame tap his head. He demanded his coat, brushed her aside, and walked into the apartment.

Mamì watched him as he stalked through the living room, pausing to glance through each door. Vasquez trailed him in bewilderment. He found her bedroom. Together, they barely fit in the tiny room. He said nothing, frowning as he studied her messy dresser, the spilled contents of her closet, looked from her window, then grunted as he looked down onto her bed. He slid from the tan jacket he wore, dropped it on the bedpost, and stripped his peacoat from her bed. He walked from the apartment without a word as he pulled on his coat.

At the stove, Mamì nodded after the door closed. "That one, *hija*, you should tell me his name." She laughed when Vasquez slammed the door to her room.

Vasquez lay for a while in her dark, quiet bedroom, listening to the distant sounds of cars. True darkness waited beyond the cocoon of streetlight. Slowly, she stood, rummaged a bottle from the jumbled bottom drawer of her dresser, and poured a deep nightcap. The smooth rum drew down the firm blanket she wanted. The window frame glowed in the streetlights. As she fell asleep, she noticed a gray stud jutting from the mortar between two long-familiar bricks. Watching.

CHAPTER FIFTEEN

Vasquez woke early Thanksgiving morning knowing that Parson's camera would snap a picture as soon as she moved. She waved Tommy's jacket at her dresser mirror, then tucked it back under her pillow and dressed quickly. The apartment was fragrant with cooking, and Vasquez dribbled to a halt when she saw Mamì in the kitchen. Her mother watched her strap her pistols and sighed. She pointed at the table and poured coffee.

"I have to check on the boss," Vasquez said. She rolled her trench coat into a bundle.

Mamì nodded. "Roberto is coming," she said, and flashed a smile. "He's bringing Summer." Her middle sons, Indio and Miguel, were troublemakers outside the house but peaceful within it. Her eldest son and her only daughter nursed a grudge that bubbled and spattered like an unlidded pot. Mamì was the lid, the smile was the warning, but Roberto's daughter Summer was the peace offering.

Vasquez's answering smile foundered quickly.

"Pastele?" she asked.

"Always." Her tone held more warning that broke through Vasquez's distraction.

"I have to check on the boss," she repeated. "I'll be back."

Vasquez regretted the promise. It clung unwanted to her as she streamed into midtown with the early traffic, shooting crosstown on Twenty-seventh Street before cutting around the Garden on Eighth Avenue to hit Thirty-fourth Street. She rushed upstairs to the dark office and found Guthrie curled in a hammock in the supply closet. She watched for several seconds before seeing the slow movement of his breathing. After easing shut the heavy wooden door to the closet, she settled in her desk chair. Relief struck her suddenly, and her mind began to work again.

The ordinary moments of her life seemed out of place compared to the immediate fear she felt about Duane Parson. Vasquez wasn't stupid. The stalker was dangerous, even if he hadn't killed Stephanie Morgan. The camera stud frightened her with the possibility that he had chosen her to replace the dead heiress. The stalker used the rear end of a van to block the entrance to his lair, moving it by hand like Mamì might move a crate of eggs or the laundry hamper. Vasquez wasn't ashamed to be afraid; she was ashamed that she had run without warning her family. She ordered breakfast and had it delivered instead of going out again.

Morgan's death canceled the operations related to Duane Parson, because Guthrie knew Parson hadn't killed Morgan. Vasquez considered the cold trails left behind. She printed the reports and spread them on her desk, drank double coffees to fire her imagination and recall abandoned plans.

Three firm leads remained untested in the operations reports. Media connections to MAGNUM and *Kaleidoscope* might offer background, while Alice Powell's murder contained physical details. Fat-Fat's new key opened MAGNUM's archive, releasing a welter of disturbing images. Parson photographed bodies and ruined buildings—Colombia, Vietnam, Germany, Israel—scattered across decades of time. Most of MAGNUM's purchases amounted to only a few photos at a time, so a single purchase of forty images in Stuttgart, Germany, made Vasquez look closely.

An unkempt blond man in a leather jacket, jeans, and engineer boots dominated the pictures. He seemed a bit above middle height, stocky, and hollow eyed. A revolver filled his right hand in most of the photos. A rough sequence began as he burst from a glass-fronted building dragging a slender woman by the hair. He jabbed her with his revolver and forced her into a taxi. The driver abandoned the taxi and they performed a Chinese fire drill. He shouted threats during negotiations with the police, and carelessly smoked a cigarette while he pinned the woman to window glass with his revolver. The woman's jaded endurance of the revolver crammed to her throat ended with the sudden finality of a shot.

The array of photographs startled Vasquez. They spanned decades, but rarely provided enough payment from MAGNUM to require taxes. The remittances formed a thin trickle with a few spikes. The attachments in the archive showed that Parson spent his time overseas. Vasquez dredged the U.S. State Department files but found no passport or visa requests. The stalker used a different name to travel overseas. The German photos detailed a sensational bank robbery from 1983 that buried her in material without providing a connection to the photographer. Each was neatly captioned: MAGNUM.

As the morning passed, Vasquez ignored her phone. She accumulated warning texts from Miguel and voice mails from Mamì, like strident heralds for the approach of the meal. She wasn't hungry. After a few doughnuts, she left the remainder untouched. Steak and pepper biscuits turned cold and greasy. When she couldn't control her feet, she stared from the windows and rechecked the lock on the office door.

Parson's work at *Kaleidoscope* existed only on the electronic masthead of the Webzine, an expression of gratitude for a contributing photographer and editor. The Webzine images were assembled from fragments of the city, ripped from ordinary context and reassembled into fanciful essays, like a pair of listless children staring through a rainy window paned by miniature avenues from a building made of tire treads and bumpers. A review of a coffee shop was a welter of images, including close-ups of steaming coffee, a glance through the window at the street outside, and a snapshot of a gleaming bathroom overlaid with a red check mark and plus sign. The masthead was a fiction of untraceable electronic names. Vasquez searched but found only ghosts that bit the ends from Fat-Fat's tracers and a cascade of unconnected hits from ordinary namesakes scattered around the country.

Hours passed. Each time Vasquez checked on the little detective, she thought he had shifted slightly on his hammock. One important similarity always remained—he was sleeping. From the office windows, she could see the gleeful scramble of crowds for the parade. Mamì's voice messages shrilled to insistence, and Vasquez went, carrying the lead weight of Parson. She scanned the traffic around her with jerky spasms as she rolled down Seventh Avenue, then looped crosstown through the Financial District to Henry Street.

The holiday meal shifted around Vasquez, who sat numbly over her plate. Mamì's *pernil y pastele* tasted like cardboard when mixed with fear. Her brothers needled and joked, talked football, and entertained an endless stream of old friends, but Vasquez felt invisible except for the brief moment she spent showing Summer how to twist and tilt her new Yankees cap while Roberto scowled. Her parents hovered with frowns, but flashed brief smiles when she looked up at them. Miguel directed her from place to place like furniture with legs, and scowled because he couldn't stir up an argument.

"Rachel, just go," Mamì said tiredly after she picked apart a plate.

"The boss needs me," Vasquez said defensively, hunching her shoulders, and moving quickly for the first time since she came home. She had never removed her bolero or her pistols. Papì turned away so he wouldn't have to see her go through the door.

A wall of dark clouds rose over the city, blackening the sky, as she drove back up to the office. On the radio, weathermen predicted varying amounts of snow. Guthrie was still asleep, despite the waves of sightseers and shoppers streaming to and from the trains. Vasquez skimmed her notes from the morning, then abandoned the electronic trails. They followed a ghost—Duane Parson—that she already knew didn't exist.

The little detective had admitted that the stalker's connection to Alice Powell might corner him, given time, then tossed the lead to the police like a long-fused bomb. Vasquez wired through Fat-Fat's trapdoor downtown. NYPD had a BOLO on Parson in the city—of interest to the Morgan investigation. The stalker wouldn't run loose in the city, but the police were only concerned with Morgan and Powell. Vasquez had it in mind that physical details from the Powell murder might connect elsewhere, possibly Arizona, since the Parson identity started in Scottsdale. The detectives had identified Gagneau using a similarly wide net.

The NYPD reports were inaccessible, wrapped beyond reach of Fat-Fat's trapdoor and tool kit. Guthrie had warned her that Inglewood would stonewall, even after warning him. She shifted her focus to Seattle PD, who suspected Parson for the Powell murder on Guthrie's tip, and was buried in lead reports detailing interviews conducted by Seattle's task force while searching for potential witnesses. Vasquez thought her eyes would bleed.

The ME in the city had a wrap on the Fifty-second Street examinations, but Seattle's ME had already surrendered Powell's file to the federal archive. Vasquez reached through the opening and extracted the file. The medical words rattled in her head like bad poetry, forcing her to rifle through a desktop dictionary. Sifting the words and diagrams prepared her for the photographs. Powell emerged from a visual puzzle of clothes, litter, and damage. Glimmers of eye and curve of teeth were visible in some photos, while others revealed a curl of ear or a dark sticky mass of hair. Her undamaged hands glowed with pale blue polish. Little blood appeared at the scene.

Powell's autopsy photographs were starkly different. Flat, plain steel replaced the shattered roadside dump site. Clinical photos didn't strip dignity; they underlined endurance with finality. The fatal blow was hidden by her hair. X-rays showed her badly damaged skull. One eyebrow was torn in half; that brow ridge was shattered beneath the puffy, swollen dome of her forehead.

Seattle's ME circled a question about a contusion on her left lower leg. A deep bruise, six inches wide, encircled the entire leg. Ragged discoloration feathered from the edges. The ME suggested the mark couldn't have come from a ligature or impact, being too broad for the first and lacking a focus or laceration to satisfy the second.

One appended note compared the mark to the impact of a car bumper. Vasquez sat quietly for a long time after she finished studying. She realized Guthrie was awake when she heard the toilet flush. The little man came out, drying his hands on the belly of his workshirt, and attended the coffeemaker. Some powdered doughnuts vanished from the box beside it.

"*Viejo*, I found a camera in my bedroom window last night."

Guthrie turned around. "One of those we took to Fat?"

She nodded.

"You sat here all day without waking me?"

She nodded.

He grunted, and glanced at the office windows. He gulped a cup of coffee as he walked over for a closer look. "Storm's coming," he said. He sniffed at the glass. "Snow."

Guthrie walked quickly back to his desk, dropped into his chair, and opened the big bottom drawer. He pulled out two shoulder harnesses, both wrapped around revolvers. He slid them on, stood, and collected the Ford's keys from the corner of her desk.

"I'm going out," he said. "You stay here." At the coatrack, he pulled on his suit coat and overcoat. He snugged his fedora atop his grizzled head.

Vasquez followed the little detective, sliding into her trench coat as she hurried to catch the door behind him. She followed him down to the street, and they threaded through a crowd hurrying to catch the A train. He paused before he opened the driver door of the Ford, and looked across the top at her.

"You may regret failing to mind me," he said.

Guthrie drove south on Seventh Avenue, grinding along with the traffic. He veered onto Bleecker in the Village, and they stopped at Joe's for pizza. Darkness swept into the city with a sprinkle of snow, then a whirl, and finally a Canyon of Heroes tickertape extravaganza. The Village sparkled. The detectives walked out with folded slices to get back on the road. Turning corners parted white curtains; they swept past City Hall in white silence, then crossed the Brooklyn Bridge.

The old factories in DUMBO wore fresh frosting. The streets shifted like slick ribbons beneath the tires of Guthrie's old blue Ford. He turned straight into the industrial knot, and the alley instantly stripped off the veneer of freshness provided by the snow. A black slash of sky followed the alley, but few flakes passed the railed parapets, pipes, and looming stonework. The little detective dimmed the headlights to a faint glow that lit only a few dozen feet. He idled the Ford around the last corner, but the tiny lot was empty. The Dumpster was alone, the break between the buildings unblocked. Guthrie killed the engine and silence descended.

The little detective drew a revolver as he climbed from the Ford. Vasquez followed, pocketing both pistols into her trench coat to keep them out of sight. He strode through the gap, looking carefully among the pipes and catwalks surrounding the concrete diamond pressed between the buildings. Snowflakes glimmered in the quiet air before vanishing on the wet concrete.

The little detective holstered his revolver and climbed a slender pipe onto the lowest catwalk. He drew his revolver again before signaling Vasquez to join him. The young detective struggled, breathing heavily when she reached the catwalk.

"I don't feel he's here," Guthrie said softly, "but it was wiser to have waited."

The detectives slipped around the diamond on the catwalk, down the service corridor, and Guthrie opened the iron door to Parson's lair. Dim light and stink drifted out. He listened, signaled Vasquez to wait, crept through the door, then listened some more. He beckoned her inside, pulled the heavy door, and wedged it. He strode down

the long gallery with his revolver jutting from his hand. After passing every concrete niche, he drew a penlight to spread a halo of light
as he holstered his revolver.

"Search it," he called.

The detectives found signs of a hasty exit—scattered food and
clothing, unsealed containers attended by celebrating rats, and computer monitors still flickering with life. In the stinking den where
Parson bedded, boxes of mothballs provided a bedside deodorizer
overpowered by body odor. A wad of bloody clothing lay beside a
washtub of rotten water. Alcohol faintly flavored the air. The clothes
were stiff with dried blood, pants and shirt both scissored for a rough
undressing. Bandages and paper packaging littered the floor.

"That was some fight," Guthrie muttered. "Somewhere. 'Cause
them kids didn't touch him on Fifty-second. Wasn't no blood in the
van."

"What do you think, *viejo*?"

"He ain't dead. I think he's hurt, though, and didn't trust sleeping
here. He knows we know this hole. Maybe he figures we'll take the
reward."

The little detective pulled a camera and began filming. He gathered bloody gauze and tucked it into a plastic bag. He stretched the
damaged clothes out on the concrete floor for a careful examination.
He found five holes—one in the bloody arm of the shirt, two in the
bloody legs of the oversized trousers, and two more in the torso of
the shirt—but those last weren't darkened by blood.

"I think my rat wore a vest," he said. He rinsed clotted blood from
his hands, then wiped his fingerprints from the water bottle.

The detectives shot a long video of the contents of the old pump-
house. Parson had five trophy galleries, each arrayed with pictures and
trinkets surrounding a single item on a pedestal. Stephanie Morgan's
gallery contained her purse; a few more small personal items perched
on a narrow shelf installed roughly on the concrete walls: a comb,
some makeup, sketches, and a scarf.

Photographs covered the walls. The detectives appeared in several,
and Swabe was prominent. Secured with dabs of epoxy, the pictures

formed a crooked scatter like leaves might make striking the ground. The oldest formed a layer of debris beneath the newest, although some photos received special consideration, uncovered by newcomers while neighbors were obliterated. After several minutes, Guthrie pointed.

"That must be the first one," he said. A roughly framed shot of a well-dressed blonde running away held a flurry of cropped close-ups in orbit: Stephanie Morgan puzzled. "She ran, then she came back."

"Maybe coming back had something to do with it," Vasquez said.

Guthrie shook his head. "He's a peeper. He likes to look. Could've just as easy been waiting on the moon."

Unease coiled in Vasquez's stomach, but she didn't argue. Her pistols hung like heavy weights in the outside pockets of her trench coat. She watched silently as Guthrie filmed each trophy room in detail. On Parson's wall, Alice Powell had the slender build of a fashion model. Somehow the pictures made her alive, even with the clinging memory of her autopsy shots.

After some slow minutes looking, Vasquez saw how people could thumb through old albums featuring bygone years. Reliving a glowing past removed the mind from a dark present. She watched Guthrie filming a record of a record, and creeped the feeling that someone else had to be watching. Her glances darted, searching for cameras.

Without turning, the little detective said, "They're everywhere. Before we leave, I'm gonna find the brain and take it. Then I'm gonna lay awake, hoping there's no backup. This rat's smart, Rachel. Somewhere in here, we're gonna find something he left for us. He's smart."

Vasquez found it while Guthrie kept filming trophies. The desktop of Parson's computer was swept clear except for two video files, showing scenes from Fifty-second Street in front of Stephanie Morgan's town house. One file showed the shooting—from a higher angle— while the other was dated three days prior to the shooting, and unwound a long, unremarkable view of Fifty-second Street. Vasquez was still watching it when Guthrie appeared at her shoulder.

"Got something?"

"I can't figure this one," Vasquez said. "The shooting, and this."

"Okay, get copies." The little detective watched the video on split while she copied the files to a flash drive. He appropriated the mouse and restarted the file. After she pocketed the copy, he pointed.

"There he is." He stopped the video, reframed, and isolated a tall man stepping from the passenger side of a Chrysler, with a square fur hat pulled firmly onto his head. "The hat."

Guthrie rolled the video again, and framed the ancient Chrysler when the traffic gapped around it. He tightened the video to read the license plate. "Okay, this rat's smart," he said. "He's sharing cheese."

After jotting the number on his notepad, he frowned. "I change my mind. Take the computer."

Vasquez bundled the computer, then followed Guthrie as he trailed the surveillance system. A warren of rooms waited behind the iron doors, divided among three levels. Rust-eaten hinges, darkness, oily smells, and rats waited in the young detective's imagination, a rerun of her previous searching.

Guthrie traced the power instead. He backtracked to the breakers and counted amps. The surveillance console filled the service niche of three interlocked freight shafts. The detectives reached it by a ladder of ancient iron rungs, with shiny conduit attached alongside.

The little detective sighed as he collected components. "I hate rats."

CHAPTER SIXTEEN

In the morning, Guthrie was double-parked on Henry Street, watching the front of the tenement apartment from the driver's seat of the old blue Ford. Wearing white in the still morning, the hardscape looked clean. The cars lining the sidewalk had a topcoat. The snow on the street had been patted tenderly down by some hours of slow driving. The little detective wore a frozen mask of frustration. A handful of pills had only postponed his insomnia. He handed Vasquez a M1911A Colt pistol loaded with black-tipped, armor-piercing bullets, after she climbed into the car.

"Those're copkillers. I figure the rat's wearing a vest. Those bullets go through it, and the pistol's clean. Keep it in your pocket," he said. "I talked to Tommy. He's coming by the office later, after he gets off work."

"Tommy Johnson," Vasquez repeated, as she slid the heavy pistol into the pocket of her trench coat. Her stomach flipped. The young man worked a few blocks away, at the downtown headquarters of NYPD. Recently, Johnson had become someone Vasquez would rather avoid.

"I asked him for whatever he can scratch up on that meth pit in the Bronx." NYPD had confiscated a middling stash of marijuana and a few grams of meth, but no cash, after a Tuesday-night mass murder in Parkchester. They responded to a shots-fired at an abandoned restaurant adjoined to an empty bodega in the small hours, and stumbled onto the bodies.

After returning to the office on Thirty-fourth Street the previous night, the detectives had traced the license on the heavyweight black Chrysler to Ricardo Sorcini, a forty-four-year-old naturalized citizen from Mexico. His placid DMV photo showed a simple black fade and neat mustache on a brown face. He was killed along with three other Mexicans at the meth pit in Parkchester. Guthrie concluded that Parson had fought the Mexicans, mostly coming out a winner—likely to avenge the insult of having Stephanie Morgan snatched from his grip.

"Could be some clue there to what Parson intended."

The detectives drove up to Morgan's town house on Fifty-second Street. A late-night call from George Livingston, tracing the solid lines of estate law, had expanded their assignment. Without an heir, Stephanie Morgan's estate became subject to intestate division—granting by law a vast fortune to the Ludlow family. Prior to the marriage, arm-twisting and a prenuptial agreement required Peter Ludlow to sign a will granting the estate to Morgan's heirs. The murders changed everything. Livingston sent electronic copies of the will and prenuptial, then commanded: "Find a way out."

A pair of security guards hired by Davis Polk followed the detectives as they surveyed the town house. Before the shootings, Guthrie had searched for cameras but paid little attention to the interior. They spent ten minutes finding Peter Ludlow's office, with neat inscriptions on the blotter matching his schedule at his office on Lexington Avenue. Guthrie confiscated his hard drive and an armload of paper records, silencing the security guards with a phone call to Sinclair's assistant that boomeranged with fresh orders to the guards.

Vasquez paced the dead couple's bedroom, studying the arrangement with a sudden obsession to lift and examine. The remnants marked a pattern of conjugal harmony, including ranks of smiling photographs, matching pairs of necessaries, and an interlaced wardrobe. A chest beneath the windowsill held bundles of handwritten notes wound in red ribbons.

Vasquez recognized the handwriting—Ludlow. Dated lead lines marked neat time up to the day of the shootings. After scanning a few, she felt sick. A glimpse of Ludlow's journal might have thrown cold water on the hot relationship traced in the sugary notes. She gathered the bundles.

In the office, Vasquez traced edges with her fingertips, delved in the drawers of the desk, and lifted each book on the rows of bookshelves. Midway on the highest shelf another journal appeared, less worn but equally full. The entries hissed like ice, a mechanical recounting of romance fashioned from the parts of the machine. She added it to Guthrie's pile of documents.

The little detective snorted. "You're gonna be doing that," he said.

Tommy Johnson strode into the Thirty-fourth Street office at a quarter past six. His glare caught on Vasquez for a moment, then jumped away before she looked up from Ludlow's journal. He hung his peacoat on the wall rack after he reached across the oxblood couch to drop a handful of files on the coffee table. Guthrie studied him for a long moment, his expression drifting from concentration to amazement.

"I'll be damned," the little man said.

"The taxi driver had a feeling about Sixth Avenue," Johnson said. "Some New Age feeling that traffic would clear up, north of Fifteenth Street. We followed his feeling all the way up here."

"No, no," Guthrie said. "You grew up. This summer you were a bundle of sticks. You look like another forty pounds—I guess I got to call you Tom, now."

The young man's golden eyebrows stood out brightly when his face reddened. He mumbled something about weight lifting, dropped onto the couch, and opened his folders. "I got some stuff on that meth pit in Parkchester," he said.

The detectives huddled around the coffee table. NYPD's Organized Crime Task Force connected the murders to El Silencio, a cross-border gang linked to one of the Mexican cartels. Johnson rattled details for the victims—a fabric of fact and speculation—and finished with a shrug.

"There was some shooting, right?" Guthrie prompted.

"That's the crazy part," Johnson said. "The first call was a shots-fired, and we found spent casings from four nine-millimeters—three recovered—but three of the victims were bludgeoned to death. They're carrying Berettas, but decide to beat each other to death. El Silencio supposedly originates with the Zetas, a sort of paramilitary organization that originated with the Mexican army. They wear buzz cuts and carry military weapons. Anyway, spatter, drag marks, pooling, blood trails—"

Johnson rearranged magazines on the coffee table to resemble a floor plan, and detailed movements with a forefinger. Spattered blood and a bloodtrail from a shattered side door suggested the entry to the abandoned restaurant. After that, mayhem tumbled between the dusty restaurant and the neighboring bodega through a pair of roughly cut doorways.

The sequence was speculation, and so Johnson detailed each room separately, drifting around the office to point out the locations of spatters on the ceiling and walls, the orientation of drags and trails, and sketch the arrangement of limbs on each victim with attendant pools of blood. His sweeping hands hypnotized Vasquez. Guthrie darkened with disgust each time he noticed her distraction.

The meth pit was wrecked, and the victims were mutilated by bludgeoning. The blood work was so extensive that the ISU lab sorted it only by type and description.

"So ISU's got no notes on gunshot injuries?" Guthrie asked.

"Some of the spatter corresponds with the casings and possible trajectories. Then one victim caught two bullets in the back, and the blood guy suggested that could be friendly fire. Eighty-two casings." Johnson looked puzzled.

"Got any blood that doesn't match type?"

"Guth, you're leading me around. This's a drug robbery. Right?"

"Sure." The little detective walked over to the office window and looked down on Thirty-fourth Street. "ISU's gonna run the blood that doesn't match bodies, right?"

"That's procedure, Guth." Johnson studied the detectives. "You could've helped me out with keeping quiet."

The little man shrugged and walked back to his desk. Some basic details had already clarified his questions before Johnson arrived. The tallest of the dead Mexicans from Parkchester was five foot seven: too short to be the Fifty-second Street shooter. Duane Parson attacked, but missed the shooter: he had escaped. Vasquez tugged at the stack of files on the coffee table. Johnson looked down at her. Her face was invisible beneath the brim of her black hat.

"Maybe I could help?" he asked.

"Autopsies," she said. "You brought the autopsies?"

He thumbed a thick folder from the bottom and passed it across the table. Vasquez retreated behind her desk, spread the file, and began studying.

"I don't stick my nose in crap," Guthrie said.

Johnson shrugged. "This looks like a casual sniff."

"You know what I'm working on?"

Johnson nodded. "Everything from Fifty-second Street is under wraps."

"This is under wraps, but you get a heads-up."

"It's something I can trade in?"

Guthrie smiled. "I dropped that first dime on Duane Parson, out in Seattle. The Ds on the Fifty-second Street shootings just switched it off, but that don't mean he ain't good for Seattle.

"Problem is, he ain't really Duane Parson. That's a cover identity. He used it to work for an agency in the city—MAGNUM—and he picks it up when he needs a clean sheet and an excuse to carry a camera. He's also mixed in with a Webzine, *Kaleidoscope*, operating in the city. I only got two hands, or I'd start digging him up." He flicked a glance at Vasquez, but she was buried in the autopsy on her desk.

"That ain't exactly a smoking gun," Johnson said.

"Try Stuttgart, Germany, on December 3, 1983," Guthrie said. "Parson was there, using some other name."

"Guth, that's thin."

"Maybe you never use it." The little man shrugged.

Vasquez tapped a photograph and looked up at Guthrie.

"A footprint?" he asked.

"You got it, *viejo*."

All of the dead Mexicans had suffered abrasions prior to death, but Ricardo Sorcini had suffered prolonged abuse that continued after his death. Multiple fractures made his skull resemble a shattered egg in a fleshy bag. His right calf had an encircling contusion, visible in the photographs, that drew no comment from the ME. The welt seemed irrrelevant compared to the mess of other damage, including shattered arms and ribs.

The little detective scanned the material, paying attention where Vasquez indicated in the autopsy notes and photos. Johnson watched them silently while they worked, weighing down his curiosity with heavy sighs that could have been equally related to the long looks he stole of Vasquez's profile while she was busy. They returned the file and he tidied it up with his other materials.

Afterward, Guthrie took them down to Dylan's in TriBeCa for steaks. The little detective wanted to celebrate the pocketful of nails they had gathered for Duane Parson's coffin. Vasquez watched his smile transform repeatedly, on the drive downtown and at the restaurant, while he cut his strip, emptied mugs of beer, and spread jokes on the tablecloth.

At the restaurant, the men traded city stories, and Vasquez studied them. Johnson had an uncanny resemblance to Guthrie in his manner—the cadence of his words, his gestures, and the way he tilted his head. Otherwise age marked them apart, with Guthrie worn smooth and unflappable as a mossy river stone, and Johnson quick and sharp like fresh-broken flint.

Wrapped in a beer buzz, with a belly full of steak and fries, Vasquez was silent. The frozen sidewalk outside the steakhouse rattled like a snare drum beneath their feet as they walked back to the car. She sat in the backseat and listened as their stories bent backward in time. They bragged about catfish, ratcheting up sizes until they swallowed cars, and about cold-water swimming in springtime, where the Big Sandy slides into bed with the Ohio.

Faintly Vasquez remembered returning to Henry Street, but lying in bed she drifted to sleep wearing a frown, unable to decide why she hadn't asked Johnson for his peacoat.

CHAPTER SEVENTEEN

Guthrie prowled Henry Street overnight. The blue Ford's slow rocking on the streets soothed him; turning the wheel was like rolling tiredly over and drawing along the blanket, settling into the neat crease of the pillow and mattress. Flickering streetlights, signs, and arcades of fractured shadow substituted for his dreams.

In the morning, Guthrie and Vasquez found NYPD detectives waiting on their doorstep in the Garment District. Ame Hernandez and Rocky Devlin popped from an unmarked red Ford and jogged up to the building as Guthrie paused outside, kicking slushy gunk from his brogans on the top step.

"We need a conversation," Hernandez said.

"Sure," Guthrie said. "Come on up."

Inside the office, the tall Dominican police detective settled on the oxblood couch without removing his coat, draping his arms along the top like wings. His expression suggested amusement mixed with annoyance, while Devlin stood again in the window-lit end of the office, arms crossed on his chest matching the twisted scowl on his bullet-scarred face. Without his dark glasses, Devlin's eyes were brilliant blue. Vasquez started a pot of coffee. Guthrie settled at his desk and dropped his brown fedora on the blotter.

"We were warned you were sharp," Hernandez said. "You even told us to look at Ludlow." He slid his fingers through the dark curls on his head and shrugged. "So now we are. His old law practice in the Bronx is suffering difficulties. Stay away from that. We don't want you in our way. You're walking along the line of obstruction already."

Guthrie smiled. "I'm sure I'll be out of your way if I keep doing what I'm doing and you keep doing what you're doing."

"This's a joke?" Devlin asked.

"No," Guthrie said. "I ain't got time for public service or I'd follow you around to make sure you don't wander into traffic. Go play, but don't call me. And don't try telling me what not to do about this Morgan thing."

"You're poking into an ongoing—"

"Shut up!" Guthrie barked. "You blew this already! First grade is out the window, boys. Concentrate on not going back to patrol."

The police detectives exchanged startled looks. Vasquez polished coffee cups and laid them out in a row. Before either policeman could insert a retort, Guthrie said, "When we talked before, you indicated you knew who had an interest in this. *Then* you pissed six days into the crapper."

Hernandez's face darkened with a furious scowl.

"Flush and walk away, will you? If you make noise about this, people downtown are gonna realize how stupid you really are. That makes *them* look stupid for not kicking straight to Major Case. Who's gonna be patsy?"

"I didn't realize a private dick could get a swelled head from working for rich people," Hernandez said. "I thought that took a hand-job. I warned you. Now my conscience is clear. When you get in my way, I'm gonna roll over you." He pressed to his feet and slipped on his calfskin gloves.

"Go do the job I'm paying my taxes for," Guthrie said. He jerked a thumb at the office door.

Vasquez sat quietly at her desk as Guthrie muttered for several minutes after the NYPD detectives left. "I gotta stop talking to people like that," he said, lurching around his desk for some coffee.

"You ain't meant to do that?"

"I gotta get some sleep," he muttered.

Guthrie spent his day filling blanks in his background on the law firm in the Bronx, looking for a useful edge. He collected watering holes, phone lists, shopping stops, spending habits, and registered property to accompany skeleton life histories—schools, past residences, and old phone numbers. He collected piles of forgotten minutiae covered with fingerprints and habits, ground it in the mill of his subconscious, then recited pin codes and passwords that came up right too often for Vasquez's comfort. The little detective had an X-ray mind.

Charles Congdon emerged from the mess smarter than he looked. His cellphone called out, but only accepted voice mail. His credit cards yielded static silence. While his coworkers remained in the grooves of their ordinary lives, Congdon had vanished. Even the little detective couldn't pinpoint him.

Vasquez raked through the material from the Morgan town house. She built a dossier on Peter Ludlow, framed with details from her meetings with the dead man. She found a man divided.

By external marks, Ludlow burned with paragon brightness. Charitable contributions, pro bono work, perfect grades, and a spotless past without arrests, tickets, or unpaid taxes matched Vasquez's memory of his cavalier manners and perfect social grace.

His handwritten journals fell beneath the brightness like a shadow. Ludlow was a decade older than Stephanie Morgan. Vasquez looked again, but the missing piece was obvious once she held it: Ludlow was a perfect man who never sought a perfect match. Ludlow was cold.

Sorting the notes Ludlow had written for Morgan, Vasquez found a smooth jukebox rotation of endearments, sexual promises, and sated gratitude—all dated with prime numbers. Ludlow wrote notes for Morgan on a prime progression of dates, coldly unerring for three years of sorted bundles. Vasquez's internal clock was a source of jokes for her few girlfriends, especially Isadora, who drifted like a cloud through endless pregnancy scares, but Vasquez only wobbled a day or so every few months. Three years of prime precision just wasn't possible.

The journals provided bitter background for the sugary notes. Each entry began with a nonsense tongue twister, a Carrollian perversion but lacking made-up words. Some phrases repeated, without sounding any clearer after repetition. Dinner dates, conversations, detailed seductions, and sexual encounters followed as mechanical recitations.

The entries used initials; the journal from Ludlow's office on Lexington Avenue used an *A*. Juxtaposed to the nonsense sentences, Vasquez originally read the initial as more nonsense. The journal from the town house used an *S*: Stephanie Morgan. Vasquez concluded that the journals recorded cold-blooded exploits with two different women, by a man with only one visible woman in his life.

The journal entries blurred as Vasquez read them, reducing sexual gymnastics to an orderly sequence of stripping, grips, and tonal evaluations of moans. The cold thrills blunted her curiosity. She scanned the prenuptual and will, caught the idea that Ludlow needed to be married to Morgan to inherit, and considered the second journal—two women.

A search in Westlaw ended the trail. Any possibility of annulment or divorce ended when the couple died, beyond an unreachable hint of false pretense. Vasquez kept reading, but after hours of reading the background, notes, and journals twisted like smoke.

Early in the afternoon, the office phone rang. Guthrie laughed, and put the call on speaker. He recognized the cellphone number on ID—Ed Pratt, an associate at Harper Congdon.

"I'm not prepared to pretend that nothing is happening," Pratt said after brief pleasantries. The lawyer's voice was a high tenor that peaked under stress. Some words disappeared into squeaks.

"I'm with you, counselor," Guthrie said. "How can I help?"

"Find the killer!" Pratt blurted, then laughed uneasily. "Or killers. I have some suggestions." The lawyer rattled out the names of Myster Reed's crew, missing one name, but adding two others.

Guthrie jotted notes, allowing a pause to build, then said, "I think these kids are in the clear, Mr. Pratt."

"Maybe you don't know the entire story."

"Okay, help me out."

"That's exactly what I don't need—loose information. You have a reputation for discretion, Mr. Guthrie. You wouldn't work for those people downtown without that discretion. Do you see what I mean? If I wanted a messy job of taking out the trash, I could talk to the police detectives that are knocking on my door."

The little detective grinned. "I got some discretion, that's true—I tend to know things I shouldn't. First, these kids are in the clear. It's somebody else connected to your firm that's the problem. I need access."

"Access?" Pratt's question disappeared into a squeak.

"Like a list of clients, old and new, mostly old, nothing borrowed, nothing blue—"

"How do you know Reed isn't involved? He's terrified that the Fifty-second Street murders will fall on him."

"A frightened client is a guilty client," Guthrie said. "I understand. In this case, he might be smart enough to see how big the mess is, but NYPD just isn't interested in his crew. A nosy Italian saved him."

"He doesn't know that," Pratt murmured. "But that doesn't mean he's not involved."

"So you don't see these two things together?"

"I didn't say that!"

"So you figure he's scared enough to kill you, if you won't help him dodge a mess he ain't even caught in—or keep killing you—that's how you want to angle this?"

"He's not alone," Pratt said sharply. "Nor is he completely in control. Nor do I think I know everything at issue—a mistake you seem prone to making, Mr. Guthrie. Knowing something creates a logical pitfall of assuming total knowledge. Who killed Peter Ludlow? Why? Reed is terrified. Is he involved or does he know something he ought not?"

"You got my attention, Mr. Pratt. Say with it my discretion and co-operation. I'll deal with Reed, but on my end, I want access."

The lawyer sighed. "We'll need to meet," he said. A pause stretched. "I need to communicate with my partners. I can't open our files to you without permission. I certainly won't sneak you into the office."

"When and where?"

"Six o'clock," Pratt said. "You know the Terminal Market, under the stadium?"

"Sure," Guthrie said.

Guthrie called Todd Royal. Besides working as a night prowler at Morgan's town house his background included a Westchester gang. The little detective figured him for the quickest connection to the Tremont gangsters.

"Yo, what time is it?" the young man growled on speaker, his voice thick with sleep.

"Past two," Guthrie answered.

After a pause, "What d'you want, anyway?"

"A connection to a banger up there, a street lieutenant in Tremont. Myster Reed, aka Ready—"

"Seriously?"

"Seriously. I don't do much joking."

"You know what—" Shouting erupted on the phone, quickly muted with a hand but still identifiable as curses and threats. After a few minutes, clearly, "And fuck him, too. You still there?"

"I'm patient."

"You ain't even come by here to see how much of my ass them dogs bit off, and forget waiting at the hospital, *then* you call me at two—"

"If you wanted me to hold your hand, you should've looked more like a girl," Guthrie interjected. "How's the worker's compensation working out?"

"I know that's right!" More cursing erupted, and then a low house beat smoothed the angry voices.

"How about Myster Reed, aka Ready?" Guthrie asked.

House music played for a long pause, like the phone was suddenly on hold while someone shouted for the manager to assist with a tough question.

"You know what," Royal said softly. "I could give a fuck. I been wondered about you, about how P-Lo got hooked up with you. So say this: I appreciate you bailing me out of jail, that lawyer that brushed dirt off me, and the legit shit. Hey, worker's compensation! Whatever . . ." Empty bottles rang, gathered together, then thunked into a plastic garbage can.

"Still, you some stupid-ass old cracker looking to uplift the down-trodden Negro, trying to compensate for killing my fucking brother! Are you serious?"

"Chill, chill!" A racket of voices sounded over the phone.

"Fuck it, you know what? Make some proper noise with your mouth, explain how it ain't like that, and I ride with you," Royal said. "Otherwise . . ."

Guthrie pulled off his fedora and dropped it to rest on the corner of his desk. Vasquez stared from the office window. The office hummed with the awed expectation of a falling man during those long moments it needed for his body to drop.

"I reckon you figure you got a choice in the matter," Guthrie said. "Maybe by a few years from now you'll see that ain't the case. I suppose I can make this clearer by explaining how I got fourteen uncles.

"First thing would come to mind was that my grandma was a busy woman, but I only have three uncles that way," he said. "The other eleven were all born in 1970, near Dac To in Vietnam. I was nine years old. They didn't *choose* to be my uncles, any more than my father's brothers did, but a man ain't gonna stop doing for spite.

"I guess my father was closest to the grenade when it sailed in, or moved the quickest, or maybe the dumb bastard slipped when he tried to jump from the window. I don't know. He covered the grenade. Eleven men lived." House music played while Guthrie picked up his brown fedora and fretted the brim.

"Your foster brother stood with me on account of Gagneau killing your mother. I know you remember that, but I owe him blood. I'll do by you what I can, for that. I don't even need for you to like it. That don't mean I won't beat the shit outta you next time I catch you, for being smart with that mouthful of crap. You hear?"

"You too little," Royal said.

"Don't try me, nephew. I got tricks that'll make you worse off."

"Fuck it. Least I ain't end up with an aunt."

An off-key bray of laughter burst from the speaker.

"Chill, let me get this," Royal said. "I know your set over in Tremont. They tight because that's mostly Puerto Ricans over there. Ready, he's live. Funnyhead, Troop, Gonzo, D-Black. And Will, he's live. I don't know they government shits, right? They was under Longball, back a few years ago. He went Upstate, now they whatever. I hear mostly they jackboys. The spics got the corners over there. They trip at China's on 174th. Then what?"

"Tell 'em they're clear on Fifty-second Street," Guthrie said.

Vasquez crept to the window while she swallowed her anger. A motley army of shoppers marched along the north side of Thirty-fourth Street toward Macy's, carrying umbrellas instead of popguns to win the never-ending war on high prices. Phillip Linney, aka P-Lo, was shot to death by Marc Lucas Gagneau during the takedown operation that ended with her own near-death experience. A blow to the head and a resulting concussion might have twisted Royal's memory, maybe erasing the part where Linney came along for his own reasons. Guthrie didn't ask for volunteers. Everyone did what they wanted. She glanced back at him, sitting motionless at his desk. The little man looked like bones wrapped in cloth. With pretense and trickery stripped away by exhaustion, he should've been different. Vasquez realized she had been counting on that; deep down, Guthrie should have a soft spot in the middle. The truth was that hard went clean down to the bone.

The little detective checked the grab bag for marshmallows, then settled for a Three Musketeers candy bar. Cold air tainted with bitter smoke whipped through the open driver door of the Ford.

"Forget it," Vasquez said. "Those firemen ain't gonna let you get close enough to toast that."

One truck with whirling lights aimed water at a runaway fire consuming the offices of Harper Congdon and Lynch. They sprayed water on the neighboring buildings for containment. The law offices were a loss, a retro-eighties flare-up in the firework intensity that once made the Bronx famous.

After spending the day collecting information, the detectives drove up to the Bronx in time to follow the fire engines to the law firm's meltdown. The coincidence led Guthrie to point a finger at Donald Harper. The lawyer was tall enough, and after a few decades of criminal practice in the city, maybe ballsy enough to settle scores for himself.

"Ain't no way," Vasquez said. "He's a lawyer, *viejo*. He's gonna know better than to shoot Stephanie Morgan, even if he did shoot his old partner. The Morgan murder won't ever go away."

"Criminals ain't bright people," the little detective said. "But even if he's clean on that, he's behind this burnout. There's something in there these lawyers were afraid about—all of them. Maybe what these Mexicans were mixed in."

Vasquez shrugged.

The detectives left before the crowd grew bored and drifted away, but not before a patrolman made a circuit writing down license tags around the fire, to Guthrie's disgust. On the drive south to the old market complex, he called Ed Pratt but reached voice mail. The market spread along a handful of blocks of Harlem River waterfront, mostly in one old, long building that served as an indoor market before chain retailers devoured all of the competition.

Daylight wound down. Shallow lots edged with hurricane fence studded the market, masking loading docks and roll-up doors. The surrounding blocks held more small lots, grimy with windblown litter and gray snow. The dull, silent cars sat like paintings in empty rooms. Guthrie patrolled, calling Pratt again. As streetlights lit, the market gained solidity by flexing straight brick lines and breaks marked with iron gutters and pipes beneath long rows of tall windows.

Vasquez pointed into a lot stubbed on 150th Street. "That's a red 500," she said.

The little detective grunted and swung around. Pratt owned a red BMW 500-series. A fence and a gapped-up line of cars screened the back of the lot, where the 500 sat between a Toyota SUV and a rusted Ford station wagon. Guthrie slid to a halt at the nose of the 500.

In the driver's seat, a man leaned forward against the steering wheel. The detectives hopped from the Ford and walked over to the doors of the BMW. Guthrie spit out a string of curses. The driver had a bullet hole in his neck, like a misplaced piece of junk jewelry. Looking closer, he decided the corpse was Ed Pratt. Vasquez checked the license plate and matched Pratt's DMV information. Guthrie added more curses.

"What's the problem, *viejo*?" Vasquez asked. "I don't think I mind running out of lawyers—"

He laughed. "Okay, I got you. But maybe this one did something for us if he lived a little longer."

"He warned Harper." Vasquez stared through the windshield. Isolated behind the glass, the body didn't seem real. She stepped back, wanting it to stay that way.

"Maybe Harper did this." Guthrie studied the car and body without touching. "Once in the neck and posed the body. Pratt must've known the shooter, because he didn't panic."

Vasquez pulled out her phone. Guthrie shook his finger. "No way," he said. "I'm not going to jail tonight. Tomorrow, maybe, but not tonight."

She hesitated, but he walked back to the Ford and climbed into the driver's seat. "If we call the cops, it won't matter who catches the squeal. This falls straight into Hernandez's lap—he's the primary. We'll be sitting in his house all night while he thinks up questions to ask. There's time enough for that tomorrow."

"How's it gonna connect tomorrow, if we don't call 911?"

"We talked to him on the phone," Guthrie replied. "That's gonna get a conversation, complete with lawyers. I just pissed on Hernandez's blue suede shoes this morning."

"I told you not to do that," Vasquez muttered.

The little detective shrugged. Clogging up in traffic on the drive back into the city poured gravy on top of coming away with nothing. Back in the office they played connect the dots and argued about suspects. They marked up paper destined for the trash. More snow whirled down from the darkness. Outside the office windows, the city's lights shrank until they were small enough to cup in a hand.

CHAPTER EIGHTEEN

"I understand why you wouldn't mention your conversation with Ed Pratt," Hernandez said. The Dominican detective sucked his lips to kill the smile trying to emerge on his face. He nodded sympathetically. "I understand."

Lawyers and cops packed the conference room at the 55th Precinct. Three Italian lawyers from Brooklyn, William Sinclair from Davis Polk, a detective from Bronx Homicide, Ame Hernandez and Rocky Devlin, two detectives and the lieutenant from the 55th squad, the chief of detectives, and Eliot Wilkins, a detective from Major Case, crowded the table with Guthrie and Vasquez. The chief ordered a combined interview to prevent a multihour interview where the Italian lawyers took turns passing information and questions. Wilkins, the Major Case detective, watched with tired disinterest.

"You didn't ask," Guthrie said. "I offered you some answers in a previous conversation—you dropped them. I ain't handing you something you're gonna drop."

Hernandez smirked. "So Pratt called you?"

"That's right."

"To set up a meeting?"

"That's right."

"At the Terminal Market on 150th Street?"

"The market. He didn't name a street."

Hernandez nodded. "You know, I had a teacher at John Jay tell me that I should never overlook the possibility of coincidence."

Smiles and chuckles drifted through the detectives in the room. None of them believed in coincidence. They solved cases by connecting things that seemed unconnected. "There's a teacher looking for another job," one offered.

"Exactly," Hernandez said. "What did Pratt have to say when you talked with him?"

"I didn't talk to him," Guthrie said.

"You drove up to the Bronx for a meeting but changed your mind?"

"I didn't talk to him. I called him, and cruised the market looking for him. He stood me up. I decided he was playing some game connected to the fire at his office that evening. I drove back into the city."

"There was a fire?" Devlin asked.

"Don't play with me," Guthrie asked. "I ain't slept. I ain't in the mood. A uniform took my plate across the street from the fire that sure looked like some arson."

"I guess that's another coincidence," Hernandez said, "being on time to catch the fire. You do seem to show up in all of the right places, at the right times. Or sooner. Everywhere I go, working this case, I run into you coming out. Three lawyers connected to Harper Congdon are dead. Clayton Guthrie connects up neatly."

The little detective shrugged; opportunity netted innocent with guilty. Vasquez traced circles on the tabletop with a fingertip. On the street, opportunity was a hard truth about the usual suspects. Her brothers stood in lineups and shrugged off questions with ritual indifference. They looked guilty, mostly for trips that never caught up with them. The shoe was an uncomfortable fit with an audience of silent police detectives.

"I'm trailing a killer that started something on Fifty-second

Street," Guthrie said. "He killed Ludlow on something that seems connected to his old criminal practice in the Bronx. You took a few days off before you started looking. You're following me."

"That's all it is?" Hernandez asked. "Here's what it looks like to me: Ludlow did something to Stephanie Morgan, or meant to do something to Stephanie Morgan." He fingered his silver cuff links, then sat back in his chair.

"Ludlow had to go. You arranged it, but something went wrong. His old firm was his safety net. You're cutting it down." Hernandez made a pistol with his forefinger, pointed, and mouthed, Bang.

"You get all this from me being in front of you, you got some imagination," Guthrie said. "Now I'm thinking I screwed up. I came here thinking it would make you feel better on your feelings being hurt. Now? Get a warrant."

"That's happening right now," Hernandez said.

"Talk faster," Guthrie said.

"Ed Pratt was shot to death last night. He met somebody at the Terminal Market, had a conversation, and wound up dead."

"I didn't talk to him," Guthrie said sharply.

"He stood you up, I remember. Pratt, interestingly enough, met at least two people." He extended a finger that wavered between Guthrie and Vasquez. "Someone was sitting in the car with Pratt when he took the bullet."

Hernandez paused, nodding. "You know what a void is, right? A spatter-and-residue void, right there on the passenger side." His gaze drifted to Vasquez. "I like your new hat. Did something happen to that Yankees cap you wear?"

Rocky Devlin grinned, studying his cellphone. "We have the paperwork," he said. "Both residences, the office, and the car."

"Search warrants," Hernandez said. "We'll find the clothes. *Then* we'll do arrest warrants."

Guthrie sighed. "You're an idiot," he said quietly. "Wilkins . . ."

The skinny black detective from Major Case sat forward. His skull had a gleam of baldness on top explaining the clean shave on the sides. He frowned doubtfully.

"Wilkins, you oughtta take this over before this guy wastes any more time. Do me the favor of calling me when you're done with my car." He pushed the keys onto the table. "I'm getting back to work. Those lawyers are into something dirty, and it's killing them."

Hernandez laughed. "You really think a head start is going to help you?" he asked, sliding into his overcoat. Devlin slipped on a pair of dark glasses.

The little detective looked into the corner of the room, without letting his expression change, then stood and tugged his fedora onto his head. He motioned Vasquez to get up. In the corner, William Sinclair was whispering to the chief of detectives. Wilkins watched. He shrugged when Hernandez lit with astonishment.

"Cut them loose," the chief said.

Guthrie and Vasquez walked from the precinct surrounded by lawyers.

NYPD executed their search warrants. For the detectives, that meant a slow rotation between standing on Thirty-fourth Street and walking up to the frosted-glass door for a frustrated glance at the uniformed officer securing the premises, like laboratory animals doomed to repeat the same section of the maze again and again. Guthrie wouldn't go inside.

"Believe me," he said, "watching them do it is worse. You can't stop them. Some of the freakish pieces of crap get kicks feeling for a soft spot. They're reading you."

Before the call came that NYPD was finished processing the Ford, an Italian kid paused on Thirty-fourth Street in an Escalade to give the detectives a lift to the end of the block. They climbed out of the vehicle with new pistols. Guthrie took chrome Security Sixes in .44 caliber, and Vasquez took another pair of Smith & Wesson Chief's Special semiautomatics. Then they rode the train up to the Bronx, finishing the ride in a taxi to retrieve the car.

The old Ford looked worse molested than some badly twisted underwear. Guthrie rummaged, sorting tools, papers, and clothes. Vasquez supervised the coffee and doughnuts. She slid the Colt pistol back into her trench coat pocket after retrieving it from the untouched lockout. She tossed a bite of doughnut into the gutter when she answered a call from Indio.

"*Chica*, I got to hand you this one," he said.

"The cops are there," she said.

"Oh my, yes," he said. "Many cops are here. Cops are searching the bedroom you haven't cleaned in three weeks. Cops are checking how well Mamì has done laundry. Cops are snaking the drains in the bathroom. Cops are knocking on our neighbors' doors with questions. These questions usually include the words *Rachel* and *Vasquez*. They wonder when you come home at night." Indio's voice was smooth. Miguel called him big, dumb, and slow, but he was always convincing. Detailing the search, he sounded snide.

"This's good?" Vasquez demanded.

"*Chica*, it's hysterical," Indio said. "I've never seen Papì look like this. His face is so dark, he almost looks like a *moreno* with golden hair. He is going to burst into flames. One of the cops waved some underwear at him and asked if it was yours or Mamì's."

Vasquez cursed, darting glances at Guthrie as he counted the pieces of a toolbox he kept in the trunk, crouched beside the curbside ridge of dirty snow with his overcoat trailing into the slush on the sidewalk.

"A tall black bastard with scars in his eyebrows—" Indio said.

"Hernandez!" Vasquez hissed.

"—came out of your bedroom with your Yankees cap on the end of a pen like he had a Lotto winner."

She cursed again.

"I hope that's not bad news," he said. "That received a signed plastic bag, a clipboard entry, signatures and smiles all around. I thought they would hold it up and pose for a picture, but they had more searching to do. So . . ."

"Indio, I didn't do anything."

"You mean this isn't about whoever you shot in the Bronx?"

"I didn't shoot anybody in the Bronx!"

Indio laughed. "*Si.* That was *last* month."

"I'm gonna hang up on you!"

"*Chica*, I called to warn you," Indio said, his voice suddenly serious. "You don't want to come home tonight. Papì will kill you. He won't mean to. He will even regret it. First Thanksgiving, now this?"

Vasquez sighed. Her brother would know. Indio and Miguel had fought her father over every scrap of teenage independance, mostly related to their gang allegiance, arrests, and occasional jail terms. Both of her middle brothers had spent time on Rikers Island. They read Papì's moods like a weather report.

"What am I gonna do?" she asked. Once the question slipped out, she remembered that asking advice provided her brothers' favorite setup for a prank; her middle brothers were old enough to help, when she was a little girl, but young enough to prefer mischief.

"I don't know," Indio began, with a speculative edge to his voice, then finished, "no, *chica*. Play it safe. Maybe a few days."

After she pocketed her phone, Vasquez watched Guthrie finish assembling the puzzle of trinkets in his old blue Ford. When she took the job with Guthrie that spring, she wondered why he kept such a ratty, beat-up old car. Driving in the city was a headache that rarely became a reward—late at night, or in a moment where everyone else turned and left you to hit all the lights by yourself. A *relief* from continual pressure substituted for pleasure.

Guthrie's Ford was more, a hotrod wearing a rusty disguise and a rolling warehouse of tricks—tools, gear, clothes, and room for more. The armored lockout opened neatly after a precise sequence of mechanical and electrical keys. The old car was everything but a place to stay. Vasquez mentally counted the money in her pocket without liking the result.

"Something eating you?" Guthrie asked. He took off his fedora, and scrubbed his eyes with the sleeve of his overcoat.

The detectives drove back over to the city under a sky that looked like steel wool, foamy with dirty soap. Charles Congdon still refused to return calls. Guthrie focused on the runaway lawyer all afternoon, listing leads and rubbing out false trails while Vasquez puzzled at the notations in Ludlow's journals. The entries lined up dreary foulness—recitals of champagne cocktails, prime steak, and nights of cold seduction.

Gray daylight still lit the tall office windows when Tommy Johnson pushed through the frosted-glass door. He glanced at Vasquez, then circled the oxblood couch and sat down. He folded his peacoat on the arm. Guthrie looked up from his computer with a sigh and rubbed his eyes.

"You're clear," Johnson said. "The warrants came up dry. That dick from the One-Seven walked your Yankees cap to the lab, but it was clean. Wilkins took primary on Morgan—Manhattan South is off."

Guthrie smiled. "So they pulled the cruiser from out front?"

"I didn't see one." Johnson bounced up from the couch, walked to the window, and studied the street. He shook his head.

"You seen anything on that Pratt murder?" Guthrie asked.

"Guth, you could buy a fellow dinner first," Johnson said. The big young man smiled as he walked back to the couch.

"I got plans with Monica."

"You were pretty sure to clear, huh?"

Guthrie smiled. "I'm hoping for a night's sleep."

"Then you need a different girlfriend," Johnson said.

Vasquez nodded agreement, but didn't say anything. Monica worked for NYPD as a computer analyst at headquarters. She dressed like an office drone, using glasses and a square haircut to hide her looks. She liked lemonade, quiet sarcasm, chocolate, and Clayton Guthrie. The little man's phone conversations with her rode on murmurs and laughter.

"What about Pratt?" Guthrie asked again.

Johnson settled back on the couch. "Shot once in the neck with a nine-millimeter while he sat in his vehicle. Spatter in the compartment puts someone in the front with him. They took some souvenirs away. That's what the dick from the One-Seven was after."

"That's it?"

"Some speculations. The shooter had to open the driver door, or the window, or sit in the back and fire with a twisted wrist. Or someone in the front seat was struggling with Pratt, and that created an opening. Pratt was in the driver seat, and there was a passenger and a shooter."

Guthrie relaxed back in his chair. "You want suspects?"

"Bronx is looking at his coworkers. They don't need me for that."

"Tell them to scratch Congdon off their list."

Johnson grunted. "That's what you're working on?"

"It's related." The little detective groaned to his feet and stretched his back. He pulled some money from his pocket and handed it across to Vasquez. "Do the honors. Take Tom out someplace fancy." He pocketed the keys to the Ford, took his overcoat from the rack, and walked out while she was still staring at him.

CHAPTER NINETEEN

Tommy Johnson tapped into an app on his phone, quizzed her on preferences, and landed impossible reservations at Acappella while Vasquez was still considering how to fight through the theater district to reach Edison's for lox. The efficiency needled Vasquez. Johnson loomed as he strolled around the office with his phone, managing details, another card in the same suit as listening to Guthrie, and rolling smoothly in the rut of her teenage life at home—squabbling with her brothers, reading notes from Mamì, and dodging storms of displeasure from Papì. Vasquez didn't make many decisions, so once she noticed Johnson leading the way, she dug in her heels. That seemed as natural as breathing.

Traffic vanished as they drove down to TriBeCa. The rusty Challenger's engine rumbled beneath Johnson's questions while he pried ineffectually at Vasquez. Her smalltalk lurched out in broken pieces, punctuated by hissing curses in Spanish that he didn't understand but drew out his smile. Vasquez was relieved and annoyed. She didn't want him inside her head, beyond snapshot glimpses of his sharp profile and blond fade. At least her language was beyond his reach. He kept shuffling his questions, while he slid his hands smoothly on the steering wheel.

She didn't want to talk about her family, the weather, or the holidays. She hadn't been shopping. Along the drive she realized that over the summer she had abandoned all of that. She saw Isadora when Isadora came to see her, or Miguel when he poked his head into her room. Only a long handful of overnights from Skinny's broke the blur of October, September, and November spent sitting on the side of her bed without bothering to turn on the television. Sometimes she didn't even take off her boots before she curled on the bed. She thought about that as she threw broken answers at his questions and stared out into the cold pools of streetlight in the city.

Johnson parked on Chambers Street, and as they walked down to Hudson Street, Vasquez stumbled onto her anger like an underwater rock. As quick as a footfall, she felt like she was bleeding. "What about you?" she demanded.

Johnson missed a step, caught by surprise. Freezing slush crackled beneath their feet. "I want to keep doing this without going back to school," he said. The words came out softly, pillowed on a burst of misty breath. "I don't think that's going to work." His gaze dragged along the pavement.

Acappella threw a circle of light onto the sidewalk ahead of them from low, gold-lettered windows fringed with green curtains at the top. A hint of basil and tomato rode the biting air.

"So?"

"I like the job, but I can't go up. I need that degree."

"I can see that," Vasquez said. She lunged forward to catch the door, opened it, and bit off a laugh as his hand fell back to his side. Slow violin and bel canto accompanied the invitation of tomato sauce.

The waiter led them to a round table at the window, offered a smile, and recited the names of the night's specials. The table was small enough for Johnson to reach across. The waiter returned quickly with a basket of bread, and a candle for the "bella donna." Johnson fussed with his silverware and napkin. His hair seemed more softly golden in dim light.

"You aren't satisfied where you're at?" Vasquez asked. "You have to go up?"

Johnson smiled. "I better. I live in a walkup in Queens, full of nosy neighbors. I have an old woman on each end of the hall. One burns cat food, and the other one cooks like an angel. They're having some sort of war over me. I better go up."

"Even if somebody else has to come down?" Vasquez's glare was sharper than the question. He ducked his head.

She flapped her menu open. "Maybe it don't matter," she said. "Up or down, my nose still winds up in the sewer. If what I wanted mattered, I wouldn't be in this mess. This city has some rotten sewers. Has Guthrie bothered to tell you about Duane Parson?"

Johnson shook his head uneasily. His eyes bored into his menu, but he flicked glances at her each time her voice sharpened.

"He's a murdering piece of shit," she said. "He killed a girl from Brooklyn over the summer. That's what sent Hernandez in the wrong direction. No hard proof—" The autopsy photographs blurred in her mind, comparing wide, encircling bruises on Powell and Sorcini. "That piece of shit kills like you and me breathe. No, he enjoys it. Powell ain't alone in his trophy case.

"Parson? That's not his name. *Viejo* sent you on a wild-goose chase in Stuttgart. He's probably Albert Sidney Hunter the Third, from the Westchester Hunters—you know, the cousins of the Albany Hunters."

The waiter slid to a stop at their table. He offered a smile and a mouthful of smooth Italian. Soft music and conversation underscored one recognizable phrase of English: "You are ready to order?" They ordered veal and linguini with a Barolo recommended by the waiter.

Vasquez watched Johnson while they waited for the bottle of wine. Frowns raced across his face, mixed with glances out the window. Finally, she said, "What's the matter, *chico*? This's the part where you nod your head and smile, and agree with whatever I say. You ain't gonna agree with me?"

"No."

The waiter swept up to the table, poured wine, and departed. Beyond the misty glass, a ghost of Hudson Street faded distantly. Vasquez stared across the little table at Johnson, wondering at the sad, confused expression on his face. She drank wine. The Barolo cut her tongue, unlocking something inside her head with a dead-bolt slide and snap.

Vasquez talked. Her words fell into Johnson like a stream into a pool. Questions left eddies that filled with a rush. They ate.

Food and wine disappeared from the table; a second bottle arrived and emptied. Vasquez talked, wandering randomly through memories snipped like ornaments from a Christmas tree, and watched Johnson's expression change until it settled on wonder. She looked inside herself. The fire was out, leaving ashes on cold embers. She was sleepy.

Outside, the night air was crisp, too cold to feel damp. Johnson cranked the engine of his Challenger and they sat silently on cold leather seats for a minute while the heater fought the chill. Handfuls of bundled people darted between cars and restaurants, silent beyond the glass.

"Henry Street?" Johnson asked.

"Can't go home," Vasquez said. "Papì's gonna kill me."

He nodded. The Challenger's engine rumbled as he drove. With her face leaned against the chill glass, Vasquez watched the blocks slide along. They crossed the Williamsburg Bridge.

"Where are we going?" Vasquez asked.

"Corona."

"I like Queens," she said brightly.

The street was quiet when they parked. Hardened snow hung on to some windowsills and rails, but mostly the dark red bricks shrugged off the brightness of the streetlights. Apartment windows glowed overhead, like posters advertising warmth and comfort. Vasquez followed Johnson to the fourth floor of a five-floor walkup. The next block had suburban brick homes, but his block was an alley-pierced miniature of the city. Vasquez sniffed warmed-over *pernil*, then wrinkled her nose when she found the cat food.

Johnson circled his apartment, turning on lights. An island counter with louvered folding doors on top separated the kitchen from the front room. Dishes waited in a drying rack, and a few pans hung in a cluster from a chain hooked to the ceiling. A microwave, toaster, and Crock-Pot lined the narrow counter.

Vasquez stripped from her trench coat. "I can't believe you live in Corona and don't speak any Spanish," she said.

He shrugged. He hung his coat from a peg. "I recognize a few words. If I'm listening." He poked into a closet and pulled out sheets, a blanket, and a pillow. In the front room, textbooks covered one edge of the coffee table. Two end tables held lamps. Along one wall, a crude wooden table held a neat array of tools and machine parts, including a transmission shroud. A cheap throw rug covered some of the hardwood floor.

"That looks like mine," Vasquez said, nodding at the bedroom—a strip of bare floor surrounding a bed.

Johnson snorted. He dropped sheets, blanket, and pillow on the couch. "Yours is bigger. Remember, I've seen it."

Vasquez glanced at the couch. "You're gonna sleep there? You're gonna stick off both ends." She sailed her black hat through the bedroom door. It landed on the bed. She lifted her chin and gave him a challenging glare.

His face hardened with a frown that reminded her of Clayton Guthrie: unbreakable. "I ain't interested in nothing casual with you, Rachel."

"What?" Vasquez's anger returned with a rush, pounding her heart until she trembled. "I guess you lost interest when my face got fucked up, beyond being sorry for me." She ran short of breath. Her eyes burned, but she wasn't drunk enough to cry.

"What in the hell are you talking about?"

"Don't play me stupid, *chico*. I know why you don't want me."

"I ain't interested in nothing *casual*!" Johnson lunged across the room and grabbed her arm. "You can't be serious, can you? I know the kind of mess a man finds with a woman who don't want him. I'd rather eat my heart out." He shook her, then let her go. She stumbled away.

"Doesn't matter," Vasquez hissed. "The shit's over for me, right? I got to take what I can get."

Johnson stiffened, then drooped. With a broken smile, he walked into the kitchen. Through the space above the counter, she watched him open a cabinet.

"Maybe this sounds familiar, *chico:* some dumb Puerto Rican girl kisses Prince Snow White, then *somebody* turns into a frog. I been noticing lately white girls catch the same hell. So it don't matter! You get that?"

Johnson strode back into the room. He poked two glasses down onto the coffee table, then paused for a silent moment with an unopened bottle of Maker's Mark in his hand. He split the wax and wrenched the cork free with a single smooth twist. He poured. "Would a prince do this," he muttered.

"*Chico, stop*, I know you can't drink no whiskey," Vasquez said thickly. She stepped close to him and took the bottle from his hand. She took the glasses, dodged around the counter, and dropped it all into the sink.

He scowled. "I can't drink, and I can't understand why you need to get drunk," he growled as she drifted back into the front room. With a quick step, he reached, caught her hand, and tugged her to him. He brushed at the string of beads in her hair. "I liked the feather."

Vasquez laughed.

"I thought you liked me, Rachel."

"I do, *chico*, I just—"

"Call me *Tommy*," he demanded.

After a pause, she whispered, "Tommy."

His long hands softly framed her face as he kissed her. She gripped at his shoulders, and he whirled her with short steps into the bedroom. The zipper of her blue jeans purred when he pulled it. They corkscrewed slowly down toward his bed, shedding clothes as they descended. The tiny space and the single night broke open to reveal wide, icy stars and endless time spread above the blanket of Tommy's fiery skin.

Floating half awake in the deep dark of the morning, Vasquez saw why Ludlow wrote and wrote. He detailed and measured, but he had it all wrong. Words could only cast a faint, distorted shadow of glowing madness, because after it was over, it was gone.

CHAPTER TWENTY

Johnson drove Vasquez in from Corona early in the morning. When he slowed his Challenger to a stop in front of the office on Thirty-fourth Street, she bolted from the car without a good-bye. At a fast food breakfast passing through Williamsburg, she served averted eyes and broken sentences while he clenched a trembling fist beneath the table. She wouldn't talk. A night with Tommy Johnson had ripped aside her rum-hazed satisfaction with overnights from Skinny's. The revelation panicked her. She tried to turn around, but the door of drunken forgetfulness had locked behind her. She shut down.

Vasquez forgot about the scramble from Queens into the city once she arrived at the office. Only two lawyers remained in the Bronx firm, and Guthrie was desperate to gain an edge before the case slipped away. The detectives drove up to Pelham again, where the snow had already slipped on a coat of smoky gray Bronx grime. Guthrie's deep background search had unearthed one thin bone in the lawyer's past—racquetball. Congdon had been buying racquetballs by the dozen, plus racquets, shoes, sweats, and other trivial purchases in a steady trickle for twenty-five years. His chin and chest jutted proudly in trophy photographs from tournaments. A few late payments on his mortgage, credit cards, and car loans marred excellent credit, but he had never run late on his gym fees. His current spot was a sports complex in Co-op City.

"C.C. probably took half his showers at the gym, anyway," Guthrie said as they drove along Southern Boulevard. "He felt at home. Big places like this got food, they're open all night. He could have friends there."

"C.C.?" Vasquez asked. The lawyer had less personality than a bowling ball. Guthrie shrugged.

The detectives drove around the sports complex—a vast brick wall camouflaged with posters offering gymnastics, martial arts and yoga training, coaching for an endless variety of ball games, personal trainers, massage therapy, and nutritious food, heavily laced throughout with inducements to relax and enjoy. Vasquez spotted directions to the free parking. The lot led to an underground entrance opening into a brightly lit glass and aqua tile lobby that smelled of chlorine and fruit yogurt.

A pretty, cocoa-skinned West Indian woman at the desk watched them for a moment as they examined the lobby. She wore a navy track suit with crimson accents and a name tag that read *Sara Desir*. She settled on polite suspicion and offered help. Guthrie grilled her for the layout of the complex, gaining a brief description of the floor plan, staff, and membership while Sara's expression progressed into annoyance. Vasquez nodded along with the question-and-answer, surprised that the woman kept a polite tone.

"Sara, you almost convinced me to join," Guthrie said, "but I'm really just looking for someone—a tall, middle-aged white man who likes to play racquetball." He grinned. "That ain't sounded right. I don't want to marry him. I just got some questions."

"Well—" She glanced at Vasquez.

"Let's narrow it down," Guthrie said. "Booming voice, stands too close to people, actually wins games of racquetball—"

Sara's eyes lit with recognition, but before she could speak, Vasquez said, "With that, is anybody else asking about him? He could suddenly have a lot of friends."

Guthrie sighed when the dark-skinned woman paused to consider. Vasquez shrugged. Later, she would get a lecture. That one was a jukebox favorite: don't tilt the deal. The little detective sometimes buttered both sides of a slice of bread to show her how to do it, but when he meant business he never switched directions until he ran into a wall. He demonstrated, then tested her with hard-eyed clerks at the bodegas in *El Barrio*. The clerks sensed con from long, bitter practice, forcing Vasquez to measure every nuance of word, tone, and gesture. Guthrie's sigh marked failure.

The little detective fished a pair of folded fifties from his trouser pocket, and left the corners of the bills peeking from the loose fist he dropped on the counter top. "I swear to you that we're not C.C.'s problem," he said softly. "We're the solution. He needs a lifeline."

"He's been in *a lot*," she said. "More than usual. I knew something was wrong—he's been quiet."

The little detective nodded. "He talks to somebody here?"

"You want Rick Martini. He's one of the personal trainers." She frowned. "No one's asked for him."

He smiled. "That's good news." He fished two more fifties from his pocket, and folded them up for two pairs. He added a business card. "I'm Clayton Guthrie. If the police ask who asked about C.C., give them my name. If somebody scary asks about him, give me a call."

Sara took the money, studied the card, and gave them directions to the courts and weight rooms on the second floor. The detectives went upstairs. The complex had thin blue carpets, mirrored hallways, and a continuous wooden banister. Reflections watched Vasquez at every step. One court in the quiet block was occupied.

The racquetball game thundered at high velocity. Martini, a heavily muscled dark-haired man in his thirties, had a thick belly bulging his white T-shirt. Congdon had a similarly mismatched physique, with hyperdefined arms and calves bookending his belly. Guthrie watched through the door.

At the end of a second game, Congdon noticed the little detective. The lawyer's shoulders drooped, and he circled hesitantly on the hardwood floor. Martini prodded him with questions, then saw the detectives. Guthrie opened the glass door and walked inside. Vasquez lingered, holding the door open.

"You seen the papers?" Guthrie asked.

Congdon nodded, but said nothing. Martini fingered his racquet.

"The shooter hit Pratt two nights ago."

Congdon sagged against the wall of the court and slid down into a defeated sprawl. "Go away," he said.

Martini frowned, showing a deep stamp on his face from constant anger. "What's going on?" he demanded. The muscleman had a fade and a clean shave, but his jaw was dark with what would be a thick beard.

"C.C.'s having trouble accepting help," Guthrie replied. "Have you noticed in the papers about some lawyers getting shot?"

Martini shrugged.

"C.C. knows all those dead people." The little detective turned back to Congdon. "It's down to you and Harper."

"You don't want to help," the lawyer muttered.

"I want the shooter!" Guthrie's shout cracked like a whip. "If I get him before he gets you, that is help."

Congdon shook his head helplessly.

"You would rather be dead?"

"You don't understand!" Congdon cried.

"And while your mouth stays shut, I never will," Guthrie said. He waited, watching Congdon hide beneath a forearm propped on an upthrust knee. He shook his head.

The lawyer answered with silence. Martini studied him.

"That means Harper finds you. I think he killed Ed Pratt." The little detective pulled a business card and dropped it on the court. "In case you lost the last one."

Guthrie was quiet as they walked out. Vasquez watched him brood, and decided he was wondering what she was wondering: How could the lawyer sit still rather than save himself. Between the mirrored walls, the detectives became a crowd of people abandoning Congdon to his fate.

Vasquez had never seen a muchacho freeze in front of danger like that. Hazily, she remembered that an old woman in the neighborhood, Esmerelda Nuñez, sat silently waiting for cancer to kill her. Long before the disease arrived, the *abuela* was afraid of doctors and hospitals. She relied on old remedies from the island, some so foul a *jíbaro* would rather cut cane for a week than drink. When the cancer came, Nuñez was forced to the hospital by an insistent crowd of children and grandchildren, but at length told them *no más*. She curled up like an old cat, immune to comfort. No muchacho would ever do that. If a hundred enemies waited out in the street, a muchacho would run out with his pistol to get them first.

After Guthrie started the old Ford's engine, he paused. "If he had any clue who it was, I think he would tell," he said. "That's his trouble. This has to be some client he did dirt—he don't know which one."

"What do you mean, *viejo*?"

"I think he screwed all of them, and now he can't pick."

After locating Congdon's Infiniti in the underground garage, the little detective parked in the back row of a shallow lot down the street, with a slim view of the garage entrance.

Vasquez wasted some time griping, but they were watching Congdon. The little detective knew she hated stakeouts, so he called her a taxi to ride around and gather a grab bag. While she was gone, he took a quick walk up and down the street, looking for a better place to park. He found nothing. A line of stores retailed discount clothing, shoes, and packaging. A few vending machines crowded a small plaza, with benches and a miniature fountain, directly across from the main entrance of the center. Street parking was the only other option. Vasquez came back with the grab bag and found him sitting in the Ford, spinning his fedora in his hands.

The young detective hated stakeouts for being long, usually pointless waits. Over the months working for Guthrie, she was forced to admit that stakeouts served a purpose, but mainly marked what would have been a good time for a nap or a long bathroom break.

A trickle of shoppers trudged back and forth on the sidewalk while the cars in the lot slowly shuffled and exchanged places during the passing hours.

"Now I feel like I missed this on my first pass," the little detective said. "Wasserman wouldn't have missed it. That old man was sharp. One time we were picking up a car. Nothing serious, just a little repossession to twist a screw on someone who crossed somebody high up.

"Anyway, this Italian knows the car is due, from getting notices, so he keeps it hidden. Wasserman lifts the lid on the Italian's garbage can and glances inside. I swear, he didn't even rummage around. Then we took a train ride, and walked over to an Irish grill on the edge of Hell's Kitchen. The Mercedes is in the parking lot. We jumped in and left."

Vasquez shook her head. The little detective cracked stories about his predecessor, Wasserman, the same way some muchachos tripped war stories about street heroes. Wasserman had worked for the Whitney family, doing the same business Guthrie did, up until the early 1990s when he passed the torch. Vasquez doubted that all the stories were completely true, but she knew her part in a dangling finish— she asked for the punch line.

"All right, how did he find it?"

"He said he saw a matchbook in the trash." Guthrie shrugged. "One hair—nine oxen. That's the simplest way to say it. Wasserman was sharp."

Vasquez didn't argue. The detectives waited as the afternoon slowly passed, punctuated by rummages in the grab bag for fruit and candy, a slow parade of shoppers chipping away at Christmas lists, and gusts of wind brooming loose trash down the street.

At four o'clock, Harper parked a green Ford Taurus on the street in front of the center. Guthrie shot video and noted the time. The lawyer pulled an in-and-out at the center, emerging from the garage entrance, and walked back across the street. He dipped around the Taurus and disappeared. Guthrie ran the plate on the Taurus, and came up with a rental agency.

The little detective grunted. "He's been waiting to do this, I think. I'm gonna go see which store he ducked in, maybe." He climbed from the Ford, glanced down the sidewalk before hopping the steel cables fencing the parking lot, and darted across the street.

Vasquez watched him, growing queasy from the whiff of exhaust and icy air when he opened the car door. She checked her pistols. The little detective eased slowly down the sidewalk, craning his head for a view at every half-step. He looked like a bad mime, facing the wrong way to be pretending to look at the posters plastered on the brick wall of the sports center. He stopped, scowled, and hurried back to the car.

"Waiting in that little plaza," he said, after he slammed the door.

"So?"

"I guess he waits until C.C. comes out for supper, trails him to a restaurant, and whacks him."

She drew a quick breath to object, but bit her lip, then said, "A matchbook?"

"C.C. eats out. Never cooks. Usually it's a credit card, but he's hitting ATMs for cash to keep from leaving tracks." Guthrie sighed. "Lawyers are only dumb when you need them smart."

Her hand dropped gently onto the Colt in her trench coat pocket. "Now what?"

"We stop him."

CHAPTER TWENTY-ONE

The darkness of the November night pressed down on the Bronx before Congdon drove from the sports center's garage. Guthrie started the old blue Ford, and pulled slowly from the shallow lot to give Harper time to reach the rented Taurus and follow his partner. They fell together with the precision of gears in a watch. Smooth nighttime traffic cloaked the cross-Bronx chase—unnecessarily—because both lawyers drove with their eyes determinedly ahead, forging toward conclusions with the single-minded fervor of accountants.

"*Viejo*, you always end up with the easy one," Vasquez said.

The little man grinned.

Driving practice for Vasquez meant following taxis in the city. The gypsies would turn and bolt at any moment, driven by paranoia. Legitimate taxis made sudden radio turnarounds, and took it personally when they noticed the detectives on their bumper. After she mastered timing streetlights, and lulling suspicion by changing her distance, Guthrie made her chase the fares after they left the taxi to find out what they were doing. An easy one ended right at a door.

The chase ended in Norwood, above the Garden. Congdon barreled into a parking lot, bounced from his Infiniti, and strode briskly onto the sidewalk. The pursuit bunched up as Congdon walked back toward them; Vasquez had a sinking moment when Harper surged forward in his rental car toward Congdon approaching on the sidewalk, but his brake lights flared, and then he cruised slowly down the street, craning his head to watch Congdon. Guthrie mumbled some insults to the Ford's steering wheel. Congdon hurried past, darted across the street, then walked into Naruli, an Indian restaurant. Guthrie sighed.

The detectives played hide-and-seek with Harper, parking briefly on the street when he cruised the parking lot, ducking the dashboard when his head swiveled past them, and followed him twice around the block. The evening traffic was a thin trickle of couples landing in restaurants and an occasional truck whishing past, crowded to the middle of the street. Harper parked around the corner, then walked into an alley that cut through the block.

Guthrie drove back around to the parking lot, pulled in, and parked with a view of Congdon's Infiniti and a long slice of the street. The detectives watched Harper stroll into the lot, find Congdon's car, and kneel to slash the tires. Guthrie shot video and noted the time. Harper walked back out to the street. He settled across the street in the unlit doorway of a hair salon, where a sagging blue banner and awning blocked the light cast by the streetlamps.

"*Viejo*, this ain't right."

He glanced over at her, then turned back to watch Harper. "That is?"

"He's gonna nail C.C."

He nodded.

"I ain't gonna sit here—" she said, opening the passenger door.

He caught her wrist and jerked so hard that he snatched the passenger door shut, rocking her in the seat. "You're gonna distract me," he hissed. "Quit screwing around, will you?"

After a pause, he continued, "Take the camera and catch Harper when he makes his move. I got this, being one of the times where it's tricky. Right now, Harper's a suspicious-looking vandal. That changes if he nerves up and takes a shot. I already know there ain't no room for mistakes, all right?"

Vasquez settled into the seat, and tilted her black felt hat. "You could say something," she muttered.

He grunted. "Okay. I slept last night. I could still be a little off center from last week."

Vasquez shrugged, and pulled the grab bag from the backseat. They watched. Harper waited in the doorway of the salon, while the traffic on the street measured the frequency of the lights. Harper rotated through slow changes of position and sometimes stamped his feet on the cold pavement. An hour passed, then he stirred expectantly.

The entrance at Naruli fluttered open and shut hesitantly. Congdon walked out. A slim dark man followed him onto the sidewalk. They talked, punctuated with gestures and plumes of misty breath, then finished with bows and pressed palms.

Guthrie disabled the dome light in the Ford, slid from the driver's seat, and pressed the door shut without latching it. Vasquez shot video, panning between Congdon and the shadowy entrance of the hair salon, where Harper was a tall, tense shadow. Congdon turned and strode toward the parking lot, picked a moment, and dashed across the street.

Crouching, Guthrie slipped between the cars for a clearer vantage. He drew his revolver. Harper muffled his face while he watched Congdon on the opposite sidewalk. After Congdon passed, Harper trotted across the street and hustled into the parking lot behind him. Vasquez opened the passenger door of the Ford and squeezed out to shoot video across the hood, with both lawyers converging on the Infiniti. Congdon erupted with curses after noticing the tires. Harper drew a pistol.

At the first shot, Congdon sprang into a run like an electrocuted man. Guthrie ordered Harper to drop his gun, extending his revolver. Congdon bolted directly into a parked Toyota, rang the quarter-panel, whirled around the bumper, and sprinted across the graveled lot. Harper threw two more shots at the dodging man, then Guthrie fired once, smashing the semiautomatic pistol from his hand.

Harper tucked his hand and fled. Congdon bolted through the line of cars parked on the street, then pirouetted for a glance back into the parking lot. Guthrie shouted, but Congdon finished his spin and rushed into the street. A speeding truck scooped him from the asphalt with only a brief squeal of brakes.

The little detective spit curses. He rushed out to the sidewalk as Harper disappeared into the alley. Congdon was a jumbled pile on the strip of dirty, clotted snow decorating the painted median. The truck swished slowly to a halt a hundred feet down the street. Vasquez walked from the parking lot, still shooting video. A siren lit to a wail in the distance, and onlookers gathered like a sudden flurry of snow.

The detectives walked out and paused over Congdon's body. Guthrie scowled up at Vasquez after he knelt to check the lawyer's pulse. "Keep quiet about how we got on this trail," he said. "And forget selling that clip to Gawker."

While staring at the blank stone wall of a jail cell in the Bronx, Vasquez connected a handful of missing dots. Her thoughts tightened around Peter Ludlow like a noose as the elaborate, senseless opening sentences in his notebooks resolved into a key. She sat wide awake in the darkened cell, with her gaze bouncing around in the confinement like a maddened gerbil doing midnight gymnastics, but she needed the notebooks to test her inspiration.

Before she wound down to frustration, footsteps echoed in the quiet hall, the lock on her cell door ground open, and she was called out. Sullenly, an officer returned her pocket money, palmtop, phone, identification, and pistols, and she was escorted to the precinct lobby. Guthrie emerged a handful of minutes later, while the desk sergeant's clock counted slow, early-morning time above the desk.

Outside, some traffic eased along in the cold, dark November morning. Mike Inglewood, a detective from NYPD's Major Case squad, plodded up to the detectives as they came down the precinct-house steps. He pushed taped-together glasses up his nose and sighed, looking down at Guthrie. The policeman was tall and heavy bellied like an old, retired bull.

"I came up here to help you out, Guthrie," he said, "but I wonder if it'll do any good."

"Is that so?" the little detective asked. He snapped the brim of his fedora. "I'm up to here with cops right now, Mike. You could do me a favor and put away the badge?"

Inglewood smoothed his ginger mustache, unsuccessfully trying to hide a smile. "Sorry, I had that tattooed when they pumped in the blue blood."

Guthrie pulled his phone and started to call a taxi.

"Forget the cab, I'll give you a ride," Inglewood said. He pointed down the line of cars parked on the street, and started walking.

The detectives followed him. Inglewood's mouth twisted and settled a few times, with glances at Guthrie followed by shakes of the head.

"Just say it, will you?" Guthrie said. "You're killing me."

"Why don't you stay outta the Bronx?" Inglewood blurted. "You're messing up, Guthrie. The Bronx is the drain de la drain of the city. It's about to suck you down."

"Now that I handed Harper over on a platter?"

Inglewood sighed a long plume of mist. "People downtown are talking. I hear suggestions that people you work for are burying some sort of mess the hard way. You think a miss on the Pratt warrant clears that up? Then your face pops up for more news the next day?" he continued. "Who could forget so quick? You know what I'm talking about?"

Both detectives nodded, and Inglewood lit with surprise. "You're in this up to your eyes," he muttered. "Both of you."

"Not that NYPD bothered, but Ludlow was dirty," Guthrie said.

"Now you want the victim on trial?"

Vasquez scowled, fighting the urge to recite a list of complaints against Peter Ludlow. Inglewood sighed after glancing at her. He pulled his keys and opened both passenger doors of his unmarked car. Radio whips stood at silent attention for the passing traffic. He walked around and unlocked the driver door, but he paused before he climbed into the seat.

"I get it. I don't know everything," he said. "But right now you're both looking like hired thugs. I guess I've known you for a long time, Guthrie. We've traded jabs and so forth. I ain't never thought you were dirty—just a little too determined." His gaze strayed to Vasquez, but he looked quickly away.

"We ain't drove that thing in the Bronx," Guthrie said quietly.

"I wouldn't be here if I thought that." Inglewood shrugged. "Maybe you forget that appearances matter—but how could you, with who you work for?"

The little detective took a quick look at the gutter.

"Then after that, what happens with a dirty rag once you're done cleaning up? Wringing out's the best it's got coming. I'm just saying." He ducked into the car and yanked the door shut. A truck groaned by heavy with merchandise, and then the detectives climbed into the car for the ride.

CHAPTER TWENTY-TWO

The little detective picked Vasquez up at her parents' tenement on Henry Street at mid-morning, a late start to make up for some lost sleep spent sitting in the Bronx after Congdon's departure. He looked calm. Vasquez was exhausted but relieved. Forgetting Indio's warning, she had gone home after getting out of jail. Both of her brothers had crept heroically from the apartment once Papì woke up and began yelling. Mamì watched, arms crossed on her chest, while Vasquez sorted the clothes NYPD dumped onto her bed. Papì helped her organize by kicking her things from one pile to another. Apologies made him more angry. Papì mixed frightening outbursts with his lectures. His hands dangled from the end of massive arms like old, scarred shovelblades; every angry gesture threatened decapitation. Vasquez slept uneasily afterward, then fled when the old Ford's horn blew in the street. Guthrie was oblivious. Without a pause at the office, he drove back to Co-op City. He used the free parking at the sports center.

The detectives went inside and found Rick Martini, Congdon's dark-haired racquetball opponent. The man flared with anger when

Guthrie told him about his friend's death, then locked his jaw on a sullen scowl. Guthrie wasn't deterred. He used video clips for show-and-tell, mixed in Harper's DMV photo with some publicity shots from the Bronx law firm, and narrated the night's adventure with the determination of a high-priced lawyer. By the end of the final film from the parking lot, Martini's expression had softened.

Martini pulled a key ring from his pocket, and led them to the main locker room. He opened one of the coin-operated lockers after removing the key from his ring. A laptop waited, turned on edge among a thick sheaf of sealed yellow envelopes. Each envelope bore the neatly lettered name of one of Congdon's partners or associates.

"You tried," Martini said, watching the little detective empty the locker. "C.C. just couldn't trust you. He didn't trust people that had something at stake."

"Like clients?"

Martini nodded.

After returning to the office, Vasquez ignored the little detective's instructions, settled behind her desk, and pulled out both of Ludlow's hardbound journals. He shrugged and started coffee before opening Congdon's laptop. Fat-Fat's tool kit laid bare a pedestrian hard drive without hidden caches of memory. He browsed the files, then dumped them onto his desktop for more speed.

Congdon's transcription of records fell three years short of being complete, but contained some files of recent vintage that Guthrie suspected were connected to the stack of insurance envelopes. Many skeletal files held only names, dates, and billing information. Others bulged with briefs, notes, and orders. Guthrie culled the files, reducing to clients with Spanish names: The first footprint on the trail was the Mexican connection provided by Duane Parson. The cull reduced the files from many hundreds to less than two hundred. The little detective began to read and take notes.

At her desk, Vasquez copied and rearranged sentences from the journals, scratched out notes, and mumbled to herself. Her early-morning idea floated beyond her grasp, beckoning from among the nonsense sentences in Ludlow's journals. She ignored her cellphone, buzzing periodically on her desktop. Trahn, the Vietnamese boy that delivered Guthrie's lunchtime pizza, left after a one-sided conversation that the detectives ignored. Vasquez ate the misplaced slice with the ring of pineapple before Guthrie stirred from his desk. Traffic drifted along on Thirty-fourth Street without disturbing them.

The little detective raked the files for names and addresses, then went to the DMV for photos. Rough groups emerged as he compared addresses to a map of the Bronx, and faces with names—Puerto Ricans, Dominicans, and anyone else. He divided his groups again between more and less serious felonies and sentencing orders. Unknowns formed another group that sent him to the NCIC. He searched tax records to confirm addresses. The sky brightened with early afternoon, and he paced the office to stretch his legs. He paused at the windows to look down at Thirty-fourth Street, where sidewalk crowds marched in the cold for bargains.

"Entiendo!" Vasquez shouted. "That piece of shit is mine!"

The little detective scowled, peering through the window. "Wait a minute, Rachel, don't say nothing else," he commanded.

Vasquez paused with an upraised finger and smile, then stopped as he unlocked and threw up the window sash. Cold air and traffic noise poured into the office. He strode across the office, disappeared into the supply closet, and then reemerged with a steel toolbox. Vasquez followed him back to the window. He pulled needle-nose pliers from the toolbox. She saw the camera stud in the windowframe a moment before he gripped it and wrenched.

"You know what?" he muttered. "Maybe it don't matter. It hit me like a flash that he could be using bugs along with the cameras. I can't decide what he's likely seen or heard, here at the office."

Vasquez nodded. Guthrie dropped Parson's camera into her hand, and she shook it like a peanut. He slammed the window shut, then stepped over and examined the other frame. It was clean. He dropped the pliers into the toolbox, closed it, and picked it up.

"So what is it?" he asked. "You're working on Ludlow, right?"

She grinned. "I got him, *viejo*."

Guthrie followed her back to her desk. She opened the journals and lined up her notes. With a jabbing forefinger, she demonstrated how correspondences between the nonsense sections beginning each journal entry provided dates and locations. Guthrie reopened the journals randomly, tried the ciphers, and learned new dates and locations.

"All right, that's exciting," he said.

Vasquez laughed. "If we only had one journal, it wouldn't matter," she said, "but he was an asshole twice. Then I was bored enough to read the twisted bastard's nightlife."

He shrugged, adding a blank stare.

"Both journals contain a marriage," Vasquez said. "When I did his background, I didn't find a marriage or divorce. Who is the other woman?" She spread the journals and demonstrated dates. "These dates match his relationship with Stephanie Morgan. Their marriage day is a ringer. This one covers something that started twenty years ago."

"With another marriage?"

"Sí. Ludlow was in college. C.C. said he was a ladies' man, so I don't think this is wishful thinking. This is a record of his exploits—how and what he did to these women. The journal with Stephanie lacks some . . . Ludlow was twisted. Her journal was unfinished, but the earlier journal was full and had a sense of finality."

"He had some unfinished plans?"

"Or hesitated to use the same tricks on her," Vasquez said. "I think the first marriage was as real as Ludlow's marriage to Morgan."

A smile spread slowly across the little detective's face. "This's your operation," he said. "Put it together."

Vasquez paused to check her phone and found a long list of identical texts from Tommy Johnson: *Call me.* The splash of memory jerked her heartbeat into a disjointed rhythm and whirled her stomach in quick circles. Mostly she remembered a sharp chin and blue eyes, cut into slices by streetlight through the venetian blinds in his tiny bedroom, before she began riffling helplessly through memories of blue, looking for anything that compared to the eyes glowing in her imagination.

She jabbed repeatedly at her phone—no ring, no vibrate, no messages, *off*—and slammed it into a desk drawer, more successfully than she slammed a lid on her memory. She opened one of Ludlow's journals at random, and splashed for a few minutes in the cold water of his mechanical recitals before she could work purposefully at decoding the dates, times, and places. The work drew her back into the reality of the quiet office.

Guthrie arranged an after-hours house call from Fat-Fat, with an instruction to "bring a vacuum cleaner," then settled at his computer. With a tapestry of Harper Congdon's clients in hand, he tried to cross-connect the four Mexicans killed at the Parkchester meth pit. No names or addresses produced an immediate match. He searched DMV records for registrations and old traffic tickets. He eliminated a long list of nicknames. The afternoon slid past.

Fat-Fat arrived with a suitcase of equipment and demanded food. Guthrie ordered from Shun Lee. The big Korean shrugged, opened his suitcase atop the low coffee table in the middle of the office, and ran electricity for an array of scanners.

The detectives watched as Fat-Fat swept, quickly focusing on the wall outlet near the frosted-glass office door. He opened it and gestured magnanimously. Guthrie sighed. The big Korean removed the bug and resealed the outlet. He studied it with approval, then dropped it on Guthrie's desk like a dead mouse.

"All right, you get vodka."

Fat-Fat rubbed his belly and grinned. He claimed a handful of fifties from Guthrie's outstretched hand, then settled onto the oxblood couch. Vasquez offered him a quick outline of their dealings with Parson while they waited on the food. The little detective gathered phone numbers for the Mexicans and began cross-logging against Harper Congdon's clients.

A long, jagged string of calls to Mexico emerged, aimed at Tamaulipas, Chiapas, and Tabasco, but matched no clients. With a sigh, he began cross-logging the clients. The food arrived, and the little detective aimed his scowl at his *kung pow* for several minutes.

"I got something else," Guthrie muttered. "Fat, while you're here, I want to get into NYPD's system."

The big Korean grinned. He liked extras, but the task was too simple. Guthrie wanted information from the organized-crime database, where NYPD collected intelligence on known and suspected gangsters. He lifted the files that matched Harper Congdon clients, and the files on all four Mexicans from Parkchester. One Mexican shared a street name with one client, and a note of affiliation to El Silencio: El Primero. With a shortlisted name, Guthrie dug through the backclutter and found a common phone-log number in Chiapas.

"Those calls are seven years apart, *viejo*," Vasquez said.

"Rafael Morales is our man," Guthrie said. "He'll know something. Besides, I don't think that aka is a street name. I think it's a title—like a 426, a Red Pole."

The little detective tapped on his blotter with a pen for a minute. "Something else. Our shooter's been calling Ricardo Sorcini. I bet one of the numbers on his log recently is the shooter."

The detectives unrolled the phone log. Fat-Fat grunted encouragement while he finished the takeout. Within a quarter hour, the detectives found a repeating number, but the provider refused answers despite Fat-Fat's tool kit. The detectives couldn't attach a name to the phone number. The big Korean was amused.

"I'll ask nice," he said when he settled at Guthrie's computer. The chair creaked beneath him.

While he worked, Vasquez continued identifying the other numbers on Sorcini's log. A double handful were cellphones registered in Texas and New York to fictitious identities. She noted those numbers alongside the Mexican numbers. They could be unmasked with crank calls or activity-tracking, an ugly and time-consuming but effective trick.

"Yo, Guth, I'm backing out, here," Fat-Fat said softly. "I walked around a few corners before I knocked on the door. That saves your desktop."

The little man frowned.

"The phone's a satellite job. It can go anywhere, and run through local towers and relays, but it hops up into the sky before it lands."

"This means?"

"It's a hardware thing. That firewall's murder, probably unless you're using the right key. Those sort of phones are proprietary, like, they'll speak English, but they prefer Latin, and you won't get answers if you speak English."

"And that bit about saving my desktop?"

"That firewall had claws. I'm going to ask around, and get back to you. I'll get you in—don't worry." Fat-Fat creaked up from the desk chair, gathered his gear, and rumbled out.

The detectives shuffled and scraped the background on Rafael Morales without uncovering any more ideas. The other Mexicans from Parkchester received their own face peels, followed by comparison.

"Morales wins the beauty contest," Guthrie said. "We talk to him."

"What's to talk about?" Vasquez asked. "Rafael Morales is locked up in Sing Sing. He didn't shoot Morgan. We have a *picture*." She slapped a print from the video of the Fifty-second Street shootings against the edge of her desk, then studied the masked face again, the long coat and blocky fur hat. She shrugged. A seven-year-old phone call to Mexico wasn't a shortcut to the shooter.

He picked up the phone. "I'm gonna kick Morales and see if anything drops out. We need more than this paper." Congdon's files had a heavy stack of legal notes and filings related to Morales. A brief study convinced Guthrie that a good legal case had dead-ended for no reason—except for some billing notations in Harper Congdon's records. "That payoff leads into a mess. Trust me. We got to talk to him eventually." He smiled. "Don't worry so much. This's been a good day's work."

Vasquez had to agree. The dates and places in the old journal pointed to a beginning in western Pennsylvania during Ludlow's college years at Pitt. The young detective felt that the other woman was a local, and she wanted yearbooks to help with the search. The journal led overseas three times—to Italy, France, and Spain. She meant to cross-reference visas against the yearbook photos for a match. She wrote the report and Guthrie cleared her to hire a detective in Pennsylvania for legwork.

An icy feeling remained to chill the triumph for Vasquez. She took the grilled listening device from Guthrie's desk, and compared it to the camera stud. The devices were finished with the perfection of jewelwork. Duane Parson was a perfectionist. Even the wires for attachment wore cunning hooks to ensure a grip. Duane Parson wasn't a man that let go of anything.

CHAPTER TWENTY-THREE

In the morning, Vasquez snatched for the distraction her job offered from the rest of her life. After the search warrant and arrest her parents' tenement apartment contained a fragile silence that still echoed from Papì's shouting the night before. Vasquez took a cue and went early to bed. While she lingered on the edge of sleep, a disembodied argument between her brothers came to an abrupt end with a slammed door.

"*Hija?*" Mamì asked sharply. Vasquez peeked from beneath her blanket. A bar of light spilled into her bedroom past her mother, who pointed at the window. The door clicked shut while she sat up, looked out, and spent a long moment assembling her scattered thoughts into a focus on the street. Her heart sank.

Lines of old tenements grilled with fire escapes faced each other across Henry Street, with a broken double line of cars parked beneath them like toys. A loose neighborhood crowd, small with the distance of three stories, hustled around the edges for a better view of Vasquez's loco brothers arguing with Tommy Johnson.

Johnson's rusted Challenger sat on the other side of the street, in old Mr. Esteban's space. Indio, being bigger, confronted Tommy. Miguel circled at a little distance in the corner of Tommy's eye, the street reminder of standing in the wrong spot. Indio punctuated with a forefinger, but kept back an arm's length of clean sidewalk, then swept a hand to indicate the Challenger and pointed up at Esteban's apartment.

Tommy shrugged. He leaned against his bumper and glanced up at her window, a man going nowhere on account of Mr. Esteban or the neighborhood parking police. Miguel and Indio switched places.

The switchup served as a warning; Miguel was faster, more likely to throw a punch, and started most of the trouble to get Indio a clean shot at any sucker standing on deck. The crowd thickened as Tommy shouted back at Miguel. Miguel jerked a thumb across the street at their tenement and shook his head with exaggerated sarcasm. Tommy shrugged from his peacoat with a smooth roll, draped it on the Challenger's roof, and stepped onto the sidewalk. He rolled his neck and scowled. Miguel drifted back a step, looking up at Tommy. Indio circled.

Vasquez pounded the window, brightening with realization that her brothers were about to jump Tommy, or Tommy was about to punch Miguel into the gutter. She snapped the lock, lifted the window, and screamed curses down at the street. She threw down what she could reach; a pair of blue jeans didn't make much distance, some unused lipstick and mascara vanished noiselessly, and a boot bounced from the hood of a car, but a half-empty pint of dark rum shattered on the asphalt and froze the action.

"Are you *stupid*?" Vasquez shouted at the upturned faces. "No, wait—I know the answer to that one! Next question: Do you want me to go get my pistols?"

Miguel, Indio, and Tommy spent one long moment staring up at her, then her brothers ducked their heads and slouched across the street, while Tommy rescued his peacoat, slid into his Dodge, and started the engine. The crowd chattered and laughed as it fragmented.

Vasquez lowered her window, then untangled her sheet and blanket. Trembling, she stretched out again. After a few minutes, a brief hiss of argument paused outside her door. The door cracked and her boot and blue jeans hit the floor. Miguel laughed softly before he walked away. She circled and curled around one thought, *impossible*, until she eventually slept.

Vasquez woke the next morning gasping for air like she was breaking the surface of deep water. Mamì poured her a cup of coffee in the morning-dark kitchen while she laced her boots, and drew breath several times with a burden of words, but stayed silent in answer to Vasquez's unspoken prayers. The young detective bolted the kitchen when the Ford's horn blew.

Overnight, Brooklyn patrol officers had responded to a shots-fired and found a crowd assembled around the bullet-pocked apartment door of Marie Tyminska, an Internet boudoir queen. Tyminska was deceased inside with Donald Harper, whose corpse sported a badly bruised finger from having a pistol shot from his hand in the Bronx. The crowd of neighbors reported angry shouts prior to an exchange of gunfire.

Harper's death tugged the last brick from the wall of the Bronx law firm. A brief survey of C.C.'s envelopes revealed a long-running over-billing scheme and some spectacular examples of buried evidence. The details sickened Vasquez. Her opinion of lawyers sank deeper in the fresh grime. Losing the luxury of time angered the little detective, forcing him to press his last button.

He called William Sinclair at Davis Polk and Wardwell and borrowed a junior associate, Joseph Craig. On the drive north to meet the detectives at Ossining, Craig arranged a visit at Sing Sing. The vast brick wall encircling the prison kept the ghosts inside from peering out onto the broad parking lot. Vasquez was relieved to surrender her cellphone. Her voice mail and in-box were crammed with messages from Tommy Johnson. The prison guards focused puzzled stares on the mismatched detectives, without a second glance for the power-suited lawyer.

The prison visiting room flaunted bare conduit leading to fluorescent lights and a scarred stone floor with a single long, bolted-down table and jutting benches. A heavy steel door with a grilled viewport clamped shut after Morales limped inside and sank onto a bench. Bright scrapes decorated the Mexican gangster's forehead, and a purple bruise hollowed one of his eyes. He stared intently at the lawyer, Craig, dismissed him with a contemptuous sniff, glanced over Guthrie, then settled his gaze on Vasquez. He winced when a slow smile stretched his split lip, almost hidden beneath his thick mustache, but sighed out the pain. Guthrie studied him quietly.

"You ran into some trouble, Mr. Morales?" the little detective asked.

"Too much partying in here," the gangster purred. "Sometimes when I stay out too late I can't remember everything I did." He flicked a glance at the lawyer, Craig, and added a lopsided smile. "I don't remember you, *señor abogado*, but that don't matter. The party will reach your doorstep soon enough."

The lawyer crossed his arms and frowned. The creases in his suit looked misplaced in the steel-on-stone decor. "You're in a bad spot to threaten someone. I think you could actually use some help. Ask."

"Don't look that way to me," Morales said. "You had a nice drive up from the city? I think more snow could be coming."

The little detective shook his head. "Seeing you like this is a slap in the face, Morales. A man who can reach through a prison wall should be celebrating, but you're fighting for your life. What did you do, whistle at the wrong pretty boy? Or you wouldn't step out of the way when the captain strolled down the block? A veteran shouldn't make mistakes like that, Morales."

The gangster's face darkened. "This is nothing," he said. "You gringos know shit. In this country, everything is easy. For me, this is nothing."

"Nothing?" Craig asked. He looked the gangster over and nodded sagely.

A smile crept across the gangster's face. He slapped the tabletop. "El Primero earns decorations when he comes out on top. Seven years, *señor abogado*, and thirteen more to go. You know something now, I see, about the sleepless nights and darkness filled with lurking *gatilleros*. In my country, a man learns these lessons early."

"You know, I told him he would be wasting his time, Morales," the little detective said. "Men like you don't want help—you like being in a garbage can. You knew there was a problem with your case, then you would rather send it to the grave than fix it. A man with some sense would've waved a flag, then offered an explanation. But you would rather stay in Sing Sing." He paused with a shrug. "Like it matters. You're serving us everything you got in the city. You're naked now. Look at you. You bit the hand that feeds. Why make you an offer?"

"An offer?" Morales said. "Who cares? Thirteen more? Who cares? You *want* an offer, so you come to El Primero. In Mexico, a man is a man. He has a belly full of fire, like a volcano. A man who burns is destined for great things."

"Destined for thirteen more years," Guthrie said.

Morales shrugged. "A man can't change his fate. I am strengthened by darkness—my fate. El Balam marked me when I was fifteen. You understand? I chose to be a narco, but then El Balam marked me." He glanced at the lawyer. "Soon . . ."

Guthrie waited, glancing to quiet the lawyer when he drew breath to speak. The gangster was turning something over in his mind. During the ride up from the city, Guthrie had explained that the visit turned on baiting the gangster's pride. With a hole poked by anger, his reasons could pour out. He spelled out the lawyer's angle, but the gangster's sly threat turned one final card: He threatened Craig because he didn't know the game was already finished. He didn't know Harper was dead.

"Soon you will understand that you cannot escape the darkness, *señor abogado*," Morales said. "In my beginning, I trafficked cocaine across the river, another soldier for the plaza. When we moved, eyes watched the jungle for kilometers in every direction while burros carried the cocaine along the ancient tracks. All of this was good, even the jungle at night full of mosquitoes, and vines so thick that by morning a machete had less edge than an old rubber tire. El Balam waited until the night I brought Ramon with me." Morales shrugged. "I was proud. He was curious. El Balam was waiting.

"Guatemalan guerillas waited along the causeway beneath the bushes. After a few shouts, some men lost patience." Morales drummed the table with his fingertips, and continued softly, "Bullets fell like rain. The burros scattered. Gunfire stripped the trees naked. Running away went around in circles, because the Guatemalans were everywhere. *¡Viva la revolución!*" His hands rose up in outstretched salutes.

"I squatted with Ramon between two mounds and watched. Screams and laughter took bites from the silence. The guerillas and narcos fired whenever some brave soul tried to carry away a package. The cocaine bound everyone like chains.

"Ramon recovered his spirit while we watched. He climbed around the mounds spotting for guerillas. El Balam swallowed everything but his scream. That frightened me: His voice became a tiny thing, like an insect. Waiting in the dark for more shooting, I searched with my hands on the floor of the jungle.

"More trouble came," Morales said. "Like moths swooping onto the reflection of the moon in still water. Guatemalan soldiers came chasing the guerillas, who were chasing the narcos, who were guiding the burros, while everywhere men reached hesitantly for fallen blocks of cocaine. Ramon was frightened. His screams oozed from a hole like my two hands—"

He stretched his fingers taut and pressed them onto the tabletop to fill a hole in his memory. "Pure darkness and the smell of earth. So I slid down El Balam's gullet to find him."

Morales shrugged. "Ramon stopped screaming when he heard me coming down, but he ran in circles. He broke and crushed the dishes, scattered the bones, knocked against the walls . . . by the time I reached him and struck my lighter, he looked beaten and bloody, but that was cinnabar. The walls glowed like bloody intestines, wound like ropes around us."

Morales fingered a leather thong around his neck. A chip of glistening jade rolled between his thumb and forefinger. "We passed through the madness in the belly of El Balam. No water, no food, no light after the lighter burned low. Snapshot glimpses with the spark of the flint. No air. At night, the darkness was complete."

The gangster's eyes burned dark and hard. "Three days spent in his world gave me eyes that see in the dark. Ramon never screamed again. His fear was gone." A smile slid onto his face as he looked at the lawyer. "Soon, the darkness will find you."

The little detective nodded. "I didn't drive up here to listen to nursery stories. I told him he was wasting his time on a stupid man—you don't even think to wonder why I'm here. That leaves me telling you."

Morales darkened. He began a gesture, but the little detective continued, "You think I'm here for my health? I'm going to get your killer. You understand? I found you, I'll find him. That's what I do, and I ain't got to wait until it's dark and they pull down their pants. You understand?"

"*Cuidese, gringo,*" Morales said sharply. "*Mi hermano es la muerte.*" The gangster allowed himself another long look at Vasquez, and kept looking in sips until the guards took him out. The heavy door sealed on his laughter.

The clang of steel doors and gates, footsteps on concrete, and the sharp odor of fresh paint escorted them outside. The little detective paused to offer Craig an apology for the wasted trip, parrying his complaints with reassurances, while Vasquez hid a smile at the lies smoothly rolling from the little man's tongue. Past the encircling brick walls of Sing Sing, the lawyer rushed to his car to return to the city. Vasquez opened her palmtop and tested the signal.

"Ain't no need to hurry," Guthrie said. "Morales might not use the phone for hours." Cold wind rushed through the parking lot, sweeping stale air from the interior of the Ford. Trash rattled on the floorboard. The little detective paused to gather it into a paper bag.

"Maybe," she said. "And maybe he's already calling."

He smiled. "I thought I got to him, too. I can't believe he gave up his own family like that."

Vasquez paused. "*Viejo*, he wasn't being literal. Bangers are like that. They like to talk in riddles."

"Morales fingered his brother. Once we crosscheck the background, it'll jump out." He shrugged, shouldering aside her incredulous glance. "You heard him. He's a smart guy in his moments. That's how he rose so high in that organization—he's some sort of criminal supergenius. About the ordinary things, he's just as dumb as the rest of us. We want Morales's brother."

CHAPTER TWENTY-FOUR

Vasquez searched phone logs on the drive south into the city. Even with a cross-logged list from Harper Congdon and the Mexicans, she felt tricked into fishing in an empty bathtub. Her list of false-registered cells and the untouchable satellite phone were prime suspects, and she only needed to search calls through the tower nearest Sing Sing, but nothing surfaced. Guthrie expected a callback, a connection between two previously connected numbers, in a torrent of numbers that created an electronic smear. He glanced at her occasionally during the drive. The wide skies of Westchester disappeared behind the grim, piled bricks as they swept into the city. The sidewalk in front of the office bustled like a parade.

"I'm gonna make a quick call before I run you down to the LES," Guthrie said. He shed his overcoat, dropped it on the back of the oxblood couch, and strode to his desk. "Your choice of early afternoon or long day, because the shooter's probably leaving the city right now—or gone. Harper's dead, so that part of the game is over."

"Maybe," Vasquez said. Her cellphone buzzed in her pocket again, and she turned it off with a quick, well-rehearsed fingertip. Her heartbeat swooped and circled.

The little detective dropped into his chair, woke his desktop computer, and searched for phone numbers. The day was still young in Mexico City. He noted down a list of private detectives in the Mexican capital from the register of the world organization.

"Alberto Guzman," he muttered as he dialed the first number.

"You're hiring someone in Mexico?" Vasquez asked.

Guthrie nodded. "For background. And I want a local if I need to go down there."

Vasquez's stomach sank. She turned away to look from the window, surprised to be left on the carousel like unwanted baggage. She had counted on Guthrie to need a sidekick, even if that hurt. Being the sidekick was better than nothing. Shoppers marched on Thirty-fourth Street, thicker on the Seventh Avenue end of the block.

She sneered at the cold glass as Guzman refused the offer of work and Guthrie tried another number on his list. She watched his reflection, bent busily at the computer with the phone uncradled on the desk, and tapped the windowsill in frustration. She didn't want to be left behind in the city when the little detective flew to Mexico for heavy lifting. Another quick phone call passed. Vasquez clenched her teeth to hold in laughter. Maybe all of the detectives in Mexico would be unavailable, and then she would be good enough to go along.

"Carlos Abaroa?" Guthrie asked.

"*Sí?*" The speakerphone sounded clear in the quiet office. The conversation unrolled in Spanish. Abaroa wanted the work. Vasquez frowned through the window at the blameless traffic on Thirty-fourth Street.

"Mr. Guthrie, you are a member of the world organization?"

"Yes." The little detective tapped at the heavy glass paperweight on his blotter as a pause stretched.

"Very good. Will you detail for me what you wish?"

Vasquez listened to the little detective's checklist for Rafael Morales's background and Abaroa's carefully offered additions. She shook her head, listening to their operation plan unwind in neat overlooked tracks just like those she missed when searching for Duane Parson in Seattle after blanking in the city. Abaroa asked for nicknames and offered several common alternates; Mexicans used nicknames as often as they used real names. Vasquez tapped quietly at the windowpane during the recital.

As the men argued about banking records—Guthrie suggested Morales could have drug money—Vasquez realized she would be better off not going. Staying away from Mexico was one less chance to screw up. She collected her trench coat, wound it around her arm, and settled on the arm of the ratty old brown faux-fur couch, nearest to the frosted-glass door of the office. She slumped around her trench coat, thinking about the last quarter bottle of Golden Reserve rum in the bottom drawer of her dresser, worth one sleep of drunken oblivion. She slid into the soft grip of the couch.

Guthrie wired a retainer fee to finish the arrangement with Abaroa, then relaxed in his desk chair. "It's early," he said. "HP could buy us supper before I drive you home. Where do you want to go?"

"I just want to go home," Vasquez said woodenly.

Guthrie frowned. He peered across the desk at her, balled around her trench coat on the couch. "We could go to that Cuban place in the Village?"

After waiting through a moment of sullen silence, he said, "You look like somebody threw water on you. Who did you talk to on the phone while I was busy?"

"Nobody."

Guthrie's face lit with another question, but he turned to his computer instead of speaking. He focused on the monitor while his hands worked.

"What are you doing?" Vasquez demanded. "You're looking at my log?"

He shrugged.

"I didn't talk to nobody!"

A scowl sharpened his bricklike face. "You didn't *talk* to anybody—I see that."

Vasquez wavered between bitterness and the pitiful gladness of at least being worth a snoop, then settled on anger. She sprang from the couch and flung her trench coat onto the coffee table. "When is it your business who I call?" she demanded.

"You're distracted!" he barked. "You're wearing that same bent look you had on all autumn. I can't have you going limp and useless on me right now. Then Tommy's mixed up in this, so I'm gonna beat his ass." He shrugged.

"What!"

"I ain't stupid, Rachel. You two have danced around like mismatched magnets since I hired you. Lately, I thought you two were into something. He is. That shit's harassment. Look at all those messages, every damn quarter hour, I'm gonna—"

"No!" A brief image of the little detective punching Tommy wrung the shout from her, because she knew the truth. Tommy wasn't harassing her; she was ignoring him.

"Then what? Because from what I see, the result is the same. Right now my finger is on Tommy. Something's got to give."

Vasquez dropped back onto the couch. She felt completely empty, like a ghost with a set of functional eyes and nothing else. After a moment, her voice worked, but distantly, like somebody else's mouth. She spit out the truth to save Tommy. "What's it matter? You can just get another sidekick, right? If I don't work right, just get somebody else. Abaroa breaks ice in Mexico—that's a start."

Guthrie snapped to his feet and jabbed a finger across the desk. "I ain't getting somebody else! You ain't quitting!" His mouth settled into a grim line for a moment, and then he stared down at his desk. "I know you've been having a hard time, but that's something you have to learn to deal with. That's life. But you keep going off on angles and losing focus. That ain't something you can do in a crisis. If we end up in Mexico, it won't be easy."

"You don't have to take me to Mexico because you feel sorry for me! That's stupid. I mean, what use will I be? You won't need a fashion plate to distract anyone."

"Unbelievable!" Guthrie hissed. He sat down. "We ain't going to Mexico," he continued softly, "but if we do, you're going. I'll be the first to admit that you screw up every now and again. Then along comes a time where you save my ass. Or cover my mistakes. A detective can't walk around bare-ass naked. That sort of thing only works in Hollywood."

"You don't make any mistakes," Vasquez muttered.

Guthrie snorted. "I just lost a client. I stood down the street, watching the wrong thing, while Stephanie Morgan was shot to death," he said. "I would've lost another client this summer. You remember Greg Olsen, don't you? You saved his life in August when you pulled him into that storeroom. You stood over him and fought Gagneau to keep him alive. Did a couple of weeks in the hospital make you forget?"

Vasquez cupped her jaw with the palm of her hand, tucking her elbow into her belly. At the end of the summer, after the bandages stopped camouflaging the disfigurement, she discovered in the mirror how to place her hand to cover the bend in her jaw. She could stare at herself and almost feel normal.

"He was going to kill me," she muttered. The drumroll of gunfire unwound in her memory—all misses. Gagneau's knife gleamed. "I screwed up and you had to save me."

"You remember Gagneau has 187 bodies and counting?" Guthrie asked. "He killed Linney, you remember? We're lucky he didn't get us *and* Olsen."

"I missed him every time," she whispered.

"He missed, too."

Vasquez gathered her trench coat into her lap and squeezed it into a ball while Guthrie glared at her. The city's lights glowed late-afternoon dull in the tall, dark windows at the far end of the office. Traffic muttered a lullaby.

"Rachel, you take the city for granted," the little detective said. "You don't see it because it ain't ever been any other way for you. Mostly that's good, understand? You're right on time. You talk a streak when they're listening, and step to the side when a punch is coming.

"And then you expect to shine. The city doesn't accept less. You're the headline, or nothing. You're built around that. That's only trouble when you're thinking you don't measure up, or when you reach out too far past the window ledge for the fattest snowflake drifting down. You don't see that, either.

"That ain't quite how the world really works all the time," he said. "Bullets ain't never cared who's best. And a dog's gonna love you no matter what."

Vasquez burst briefly with laughter. "You sure about that one, *viejo*?"

"No," he answered. "I ain't sure about nothing. Maybe this: Leave being Superman to Clark Kent. He has that covered. You're a smart girl, Rachel. You're gonna figure it out."

Vasquez pushed her trench coat onto the cushion beside her. The little detective grunted.

"We got some work to do, if you're game," he said. "Then maybe a late supper."

Vasquez nodded. She felt wrung dry, and already shaken, but wide awake. The quiet office wrapped her like a warm blanket. Her desk seemed better than a bed, the hum of her computer smoother and hotter than a rum and Coke.

CHAPTER TWENTY-FIVE

Clayton Guthrie wanted a recognizable photograph of the Fifty-second Street shooter. Video clips from Parson's DUMBO trophy hall pinpointed the shooter twice in time and place without unmasking him. Fat-Fat's skeleton keys opened surveillance servers surrounding Fifty-second Street, and even tracked the assassin to Grand Central Terminal with numerous clips of his blocky fur hat, but a clear mug shot didn't surface.

Vasquez watched the Fifty-second Street clip again and wished for supper. She switched to the sequence of Grand Central clips, watched them again, and compared the printed image from Parson's video outside the town house.

"Nice boots," she said.

"What's that?" Guthrie asked.

She looked down her nose at his brogans. "I would ask you how much his boots cost, but somehow I don't think you'll know."

The little detective walked over from the window and watched while she ran the Grand Central clips again, pausing and pointing. "Look at the boots," she said. "His coat's nice, too. The hat—"

"We got an overdressed assassin?"

"A coat like that could be five thousand," she said, thinking about the designer clothes crammed into her closet. "Cheaper if it's used, or a knockoff. The boots? I don't really know about men's stuff."

"You think you can find where he bought it?"

Vasquez shrugged. "That's a lot of places, but maybe better than watching train platforms until supper. I could ask some people about the boots."

"Do it," he said. "I got this." The little detective walked back around to his desk and settled behind the computer.

The early evening was dark and cold when Vasquez arrived at Henri Bendel. A massive lid of clouds enclosed the lights and panted wet breath down onto the city. Bendel's held an edge of hysteria as shoppers rustled on the main floor wrapped in the scent of linen, spices, and money.

Samuel, neat in gray wool slacks and a knit vest, darted from behind the showcases at the street window when she walked inside. "Rachel!" he cried, halting like a mannequin with a frozen, anxious smile before he extended his hand. "I think I thought I would never see you again."

Vasquez shook his hand, and abandoned the lies she had rehearsed on the drive uptown. "I'm sorry," she said. "I guess we're from different worlds, right?" Studying his smooth face, she realized she felt years older than when she first met him. "Can we go upstairs?"

Samuel glanced at her stark black hat. "You liked it," he said.

She grinned. "Are you kidding? It's perfect."

His eyes lit. "Come on, then. You'll tell us what happened."

In the upstairs loft, the mirrored stage glowed unnecessarily with light while Gail and Bonnie worked on a rackful of alterations. The work stopped, and the fashionistas shared hot chocolate while Vasquez retraced her steps since the Art Commission dinner. She went back and forth in time, digging out her memories of Abraham Swabe, the shooting, and the dirty lawyers from the Bronx. She finished in whispers reminiscent of ghost stories.

"I knew he was wrong for her," Bonnie said, winding a measuring tape around her fingers.

"He had more kink than a leatherhead," Samuel said. "Off in a bad way. We were right, but what can you say?"

"We were watching the stalker," Vasquez said. "We screwed up."

"But you know who did it," Samuel said.

"Yes and no. That's why I called." Vasquez studied their puzzled faces. She emptied prints from the pocket of her trench coat. "I have pictures," she offered. "What do you think about the boots?"

The fashionistas studied the pictures and made rude comments. The shooter had too much money and too much gaudy bad taste. They laughed away some of the bitterness over more cups of hot chocolate.

"Enough," Samuel said. "This is about Stephanie Morgan. She was one of the good ones." Gail and Bonnie agreed with silent nods.

"We're little people," he said. "We play dress up for the big people, but most of them are pissy snobs. Stephanie—"

"She was sweet," Gail said. "We were careful when we dressed you because she asked."

Samuel opened his wallet and pulled out a business card. A small ink portrait on the back depicted Samuel in full cockscomb glory. "Stephanie drew that in twenty minutes," he whispered.

"She was an artist," Vasquez said. "I saw some of her work at her town house."

"There's that," he said. "But I think about her sitting at that table and spending twenty minutes drawing yours truly—Stephanie *Morgan*."

"I guess she liked you."

"She didn't deserve that evil bastard," Samuel said. He lifted one of the prints. "The coat and boots could've come from anywhere, Rachel. They're expensive, but the city is full of expensive. That hat might be a different story."

The best furriers in the city did business in Chelsea, opening the door for several sly comments from Samuel. Gail pelted him with plastic buttons as he made phone calls. After some whispered conversation, a clerk at Hennessy named Mickey appraised the square fur hat, an *ushanka*, as premium sable from a cellphone picture. Hennessy hadn't sold one recently. "Not cheap," Mickey offered. "A walk-in customer could pay five figures."

Gail and Bonnie recited the names of furriers in the city, and questioned whether the hat was purchased in the city at all. Vasquez shrugged. Samuel called Goodman, the other premium furrier in Chelsea, and fought a war of name-dropping to reach the manager. While he curried favor, the women pried at Vasquez.

"This's a big city," Gail said. "I smell a wild goose."

"The shooter is Mexican," Vasquez said. "Mexicans don't wear fur hats. He came to the city in November, it's cold, maybe he bought the hat . . ." Spoken aloud, her suspicion turned to vapor.

"That's it?" Gail's round face sharpened with annoyance. "I knew I should've gone to the spa. I could be getting a rub."

Bonnie turned back to the worktable. "Maybe," she said.

In the following quiet, Samuel's conversation—narrated by exasperated miming—became the focus of the long workroom. Traffic sounds from the avenue spattered against the narrow windows. The manager struck a deal; Samuel sent the picture.

The manager wanted payment in gossip; using a shield of "client confidentiality" for a fortress, he exchanged tidbits through the phone. Samuel fenced details of Morgan's murder—an unnamed "victim"— and the resulting chaos in the Bronx. Goodman had sold the sable *ushanka* to a tall Hispanic man. He paid a huge wad of cash without quibbling, and bought a matching *eskimoska*. The manager admitted a substantial digital backlog for the security system.

"I've had quite enough innuendo, my dear boy," the manager said finally. "It's time to take your clothes off. I want the real victim's name. My sales rep had some serious smile after that man left $24,000 in his hand. Make *me* smile."

Samuel covered the phone. "Can I tell him?"

Vasquez nodded. Gossip was cheap trade and made friends, even if

Fat-Fat's tool kit could raid the furrier's system. The manager sent the video clip by phone: a sharp-featured Mexican with a drooping mustache, dark eyes, brown skin, and thick, angled eyebrows. Vasquez studied it briefly, satisfied with the matching stride on the surveillance camera, but was still disappointed. The man looked nothing like Rafael Morales beyond a similar build. Her mood dampened the victory celebration at Henri Bendel, where the fashionistas toasted hot chocolate.

"Stephanie's still dead, isn't she?" Samuel said quietly.

Vasquez nodded.

Before the detectives could print copies of the image from Gus Goodman, Miriam Weitz opened the door and walked into the office. She wore black leather gloves, a long black coat, and a black muffler with her dark hair clipped paratrooper-short. Her eyes hid in tired, dark hollows.

Guthrie looked her over. "You're doing okay?"

She shrugged. "I'm finished scheming how to kill you, if you're worried."

"Meaning you decided how to do it?"

"Neyn," she said. "You have another pass."

The little detective smiled. "That adds up to more lives than a cat."

"I think you're wasting another one," she said. She scanned his monitor, then glanced at Vasquez. "There's a freak outside watching you, Guthrie. He kind of reminds me of Frankenstein." She read his astonishment, and continued, "I *knew* you were wasting it. When I give you another chance at life, you waste it on some freak."

The detectives exchanged a glance. "Duane Parson," Guthrie said. "You sure he's following me? Not her?"

Vasquez's stomach did a sick descent. Of course Parson was following her; he would never forget, never stop watching. Morgan's killer was a distraction that wouldn't last forever.

"He's locked onto you, Guthrie. I noticed him earlier but I wasn't sure. He looks like some stalker freak that likes little girls—" Weitz smiled at Vasquez. "No offense. But he stayed here when she left earlier. He followed you to Ossining today. He's your shadow."

Guthrie frowned, and studied the windows at the far end of the office. "I appreciate the warning. I had the office swept, and stayed on top of that. I didn't peg him for stalking me, though. I guess it's time to send him to jail. I'll go see Mike tomorrow."

"You know what he wants?"

He nodded.

After a long minute of silence, Weitz smiled. "Same old Guthrie. Some things never change." She settled on the furry brown couch without removing her coat. "Are you working on something, or is that busywork on your computer?"

"Miriam, you're staying out of this," he growled.

She thrust her chin out. "You made that clear. But I want to know. You could owe me, you know? For Frankenstein."

The little man sighed.

Weitz smiled, flashing beauty through hollowed-out grief and dark simplicity. When the smile disappeared, a handful of tears replaced it. She wiped them away on her coat sleeve. "I'm all right," she said. "I got it, all right?"

He paused, watching her, then said, "We got a good picture. Rachel just brought it back. We ain't even printed it yet. And we got his brother—" He jabbed a thumb at Vasquez. "She thinks I'm dreaming. I hired someone in Mexico to dig for his background. Then I sorted the recent visa applications while she was driving back. He's wearing a five-thousand-dollar coat and a twelve-thousand-dollar hat. I think he flew into the country first class. We're about to find out."

"False ID?"

He shrugged. "Maybe he uses the real thing if he's not wanted. Either way, the picture matches the ID he *is* using."

The detectives loaded the security images from Gus Goodman. Guthrie printed a handful, tossed one to Weitz, and laid another beside the masked Fifty-second Street print on his blotter. He nodded approval. "That's him."

Guthrie confined the visa search to men over five six that had entered the country since the beginning of September, allowing the shooter plenty of time to get acquainted with New York City before he began killing. Vasquez began at the end of the alphabet and worked forward toward him, comparing passport photos. The office filled with silence, concentration, and keyboard riffs like slow jazz drumwork. Weitz pulled off her gloves and coat, then stretched out on the furry brown couch.

"Got him," Vasquez muttered, ninety minutes later. Her voice was muffled with disuse. She darted a glance at Weitz, but the young woman didn't move. Guthrie walked around to her desk. The shooter had landed at Boston using a Guatemalan passport with the name Carlos Riva Palacio. The photo showed the same determination as in the other images.

Guthrie tucked a sheet around Weitz, and then the detectives slipped quietly from the office. During a late supper at Maxie's, Vasquez tossed him questions about his former operative. Mostly he set them aside untouched, just like his salad. The little detective was an expert at ignoring unwanted questions and healthy food. While they waited for the dessert to arrive, he admitted that Weitz still kept a key to the office. For a year or so, she had slept mostly on the brown couch at night. Then he stared down at his cheesecake for a long silent minute.

"Why don't she work for you no more?" Vasquez asked.

"She was short on some understanding," he said.

CHAPTER TWENTY-SIX

The next morning, the detectives worked on the Guatemalan passport. They found an electronic web of connected points in the city, a neat trail smoother than the polished explanations in a history book. The after-the-fact summary felt like eating dust from the winning car. Fat-Fat called, supplied a lock pick for the satellite phone, and added a warning. "This pick is trouble, Guth," the Korean geek said.

"How's that?"

"Don't use it from your desktop. Use one of your clean decks—then keep it turned off, and ditch it when you finish scraping the provider."

The little detective kept a handful of brand-new laptops in the office, all clean of everything except commercial software. They came out when he tiptoed on the edge of privacy laws. "I got you," he said.

"The provider is tough," Fat-Fat said, "like I said, proprietary, but not really the problem. Their webmaster is a hacker named Tinkerslink."

Guthrie let the comment dangle for a moment. "That should mean something to me?"

A trill of high-pitched laughter burst from the speakerphone. "No, not really. Just use a clean deck. And you owe me a stack. I had to buy one of their phones for a Trojan horse to build the lock pick. Don't plan on a long shelf life; maybe five days. You hear me, old man?"

"I hear you." Guthrie disconnected before Fat-Fat could add another comment, then disappeared into the storage room to retrieve a laptop. The street outside growled with a bellyful of trucks.

The cell tower in Ossining produced a connect between the satellite phone and a dead-end prison cell phone. Vasquez logged the anonymous cell and hit the sat phone's number repeatedly in a seven-month span. Guthrie logged the sat phone, scraped a year of connections from the provider, and then transferred the file onto a drive and disabled the laptop. He noted the time on his blotter. The log crossconnected with the electronic footprints in the city, and added a thick trail in southern Mexico, Guatemala, Honduras, and Belize.

"He's gone to Mexico," Guthrie said with finality.

While Guthrie wrote summary reports, Vasquez called the operative she hired in Pittsburgh to uncover Ludlow's college background. The detective, Earl Watkins, had already accumulated a massive electronic file. Argument followed. Vasquez wanted printed high school yearbooks from western Pennsylvania; actual pictures negated electronic invisibility, a natural result of being twenty years in the past.

An elliptical list of grumbles beginning with the death of middleclass Pennsylvania due to coal, steel, and railroad collapse, Sun Belt flight caused by bad weather, the drop-off from the baby boom, and continuing through school consolidation from lost tax base and rundown infrastructure, all slowly softened once Watkins was reassured about payment. After Vasquez cradled the phone, she wondered if she had been gulled.

The little detective grinned. "Wouldn't no bumpkin try that with some sophisticated New Yorker, right?"

The detectives hammered out differences in their reports—writing, revising, and documenting. Guthrie called George Livingston while they ate the midday pizza and wired him a preliminary report on the Fifty-second Street shooting. More comparison, revision, and writing followed. During pauses, they rechecked details, assembled final backgrounds, and argued about wording.

Guthrie folded the work away in the late afternoon, and the detectives went for an early supper. They drifted with the traffic down Seventh Avenue toward the Financial District. Vasquez had never felt that something was beyond Guthrie's grasp before. Knowing too much settled an uncomfortable weight on her neck. She watched him drive, clenching his teeth on unspoken words, and wondered if life would always be larger than the people in it. He parked off Whitehall Street. They walked a block in the chilly evening to reach Mako's, a sports bar down near the Battery full of middle-aged men avoiding home during the holiday season.

The detectives pushed through the crowd, stopped a waitress to order steak sandwiches and a pitcher of beer, and nosed around until they found Mike Inglewood. The ginger-haired detective filled the corner of a booth in the back. His partner, Eric Landry, perched at the diagonal. The younger man wore blue jeans, a Dodgers cap and jacket, and a scowl.

Landry jerked when the little detective tapped his shoulder, then rotated past him into the booth. Vasquez slid onto the other bench. The waitress unloaded two pitchers and two mugs onto the table.

"Guthrie, we were just flogging you," Inglewood said. "You should try harder to make friends in the department, or I ain't gonna keep taking your calls—and forget all this public handholding."

"I don't get points for the chief of d's?" Guthrie asked as he poured a mug of beer.

"Bosses don't count," Inglewood said. Landry smiled.

The detectives sat back quietly for a few minutes, drinking beer, eating chips, and watching the crowd swirl in Mako's. The waitress brought sandwiches and steak fries. Landry flicked glances at Vasquez while she ate.

"This isn't helping you," Inglewood said, "but you're pretty much clear on everything in the Bronx. That's sick, but that's how you have it. You didn't help yourself by kicking Devlin and Hernandez in the balls."

Inglewood raised a hand to block a retort, then pressed his glasses back up his nose. "I'm not saying they didn't deserve it, but you know, the job is tough."

The little detective shrugged. "How'd we clear?" he asked.

"When the lab worked up Tyminska—the one in the apartment with Harper—she had sunglasses, *inside* a case, *inside* her pocket. When they did blood, the glasses lit up to the scope. They took a droplet of dried blood from the hinge, tested it, and it came back to Ed Pratt. That put Tyminska in the blood void on that execution. *Then* the snuff flick from Norwood. That was cute, Guthrie. You got a lot of fans lining up for a bite of you."

Vasquez finished her sandwich, then refilled her mug. The tingle from the beer fell short of rum's burning glide, but she bit back the urge to call the waitress. Landry scowled at her hopefully. She shook her head. He had another beer. She felt a creeping sense of isolation in the crowded bar, faceless and unwanted even after Landry's feeble effort to connect. The older men clinked mugs and continued sparring.

"This leads me to believe that my other eye is black after tonight," Guthrie said. "You remember Duane Parson, the stalker at the front end of the Morgan case?"

Inglewood nodded. Landry turned back to face the little detective.

"He's still an attention grabber because of Alice Powell, I guess. Those two idiots didn't know I handed that to Seattle in the first place, and I knew what they were sniffing after before they walked into my office. Mike, you gotta get some better help. Did you ever manage to bring him in, or did you fall short of having enough for a conversation?"

"Your point?"

"Okay, he's probably outside watching the front of Mako's right now."

"I'm seriously not taking a complaint over some beers—"

"Listen, will you?" Guthrie sharpened his glance at Inglewood. The big man tossed his hands up for a shrug.

"I looked at him close while I was fitting him for the stalking. He connects up to something in the Bronx that might get me dirty for showing how I caught on to it." He paused for a swig of beer. "There's details that put him with Powell and some others."

Landry laughed. "You're too damned smart for your own good, man."

"Now he's following your girl?" Inglewood frowned.

Landry fell quiet, and his gaze darted to Vasquez before dropping to the tabletop. The detectives drank more beer, and wiped out the steak fries. The waitress brought another pitcher. Guthrie ordered more fries.

"What kind of jackpot are you looking at?" Inglewood asked.

"Trespass, maybe burglary," Guthrie said. "That's my license. But Parson does multiple homicide, guaranteed. Serial could be the bonus."

Inglewood grunted. "First grade," he said.

"That's right." Both older men turned to consider Landry.

"Aw, shit," he muttered.

The men put their heads together and made plans. Vasquez concentrated her attention on the pitcher of beer until she hit a 911 chime on her phone: Isadora.

"*Chica*, you are one long mess since this summer."

Vasquez laughed, and offered a toast with her mug that the men ignored after a glance at the phone she held to her ear.

"I *think* I have this figured out," Isadora continued. "Let me tell you what I think. This problem is because you don't know the rules. Your mother caught me earlier, when I made the mistake of knocking on your door to look for you—or maybe you could start with explaining why you won't answer your phone, that caught me in that trap?"

"I've been *busy*," Vasquez said, and paused for some beer. "I didn't want to be bothered, you know?"

"*Chica*, you're lying to me—to *me*. Your mother twisted my ears.

The next time I sit down with her, I'm going to give you up. I swear I will come clean with your mother. The problem is you don't know the rules, and she doesn't know that part, does she? I could kill your brothers. But maybe I won't have to. This muchacho will do it for me."

"What are you talking about?"

"A tall blond muchacho wearing a long blue coat. He's almost as pretty as you are, Rachel."

Vasquez tucked the phone hard against her ear and ducked her head almost beneath the tabletop, recognizing a description of Tommy Johnson. She glanced quickly around the bar before she bit down on the paranoia. He wasn't there.

"You didn't pick that one up at Skinny's. You went on a date."

"*No.* Not really. I mean, I took him out to dinner on the boss. He handed us some information, so—"

"That's a date, Rachel, and from the look on that muchacho's face, you stayed over. Right? Don't lie to me. I could walk right back up there and talk to your mother again."

Vasquez checked the detectives. They were deep in the booth, huddled around a map doodled on a smoothed-out napkin. Sharp whispers mixed with jabbing fingers. "I kind of knew him already," she said softly.

"You messed up. You hooked him. You pick some guy up at Skinny's, he don't expect nothing but a long night, you're drunk, it don't matter. A date? That's *different.*"

"He's just a boy."

"*¿En serio?* You're gonna stop lying to me. You are so dumb sometimes. Look, this muchacho is parked across from your stoop, leaned against the end of a broken-down Dodge, staring across the street at your brothers. This looks like some old Western movie, except the wind is cold—"

"He's there?"

"*Chica*, I didn't see him in my dreams. I'm looking at him now. He's pissed, and he's ready to take it out on your brothers. You can't hook no muchacho like this one and dangle him. When was the last time you talked to him?"

"I don't know. The next morning, when he dropped me at work? Three days ago—four days?"

Isadora laughed. "You are a mess. You can't do no muchacho like that. I mean, you *like* him. What are you scared of?"

"I'm not scared," Vasquez said automatically.

"You should be," Isadora said. "High noon, *chica*. Your brothers are crossing the street. Your muchacho just took off his coat. The ringside is crowded. He parked in Esteban's space."

Vasquez groaned. "Stop them," she said.

"Little me? Indio, Miguel, and this muchacho bigger than both of them?"

"Isadora!" Vasquez paused to face down stares from the detectives in the booth. They restarted their conversation with sidelong looks.

Vasquez listened intently to shouting on the phone, a mix of Spanish and English, car horns, jeers, and a string of commands from Isadora. She rocked, bending herself around the phone. Isadora laughed. "*Chica*, you are so lucky you have me," she said. "Now you talk to the muchacho."

Vasquez's heartbeat accelerated into the space suddenly abandoned by her stomach. Her voice didn't work.

"Rachel?" Tommy demanded.

His voice squeezed her like a giant fist. She started to shake. "Do you know Mako's, down by the Battery?" she asked.

"Sure," he said.

"Come here," she said.

CHAPTER TWENTY-SEVEN

Guthrie arrived late the next morning at the office on Thirty-fourth Street. Vasquez was drifting in the office like a ghost, halfway through a pot of coffee, at war with herself about Tommy Johnson. Before daylight, she scampered from his apartment with her trench coat and guns over her arm. Tommy chased her and forced her to accept a ride back into the city. Needing a ride embarrassed her, but wanting to stay in Corona frightened her—Tommy was too comfortable, a chunk of Middle America with a golden-brown fade and prickly morning chin that smelled like *pernil y pastele*—she had to run. The spectacle resembled an ordinary getaway from an overnight except that when he idled his Dodge Challenger in front of the office, Tommy caught her wrist and tugged her back into the car for a kiss like hot fudge. Nothing started cold with him. Vibrating around the office after she escaped, clips from their conversations remixed in her ears, and she couldn't sit still until Guthrie arrived like a bucket of ice water.

"Landry moved on Parson this morning," the little detective said. "That started a little after six. Landry called me while I was shaving and asked when I was gonna come out."

"So what happened?"

"Parson was parked in an alley cutting around that old supermarket on Forty-ninth Street, across Tenth Avenue. Now there's a warehouse with some promises of a minimall along the lines of a bazaar. On the other side, each corner has one bodega, with a Mexican restaurant sandwiched between them—I think they split the crap from the old supermarket. There was a nice deli back in the nineties. I used to—" He sighed.

"Anyway, on account of the alley, Landry figured the rat would bolt out of the other side when the trap clapped shut. Parson had a big white Lincoln, registered to a rental agency on Thirty-ninth Street. The rat has moved to my neighborhood. Well, the agency had the same SRO address in Brownsville that he gave NYPD on Powell. Okay."

Vasquez frowned. "You live in Hell's Kitchen?"

"Sure. Wasserman's old place. The keys were on the key ring he threw me when he walked out." He laughed. "I didn't know. The bills kept coming to the office, and I paid them from the retainer. Eventually I turned curious, went over there, and found a layer of dust. I don't think he even went back there when he walked out.

"The old place is big. I don't use all of it. I use the front door— that's a walk up to the second floor—there's a blind loft, and then a back stair to the old restaurant. The windows are painted black down there. Lots of ghosts in that place. The old man has more Nazi memorabilia than a cell of white supremacists. I still got it crated up down there. I don't know what to do with it."

"Burn it?" Vasquez suggested.

Guthrie shook his head. "Wasserman wanted it for something. I ain't gonna be the dumbass that threw it away when he walks back through the door wanting it, right?"

She laughed. "How old is he gonna be, *viejo*?"

Guthrie reddened after a moment of thought. "Somewhere in his eighties or nineties, I guess. You could be right, but I'm not gonna touch it. I might use one of the pistols if I needed it, but otherwise it stays.

"So Landry waited until I was ready to roll out at my usual time. He was working with four patrol cars from Midtown North to trap Parson. He corked the alley around the supermarket with one, but the alley forks off into Tenth Avenue and Forty-eighth Street, so the patrol had to ease up the alley, and then I trotted down the stairs and walked out.

"The front of my building is covered with the usual trash. Not garbage; that gets picked up on Tuesday. Forty-ninth Street has a regiment of slackers wearing used desert-camouflage BDUs, some new fashion statement. I glanced at the alley. The nose of the Lincoln and a trickle of exhaust are poking out. Then a cruiser squirts from the oncoming traffic and clamps its teeth on the mouth of the alley.

"Perfect timing," Guthrie muttered. He drummed the blotter. "I think Landry expected him to back up the alley, get boxed, and surrender from the vehicle. I'm speculating. I didn't get a briefing."

Vasquez's stomach sank. "They didn't get him."

"Parson bolted from the Lincoln and ran down Forty-ninth Street toward Eleventh Avenue," Guthrie said. His hands floated, emulating turns and velocity. "He's faster than you think. Slackers dive out of the way—they know a takedown when they see one—and the other cruiser roared along Forty-ninth Street to cut in front of him. Parson slid right across the hood. The whole thing was hopeless. When he made it partway down the block, he turned into Big Boobs—not Big Bob's—that XXX gallery with microbooth reels and glass dancers.

"The cops searched, but he's gone. As it turns out, there's a service door to a coin-op laundry that fronts on Forty-eighth Street. The building super has the key, but since the rat's not in the building, just maybe he went through that door."

The little detective shrugged. "No, they didn't get him. The boys in blue should be working for the circus. When I walked back down from Big Boobs, a transit cop was writing a ticket on the Lincoln."

———

At mid-morning, the detectives went to H. P. Whitridge's eagle-aerie office high above Park Avenue. Waiting with George Livingston and Whitridge, William Sinclair was settled in a dark leather wingback below the window in the office while H. P. propped against his desk with his arms crossed on the breast of his charcoal suit. Livingston sat forward, resting his elbows on his knees to lean over the coffee table in front of the leather couch.

"You proved formidable while dealing with the situation in the Bronx," Sinclair said. "You identified Carlos Riva Palacio when the police didn't bother to search for a second killer. The police would've been satisfied with holding Donald Harper responsible for the deaths of the lawyers from his firm." He paused. "But before you supply your report to the police, Mexico needs a similar, effective solution."

"Ain't a thing in Mexico would compare to the Bronx, except dirty and ugly," Guthrie said. "I would poke out like a raccoon at a dog show. You had any thought for how that works?"

"We can support you," Sinclair said. "We do have some understanding about Third-world difficulties, and—"

"You'll pull cards until you get to the bottom of the deck, Mr. Sinclair, but here's the last one: I'm not a hired killer."

"We understand you'll need legitimacy, outside the United States," Sinclair said after a very slight pause. "You'll have a sealed indictment from a federal grand jury here in Manhattan—your preliminary report provides sufficient evidence for that. We know Mexico is corrupt. We'll either find a clean policeman or buy a dirty one, but you'll have a policeman to cover you."

"My operation," Guthrie said softly. "No one else has a nose in it."

"Do whatever you need to do," Whitridge said, "but I want the man that killed Stephanie."

The little detective studied the silver-haired aristocrat. Whitridge didn't flinch. Vasquez watched the other lawyers trade looks tainted with the anxiety of needing to reach up to touch cards on the big table. Guthrie nodded, and they relaxed.

"I got something I'll try beforehand," he said, "and maybe save a trip to Mexico. Wait on those things until I tell you."

As the detectives walked back down from Whitridge's office, Vasquez decided that Guthrie was angry. He plunged down stairwells as if other people were invisible, then strode briskly across the marble lobby and out onto Park Avenue. A gray-haired security guard waved at the little detective as he passed, then shrugged, unacknowledged. A sprinkle of pedestrians floated on the sidewalk, tossing glances at the ornate façade of the building. Guthrie paused, and seemed to deflate.

"I don't get it," Vasquez said. "They tried to give you a license, *viejo*. I know you want Carlos Riva, because of Avram. Why are you making it difficult?"

The little detective rounded on Vasquez as he settled his brown fedora on his grizzled head. "You didn't listen to what I said in there?"

Vasquez hesitated.

"I don't think I appreciate that, Rachel," he said. "Someone else might go preaching consequences at you—a mouthful or two of something about prison sentences and lawyer's fees. That's crap. That's going to encourage you to think that shooting people is what you do if you figure to get away with it."

He turned away and walked down the street toward the Ford parked a half block away. Vasquez hurried behind him again.

"*Viejo*, I didn't mean—"

"Didn't you? This's my blame, here. I handed you the pistol. I took you places where you ended up using it. I knew that might happen."

"What do you want?" she shouted. Months ago, her brother Miguel had said almost the same thing about Guthrie. He accused the little man of putting a gun in her hand and then putting her in danger. That was true, but there was more truth: She accepted it. "You expect me to do something different?"

Guthrie turned and caught her by the shoulders. "This ain't the kind of choice I want you to have to make," he said. "Detective work is a dirty game of thrills. Every day, you're looking at it, sifting through it, rubbing against it, reaching for it. You get dirty. I got some foolish, romantic notion that a young woman ought to be shiny and clean—but then I brought you here. I could be sick. Or I could also be carrying the notion that you need to be sharp and hard to survive this world, and feel I'm doing you a good turn." His hands dropped from her shoulders, and he sighed.

"There's more. Tracking some piece of crap you'll come to the easy conclusion that you can work it out by shooting him. If you saw a mad dog in the street, you would hesitate? Some things have to be done, right? Wasserman may've done that some times too often, and ended up running into himself one day when he turned a corner too quick. That's a point where a man might decide to turn a pistol on himself, when he's made a habit of shooting pieces of crap: He catches sight of himself in a mirror.

"You're gonna make amends how, when you screw up and kill the wrong man?" he asked softly. "You wouldn't choose to make a ghost to haunt you."

Vasquez stared. Traffic flowed past. "What're we gonna do, *viejo*?"

"I promised Miriam to do worse than that. Wasserman had a list of men he visited in prison every year. Some of them would piss themselves when they saw that old man step into the room. I made rounds with him, back then. Now I just send them cards." The little man's face twisted, then settled back to brick.

"When Wasserman had one he hated, he brought him in alive and dumped him in a prison. The old man didn't believe in God. I needed some time before I realized that." He turned and strode for the Ford, pausing briefly to groan.

"What?" she asked.

"Parson," he said, flicking a finger down the avenue. "He just dodged around the corner."

CHAPTER TWENTY-EIGHT

The detectives moved quickly after spotting Parson. Vasquez spent some time on the phone reminding Eric Landry that the stalker remained at large, while Guthrie drove to Newark. They left the Ford in long-term parking and paid cash for tickets to Huntington, West Virginia. The plane landed before midnight and Guthrie rented a Jeep for the drive south.

Outside the airport, the reality of winter hammered at them. Endless dark sky stretched over an undulating sweep of white bordered to the west by the Big Sandy. Highway 52 cut dark slashes, swept through curves, and plunged through naked timber among flurries of houses, outbuildings, and endless fences. Cold wind moaned outside the Jeep. Vasquez slept fitfully.

Each time she woke, she glimpsed Guthrie floating in the glow of the dashboard instruments, while the Jeep rushed or cranked along like a roller-coaster in a frozen hell.

In the small hours of the morning, the detectives reached a clapboard farmhouse with drooping icicle whiskers, after an hour of catback roads and sidelong veers in thick darkness. Vasquez was wide awake by then, her fingers thrumming from her grips on the dash-board and door handle. The farmyard felt cottony soft beneath her jungle boots. A young woman swept them inside with whispers, handed out blankets and pillows, then left them to a pair of rumpled couches that stank of cat fur, and a ticking potbellied stove. Cheap translucent vinyl blinded the windows but glowed with snow light.

Vasquez woke when Guthrie shook her. Footsteps and quiet voices moved in the farmhouse around them. They rotated in the downstairs bathroom. The young Puerto Rican experimented with the creaking taps in the clawfoot bathtub, but settled for splashing her face when she discovered that all the water was cold. Bacon, fried eggs, stewed tomatoes, gravy, and biscuits covered a breakfast table surrounded by a rough brood of gawking kids. A mudslide of names buried Vasquez; she never recovered.

"Clayton, you'll eat more than that this morning, or you won't leave this house." The woman at the stove peered over at the table. A bad rinse had turned her pale hair pink. Some layers of bathrobe made her seem bulky despite slender wrists.

Guthrie meekly added more bacon and eggs to his plate, then grinned as he loaded a plate for Vasquez. "Tim, we need some guns," he said.

A short, stocky red-haired man near the head of the long table glanced up at him. "Pop's just up Drip Rock," he said. "Scariest thing up that way is Angel."

Guthrie sighed. Before he could speak again, Tim said, "All right. Colts?"

Guthrie nodded.

After a glance from the red-haired man, a younger boy left the table, scooping a hasty forkful of eggs into his mouth before he clat-tered away.

"Somebody behind you?" Tim asked.

"He's about seven feet tall and almost four hundred pounds."

Tim laughed, then fell quickly silent and stared.

"I'm starting to think he's reading my mind," Guthrie said. "I can't shake him."

"Should I set the dogs out?" The men around the table shifted.

Guthrie shook his head. Breakfast continued as hardscrabble eating with a few glances spared for the conversation. The boy returned with two Colt semiautomatic pistols, and a spare clip for each. Guthrie checked the ammunition at the table, then handed Vasquez one pistol and one spare. She pocketed it in her trench coat after she balanced the last of her eggs atop a final scrap of biscuit, and snapped it from her fingertips while another dirty-faced red-haired boy watched. The platters on the table were empty.

The kitchen emptied like a fire drill after the old woman chose a boy and a girl to clean the table. Insults, thanks, day plans, and questions drifted behind them. Guthrie took a hug from the old woman, then followed Tim through the back door onto a long, railed porch, beckoning for Vasquez to follow. Tim paused at the rail, searched his teeth with a fingertip, and spit into the yard. The cold morning was a smack in the face after the warm, fragrant kitchen.

"You figure he's back before noon?" Guthrie asked.

Tim shook his head.

"We'll go up, then," Guthrie said. "Call us up on that 77, will you?"

Tim nodded.

The slow drive up Drip Rock lifted Vasquez by degrees above the mud, slush, and snow of the earth. Turns opened curtains of naked timber and flashed brief glimpses of the furrowed hills. From up high, the hills rolled into misty distance, a blended heaven and earth beyond the hand of man. Guthrie's stony face settled into peacefulness.

The Jeep toiled along a tilted road, thick with rounded stones, swept past the pale, frosted face of the mountain, entered a tunnel of dark cedar, hemlock, and spruce, and then floated out onto a gently rolling table surrounded by vast space. A long, low house leaned drunkenly against an outcrop of pale limestone. Two old men, one light and one dark, sat on the crooked porch. A trail of blue smoke rose from the chimney before sprinting away.

Guthrie parked the Jeep beside a pair of rusted Ford pickups settled on a dirty bed of gravel. The mountaintop swallowed the sound of the slamming doors with a breezy sigh. Both old men, wearing overalls, long-handled underwear, and brogans, stood as the detectives climbed the porch.

"Morning, Danny," Guthrie said. "You too, Angel. I guess you slipped out of the house on me."

"I slept up here," Walker said. Eyes like green crystals burned in his long brown face, beneath jet-black eyebrows and a jutting corn-shock of black hair threaded with silver. The old white man had a wisp of failing hair above his ears, and bright blue eyes in a round face. He nodded silently. The men circled warily, then hammered each other with hugs and briefly cracked smiles.

"This's Rachel Vasquez. She's learning to trail," Guthrie said. He pointed between the old men. "This here's my uncle Danny Rice, and Angel Walker."

The old men looked her over, like she had magically appeared only after Guthrie mentioned her name. Their breath billowed in the frosty air. "Another one of them dark-haired New York girls, I reckon," Rice said, and nodded briefly.

Walker snorted. "With how she's tucked that pistol in her pocket, she's bound to have that difficulty Trey Rawls ended with."

Rice laughed. "I don't think she'll pull nothing out of her pants, Angel. That was Trey's problem. You remember that, Little Clay?"

The little detective rolled his eyes and bit back a mutter. Vasquez scowled at the old men.

Rice laughed again. "Trey was a fool," he said. "He moved up here to get at a MacGuire girl. That was before the war. Her brothers were gonna kill him, but they waited and he turned out to be a fair carpenter. He kept a cabinet shop right in Kilkenny, and carried his pistol in his front pocket right like that." He pointed at the Colt bulging out Vasquez's trench coat.

"He had a Walther, though, that he brought back from the war. He fought with the Thunderbirds, like Angel's daddy. That's a little pistol, and it fit neat in his pocket. Trey kept it cocked, to shoot a little quicker—"

"Don't say it," Guthrie growled.

Both old men hooted with laughter.

"Anyway, the toilet in that cabinet shop was built up on a platform," Rice said. He traced a rough stairstep in the air with his thick hands. "A man didn't have to reach down far for it. So he had a handful of us in there quartersawing while he sat to drink beer. On one of his trips to the toilet, a shot rang out. We all stopped. Trey came flying from the bathroom with his overalls hanging and a flood of water chasing behind him. 'Oh. God, is it still there? I can't look!'"

The old men shared a round of laughter. Guthrie shook his head, but a smile gleamed on his face.

"Nearest we could figure, he tapped the barrel of the pistol on the toilet. Shot it clean in half, and poked a hole in his overall pocket. He still had his cock. Wouldn't have lost much—"

Rice and Walker roared with laughter. They danced a do-si-do around the creaking porch. Guthrie sighed.

"Don't mind him, Rachel," the little detective said. "He just likes to hear himself talk."

"Ooo! Mind Little Clay! Last time you called it cost me some fair amount of whiskey." The men traded glares, then clapped hands together for a fierce handshake. They parted and studied each other for a moment. Walker grinned at them, showing some broken teeth scattered in his smile.

"Well, come in and have some coffee," Rice said, "and get to what brung you."

The wooden floor inside fit together better than the gap-planked porch, but a sweeper still didn't need a dustpan. A potbellied stove glowed in the front room, whispering as it tumbled chunks of coal. The roof creaked evenly in the grip of the wind, like a good rocking chair. Walker poured coffee. The detectives sat at the table on a trestle bench worn from decades of sitting. Rice and Walker listened while Guthrie recounted the case. Their eyes flicked to Vasquez for fresh measure each time a crumb of praise fell on her. Her face warmed slowly as Guthrie spoke, and stillness crept over her until she felt like sleeping. He drank a second cup of coffee to keep his voice oiled, and was idly turning the empty mug in his hand before he finished. They listened to the hiss of the stove for a minute afterward.

"I want the shooter, the Mexican," Guthrie said.

The old men nodded.

"I know some Mexicans," Rice said quietly. "I reckon that's what you were hoping. The people I traffic with are Sinaloans, Guzman's people. I might know some Zetas, but I doubt it would do any good."

Guthrie drooped on the trestle, and smoothed the brim of his brown fedora, easing it slowly across the tabletop.

"Well, you ain't surprised. The Mexicans are more like us. A man couldn't call me and ask about you or Angel."

Guthrie nodded.

"The Italians would put business first. About business, I think this man put his foot wrong. Something sounds off about some of that. I think he tried to rub out his trail. You might sit back and watch them kill each other."

Walker glared, and Rice paused to look him over. "The Mexicans don't do much on this side of the border—not after butting heads over that Camerena killing. Not that they won't touch a gringo, but they're careful about it. This here sounds more like what they're doing down there, Clay.

"You've likely heard how they're killing down there. They'll use a hand grenade or an assault rifle as quick as they'll handcuff a man and hack him apart with machetes. The Zetas are at war with everybody down there, but the Mexicans are proud of their people."

Guthrie nodded. "I got you. I wouldn't expect a MacGuire to give you up, even after all that on Blair Mountain. You saw my other difficulty. I ain't sure how he connects up after that mess in the Bronx. I'm speculating he's Morales's brother—Morales is a Zeta—but he might not be. I put him in Tabasco, but I want to see for certain how he connects."

"I think if I poked in that, I'd leave you worse off," Rice said. He paused to consider as Walker made another pot of coffee. "I connect with them. They'll stir up with looking and asking, more than they will already. It ain't no bet whether they know about that mess in New

York. That Camarena killing is decades old, and they're still careful. They'll be expecting something to come of that mess in New York. You could wait."

Walker glared again, then bent over the pot. "I'm too old, or you ain't old enough, Angel," Rice said, then turned back to Guthrie. "You're gonna go down there. You ain't a man to leave that alone. At least right now no one sees you coming. If I'm choosing, I'm sending an army. I'll call across the water and have a few companies of Vietnamese here in a handful of days."

Rice shrugged after Guthrie shook his head. "You want him alive, don't you? Well, you got them fool notions honest."

The old men stared across the table at each other. The stove hissed. Walker sat down.

"That down there is godless country, Clay. They ain't got no commandments. There's men down there taking wrong for right, and right for wrong, and maybe not seeing a difference to begin. Maybe I send a handful of good men with you—"

"No, I'll go," Walker said.

The old white man was startled. He clamped his mouth shut and stared.

"I'll go. I'm wasting up here."

"We ain't trailed together in a long time," Guthrie said.

Walker's eyes glittered. "I chose to stay."

"I don't begrudge you that," Guthrie said.

The old white man studied them. "I knew there was a rock in the river."

"This's your trail, Clay," Walker said.

"Come on, then. I reckon a halfblood Cherokee might be some help."

Walker grinned. "Three quarters. My mother was only half white."

"Quit lying so much, Angel. Her skin looked like milk."

CHAPTER TWENTY-NINE

The plane from Huntington landed at Newark two hours after lunch, but Vasquez felt dirty before then. Reconstructing her parents' whispered conversations about lost years in Puerto Rico, and deciphering the signals, command structure, and knowledge of her brothers' gang was grade-school effort compared to the sudden intensity she focused on Walker and Guthrie. Detective work was dirtiest when it was closest.

Aided by vivid imagination, she wrote and rewrote Walker's life story from the details of his conversations with Guthrie. The men paid little attention to her while they prodded and sparred, reconnecting after separation. Walker was older by a few years, an estimate she based on Guthrie's swings between deference and defiance—exactly like Miguel standing in Indio's shadow. The quick familiarity marked them as raised in the same kitchen, even if they weren't brothers.

The old white man in West Virginia, Danny Rice, trafficked with the Mexicans. Walker surrendered a pair of Colt pistols with a string of muttered warnings to Tim before the drive up to Huntington; the red-haired man handled the pistols like ticking bombs, unlike the casual cuff and tuck he accorded the pistols returned by the detectives. These sketchy dots connected somewhere behind Guthrie like an old, dusty photograph in an album.

The conversations floated without regard for beginning, middle, or end: rapidfire details about shootings in the Bronx, weather in the city and Mexico, hunting trips that concentrated on the rifle shots that felled the deer, and echoes of ancient regret about some woman named Debra. Vasquez decided finally that Walker was about fifty years old, almost six feet tall, mostly quiet, and absolutely had green eyes.

The city wrapped them in a cold and stony grip after they surfaced from beneath the Hudson. News was bad. NYPD's ongoing search for Duane Parson was stalled. Landry's arrest warrant came from "a reliable informant," incidentally reinforced by an off-the-record DNA match between Guthrie's sample from DUMBO and blood spatter from the meth pit in Parkchester. The connection Vasquez revealed, matching trauma on Powell and Sorcini, was a tightly wrapped secret. The patrol officers and detectives felt the urgency, but they had no leads.

Inglewood shrugged off the failure. "We're fishing with an empty hook, here," he said. "Now that our bait's back in town, we'll get a hit. Don't worry, Guthrie, we got it."

The little detective called George Livingston and sent a go-ahead for legal preparations for Mexico. Vasquez had a backlog of 411 texts from Tommy Johnson. After some whispered conversations and laughter, she handed him on to the little detective. Using the Stuttgart footprint, Johnson had found a possible second identity for the stalker: Uwe van der Haas, a 157-kilogram, 209-centimeter Dutchman resident in Germany in 1983.

Guthrie sighed. "You got to be quicker than this, boy," he said. "You give this to your boss yet? That's Whitcomb, right? Give this to her, then call Mike Inglewood at Major Case and hand it to him, too."

After he disconnected the phone, he said, "I've been playing catch-up a little too much, lately. I feel like I'm waking up from a bad nap."

Walker chuckled.

"You should've called me on this earlier, Guth," Fat-Fat said. "You old guys walk around with a mechanistic view of the world that's out of synch with today's reality." The big Korean peered through the office window onto Thirty-fourth Street, studied the traffic, then warily scanned the buildings on the opposite side of the street. He had found another device planted from the hallway outside, listening through a neatly drilled hole in the plaster.

"See, the cops scared him off," Fat-Fat said. "This hardwired office saved your ass—the first I ever heard a dinosaur having a survival advantage—but now it's time to do this my way. Your stalker is riding the wires—he's watching from the Net. You do this stuff all the time, Guth, but I guess you figure nobody looks back."

The detectives exchanged a glance. They had spent some hours Net-tracking the shooter across midtown before Vasquez broke his identity with the overpriced sable *ushanka*. Walker glanced up from the coffee table. Sorted parts from twenty disassembled Colt pistols covered the table. A smile slid across his face, and he pointed a finger at Guthrie. The little detective grunted.

Fat-Fat grinned. "This isn't television. In the real world, a server could mainline feeds from every source in the city, but all that data is white noise. Nothing can pick his face from the blur. You need a starting point where the stalker showed his face."

"Okay, then, smart guy, what's the trap?"

"This doesn't need smarts, Guth. Remember, I do this in my spare time. My real job is repairing toasters." The big Korean eased down onto the oxblood couch, and watched Walker roll slide springs between his fingers until finding two he wanted from the pile.

While Walker wiped grease from his fingers with a handkerchief, Fat-Fat said, "The trap is easy. I'll slide a spyware into a terminal the stalker will visit—and it won't wipe off with a rag."

"I love when you talk nonsense to me," Guthrie muttered.

While Fat-Fat solidified his trap, Guthrie made preparations for Mexico. Walker built two carefully gauged Colt pistols from the collection in the office holdout, then reassembled the remainder. Guthrie took three Colt pistols, two Garand rifles, and a selection of ammunition. An hour on the telephone and some hefty bribes secured permits for Mexico. Walker refused a utility vest, but Vasquez took it for a better place than her coat pocket to tuck her Colt pistol. Guthrie retrieved a high-powered air pistol from the storage room, and tranquilizer darts intended to sedate attack dogs. His final addition was a bottle of Rohypnol and a lecture on how and when to administer the drug to keep a man sleeping safely.

Late in the afternoon, Fat-Fat said, "This could be a little easier if I knew what the stalker wanted from you, Guth."

"He knows the shooter is Spanish, but maybe not Mexican," Guthrie said, then shook his head quickly. "No, it's time to stop underestimating the rat."

"Your firewall held up," Fat-Fat said. "He hasn't hacked your desk."

The little detective nodded. "That would be the end of the game."

Fat-Fat stared into space. "We stage a meeting with your power brokers. He'll ride the wires to be there. He saw you there before. That's where I tag him."

Flurries of snow swept along Park Avenue when the detectives arrived at Whitridge's office at mid-morning. After installing some software additions on the office security system overnight, Fat-Fat waited at his computer in Brooklyn. William Sinclair, H. P. Whitridge, and George Livingston reminisced about their separate college days in the Ivy League while Guthrie waited for a call-through on a clean cellphone. Whitridge's assistant supplied trays of snacks and pots of coffee.

The dark wood and leather office peered down on the avenue from high, narrow windows. Vasquez felt like a gargoyle, waiting unseen high above the city for Fat-Fat's trap to spring. Everyone stopped when the cellphone buzzed.

"Your stalker is wearing new clothes," Fat-Fat said, "but he's hiding in Penn Station. That's rough, but we can scan around to catch him going in and out.

"Come to Brooklyn," Fat-Fat finished. "I have more equipment."

After thanking the lawyers, Guthrie and Vasquez drove to Brooklyn, where Fat-Fat worked at Barney Miller's. The Korean geek had a powerful system hidden among a mass of components awaiting repair and salvage. With some rearrangement, a bank of monitors allowed them to scan together, watching a dozen simultaneous video feeds. The detectives eased into chairs.

The afternoon drained away while they watched silent video to a background of stoner music played by the band of retread hippies rummaging the record bins in the emporium alongside Fat's hidden den. The big Korean grumbled occasionally, but didn't kill their power.

"That's him," Vasquez whispered. She pointed with a collapsible antenna without shifting in her chair.

On the video, a hulking man wearing a coverall rolled a dolly through a flurry of activity in a warehouse on Thirty-fifth Street. His stride had a hitch. Guthrie noted the address and time, then compared it against the service grid, tracing it to a telephone line before reaching the connection under Penn Station.

"Your guy is something," Fat-Fat said. "How'd he find it?"

"Backward," Guthrie said. "He ain't looking from the skin in. He's using the service grid, then cross-checking the addresses." He shrugged. "The uniform coverall was a nice touch. He must've done that same thing to find the spot in DUMBO."

The little detective called Landry and served up the stalker's location with a side of razz. NYPD had blank, but had enough manpower to surround the stalker. The detectives needed their help; Guthrie and Vasquez together might've been too small to corner one determined alley cat. The little detective gave Fat-Fat a double handful of fifties and suggested a cheap liquor store. Fat-Fat never drew invitations to dinner; the little detective thought he was big enough without feeding him. The detectives drove back into the city, picked Walker up at the office, then went to Cité for steaks. Before they were drunk, Mike Inglewood called.

"Where the hell are you?" the ginger-haired detective shouted. The restaurant was full of couples skipping the early shows in favor of food. With the cellphone on speaker and centered on the table for an ornament, everyone had their hands free for more wine.

"At a steakhouse above the Theater District," Guthrie said. "You got Parson?"

"I was gonna get to that," Inglewood said.

"Mike, you're kidding me! It's time for a new partner—"

"Not his fault! I'm telling you, that skel had the place wired."

"I told you he was gonna do that."

Vasquez downed a glass of wine, refilled, then slowly cut at her strip. Walker studied her disgusted expression. He shrugged and emptied his own glass. Guthrie sighed.

"There was too many ways out," Inglewood said. "I don't think we ever had a chance except sitting for him to come out, but the bosses were having none of that after that screwup on Forty-ninth Street. You know? Our hands were tied."

"So what happened?"

"Well, once a handful of bosses mixed in, the operation turned into the usual bright-idea contest that included yours truly sucking his thumb covering a tunnel in Penn. ESU did the heavy lifting. I got to see it on camera after the dust settled, and it looked like three fat guys trying to tackle the same gerbil. He got away, you know? He hopped a taxi on Thirtieth, then rode the L into Brooklyn before the geeks caught up with him. Never stopped moving. He went right up the island until he disappeared. He knows the rules."

"He saw you coming, right?"

"From a mile."

"Well, that's it? You got a lead to Long Island?"

"They're chasing, but you know, the skel looked like he was laughing the entire time."

"Laughing?"

"He thought something was funny."

Vasquez scowled. The rat laughed when he had a plan.

"Anyway, I went down there and had a look," Inglewood said.

"The skel was working from an old storage room. He left behind some equipment and some dog biscuits. ISU swept up and they found samples—that's the good news. We probably reach a fresh warrant on the DNA and trespass that clears any mess you made."

Inglewood sighed before they could celebrate. The smile died from Guthrie's face. In the pause, he heard bad news.

"So the skel is staying on form with another wired-up bolt-hole. Your girl around anywhere? The skel had an altar in one corner, plastered with a collage of her pictures. So it's a good thing I went down and got the ID."

"Detail that, will you?" Guthrie demanded.

"Okay, the thing was diagonal from his sleeping arrangement. The pictures radiated halfway along each wall from the corner, like some—It wasn't no pervert show or nothing, but that girl can't help being beautiful. He caught her moods. He's some sort of artist, right? He looked to be building a picture *out of* pictures on the back wall. Well, I kinda saw it when I squinted my eyes hard."

Vasquez slouched down into the booth. She emptied her wine glass, but Walker took it from her before she could refill it. She glared. She felt like her eyes were full of glass, and the rest of her steak looked like painted lead on the table. The laughter swirling in the noisy restaurant turned to mockery. She wanted Parson to be dead. When she'd made the mistake, before, of not shooting Gagneau when she had the chance, she lurched away from death by one gunshot-shortened knife swing. She had had her chance with Parson when they bumped into him in DUMBO; she knew he was dangerous when he loomed suddenly over her—but she passed. She glared at the little detective while he concentrated on Inglewood's words. Parson was too big for a quick shot and a kick in the face.

"Just pictures?" Guthrie demanded.

"Well, there was a little shelf about midway up the wall. That was real narrow, just a few inches, but it had some crap on it—a leather belt, a pen, that's all."

Vasquez took it like a kick in the stomach. She had tricked herself into thinking that the belt went missing on an overnight from Skinny's.

"Was there a pedestal?"

"Like a little one-legged end table, about enough to hold a beer," Inglewood said.

"What was on it?" Guthrie barked.

"Nothing. Nothing on the pedestal. Should there be?"

"He ain't done, Mike."

The heavy detective floated another sigh. "Just because I play for NYPD don't mean I'm short on brains, Guthrie. Somebody's got to do the work nobody's paying for. Call me if you get something." The digital disconnect was silent, leaving room for hope that more remained to be said, but the drunken crowd at Cité filled it with an impromptu chorus from *Cats!* and a sprinkled-on mixture of jeers and bravos.

Vasquez stared into the celebration. Since she'd run over to Corona when they came back from West Virginia, waiting for Fat-Fat to set his trap, the glow of Tommy's skin was alive in her memory. She wanted him, but Parson made her feel sick. She texted Tommy and canceled, was torn by a pang, then called Mamì to explain she had business. The soft purr of Spanish and her mother's lightness somersaulted her mood, but she had already decided to sleep in the office.

Guthrie and Walker saved her from herself. The men had no intention of waiting to finish the Mexican business. The little detective rousted the pilot he had hired for the flight to Tabasco, and then they took their accumulated gear to Teterboro. The jet was airborne before midnight.

CHAPTER THIRTY

The jet floated down onto Villahermosa, a brilliant swirl from high above that clarified into an oily mud puddle during the final approach. A looping handful of asphalt roads held a congealed mass of mud-spattered concrete-block shacks around an island of squat, toad-like official buildings and an impoverished university, between the blubbery lips of two slow, muddy rivers wandering on a flat, wet sheet of hazy greenery. Consular agents, a game warden, and a deputy mayor rushed the jet with a motorcade to welcome Señor Guthrie.

A polite inspection followed like a parade. The pilots watched with weary resignation that turned to amazement while the game warden inspected, logged, receipted, and returned the firearms with a loud proclamation of good wishes for their hunting. Vasquez watched, absorbing the unguarded, nasal Spanish of the Mexican soldiers and agents while they gossiped about the rich gringos, eyes glowing as they examined bundles of currency in hundred, five-hundred, and thousand-peso notes, and tried to guess the size of the bribes changing hands. Swiftly they unloaded, the detectives filling a single dusty sedan in the gleaming official motorcade. Dust plumed on the gravel tarmac as they drove to the commercial terminal. They paused to exchange a long round of effusive thanks and farewells with Guthrie, before the officials hurried away to examine the numerous cases of whiskey they had been, regrettably, forced to confiscate.

Once the gleaming officials drained from the terminal concourse, the background of loudspeakers and waiting crowds resurfaced. Fatigue and boredom etched lonely brown faces among the rush of frantic hustlers. Pale golden straw hats floated above every dark face. The men wore pipestem pants and roadruined shoes. The women were wrapped in color: red threaded with green, black, and yellow, or yellow bordered with blue and green with patterns interlaced by some cunning hand and eye. Children raced among the baggage.

Vasquez felt the throngs of eyes like clinging hands, but Guthrie clowned at being gringo. He craned his neck and gawked with an open mouth. Walker blended in wearing blue jeans and dusty boots, but she felt overdressed in the stark black hat and black bolero that hid the pistols on her kidney belt. The hustlers grew bolder as Guthrie leaned against the counter to rent a car. Some whispered offers for tours, artifacts, drugs, food, and companionship, while others simply stared.

One dark Mexican, missing an eyetooth from the sly grin beneath his narrow mustache, edged forward while tapping dust from oxblood cowboy boots. A silver buckle on his belt was larger than an outspread hand, but his blue jeans were dusty and his straw hat had more gaps than his smile. He hesitated, then dipped back when a tall, slim Mexican wearing a blue suit and cream shirt marched from the crowd.

The tall man wore dark glasses and a drooping mustache. His shoes glowed like patent leather. Guthrie turned and saw him as he hesitated a few feet from the knot of gringos. The little detective smiled and thrust out a hand.

"Señor Abaroa?" he asked. "You seem younger than your picture."

They exchanged pleasantries and a round of introductions; Guthrie tagged Walker and Vasquez as operatives, then pocketed the keys of a blue Range Rover and strode away from the counter beside the

Mexican detective. Walker drove the Range Rover, following Abaroa to drop the detective at the Nuevo Hotel Manzur before going to the plaza to shop.

A gleaming stucco wall with dark, narrow windows on the second floor looked across the avenida Francisco I. Madera into the parking lot. The detectives dashed across the street, through an arched entry lined with old portraits, and into a cool, dark lobby full of old woodwork and worn black and white ceramic tile. A mezzanine looked down onto the lobby like a threadbare gentleman. The manager gently dismissed both decks of rooms in the ancient central wing, and placed them upstairs on the south side of the colonnaded courtyard, where a creaking set of stairs provided another way down at the far end. Exposed posts and beams showed like dark bones in the corridor. The floor sighed beneath each footstep.

"Señor, this was a difficult task," Abaroa said after the detectives surrounded the small table in Guthrie's room. His English was a sonorous whisper framed in halting enunciation. "In your country, you might have this information with the touch of a button, but in Mexico, some old-fashioned methods were required." He opened his briefcase and slid out a thick file. "You read Spanish?"

"Sure," Guthrie said, offering a smile as he accepted the paperwork.

A brief false smile interrupted Abaroa's frown of suspicion. "I have concern that you came to Mexico on a matter ending so straightforwardly. I have an electronic copy which I could have sent to you, but then you wished suddenly to come to Villahermosa. This was convenient only because I had already traveled to Chiapas, an expense you authorized previously. Perhaps I have misunderstood your intentions?" Despite the drooping mustache, a slick headful of black hair, thick eyebrows, and dark chocolate eyes suggested a university student, not a detective.

"I asked for a thorough background on Rafael Morales Allende, born in Puerto Cate, Chiapas, with a thorough decription of his entire family." Guthrie tapped the file with a fingertip, and opened it to reveal the operation report at the front.

"You are aware that Rafael Morales is in prison in the United States of America?"

"Sure."

Abaroa's face darkened.

"You got pictures of the Morales family?" Guthrie flipped idly through the pages of the background report.

Abaroa nodded, his face hardening. He pulled a packet from his briefcase, heavy with glossy prints. He tapped it once on the tabletop before handing it across. The little detective opened it, swept a space on the tabletop, and fanned the photographs. The shooter peered up from several—as an unsmiling boy, a uniformed army recruit, and a hardened veteran. The little detective grunted.

"This one," he said, pointing.

"Ramon Morales," Abaroa said. "The youngest son of Joaquin Morales." The Mexican detective pulled a notebook. "He joined the army in 1998, then discharged in 2003 as a sergeant. He has no employment but appears to live at ease. He could be a narco, but he has no arrests or suspicion."

He shrugged and continued. "Rafael Morales was wild and violent before his father's death. He kept all hours, refused to work, then disappeared for days at a time and returned with money. Of course he was a narco. He appears in official documents—police roundups, warrants, and intelligence reports. He is suspected of murder and terrorism during the cartel war, and being rewarded with the assignment in New York City by Los Zetas.

"So I have provided background on the family of an incarcerated career criminal," Abaroa finished. "Moreover, this is suddenly important enough to bring the man who hired me to Mexico. One can imagine my curiosity. And quite naturally, I could peer into New York City far more easily than I could gather this material in Mexico. At the press of a button, no less. You are justly famous, Señor Guthrie. Señorita Vasquez. You find Rafael Morales somewhere in the background of your killings in New York? I ask because I wish to help you."

"I need to find *Ramon* Morales," Guthrie said. "Quietly. I can accept your assumption that he's a narco, perhaps a Zeta, and untouchable by the police in Chiapas and Tabasco. An exceedingly dangerous man."

"Ramon," the Mexican detective repeated. He glanced at Vasquez. After a moment, he continued, "We should begin in Chiapas. We could watch his sisters, or his brother Ernesto. Such men are *sinvergüenza* . . . and Ramon is unwanted—"

"He came to Villahermosa," Guthrie said. "I expect to find his trail here."

Abaroa smiled, almost breaking into laughter. "This is not your country, Señor Guthrie. Things are done in a very simple manner here, usually by walking, talking, and looking. I cannot offer you shortcuts, and I feel it necessary to dampen your expectations. I succeeded with the background because simple people do not hide. Finding a narco is very different, very difficult." He paused. "I suppose you have some reason you expect to find him in Tabasco, not Chiapas?"

"He made local calls in Villahermosa," Guthrie said.

"Certainly?"

The little detective nodded. Six calls were connected to florists in Villahermosa, and each of those calls lasted several minutes—far more than needed for a simple questions-and-answer. The florists, doing business in cash, seemed likely to be a network of laundries for a narcotics operation. Guthrie intended to save them for last, in case a visit might ring immediate alarms with Morales. Three other calls were connected to a hotel and two restaurants.

Walker returned from the plaza with a few basketloads of serapes, wraps, cheap shoes, and straw hats. The detectives changed clothes. Vasquez added a long dress to cover her blue jeans and pistols, carefully slit at the sides so that she could reach inside, and a serape to cover her utility vest where she tucked her Colt. The tall Cherokee looked the same, but Guthrie was transformed. He looked like a Mexican farmer dressed for a weekend trip to the city, and could disappear against a wall with a slouch. Abaroa studied them, then shrugged. The men might pass, but the señorita still glowed like neon.

Hotel Emporio was two blocks from the Manzur, three tiers of square white plaster and red tile. On the street, a sheer wall confronted the sidewalk, with shuttered windows beneath awnings on the upper stories, each stepped back for a narrow railed balcony. Traffic pumped in the streets. The detectives floated into the lobby. Abaroa asked for a room.

Beyond the lobby, a colonnaded porch wrapped an interior patio, pool, and fountain. Neat rows of manicured trees left dappled bands of shade on the pool deck. Walker found the bar, settled on a stool, and cooled his hands with a beer. Vasquez watched the lobby using the glass windows in the gift shop.

After Abaroa left with a room key to explore the corridors of the hotel, the little detective slouched on a bench in the lobby and called the hotel desk. In rough Spanish, he claimed to be from Belize, and asked for Carlos Riva Palacio, explaining that he was expected in Villahermosa on business, but needed to postpone the meeting. He watched the clerk consult the register; Carlos Riva checked out the previous night.

With Morales already gone, Guthrie abandoned subtlety. He trotted over to the desk and asked to see the manager. A pair of five-hundred-peso notes peeled from a roll produced sudden comprehension. The manager graciously provided "deluxe accommodations, including descriptions of every wished-for amenity" after more banknotes changed hands.

"The gentleman left hurriedly last evening," the manager said quietly. "He arrived with eight Guatemalans, but left with only seven. And there was the beautiful señora." He flicked a finger at Vasquez, strolling the lobby. "As beautiful as the señorita, but more delicate, as small as a doll."

"You caught the señora's name?"

"Angela Olivares, or so the maids whispered. The cards among the flowers were so addressed." The manager smiled. "Many flowers—the deliveries were numerous, all to the señora's third-floor suite."

The detectives checked the restaurants after leaving Hotel Emporio. A table at Apolo Palacio had been reserved but not claimed. The restaurant served food intended for *los turistas*, heavily dosed with authenticity and prices. The afternoon was hot. Vasquez chafed under the extra clothes, but she settled quickly into the rhythm of Villahermosa's streets.

Walker tapped Guthrie's shoulder as the detectives rounded the plaza on foot. "See that kid by the fruit stand? Blue T-shirt, straddling the scooter?" He waved a fingertip along the line of vendors stretching toward the municipal building.

The skinny boy, maybe fifteen, squinted to light a cigarette while watching the detectives. He wore a tilted straw hat atop a bandanna, faded jeans, and leather sandals. Dark tattoos circled his forearms resting on the handlebars of his scooter.

"He was outside the hotel earlier," Walker said. "Same scooter."

Guthrie and Vasquez studied the boy as he tried out a series of hard expressions, using his cigarette to cover nervous glances aimed at a handful of young men lounging beneath an overhang in front of some ancient vending machines. They wore straw hats, T-shirts, jeans, and boots. Three laughed as they took turns punching each other in the shoulders and chest, while two watched the plaza. One threw dark looks at the boy while smoothing the ends of his mustache.

"The muchachos are sweating him," Vasquez said, "but he ain't alone. See there?" She pointed at a man ambling along the line of vendors, smiling to himself as he kicked slowly in dusty boots and blue jeans. His smile flared each time he measured glimpses at the young men.

"Okay, the tattoos," Walker said. "Good eyes." The smiling man had tattoos, fading to blue, circling his forearms with similar flared wings. A small bundle loosely wrapped in a blue and green serape dangled from his left hand.

"Watching them watching him watching us," Guthrie muttered.

"The kid's street," Vasquez said. "His shadow is some rank. The muchachos are just here. There'll be some more on the next corner."

"So?"

"In New York, somebody had to put some weight on it to get the rank out here in daylight," Vasquez said.

"Mexico has many thieves," Abaroa said, adding a shrug. "The police protect *los turistas*, that is true. And some Indians may consider gringos unlucky, but they are still white gold. Money is money."

The little detective grunted out a noncommittal reply. At the airport, the police and customs agents had seen plenty of cash. Walker kept an eye on the crowds; he had come to Mexico to watch Guthrie's back while he trailed Morales.

They rounded the plaza, walked down the avenue, and found another string of young men, arguing and watching outside La Virreina, riding the stale afterburn of a day-old shooting with scowls and loud stories. The detectives spread encouragement from a small roll of banknotes. The previous evening, *sicarios* riddled the patio and restaurant with bullets, killing a waiter and a Guatemalan customer, injuring three more customers and one woman walking alone on the sidewalk. Inside, Guthrie discovered that Carlos Riva had claimed his reserved table, but disappeared along with most of the other customers in the confusion of the shooting. The army had sealed the evening with hours of pointless questioning.

"Los Zetas," one waiter whispered as he pocketed a pair of five-hundred-peso bills. "Why would they kill a Guatemalan? They are harmless little clowns." He shrugged, smoothed his shirtfront, and hurried back into the kitchen.

Night closed the city, and the detectives returned to the hotel. Abaroa left them in the parking lot, climbed into his Jeep and drove away after promising to return in the morning. The hotel was off-season quiet. A bundle waited inside Guthrie's hotel room door: a green-glazed ceramic jaguar mask wrapped in a yellow and orange serape. The jaguar vomited a cheap black cellphone onto the bed after the detectives unwrapped it.

Vasquez scooped the phone from the bedcovers and examined it. One message waited, without a security code. "A phone number," she said.

Guthrie shook his head before she could dial, and took the phone. "That could be the official contact," he said. "I wondered why they ain't reached out directly, but that could be a good thing. Cops down here are as dirty as hell. I'll reach out if we run into something."

"Now what?"

Guthrie shrugged. "We got problems. First, that rat's gonna be behind us too easy. That's bound to be what he was laughing about. Look for him."

The tall Cherokee smiled.

"Not like that, Angel. We don't need a bigger mess." He settled on the bed. "We had a trail here, then it's gone. I tried the satellite phone earlier, but that laptop's been burned. Something got in it and scrambled it like an egg. So we're tracking him blind.

"I came here figuring we had a few days to put hands on Morales, but the locals had something going on for him that didn't sound like an accident. You recall Tommy said Ricardo Sorcini took bullets in the back? The *rat* didn't shoot him."

"Morales killed him?"

Guthrie shrugged. "That puts us back to nothing but his girl, this Angela Olivares that sticks out for a pretty face."

"He flew to get here," Vasquez said. "He don't like to get his boots dirty. Maybe he flies out of here."

"That's right," the little detective said. "In the morning our move is back to the airport."

CHAPTER THIRTY-ONE

Abaroa called in the early morning, while driving to the Hotel Manzur to join the detectives for breakfast. The upstairs hallway smelled of old, polished wood at daybreak when Vasquez came from her room. Around the corner, a room service cart loaded with dishes made the floor creak. Two waiters whispered insincere good wishes through a closing guest room door as they fought to turn the cart in the hallway. Walker and Guthrie joined her in the hallway, and they followed the cart until it reached the service lift. The detectives used the front stairs down to the lobby.

At the front desk, a tall silver-haired man wearing a gray suit stood fanning himself with a black hat. With an arm outstretched to press on the desktop, he studied the clerk sitting with downcast eyes. He looked like a lonely king standing on the black-and-white checkerboard of worn ceramic tile in the lobby. Guthrie and Walker paused, but Vasquez kept walking. She wanted a cup of coffee. The tall man saw them, and smiled with bright insincerity. Beneath his thick silver mustache he had a mouthful of yellow teeth.

"Mi amigos!" he said loudly. *"Me alegra verlos!"*

The antique wood-paneled lobby filled with the sound of shuffling feet like polite applause. Grim-faced men emerged from the portrait-lined entry, the colonnaded courtyard, and peered over the wooden mezzanine rail. The desk clerk stared determinedly at his blotter. Vasquez slid a hand under her serape and gripped her pistol.

"No, please," the man said. He held out empty hands. "I wish only that you will join me for breakfast and discuss your adventures."

Guthrie stepped out onto the dusty tile and approached the desk. As he walked he glanced at the watching men, each haloed with a broad-brimmed hat. "You sure brought a lot of friends," he said.

The tall man covered his silver hair with his black hat, shrugged apologetically, and straightened the sleeves on his gray suit coat. "I am Enrique Michaus Garcia," he said. He smiled again, trying for sincerity. "My employer is perhaps careful. A car is waiting for us."

Walker and Guthrie scanned the waiting men. Some carried bundles, and others waited with hands poised beneath their dark jackets. Guthrie shook his head at Vasquez. Michaus led the way with a broad, welcoming gesture, and the watching gunmen parted to allow the detectives to pass, sweeping shut behind them like curtains. More men waited on the sidewalk.

A white Escalade with blacked-out windows idled in the middle of a line of dusty Jeeps and Broncos. Leather bench seats faced each other across a small table in the rebuilt interior of the Escalade. Michaus sat in the back, and the detectives filled the bench seat facing him. As they pulled away, Vasquez saw Abaroa rush from the hotel parking lot and end in a sudden, gaping halt. He darted back from the street.

Michaus offered assurances during the drive, but Vasquez didn't trust him. He removed his hat again, in the Escalade; at arm's length, threads of black darkened his silver hair. He fell still in the padded seat. The man seemed tired, sick, and old, but filled with a gleam of manic energy that hovered like a hidden smile.

Surrounded by Jeeps and Broncos full of men, the Escalade rushed and turned through the streets of Villahermosa, then stopped in the walled courtyard of a red-tile-and-stucco mansion. A token handful of men emerged from the other vehicles to escort them into the mansion.

A polished marble floor in the broad foyer held a scattering of antique stuffed chairs. Long crimson and gold drapes hung at the windows. A grand staircase descended from a mezzanine; three half-dressed young women glided down, chattering about a bad haircut. Norteño blared from somewhere deeper inside.

A black-liveried maid attached herself quietly to Michaus and he stooped to catch a whisper. The trio of young women turned through an arch in the foyer. Two barefoot men wearing T-shirts and blue jeans lolled on the woven carpet in front of a wide-screen, shouting curses while they wrestled with game controllers. Semiautomatic pistols and AR-15s lay on the floor beside them in a litter of beer cans and candy wrappers. The young women paraded in front of the wide-screen, sparking curses and catcalls, then settled onto a couch. One of the men glanced through the arch as the detectives passed. He spit a low comment at his companion. They both laughed.

Michaus led them to a dining room dominated by a long, polished table. A stocky, middle-aged man wearing a baseball cap, fatigue pants, and a T-shirt stood at the sideboard eating a bowl of cornflakes. He wiped his drooping black mustache with a napkin when they came into the room.

"Enrique!" he said. He strode forward and studied the detectives. "There was another? Another was not a gringo?" The grip of a Beretta jutted from his belt, and another gunbutt rode in the cargo pocket of his fatigue pants. Three men drifted in through the patio door with AR-15s hanging from their shoulders.

"I found these three at the hotel." Michaus shook his head and smiled. "All gringos. The other is Mexican, but . . ." He finished with a shrug.

The stocky man nodded. "As always, you are right. I would have shot him already." He studied Walker speculatively.

"I am sorry," Michaus said. "I promised them breakfast."

The stocky man shrugged. "Sit! What will you eat?" He tugged a chair from the table, gestured, and sat down. "You may call me El Güero."

Walker strode around the long table, to sit with his back to a wall with no door. Guthrie waved Vasquez to sit beside Walker, then pulled out the chair nearest the door. Another maid in a neat black uniform brought coffee on a tray. She kept her eyes on the floor or tabletop, and never saw anyone's face. Vasquez had no appetite, but the men asked for eggs, ham, juice, and bread. They drank coffee while they waited for the food, then made thick sandwiches. The Mexicans sprinkled polite conversation on the meal.

Vasquez struggled through a sandwich, thinking about her loco brothers, Indio and Miguel. For muchachos in the city, being a man was half a game of dare: if one drunken muchacho ate a cockroach, then everyone else downed shots of rum and searched the cupboards. Watching the loco from the outside, wrapped in a girl's immunity, Vasquez despised the stupidity.

Then as she passed into the world of the *blancos*, the scowl of unearned loca became a shield and a weapon. With two loco brothers, she never heard a harsh word on the Lower East, but being Puerto Rican was a curse that blessed her when she wanted to push someone around. Vasquez used it.

At the table in Villahermosa, she had no loco brothers to smooth the way or linger nearby like stormclouds—she had a sandwich. She raced to finish, wanting to laugh at the stupidity. Guthrie and Walker beat her anyway, but the dare ignited her determination.

"The peace of my plaza has been disturbed," El Güero said. "How can I accept this?"

Vasquez licked grease from her fingers, then tossed the edge of her serape over her shoulder to make it easier to reach her pistols. She smiled. The three men with AR-15s shifted uneasily.

El Güero frowned at her. "You are gringos, you do not understand. Mexicans understand that disturbing the peace is bad manners. They understand, so I would shoot them—they have no excuses. Gringos are like children, not knowing better. You will explain why you ask about my business. *¿Sí?*"

The little detective smiled. "I ain't come here to Mexico by mistake. I came here looking for a man, and now this morning I'm wondering if you're hiding him."

"Who? Who is this?"

The little detective smiled. "I'm not here hanging in the air."

"Wait! Wait!" Michaus said. "Be patient." He mopped his forehead with his handkerchief. "I require some more explanation."

"I think I've put some of it together," the little detective said. "Now I think the man I'm after doesn't belong to you—or you got more mess than you bargained for." He paused for a swallow of coffee. "Now that you know I'm here looking for someone—"

"You came here from New York?" Michaus interjected.

Guthrie nodded.

The Mexicans exchanged a quick glance. Michaus flashed a smile. "Señor we are not involved in the unfortunate deaths of those lawyers in New York—yet your interest might substitute for proof in convincing others. This is unacceptable. If some connection existed, the result would be immediate."

"You would clean house," the little detective said.

"Of course."

They stared at each other. El Güero toyed with the grip of his Beretta. Michaus flicked a glance at him and shook his head.

"You see why I doubt you?" Guthrie asked. "Somebody's cleaning up down here, and you're hesitating."

Michaus smiled. "Of course. And I understand this hesitation more easily than your perseverance. Lawyers? Such loyalty for lawyers? I myself can admire this . . ."

"It ain't the lawyers. It's Stephanie Morgan. There ain't no getting around that, see? On account of that, we appreciate your hospitality, but we'll be about our business," the little detective said.

"I do not think you misunderstand us, señor," Michaus said. "We are not involved, and you will prove this for us, you see? You will find this man who murdered these lawyers, and your Stephanie Morgan, and also prove he is not connected to us. This is clear?"

"I hear you," Guthrie said. He stood and clapped his hat on his head. "I work for somebody already."

Michaus smiled.

El Güero began making a sandwich and said, "Enrique, send

someone to find that man you missed. I want to shoot someone today."

The little detective frowned. "I need that man," he said.

Michaus nodded. "My employer is merely enthusiastic. We would not dream of disturbing your working arrangement. Find your man, señor. Prove he is not connected to us."

El Güero smiled, took a bite from his sandwich, and spoke around the mouthful. "You would thank me for shooting this man, I think. If you change your mind." He mimed a pistol with his hand, then waved them out before walking through the patio door.

The lawyer walked them from the mansion, and lent them his driver and Escalade to return to the hotel. The bright, clear morning air smelled sweet, even in Villahermosa. The detectives relaxed in the leather seats like tycoons. Walker opened the liquor cabinet in the console, and they drank stiff shots of Michaus's expensive whiskey.

Walker paused after they climbed from the Escalade in front of Hotel Manzur. "El Güero? He didn't look blond to me."

Guthrie shrugged. "I think they mean dumb," he said. "He let you carry your pistols into the house, didn't he?"

CHAPTER THIRTY-TWO

When Vasquez downed the shot of Michaus's whiskey, Villahermosa lifted on a sudden tide of exhilaration. For the first time, she understood Miguel's endless smile. Her brothers needed no drugs—*el beso de dulce suerte* was enough. Vasquez flew with angels while the ordinary people in the ordinary street crawled blind beneath her. Magically sharp senses revealed the angle of the sun, the soundless glide of Guthrie's boots, and each subtle bend of Walker's neck as his eyes drifted behind his dark glasses. Inside the Hotel Manzur, the desk clerk bounded forward for reassurance, his eyes darting like bumblebees. The even burr of Guthrie's plainspoken replies anchored the universe. The little detective was unchanged; he stood like an upright plank, with his straw hat pulled square and firm down to his dull, bricklike face. He brushed the clerk aside after sieving his whispered explanations about *el narco:* An ordinary man was powerless.

The detectives walked back to the hotel restaurant, and the men talked about railroads and snowstorms in West Virginia. Ordinary time returned. Abaroa rushed into the restaurant. He admitted driving to the U.S. consulate, then turning away in fury. Diplomats were less help than police. "This country," he said, again and again, as he settled with relief.

"I will go to Chiapas with you," Abaroa said. "I can at least lead you to the proper places in Chiapas."

The little detective paused with his cup of coffee and studied the man. "Señor Abaroa, I appreciate your work, but we've come to a parting. I want you to go back to Mexico City and forget about what you did down here."

"Forget?" Abaroa asked, adding a frown of puzzlement. He glanced at Vasquez. "This morning you were kidnapped from the street by Los Zetas—this I know—and now you will leave Mexico?"

The little detective answered with a crooked grin. "This operation looks to turn messy anytime," he said. "I'm backtrailing, looking for a loose thread. In New York, this would be what I call a seam job. If I find that loose thread, I'll pull until it unravels. You understand?"

"And I am sure you have reasons for sending me back to the DF," Abaroa said. "Perhaps mistaken reasons. Let me speculate. After speaking with Los Zetas, you decide that I am not useful. You think they were honest with you? They play with their food. I doubt the criminals in your country are known for their honesty, but Los Zetas are cockroaches.

"Mexico is built with stories," he continued quietly. "Our singers sing and our farmers talk. We listen for rumbles of violence the way you listen for the weather—is it safe to go out, to go down this street? The narcos are *sinvergüenza*. Let me offer you a story about Los Zetas.

"Los Zetas kidnapped a banker in Mexico City. Kidnappers will cut away a finger to assist their demand for ransom, you see? This encourages prompt payment. The wife of the banker, his parents, they gathered the ransom, but this needed some time. They received two more fingers. The banker missed three fingers, and they delivered the ransom. A man can live without three fingers." Abaroa smoothed his mustache fiercely.

"So when you see someone in Mexico who is missing tips from their fingers, you know he has been ransomed. You will see the ghost of a man, a man whose mouth is full of ashes.

"But the banker was not released," Abaroa said. "His fingers continued to arrive. The wife of the banker, his parents, they begged to pay more ransom. Los Zetas cut away ten fingers. This needed nineteen days, señor. Then they cut away the head of the banker. The body was never recovered.

"Los Zetas are cockroaches, señor. I will go with you, and then I will trust one man, at least, among however many men you surround yourself with."

Guthrie nodded slowly. "Then my next move is the airport. He ain't driving over the mountains if he can fly."

Abaroa frowned. "If he did wish to fly, the narcos have their own planes."

"He's heading for a bolt-hole. Someone hit Morales as soon as he went out to dinner. He has to wonder how they touched him, unless he's mixed in that business with the Zetas one way or another."

The Mexican detective nodded agreement.

"So I got tricks for the airport that could point to his bolt-hole."

Abaroa laughed. "This, Señor Guthrie, I must see."

After Abaroa finished his late breakfast, the detectives left the hotel at mid-morning. Dusty cars and busses jammed the middle of Villahermosa. The city glowed with bright sunshine pouring from a cloudless sky. As they threaded the streets, Vasquez and Walker watched from the backseat, looking for shadows. The boy with the scooter appeared first. Speckles of spattered mud decorated his dingy T-shirt.

Paranoia pointed again and again to more faces in the crowd. Trailing drivers drew consideration and then were discarded like bad cards in gin. Every Bronco and Jeep was studied until the drivers blurred into bored eyes, ratty mustaches, missing teeth, and slow-traffic nose-picking. The drivers were no different in Manhattan. Vasquez settled on a Jeep, orange or dusty red, with a chrome grill, bumper, and rims. The driver alternated frustrated lane-changing with bored slumps, and fanned himself with a ragged straw hat at stops.

A dozen commercial planes huddled around the main terminal at the airport. The detectives parked, strolled inside, and walked the concourse. While Vasquez and Walker watched the crowd—a mix of businessmen, tourists, and dusty farmers with their families—Guthrie asked questions. Abaroa trailed him.

The little detective filled a basket with fruit and drinks, buying more when he emptied it, and handed them out to anyone who would meet his eyes. He tossed out fortune-cookie phrases of bad Spanish to disarm the crowds, but paused to question airport regulars: janitors, vendors, policemen, and clerks.

The little detective's questions about *la mujer bella* sparked long, winding conversations. He jotted notes on a rough map of the terminal and answered puzzled looks with five-hundred-peso notes wrapped around cans of lemonade. After two hours, the little detective was unhappy, but Abaroa was impressed.

"She ain't been through here," he admitted finally, while pausing to drink a lemonade.

"This is time for lunch, perhaps?" Abaroa asked.

"Something quick," he said. "The other terminal is small enough to spit across. I would've started there, but Morales landed here on a commercial flight."

The Mexican detective bought a coat pocket full of empanadas from a vendor, then strode up and down the concourse arguing violently on his cellphone. The crowd swirled fearfully around him. Guthrie and Walker wolfed down *carne asada*. While she ate, Vasquez watched the farmboys in the airport as they tried to watch her without being seen, and wondered, with a creeping sadness, whether Tommy Johnson's gruff insistence was good enough to fill her need for what was gone. "Rachel, you're crazy," he'd said. "Your face is perfect."

Once upon a time, there was no doubt. Rachel Vasquez was more than beautiful; she was *bella*, *divina*, sharp featured, with bent black eyebrows and a rosebud lip. Hissing whispers of envy erased all self-doubt. Vasquez's arrogance sprang from the perfection of a magnetic smile that had been hammered away with a pistol butt. As the farmboys in the airport snapped their dark-eyed glances away from the threat of her eyes, she wondered at what remained.

Guthrie circled the concourse to gather everyone, then they drove across to the private terminal. A jeepload of soldiers watched the tarmac between the terminals, a broad swath of bulldozed gravel alive with low clumps of grass and vine. A 737 sailed down from the clear sky and flared into a neat, screaming landing while he circled the small parking lot and found a space among the half-hundred cars and trucks glowing in the sunshine.

The terminal offered shadowy relief. A pair of bored soldiers seated on metal folding chairs watched the quiet diamond. A raised counter fronted a hand-marked flight board and weather map. Hanging signs marked the offices of the small airlines and charter services. Guthrie spent fifteen minutes and some banknotes to locate a small, beautiful woman, and received a free warning for a foolish, lovestruck gringo: Stay away from the women of other men.

The little detective ignored the warning and offered a larger bribe. A pained smile and a shrug later, a grease-stained mechanic explained that Carlos Riva was an important businessman. Early that morning, he flew to Yaxchilan on Tabasqueña de Aviación with some men and *"la mujer bella con ojos miel."* Riva often used Tabasqueña de Aviación to reach sites along the Usumacinta River, overseeing his lumber operations.

Walker supplied the turnaround—a minute of whispered nonsense in the little detective's ear—and Guthrie finished by making a show of dawning understanding and a sudden urge to relent. The Mexicans were relieved enough to joke gently at his expense while he retreated.

After the detectives left the terminal, Abaroa said, "Some of that which they said was intended as a careful warning because they suspect he is a narco." He laughed softly. "In this country, nothing may be said clearly."

"Good enough reason to come at this another way," Guthrie said. "We'll dummy up like *los turistas* and drive down there. The woman will keep sticking out. *Ojos miel.* Ain't a man alive misses that."

CHAPTER THIRTY-THREE

After tossing her clothes into a gym bag, Vasquez twisted her black hat onto her head and she crossed the hall to Guthrie's room. The wooden floor groaned like a tired man. Walker sat in a chair in the corner, watching the little detective reassemble his meticulous suitcases while they waited for Abaroa to drive back from his hotel. Guthrie had a grim certainty about the necessity of every item he packed—nothing was haphazard—but Walker bit out sour comments with each rearrangement.

Vasquez answered the door when Abaroa knocked. A laugh died in her mouth when the Mexican detective seized her wrist and yanked her into the hallway. Three more men waited beyond the door. One introduced himself with a punch. Vasquez recognized the dark tattoo encircling his wrist. She bounced from the plaster wall, but didn't fall.

"Pull her teeth," Abaroa hissed. He rammed her into the wall with his shoulder. Two stocky men wearing straw hats, dark glasses, and linen suits emptied her gunbelt. The hallway whirled as they whipped her back across to face the door of Guthrie's room. Her warning shout came out a gasp, accompanied by a mouthful of blood.

Using Vasquez as a shield, Abaroa dug his fingers into her throat and pressed the muzzle of a Beretta to her head. The tattooed man stretched his arm over her shoulder, leveling another Beretta. The serpent entwining his forearm had feathered wings. The other men gripped her wrists, spreading her arms and pinning her hands outside the door frame.

Guthrie stopped short of the door and dropped to a crouch. An extended revolver hid his hand. A snarl faded from his face. Walker had been sitting in the corner when Vasquez answered the door. He eased slowly upright, took a step toward the center of the room, and let his arms drop to his sides. Beneath his dark glasses, his face was blank. The little detective shot him a glance. "Angel, don't," he growled.

"Señor, we will come inside," Abaroa said. "Leave your pistol on the floor."

The little detective discarded his revolver gently onto the hardwood floor, uncocking the hammer before he stood up and backed away. Walker took two slow steps toward the bathroom door. His hands floated palm down, slightly above his waist. The little detective glanced at him again, then hissed out his breath.

"Angel," he warned.

Abaroa's right hand encircled most of Vasquez's neck when he firmed his grip. He pushed her into the hotel room. The Mexicans wearing linen suits pulled pistols as they brushed past Vasquez. The door clicked unhurriedly shut, but the tattooed man stayed at the door, while Abaroa pushed another step into the room.

"Remember to leave some of the *lana* behind," Abaroa said.

One of the gunmen flipped the suitcase on the bed and rummaged. Walker's face lit with a slow smile.

"I got to give it to you," Guthrie said. "You took me in with that story, earlier. You're a thief? Take the money and go."

Vasquez watched Walker's smile split open on his teeth. His hands floated. He's loco, she thought. The other gunman spared him a glance, then pointed his pistol at Guthrie.

"Money?" Abaroa asked. He unclasped Vasquez's neck, stepped closer to her, and circled her waist with his right arm. He chuckled, filling her ear with his breath. His hand wandered to her belly and he molded against her. Vasquez trembled with fire and ice; her empty holsters pressed against the small of her back.

"In your country, money buys anything. In this country, loyalty is not for sale. *La Familia tiene mi lealtad.*" Abaroa stretched out his Beretta, gesturing with the barrel. "Search them. Pull their teeth."

Vasquez dipped her finger into the compact-pocket of her blue jeans. The steel of her knife was as warm as blood, opened with a snap as she lifted her hand, then swept down on Abaroa's outstretched wrist. The blade tugged briefly. The Beretta slid from his hand as smoothly as if unrolled from a crimson handkerchief.

Guthrie charged, pulling his other revolver with his left hand. His shoulder clipped Vasquez as he passed. The gunman in the linen suit fired a shot at him. Walker spun a circle, ending the pivot in a crouch; Vasquez didn't see him draw his Colts; she couldn't count the blur of gunshots. The Mexicans threw their pistols, jerked like dancers, collapsed to the floor, and lay still.

Blood fountained from Abaroa's wrist. He stumbled to one side, ripping at Vasquez's belt. He studied his ruined hand incredulously, dangling by bits of tendon and a scrap of flesh. Blood pumped busily. Vasquez elbowed him in the neck. He sagged. She kicked him in the crotch. Vomit slid from his mouth as he curled on the floor.

After colliding with the tattooed Mexican, Guthrie rebounded from the door of the hotel room. The Mexican kept his feet by clinging to the doorknob. Guthrie slapped the Mexican's Beretta aside— two wild shots found the wall—then pressed his revolver to the end of the Mexican's drooping mustache. A gunshot erased the man's fury; his body whipped in an arc, cracking his shattered skull wetly open on top of the bureau against the wall by the door before he rolled down to the floor.

In the dusty silence afterward, heavy feet drummed the wooden floor in the hallway. The detectives paused, studying the blood-soaked Mexicans. None moved. Guthrie holstered his revolver. A door slammed nearby.

"Are you all right?" Guthrie rasped. He caught at Vasquez's sleeve.

"He fucking hit my face," she said. She felt her mouth with her fingertips, came away with blood, and cursed.

Guthrie laughed.

"You sure that's your blood?" Walker asked.

She glanced at the open knife in her hand, then noticed the blood spray on her jeans, her shirt, and her arms. "Maybe," she ventured.

Guthrie opened the door and looked into the hallway. "I thought someone was out here," he said, and frowned. "Anyway, get back to your room and get in the shower."

"My pistols—" She pointed at the stocky men in linen suits.

Walker found the pistols in their coat pockets, handed them to her on his way through the door, and walked down to the bend of the corridor. He shrugged, glancing back at Guthrie.

"Okay, Rachel, you're not going to jail in Mexico," Guthrie said. He hustled her by the arm across the hallway to her empty room. "Get cleaned up, including the clothes. Lock the door. Don't answer unless you hear me or Angel." He tossed her gym bag in behind her, shut the door, examined it, then studied the hardwood floor; it was clean.

Guthrie sent Walker back to the hotel room to straighten the luggage. He checked his pockets, then walked down to the lobby and bribed the desk clerk. The señorita was not in the hotel. He had a long conversation on the cheap cellphone while he waited in the lobby, but his hard expression never changed. At leisure, the Mexican police arrived.

Barricaded behind the bathroom door in Room 228, Vasquez discovered that the Hotel Manzur possessed an inexhaustible supply of hot water. The heat brightened her skin to pink and narrowed her thoughts down to the water swirling from the drain as she rinsed the blood from her clothes.

Eventually she noticed her knife perched on the tub corner with the blade still lolled open, as red as a tongue. She stepped from the shower, took her sharpener from her bag, and returned to the steaming water.

She stroked her knife's blade a hundred times before she returned it, still open, to the corner of the tub. Alongside the rushing shower and the whicker of her blade, Vasquez wondered why she only cut Abaroa once. Her mind fluttered like a blank page, empty of answers.

After she hung her clothes to drip, she fought the steam on the mirror for a chance to see her face. Her knife followed her to the back of the sink. Her lip throbbed, indistinct in the misty reflection. The shock evaporated with the steam, while she toweled and dressed. Vasquez ponytailed her long black hair, but left the knife-cut lock of hair to swing free along her jaw. She slid the beads into her jeans pocket, snugged her gunbelt, and holstered her pistols. Her knife slipped neatly into her pocket. Her black hat hung dripping in the shower. She pulled her straw hat from her gym bag, unlocked the bathroom door, and stepped into the hotel room.

As Vasquez walked around the corner of the bed and turned toward the door, the balcony door whooshed open, spilling light from the courtyard. The curtain whipped aside. With a glimpse of Duane Parson, she bolted for the door, tugging at a pistol. A massive hand clamped onto her elbow and her arm flared like it was suddenly dipped in fire. He lifted her effortlessly and her special tumbled to the floor.

"Don't scream," he said softly, dangling her a few inches from his misshapen face. A bright blue floral-print tourist shirt strained to contain his massive shoulders.

"You might catch the attention of the local police," he continued smoothly, "but I would simply escape." He tilted his head toward the balcony. Her hand signaled wildly at the end of her arm, contracted in a jagged rictus that burned like fire.

"Of course I would take you with me. You might need a little bit of subduing, Miss Vasquez. True? Would you rather not be subdued?"

"You freak!" she hissed. She reached for her other pistol with her left hand, but he stopped her easily with another clamping grip.

Parson sighed. "I don't want to look this way," he murmured. A shift in his grip wrung a cry of pain from her. The giant's mouth dropped in surprise, and his grip loosened until it seemed like a warm velvet cuff.

"I only want some information, Miss Vasquez," he said. "I won't hurt you unless you force me."

But you will, she thought. Photographs paraded in her memory, a blur of bruise, welt, and pallid skin. Her breath ran short. The giant's face twisted. He lowered her until her feet touched the floor.

"I don't intend to hurt you," he said.

"Like Alice Powell?" she hissed. "Like you felt all warm and fuzzy about Alice Powell? You're a monster!"

Parson flinched, but he didn't let go. His bushy eyebrows knit into a determined scowl. "I didn't hurt Miss Powell," he growled.

"Kidnapped, raped, and murdered," Vasquez spit.

"I didn't do that," he said.

"You're a liar. You killed her. You beat her to death." Vasquez's voice disappeared into a squeak. Duane Parson had gripped Alice Powell's leg and then slammed her against something that shattered her skull. The giant's hands felt like glowing irons wrapped around her elbows. The glare that met her words took her breath; she squeezed her eyes shut, but the hands and voice wouldn't go away.

"I tried to save her." With her eyes tight shut, Parson's voice sounded like rumbling stones in her ears. "In Seattle. There was a little man who liked to do dirty things. He did dirty things to her, but I found him. No one else will find him."

"You killed her." Vasquez couldn't believe the sound of her own voice. Something inside her wouldn't let her be quiet; something inside her recited a prayer for swift death followed by vengeance. Soft cries burst between her clenched teeth, riding her uneven breath.

Parson collected her wrists into a single hand, lifted her, and pinned her wrists to the wall. "The little man killed everything beautiful about Miss Powell," he grated. He turned Vasquez's chin with his free hand, forcing her to face him, but she wouldn't open her eyes. He cursed. "He killed her. I gave her rest."

"Liar," she whispered.

"I think you want to live, Miss Vasquez," Parson said. His breath flared hot on her face alongside his conversational tone. "Such a simple choice, really. Mr. Guthrie is good at what he does, you know?

Perhaps the best. He is searching for the man who killed Stephanie Morgan. He has found something. I know this because you packed your luggage, Miss Vasquez."

Silence was marred by ragged breathing and the soft cries Vasquez couldn't contain.

"I see you understand me," he continued. "Tell me about the man who killed Stephanie Morgan. For your life, Miss Vasquez." He bit off each sharp syllable a hairbreadth from her face.

She trembled. While she talked, she cried. Tears weren't currency for Vasquez, any more than she traded on smiles. She cried because for the first time in her life, she was beaten past even trying. After he had collected his answers, Parson opened the closet door, still holding her wrists with a single hand. He took her second Special, then discarded her into the closet. The door clicked shut. After Vasquez heard his heavy feet walk away, she curled into a ball. She was alive, but she wanted the darkness to hide her.

CHAPTER THIRTY-FOUR

Guthrie and Walker returned to the Hotel Manzur at nightfall. By then, the circular scrubbing of self-pity had cleaned Vasquez of all but a lingering electric tingle in her hands from Duane Parson's grip. No outward mark showed, but the stalker left a final insult behind for her to discover after she crept from the closet; her Specials, piled on the bed beneath her straw hat, were still loaded. Parson didn't even bother taking the bullets. The little detective strolled along the hotel hallway like a man coming home from a Sunday dinner, then returned to re-packing his suitcases after he and Walker carried everything to her room.

He grinned at Vasquez when she slumped in the chair in the corner of her room. "I just spent six hours in a Mexican jail, but you look worse than I feel," he said.

Vasquez flinched, and dipped her chin to hide her eyes beneath the brim of her straw hat. "Worse than the Bronx?" she asked. She quashed an urge to scan the room again for any betraying sign of Parson. Words jammed behind her teeth, but she bit down hard. After practicing a hundred explanations, she found that Guthrie's quiet good humor paralyzed her. The raw shame of being beaten by Parson was nothing against disappointing the little detective. Fear froze her tongue into silence.

The little detective paused, weighing the bottle of Rohypnol in his hand. "They could brighten it up with a little fresh paint," he said with a shrug. "We ain't seen the bad part. I tried our gift-basket cell phone. That was George Livingston's police contact. He wouldn't come down himself, but he pointed the bribe to the right pocket. We're square."

While the little detective packed, Vasquez silently rehearsed conversations about Parson that drifted further into impossibility with each passing minute. Her silence felt sealed when the last suitcase closed. The detectives walked down to the lobby, and Guthrie handed the desk clerk a roll of pesos with a nod of thanks.

Guthrie took a driving tour of Villahermosa after everything was loaded in the Range Rover. Vasquez and Walker studied the traffic as he drove. He trolled along the avenues, cut quickly back and forth on cross streets, and looped around the city through the cacao groves and canefields before returning to pass through the Plaza de Armas and park at Villahermosa's modern multiplex cinema. The streets were dark, quiet, and cool, with a spangle of stars visible in the sky. They took their luggage and walked around the corner from the parking lot.

Before Guthrie could knock, the door of a little cantina opened. Heavy curtains covered the windows, but the doorway spilled light and the sharp aroma of peppers and pork into the street around a little old man. He had a bushy white beard and wore a broad straw hat, a long-sleeved white shirt, and old jeans faded to a dusty cream. He grinned, waved them inside, and clapped the wooden door shut behind them.

One long table filled the cantina. A slim Mexican with a bottle of beer in his hand sat at the table. Vasquez had seen him twice before—at the airport when they landed in Villahermosa and paused to rent the Range Rover, and then following them in the city in a chromed Bronco. The same large silver buckle twinkled on his belt, and his sly smile missed a single tooth.

"*Hola, señores y señorita,*" he said. "*El asado, por favor.*"

The old man nodded and ambled into the back of the cantina. The slim man waved at the bottles of unopened beer on the table. The detectives joined him. Guthrie introduced him: Hector Encinas Sanchez, an agent for the AFI assigned to SIEDO, the special unit tasked to organized crime. Encinas was George Livingston's clean police contact.

"I meant to meet you at the airport, but fortunately I hesitated," Encinas said. "This private detective you hired—Carlos Abaroa, no—walked like a *boracho*, a young narco. I stepped back to protect my cover."

Guthrie shrugged. Walker tilted his beer until he emptied it, then wiped his mouth.

"Events proved me correct. Eyes watched your every step," he said. "I slipped a package into your hotel. I meant for you to call me. I would have told you my suspicions—I felt Carlos Abaroa was connected to something. He stayed too close."

"So you plant a green mask?" Vasquez asked. "Why not call?"

Encinas smiled. "El Balam," he said. "We will come to him."

"Take it easy, Rachel," Guthrie said. "We've heard it enough lately: This ain't our country."

"Are you kidding me!"

"Have another beer," Guthrie said softly, staring until she sank back into her seat. He opened another for himself. "It's been a long day, señor."

"I watched," Encinas said.

The conversation churned back and forth as Encinas prodded for an explanation about what happened earlier in the day. Guthrie refused to talk about El Güero or the fight with Abaroa. The Mexican policeman wanted confirmation for his suspicions of the unknown. Watching them jab and circle, Vasquez was gripped again with an urge to tell Guthrie about Duane Parson, but his grim reluctance to share any information with the Mexican policeman provided a final, bitter justification for silence. They ate grilled pork wrapped in soft tortillas. The whitebeard brought them chips and salsa verde, and laughed when they called for more beer.

"The result comes to the same," Encinas said. "This interests us, because now we intersect for the third time. Your killer flew to Villahermosa after some time spent in New York. Los Zetas have made many moves recently, in the reputed absence of El Balam. *Primero*.

"Los Zetas attempted to kill El Balam, after your killer arrived in Villahermosa. Coincidence? *Segundo*.

"Now you find that your killer goes to Yaxchilan," he said. "This is the stronghold of El Balam. *Tercero*." The Mexican policeman counted silently with fingertips and smiled.

"You name your killer Morales," he said. "I do not know him. His brother is a Zeta, but no longer our problem for many years. He is no one. On the other hand, El Balam is a name whispered in Chiapas and Campeche, and across the border in Guatemala, into Honduras and Belize. El Balam is a dream."

"A drug smuggler?" Guthrie asked.

"No. A killer. Los Zetas want him dead because he kills Zetas. He kills loggers, oilmen, archaeologists. He kills anyone foolish enough to stray near the Usumacinta River. Is this Morales? Is this El Balam?"

Guthrie frowned. "Rafael Morales, the older brother that's in prison in New York, told a story about being buried alive in some Mayan ruins. I've had earfuls of crap from every sort of idiot you can imagine, and I took him immediately for telling the truth—or enough of it for me. He claimed his brother was fearless. Does it matter to me if he's a notorious criminal in Mexico? No."

"I like your attitude, Señor Guthrie," the Mexican policeman said, with a bright smile. He opened a fresh beer. "If you were another man, any other gringo, I would call you a fool, laugh, and walk away. Some men here have already misjudged you."

Walker smiled.

"But you should care. We would like to have El Balam, to silence many loud voices calling for his head." The slim Mexican smiled again.

"This all sounds like good news to me," Guthrie said.

Encinas shrugged. "Less good once you understand why we will fail to capture El Balam." He drew pictures on the wooden tabletop with beer.

A coil of the Usumacinta River wrapped the partially restored ruins of Yaxchilan. Tourists visited on rafting trips, or by using a single grass airstrip. The river enclosed a knot of wild space, thick with untamed jungle, birds, snakes, and insects. The Petén wilderness of Guatemala surrounded the loop of river. "I know these things because I have made it my study," he said.

"Most important," he continued, "the Zapatistas consider El Balam a hero." He drank beer, considering. "Yaxchilan is sacred to the Indians. From the old days, El Balam, the true El Balam—that would be like Santa Muerte. El Balam is venerated—not by millions, but venerated. People believe. That is power."

Vasquez made a sour face. "Robin Hood," she muttered.

"Exactly!" Encinas cried.

"How do we get in?" Guthrie asked.

"You feel, señor, that you will go there and find him?"

The little detective scowled. "Does a bear shit in the woods?"

Encinas returned him a blank look.

"That means yes. How do we get in?"

"We drive," Encinas said. "We will drive to Chancala, then to Frontera Corozal. We will take a raft downriver to Yaxchilan. At the ruins, I have a friend." He shrugged. "This might be some small help in accomplishing the impossible: We will capture a dream."

CHAPTER THIRTY-FIVE

After an overnight spent sleeping in a hotel in Chancala, Frontera Corezal passed in a daylight blur of dusty roads sprinkled with gravel, tin-roofed block buildings, and stares from work-stained men. Walker and Guthrie were expert with the rubber raft they bought there. Vasquez and Encinas rode low in the midsection like pieces of baggage. They rode the current for some green miles below the logging settlement, then Guthrie grounded the raft on a sandbar grown thick with grasses, vines, and saplings. The men pulled the raft swiftly into the narrow interior of the sandbar, and Guthrie built a blind with loose netting and scraps of vine and branch. Dragonflies raced above the grasses piercing the sand, propelled by the adulation of a multitude of insects. They waited for the afternoon to wane.

"The water tastes right," Walker said, "but the smell is rotten."

Guthrie smiled. "Limestone ain't ever gonna change. I gotta say this music sounds like a rock concert, though."

Walker nodded. "I think this's what it was like over the water."

Guthrie grunted. His eyes dimmed. Encinas squirmed, slapped at insects, and frowned.

"You ain't got doubts, do you?" Walker asked. He waited, but the little detective didn't say anything. "Danny said that's what marked your dad out from any other man he ever met."

"Danny's full of shit," Guthrie said. "He drinks too damn much."

"Some things never change," Walker said. He glanced at Vasquez, reclining on the raft amid the baggage. The brim of her black hat covered her face except for her mouth and chin. "He still can't take a compliment, can he?"

"Doesn't hand them out, either," she murmured.

"He gets it honest," Walker said. "I didn't know him, but Danny always said Big Clay was that way. Didn't take credit or give it, never doubted himself. The Guthries got more in common with mules than men."

Vasquez smiled.

"I ain't in the mood for ghost stories, Angel," the little detective said.

"Be an end to them if you buried your dead, Clay."

The little detective's breath hissed.

"What about her?" Walker asked. "She asked for it?"

Vasquez shifted her hat. She stared at the men. They stared at each other, while Encinas concentrated carefully on insects. Birds called in the golden afternoon, leisurely about the business of harvesting insects from the swarms above the river clattering beyond the screen of grass on the sandbar. Time slid.

"Big Clay?" Vasquez asked. "How'd he get the short straw?"

"That part ain't fair," Walker said. "Danny called his dad Big Clay, joking, and him Little Clay before they ever went across the water. I think he grew to the same height, but that was already his name." He dodged the little detective's scowl with a smile. "She's family now, ain't she?"

Guthrie grunted sullen assent. "Rachel, we're gonna spend some time looking this over when we get in there," he said. "I ain't in a hurry. Señor Encinas ties him to this spot. I figure that means he keeps coming back if we don't spook him. Walker, you're playing tourist-and-guide with Encinas. I'll tap the radio every three hours—"

"Taking the night like some old mack-vee lurp," Walker muttered. "You wouldn't rather finish this by Monday?"

Guthrie considered the insects above the river. "No. I want him alive."

Walker snorted. "Nice save, though."

Vasquez stared as the two men chuckled at each other. "So this's a seam job, then?" she asked.

"Every takedown's a seam job," Guthrie said.

Vasquez settled back again, and lowered the brim of her hat to hide. After working with Guthrie for half a year, she was accustomed to watching people and waiting for them to screw up. The Morgan case felt like a mirror. Someone was watching her, waiting for her to screw up. A creeping feeling suggested that the waiting was almost over.

Lying in a raft on a sandbar in a muddy river in Central America gave Vasquez an itchy sensation of watching for a moment to spring. This stirred up some sick feelings that would've been dread, but Mexico had already created a new ordinary that walked a line separating fear from frenzy, like a lowrider revving in neutral for the light to change. She listened to the insects.

When Walker kicked her foot to wake her, the sky above the river was already dark. The men wanted her out of the rubber raft before they ported it to the sandy edge. Guthrie spent a half hour afterward erasing signs of their presence, finally slithering into the river like an otter.

The river slashed through the jungle in total darkness, disconnecting Vasquez from everything except the blind ride on the noisy water. The men were silent under the cover of the river. Drops of water from Walker's paddle lighted on her like unexpected kisses when he crossed strokes, and Guthrie whispered directions from the prow that marked progress on the shuddering water with churns when the water boiled on a turn or race.

While the raft flowed downstream, some miles along, the darkness above the river shifted like an unsettled lid. Vasquez decided the change was a figment of her imagination—insects continued to materialize from nothingness and slap her upturned hat brim and face. She felt blind. Guthrie and Walker whispered about the turns and currents of the river, but Encinas was silent. The water argued distantly with rock.

Rising sound loomed like a sheet of coolness before them. The men stroked hard with their paddles, prying at the river's determined grip. Vasquez clutched the gunwales and shielded herself with prayers. The river laughed while the men worked, then sighed while they rested. Cool shapes watched over them in the long minutes of urgency. Vasquez decided that they were rocks.

With some whispered commands, the men tucked the raft against the western bank of the Usumacinta. The raft pogoed as they climbed out. The riverbank glowed with an orchestra of sound in the darkness, layered atop the rush of water.

"Get out!" Guthrie whispered.

"*¿Qué?*" Encinas hissed.

"I can't see," Vasquez said.

Vasquez heard a splashing footstep in water before a hand clutched her mouth. "Don't talk up like that, either of you," Walker whispered. "That could get us killed. We got no idea who's out here with us." His hand disappeared, then gripped her arm and lifted. She felt Encinas beside her, and Walker guided them from the raft across a wet sand strip, then slowly among ankle-high rocks to a firm patch of leafy ground. "Close your eyes," he whispered, then vanished.

Eyes tight shut, Vasquez heard the men shift the rubber raft, less by footsteps than by faint adjustments to the background volume as curious insects paused to decide that the men were harmless. She strained after the shifting volume, like trying to decide which speaker was silent in a crowded club after someone spilled a drink on a bundle of cables. The men appeared suddenly beside her, prodding her hand with her bag.

"He's a cop—what do they know?" Walker whispered. "But you ain't taught her nothing."

"I'll be damned," Guthrie replied. "She ain't listened." His tone compressed with frustration. "Damn it, Rachel, take the switch." He prodded her with a slender branch. "There's spiders out here as wide as your face. Don't take a step without warning them."

Encinas sucked in a breath. Vasquez caught the stick. She felt hammered.

"You can't bust her cherry like this, Clay. This's crazier than splitting sweet gum for stovewood."

"This ain't her cherry," Guthrie hissed. "I don't know what's wrong with her. The past couple of months she ain't listened to a thing I said. I thought she snapped out of it a few weeks ago. I see now I was wrong."

"The clouds ain't helping," Walker breathed.

"They got us in here."

Walker grunted. The jungle wrapped them in sound. Vasquez shut her eyes again and listened. To her right the sound was less, a giant's mouthful missing from the surrounding chorus.

"All right, walk her up there where you can look out, and I'll take him along the bank," Guthrie whispered. His words sank neatly into the sound, like an expert guitarist's rhythmwork. The jungle never wavered.

"Come on, girl," Walker whispered. He tugged at her feeler-switch. "Slow-like up this hill. Lay your hand on my shoulder and you'll know when to step."

The tall Cherokee led her to her right. That quiet amid the jungle's chorus contained a hill. Vasquez guessed her steps by the rise, fall, and shift of his shoulder. She kept her eyes shut, after a glimpse contained only darkness. Once, she clipped his heel with her boot, but she softened her steps until they felt like feathers. Vasquez listened to the jungle and walked.

Walker stopped her by pressing on her shoulder. "Well, then," he whispered. "Ease down here and look about."

Vasquez floated on the darkness and sound for several minutes. Everything else disappeared. The lid of darkness above the jungle unsettled again, but she still thought the texture of the sound revealed more than the marbled darkness. A moment before Guthrie spoke, she knew he had arrived.

"I circled around here," he whispered. "Looked clean, but play it safe. When you take Encinas on downriver, get wet before you land."

"All right," Walker replied.

The little detective tapped Vasquez with his switch. "I'll grant you've had some tough days," he whispered. "I thought about that while I circled round this bit of a hill. But hugs and kisses won't make it better. There ain't no sideline out here to run past for safety. Get it together." He tapped her with the switch again, harder.

"I know," she murmured. "I'm a smart girl. I'll figure it out."

CHAPTER THIRTY-SIX

Guthrie and Vasquez slept overnight in a low cave screened by a curtain of fern, roughly centered in the web of footpaths and stone staircases interlocking the scattered ancient ruins that formed a long crescent along the river. After Walker and Encinas straggled onto the river landing in the dark, a handful of sleepy rescuers assigned them a stilted wooden cabin in the tourist village. Guthrie exchanged brief reports with Walker at midnight and three, but Vasquez slept heavily.

In the morning, Guthrie woke her early. They walked the hillside trails, and he chose each of them a perch to overwatch the ruins. They exchanged silent transmission breaks at six o'clock while they scanned with binoculars. Fog curtained the river at dawn. Vasquez ate two dry packets of instant coffee as she watched people stir at the river. The jungle around her thrummed with insistent, living music.

The cluster of tourist cabins trickled some stiff people to swirl around a shingled bathhouse pavilion. An administrative complex— one long clapboard building with a shed roof facing three snug cabins across a narrow grassy plaza—shuttled a few people from the cabins to the clapboard.

Vasquez suspected some unobserved tooth-brushing, but didn't complain on the radio. Bitter comments about boring stakeouts didn't tickle Guthrie's strange sense of humor. Encinas strolled over to the clapboard and disappeared inside like a distant, tiny puppet, and Walker hiked toward the airstrip. The sun rolled higher.

The Usumacinta boiled between towers of limestone on rough stretches, but beyond the ruined plaza, it slid along beneath out-stretched limbs and vines, twisting like a mud-colored cat with an upturned belly. Faint, drifting smoke among the ruins had a sharper tone than lingering mist. Vasquez peered through her binoculars.

Some brightly dressed Indians appeared in the ruins. A man wearing pinstriped red pants led a group of women from the ruins with a smile. Their patterned dresses shifted like a kaleidoscope around one slender woman wearing her long black hair in a loose tail. Green piping edged a red-and-gold tunic that she wore circled with a belt, above faded blue jeans and knee-high leather boots. Vasquez caught glimpses of a neatly cut jaw and dark eyebrows. Even without a picture, she decided she had found Angela Olivares.

Vasquez stung inside with a pang of loss. Olivares had the unbroken certainty and grace of beauty; she walked with the same smooth assurance that Mamì had in the city, floating on wishful glances like a carpet of flower petals. Watching another woman with it reminded Vasquez of her injury with the suddenness of an itch from a missing hand. Distantly, she realized that Morales must be in the ruins for Olivares to come out and brazenly appropriate the amenities provided for tourists and students. Her hand settled on her radio, but she didn't key a transmission.

When the women reached the pavilion, they began laughing. Their eyes died like silenced birds when Duane Parson walked from the other entrance of the bathhouse. Vasquez stopped breathing. She pulled a pistol without thinking.

The women stared at Parson as he walked past them. The giant turned smoothly on a booted foot when he passed the man in the red pants, and punched him. The small man cartwheeled from the trail and disappeared into some shaggy ferns. His straw hat settled onto the ground. Parson took two quick steps, plowing women to each side, and snatched Olivares by her arm.

On the radio, Guthrie whispered, "I got two Indians with M 16s lounging in one of the doorways of the third pyramid—north side. I doubt you can see them from that angle."

Some women fled the pavilion. A gray-haired white man walked from the bathhouse straightening his shirt, gaped, and faded back inside. The silent chaos jerked with manic frenzy through the binoculars. Parson fished a loop from his coat pocket, holding Olivares at arm's length. She flailed. Her blows fell on air and Parson's outstretched arm. She looked like a child, dangling from his grip; Vasquez dislocated for a queasy moment. While staring through the binoculars, she carefully holstered her sweat-slick pistol.

"Another one, same pyramid—higher up," Guthrie said.

Vasquez keyed her radio in her jacket pocket, then hesitated as Parson whipped the loop in his hand around Olivares's neck. The slender woman kicked like a ballet dancer. Parson gestured at the other women, then hoisted Olivares with the glinting wire in his hand. Her face brightened with blood. A moment later, she drooped, and her pantlegs darkened with piss. Parson studied her swinging figure, then gently lowered her to the dusty ground. The other woman fled.

"*Viejo*, Duane Parson just killed Angela Olivares," she whispered into her headset.

"Repeat that."

"Duane Parson—" Vasquez paused, watching with her binoculars, as Olivares rolled on the ground coughing, clawing at the wire loop on her neck. Parson snatched her to her feet by the streaming black tail of her hair. "She's alive. He's dragging her toward me."

"I see some women running into the ruins—"

"From the bathhouse. He was inside waiting like a spider," Vasquez hissed, trembling. Olivares struggled to maintain her feet, but left the ground in bounding moon-leaps as Parson hustled across the parklike open area, looping around some low knots of ruined limestone and upright stelae, carrying her mostly by her hair. His huge face was angry and grim. He never looked back. The collar of the blue floral shirt peeked like a ruffle from the fastened neck of a long, flowing tan duster.

"Okay, don't lose him," Guthrie said.

Vasquez didn't bother to reply. If Parson ran into the jungle, he would be invisible. She watched the giant while Guthrie sketched quick details about his activities in New York for Encinas. A long, massive hillock crowned with twisting vines barred the giant's path. He strode rapidly through lines of cohune palms, bouncing Olivares like a casual walking stick. Walker reported all clear from the airstrip; no airplane waited there.

Parson paused to look around, then hurried toward a broad lintel of stone layered into the hillock. Tooled limestone crawling with vine and root rose above him like a mockery of his towering forehead, and he strode into the mouth through a missing tooth: a dark square among a mismatched row of similar openings. The hillock humped farther along with hunchback shoulders, then dwindled distantly into a prostrate body. Terraces and stairs of rotten limestone marked rough layers.

"Parson went to ground in one of the ruins," she said.

"We have some more Indians," Guthrie added. "One of the women collapsed." He paused. "A lot more Indians. Not all of them are carrying M 16s."

The Indians spread like angry ants. They soon found one of the other women, who had followed and watched Parson enter the ruin. She pointed to the terrace and doorway. The silent urgency of her gestures hollowed Vasquez's guts. Walker raced back from the airstrip. Guthrie counted Indians. Smoke trickled from a dark fissure in the hillock splitting terraces of limestone like the stroke of some weighty blade.

"Something's burning inside the hill," Vasquez said.

Encinas opened the door of the clapboard building and walked out. A short, fat man wearing blue jeans and a white work shirt followed him, speaking rapidly and ticking points on his fingers.

"I got Morales," Guthrie said. "Just walked out from the north side of the pyramid. No way I get a shot from here through all those Indians."

Brightly colored Indians swirled. Three pulled the body from the ferns by the bathhouse pavilion. Parson had killed the man with a single punch. Another man claimed the pistol hidden beneath the dead man's serape. Other men drew machetes. The Indians converged on the vine-clad ruin, dividing into a half-dozen bands. Some riflemen perched nearby, while others raced around the hillock.

"Morales is going into the hill," Vasquez said. She watched the tall Mexican disappear into the same opening Parson had used. Indians slipped into other openings, while more settled to watch. The ruins fell still.

"Clever rat," Guthrie muttered on the radio. "But he ain't wiggling back out of there."

"Señores y señorita, a conversation," Encinas said. "Perhaps you will come to me here?"

"Affirmative," Walker replied.

After a pause, Guthrie agreed. Four gunshots echoed through the ruins before the detectives gathered in the clapboard building. They huddled around a tattered paper map unrolled on a tabletop. The resident archaeologist joined them, the same short, dark man with cropped black hair and a narrow mustache that Vasquez had seen with Encinas earlier. His gaze flinched away from Vasquez's bruised face; he kept his eyes on the map while they spoke.

"Dr. Gonzalez, these are the detectives from New York," Encinas said. He watched Guthrie fret beside the table, muttering while he checked his equipment, lingering over the air gun at the back of his belt. Walker studied the map after spending one glance on the little detective.

"Señor, you have plans?" Encinas asked.

"I'm going in there to get Morales."

"You are insane," Encinas said flatly.

The archaeologist flinched at the sound of a pair of muffled gunshots.

"Ain't much choice left," Guthrie said. "I didn't come down here to walk away empty-handed." The Mexican policeman's expression didn't change, so he continued. "This's what I see right now: Parson spooked the game. I don't know how in hell he got here in front of me. Maybe he dropped from the sky." Anger clipped his words, and he chopped at the air with his fingertips.

Vasquez turned and looked from the window to hide her face. Guthrie glanced at her, frowned, then said, "There's a lot of men out there. Parson thought like a killer—he went for the soft spot. That gets him a round with Morales. Sure, I could stand back and wait to see who comes out. That's what you're thinking?"

Encinas nodded, adding a shrug and upraised palms for emphasis. "You spoke earlier of this man—he is no friend. You mean to rescue him?"

"I don't see it, either," Walker said.

"I want Morales alive. He killed Abraham Swabe." Guthrie smiled, with a sad twist that made his bricklike face almost human. He kissed his fingertips.

Walker looked down quickly to study the map again. He nodded. More gunshots cracked. Vasquez watched the wind stirring the tips of the distant green jungle, blurring them into an endless dark mass. She checked her pistols again. Her hands felt as light as feathers.

"So if Morales comes out, I can see that there's more than one entrance. I can't set up on him in the open. All those men would get a shot at me. Then it's a sure thing he's bolting from here as soon as he comes out. His next move will be checking his backtrail to see how Parson got here, and he'll find our tracks in Villahermosa. I won't get a chance to take him slow again, now that Parson spooked him, and he ain't getting a chance to stalk me. I'll get him here. This is our one moment. You see that?"

"You are insane," Encinas whispered.

"You're welcome to jump from the train," Guthrie said.

Walker laughed. Guthrie grinned like a shark. The Mexicans stared. Vasquez lingered at the window, looking through it for nonexistent answers. The limestone ruins glowed in the morning sunshine like weathered bone.

The young Puerto Rican woman stood balanced on the edge of a knife. Tough talk was street music, but coming again to the moment of walking into the open with a pistol in her hand stole the strength from her legs. Fighting without a warning was easier. When Guthrie had cornered Gagneau in the Adirondacks, Vasquez didn't know better. The dark hole in the hillside beyond the window held an echoing promise of pain. She stroked her jaw with her fingertips and balanced.

"This mound lacks an impressive superstructure," Gonzalez said, tracing a shape on his map. "Looters cut into it repeatedly, but we have left it untouched—"

"Tell them about the Indians," Encinas said. "You and I are interested in this past, but we have no time to explain."

The archaeologist nodded. "The Lancandon revere Yaxchilan as the home of their ancestors. Many other Maya . . ." The short man sagged under the policeman's sharp gaze. "I apologize. The Indians come and make sacrifices like ancient pagans, but still claim to know Jesus. This mound may belong to the jaguar, the original jaguar."

He tapped the map. "Garcia Moll believed Shield Jaguar was buried beneath this structure. That old man knew more about the Maya than anyone else. An alignment of stelae includes monuments in Guatemala . . ." The short man shivered at the sound of more muffled gunshots.

"Elsewhere the Indians might sacrifice a chicken, some cornmeal, some tequila, drink *chipote*, smear blood on the altars. Here, I think they seek to fill the looters' trenches with human bones." His voice sank to a whisper. "I have seen severed hands and feet. Those did not come from monkeys."

"No one's mapped the inside of that mound?" Guthrie asked.

"Garcia Moll claimed that two staircases balanced the interior. There were chambers. He was forced to hurry." Gonzalez shrugged. "Indians."

Encinas nodded. "You understand, señores?" His gaze flicked over Guthrie and Walker.

"That don't change nothing," the little detective said. He checked the air gun tucked beneath his jacket again.

Encinas sighed. "I will call my superiors. They will send soldiers. If we wait a few hours?"

"Angel, you got enough bullets?"

Walker shrugged.

"Very well," Encinas said. "They will come eventually." He looked at Vasquez, still as sculpture at the window, and continued in a whisper, *"Al menos La Niña Blanca está con nosotros."*

CHAPTER THIRTY-SEVEN

The jungle above the ruins of Yaxchilan hovered in the watchful silence between gunshots. Tall mahoganies peered down on the open, grassy plaza where palms watched and fanned in the morning breeze. The birds were quiet. Guthrie led the way through the ruins. A few tourists, students, and scientists hiding in the clapboard building watched them go from behind dark windows.

The little detective paused behind a screening line of palms, watching the Indians knotted on the crumbled margin of the low, broad ruin. Two marksmen with M 16s were perched in doorways on the pyramid looming to the west of the ruin. The brims of straw hats hid their eyes, but they stroked their rifles with impatient brown hands.

"They thought too hard," Guthrie said on the radio. "I believe they're watching four entrances—those two doorways along that terrace, that other one high up, and that slit trench. See the other men set there?"

A few Indians waited close by each entrance, smoking cigarettes. Some strode back and forth. A few had pistols tucked in their belts, but none carried a rifle. Many carried machetes.

"Down there at the trench, I don't believe they can see that, past that stand of cedar," Guthrie said. "Take a look, Angel. What do you think?"

Walker crept forward and looked. An arm's length behind the little detective, Vasquez studied the waiting marksmen, the tangle of trees, and the trench. She smiled. The marksmen could see the doors higher on the ruin, but not the foot of the trench. Walker nodded.

The Indians watched the ruin. The detectives watched the Indians as Guthrie led them, along cover, around the tangle of cedar and thorny escoba palm. Cheap tobacco smoke floated atop an odor of rotten meat. A thin line of round lumps of limestone marked a trail through the tangle, brushed continually by the outstretched fingertips of cedar. Guthrie parted the way slowly with his switch and came to a dark disk of limestone, carved in some ancient time and now decorated with machete strokes and lingering flies.

Guthrie drew a revolver when he stepped from the thicket. Two men saw him immediately and lifted their machetes. One spared a quick glance for the gloomy depth of the trench. Guthrie waved them away with his switch. Vasquez stepped from the thicket behind him and drew a pistol. They wavered.

Another man stepped around the dull limestone pillar edging the root-twined base of the hillock. A cigarette dangled from his mouth. He snatched his machete from his belt. "*¡Por aquí, hombre!*" he shouted.

Guthrie shot him above the belt buckle and he folded with a squeal. The shot had the flat sound of a blue bullet. The other men turned and ran. One dropped his machete. Guthrie waved the other detectives toward the trench as they slipped from the thicket. They hustled across the open space. A yellow kiskadee fluttered from the root-tangled stonework as they slipped into the dark, narrow trench.

The hillock towered above them. Vasquez catfooted in the darkness an arm's length behind Guthrie, followed by Encinas and Walker. Twisted roots supported walls of raw earth that alternated with columns of neatly cut stone blocks. A rotten stench filled the narrow, sloping trench, which descended into a mess of tumbled stones and tangles of hard sticks that slithered beneath Vasquez's feet. Dust spilled from the walls when she brushed them. Encinas coughed behind her.

Dim shouts from outside chased them into deeper darkness, where scattered light from high above trickled down into the trench. After a slow curve, Guthrie paused to listen and Vasquez knelt to rest her trembling legs. Faint shouts buzzed like distant insects. The trench sighed with moving air carrying wood smoke and the smell of coconut without wiping away the rot. In the dim light, the sticks transformed into glowing bones beneath her feet. She lifted an arching rib that drank the sweat from her palm.

"There are many dead men here," Encinas said softly.

Guthrie hissed for quiet. A rattle of stones trickled along the trench from behind them. Walker tossed a bone into the dusty darkness. Gunshots banged, hellishly loud between the unevenly cut walls. Light flickered briefly.

The detectives hustled along the trench, still sloping down, and tumbled into a broad space floored with stone. The trench continued, dark across the ceiling. Faint light showed an oblong chamber with a yawning door. Guthrie rolled, and flicked a handlight: a blue and ochre mural glowed on the far plaster wall, with a long-nosed blue dancer balancing on tiptoe with a battle-axe to hold back from the ruin of the trench.

Vasquez hurried across the smooth stone and bumped into Guthrie at the doorway. He brushed her down into a crouch with an extended hand. A mutter of low words whispered in the chamber, which smelled strongly of wood smoke. Stones clattered from the trench behind them. A shouted command hammered at the darkness.

The doorway opened onto a landing. A broad stairwell zigzagged around a wide carved block of stone. Massive sigils grinned down at Vasquez, sharp-edged against dark stone in the faint light from the trench splitting the chamber ceiling. Distant gunshots sounded like handclaps escaping the earth. She decided that the smoke was coming through the doorway. A rush of footsteps sounded on the stone stairs above the landing.

Guthrie cursed softly as he frog-walked through the doorway. Light bloomed and pulsed from the higher landing.

"Which way?" Walker asked.

"We go down," Guthrie said. "They're searching above us, not finding anybody."

A crumble of masonry slid from the trench into the room. Encinas whirled through the door. Vasquez slid around the corner and pressed against the dark stones in the stairwell.

"Quite a few behind us," Walker whispered.

Guthrie gestured with his revolver. "Some more up the stairs."

"I got them here in this corner." Walker pulled a Colt from his belt.

Booted feet landed in the chamber as Guthrie considered. Walker leaned through the doorway and fired twice. The man rolled along the floor into a sprawl. Shouts, running, and a cascade of blind gunshots from the trench battered the darkness. The stairwell reverberated. The little detective caught Vasquez's sleeve, tugged, and turned down the stairs. Encinas followed. Strobes of gunfire lit their way. A rattle of automatic-rifle shots ricocheted and vanished, pluming chips from the limestone and plaster. They hurried.

The stairwell wound around a massive rectangular pillar, with stairs on each long side and landings on each short side. A pause in the gunfire lengthened into menacing quiet, broken by footsteps, bootscrapes, and heavy breathing atop a low murmur almost silent from distance. As Vasquez crossed the second landing, feeling her way with a hand on the cold stone pillar, another barrage of shots thundered in the staircase. A ricochet slapped around the stairwell like an angry hornet.

On the third landing a doorway leaked distant light. Guthrie paused at the edge of the opening. Vasquez slipped past. The opening smelled like coconut and woodsmoke: the murmur was louder.

Walker chuckled on the radio. "They could have changed their minds a little sooner," he said. "I would have come along down there, Clay."

"Right down the stairs."

Walker chuckled again. Downstairs, they listened. Gunshots came again, muffled by yards of earth, stone, and darkness. Guthrie sighed. Vasquez peered through the doorway, down a corridor of rough masonry that bent in the distance. Gaps of darkness ribbed its stony sides. Crumbled plaster softened the edges of the floor. Vague shapes rode in a long canoe in a faded remnant of mural on the wall.

The little detective shuffled forward into the corridor, leading them slowly along. He paused to listen, and studied how light leaked around the bend of the corridor without wavering. More gunshots poured down the stairs, and he led them in a rush. Vasquez paused at the inky darkness of a cross-corridor, but the air was dead and still. The murmur clarified into distinct syllables of rhythmic nonsense. Guthrie lunged forward to the corner and risked a glance. He looked very small, crouched at the corner of the rough stone wall.

Vasquez and Encinas slipped forward to join him. Walker breathed a slow whistle on the radio, then said, "I do believe there's a long line of men up here waiting for trouble. I might be encouraged to see the Mexican army."

"Maybe we should hope they bore easy and wander off," Guthrie muttered. He glanced around the corner again. The murmur drifted like an aimless conversation, or a disinterested man reading monotonously aloud from a book. The light made sharp, gruesome shadows on the glyphs carved into the corner post of the wall.

Vasquez eased into a crouch and rounded Guthrie's shoulder. A jagged doorway, black with soot stains, framed a chamber full of harsh light. The voice drifted on a stream of dark wood smoke from the chamber.

Encinas crouched behind Guthrie. "That is Maya," he whispered. "I understand some of the chant."

"Dangerous?"

The policeman shrugged. "Flowing water, earth, sky, ancient gods—"

He fell silent when Guthrie slipped forward. Vasquez followed, drawing and cuffing a pistol at her side. Harsh green light hissed from a railroad flare on the stone floor. A broad, grilled brazier glowed with heat; streaming smoke puddled on the ceiling, then poured from the chamber. Air wheezed through the doorways.

The rising light cast misplaced shadows on the walls, where the long-nosed blue dancer crept, whirled, and sang with his battle-axe. A skinny, wrinkled old man with stringy locks of white hair sat cross-legged, chanting in a hoarse voice. The low dark slab beneath him swirled with intricate carvings. He didn't notice the detectives; he was blind. A clear crystal, as bright as a soap bubble, balanced on the tip of his outstretched finger.

"Zaztun," Encinas whispered. Guthrie eased into the chamber. Vasquez and Encinas slipped in behind him. Beyond the old man a dark, open doorway beckoned.

A waist-high boy appeared in the corner, announced by a clatter of firewood dropped onto the stone floor. Bright bars of color marked his poncho and he wore a straw hat with a tightly curled brim. A heavy gourd swung by a rope at his side. A furry brown snout poked from the gourd, followed by dark eyes and small round furry ears.

The old man chanted without pausing, balancing the crystal on his finger. Guthrie walked toward the door. The boy drew a small Uzi from beneath his poncho and leveled it at the detectives. He barked a command. They froze.

Encinas raised his hands. "Raise your hands," he hissed.

The boy stabbed with the muzzle of the Uzi and barked again. A jaguarundi poured sinuously from the gourd, paused to sniff suspiciously, then padded across to the old man on his slab of dark stone. The old man chanted without breaking. Vasquez and Guthrie traded a glance, then slowly raised their hands—still holding their pistols. The boy's grim expression didn't change.

Encinas tried a hesitant phrase. The boy scowled, shook his head, and replied at length.

"What'd he say?" Guthrie asked.

"He said white people are bad luck, and I'm probably cursed." The Mexican policeman smiled unhappily. "The last white man here dropped the flare."

"Parson," Vasquez breathed.

Chanting, the old man hoisted his hand. The crystal balanced on the tip of his extended finger. Beaded sweat dripped from his forehead. The jaguarundi padded around the slab, paused, then bounded toward the detectives.

"Don't move," Encinas whispered urgently.

"You ain't gonna try more talking?" Guthrie asked. "We're gonna go with a sniff test?"

Encinas glared, then began speaking haltingly. After pausing at Guthrie's feet, the jaguarundi caught the hem of Vasquez's pantleg and tugged. She hissed at it. It looked up at her, flicked its ears, then ambled back to the boy. He smiled and spoke briefly.

"Okay, go with the sniff test," Guthrie whispered.

Encinas shook his head. He spoke some more. The boy scowled again. The old man chanted roughly, syncopated by a few muffled gunshots. Vasquez peered at the doorway beyond the old man, but the light in the chamber spoiled her vision. Faint cries of pain leaked through the darkness.

The boy spoke again, punctuating with jabs of his Uzi.

"Señor, take the flare," Encinas said. "Slowly."

The little detective nodded. He kept his hands raised while he walked, then dangled his revolver from his forefinger by the trigger guard while he bent to take the flare. Vasquez studied the boy, measuring his narrowed eyes, tightened jaw, and unmoving hands. She considered a sudden drop with her aching arm and a single shot to knock him from his feet, but waited, held fast by the Uzi's snake-eye gleam. Guthrie straightened with the flare and raised his hands.

The boy spoke. Encinas tightened. Vasquez poised with the gunshot waiting in her imagination. The old man rasped a long, sibilant phrase, lowering the crystal.

"Go," Encinas said. "Through the door."

"What is it you ain't saying?"

"He says you both can go, and take your bad luck through the door to death."

The boy barked a command.

"I have to go back, through the other door," Encinas whispered. "The door to life."

"The door we came in." Guthrie smiled. The old man chanted, dropping to a purr between clicks of his stained, ancient teeth. Encinas nodded.

Guthrie studied the boy. "He's gonna shoot us. I ain't come here to kill him, so you better go back."

The Mexican policeman nodded and turned away.

CHAPTER THIRTY-EIGHT

Beyond the door, moans and soft laughter tainted the darkness in a stone corridor running left and right. Guthrie tossed the flare. It bounced once and disappeared around the corner to the right. Vasquez slid left, staying on the outer wall until she could see past the corner. The darkness was thick. She drew back and closed her eyes, listening to orient herself. Guthrie's boots scuffed on the stone floor; she sensed him pause at the corner almost within reach.

"Stay behind me," he whispered.

Vasquez supplied the little detective with a grim look in her imagination. She opened her eyes. The far corner was backlit brilliantly by the flare. Smoke and chanting gushed from the doorway. Around the corner, a wide space opened beneath a crumbling ceiling. Debris littered the floor between some neat stacks of squared limestone blocks. Faint light from the far end of the room and two arched entryways brushed gray edges on the dark stones. The little detective slipped around the corner. Vasquez waited a moment, then followed.

Whimpers of pain drowned the old man's hoarse chanting after the detectives rounded the corner. Guthrie crept forward, watching the entryways. Behind a pile of blocks, a man lay with his hand out-stretched, clawing vainly for a machete that lay beyond his grasp. He sucked quick breaths that escaped as whimpers. A ribbon of blood darkened his lips and nose, making a cross with his narrow mustache. Vasquez paused at the pile of blocks.

Another man lay silent at the base of the wall. The limestone blocks above him were a bright, fresh machete stroke, with a drool of blood hanging from one end. Everything above the dead man's mustache was missing from his head. A broad pool of blood enclosed his body. Vasquez dodged around the pool. A burst of rough laughter came from the far entry.

"*Ella está aquí*," Parson said roughly, his voice distant.

Vasquez's blood turned cold. She drew her other pistol and pressed the cool metal to her lips like a crucifix.

"Let her go, *cabrón*!" The challenge came clearly from the near entry, and more softly from the farther one.

"Are you ready to die?" Parson demanded.

Several silent moments passed as Guthrie crept across the mouths of both arched entryways, pausing only a moment at each. A few barks of rough laughter broke the silence. Vasquez paused, heart hammering, at the first arch. She glanced into the darkness beyond the carved stone arch.

"I'm waiting . . ." Parson scraped the words out with mockery.

Vasquez spooked, dashing across the room to catch Guthrie. More laughter chased her. Morales shouted curses. The killers hunted each other beyond the entryways, but the little detective crossed to the far doorway. He drew the air pistol with the tranquilizer dart. The light in the doorway was stronger, tainted with green like from another flare. He aimed a scowl at Vasquez.

"Are you lost?" More laughter. "She is waiting, *not* so patiently." A soprano wail of fright cut the air like fingernails on a blackboard.

Thudding footsteps hammered, echoing through the entryways, then limestone smashed and shattered like glass. Gunshots boomed in the walled space. Wild laughter answered.

"Almost, little man . . . Almost." Parson sounded disappointed.

"¡*Puto animal!*"

Guthrie crept through the doorway, a small silhouette against the hissing light. A stack of skulls was carved on the door frame. The corridor beyond the door bent back, mirror shaped, a bracket for the space beyond the arches where Morales and Parson hunted. Smoke dribbled along the ceiling, already thick with soot. After the detectives entered the corridor, they heard faint whimpering. The light at the far corner burned brilliant and green.

A single gunshot boomed, hardening the following silence. Guthrie strode to the far turn of the corridor, bypassing the door that led left. He glanced around the corner, immediately ducking back. Vasquez followed. The whimper sounded like a woman. Guthrie pressed a hand to Vasquez's shoulder to hold her back. In the brilliant light, she could see blood spattered on the wall around the corner. An outstretched leg, limp as a dirty rag, nestled at the base of the wall.

The little detective slipped around the corner, and Vasquez clung to his heels, almost placing her boots beneath his feet. He didn't pause. The smoky air tasted like blood. The flare nestled against the wall beyond a battered body. Startled by the rising light, carved stone faces on the limestone wall drooled blood onto the body. The floor fell a handful of feet to a rubbled mess. A walkway clung to the walls in each direction.

At the far end of the chamber, Guthrie's discarded flare backlit the ruined chamber. The archways through the middle wall swallowed the light into endless darkness. Four massive oblong piers divided the chamber lengthwise into unequal spaces. Stacked towers of rough-cut stone dotted the gaping middle of the chamber, where the floor had been stripped away. Along the center of the chamber, broad stones paved a space like a roadway, with gaping craters of darkness that swallowed a stairway at the near end. Interlocking bars of shadow marched on the piers and walls.

An iron spike was hammered into the limestone wall, across the broad rubbled hole, between the corner and the first arched entryway. A gleaming wire hung from the spike, looped around Angela Olivares's throat. She balanced tiptoed on a short stack of rough limestone blocks, clawing fruitlessly at the wire. Her tunic was stained with blood.

A stone the size of a brick sailed from the darkness and shattered against the wall beyond her. She teetered, and Parson applauded with wild laughter. Morales cursed.

"Get some cover," Guthrie said softly as he holstered his revolver.

Vasquez abandoned the walkway at the chamber edge, dropping into the rough-floored hole. She darted for the nearest stack of stone. Guthrie drew his other revolver when she looked back, and leveled it at Olivares hanging in the back corner. Clawing at the wire looped on her throat, she didn't notice the detectives.

Vasquez slid to her knees and plowed into the stones. Guthrie fired. The flash lit a mask of fury on his face; his bullet severed the wire. Olivares dropped, rolled into a ball, and settled limply on the walkway.

Two more shots rang out. One whirled Guthrie into the wall, and the second tore a pale gouge in the limestone. The little detective bounced from the wall, losing his fedora, rolled on the walkway, and then dribbled into the pit. He aimed a puzzled look at Vasquez, gripping his revolver and the air gun.

"You didn't get him?" he demanded. Blood trickled from his mouth.

Vasquez stared. The little detective pulled himself into a crouch without releasing his weapons. He scanned the shadowy, crowded pit while he moved. The light was above them, as if they were immersed in a pool of darkness, straining upward for a breath of light. A speckle of blood darkened the shoulder of his white working shirt, beneath the edge of his dark green utility vest. More blood appeared at his waist like a crimson belt.

Guthrie scowled. "It's nothing," he said. He hustled forward to a stack of limestone blocks, and peered around the corner.

"*Lástima, mi amigo, yo creo que fallaste.*"

Morales cursed. Heavy footsteps followed, and then a stone crashed. Parson laughed. Gunshots threw light on the crumbled side of the far pier. Guthrie frog-walked to the corner of the broad pit, passing the stairwell down into darkness. He sighted along the extended barrel of the airgun, then drooped behind a towering stack of blocks, cuffing the gun. The white crescent of his shirt between his vest and pants was motley with blood.

Vasquez trailed him, but instead of passing the stairs, she darted down them. The limestone slabs roofed a wide trench leading into darkness, faintly lit at the far end where it was also uncapped. She paused on the stairs, crouching. Beneath her black hat, she vanished into the darkness. She listened.

Heavy boots scuffed on stone. A stone slapped the wall beside one arched entry, then bounced back into the pit. Vasquez fired twice with her .45-caliber Special but Parson rolled behind some stones.

"Stop it, that tickles!" He laughed.

Morales fired a barrage of shots. Bullets ricocheted before stopping in the raw earth beneath the walkway edging the wall. The following silence was grim with his determination. Guthrie slipped forward to the next stack of rough blocks, moving toward the arched entries.

Niches lined the dark trench beneath the broad slabs of limestone. Vasquez glanced down again, then scuttled beneath the overhang. Forced to crouch, her boots stirred the litter in the trench while her hat brushed at the stone above. She hurried. A heavy blanket of silence wrapped her, and darkness was her pillow. In her imagination, bones snapped beneath her boots and clung to her ankles. The light ahead seemed too far away. When she heard Parson's laughter above the slash of her footsteps in the trench litter, she paused to reload her Special. Slick palms and the uncertainty of darkness stretched the pause until her heart churned with the memory of the blood wetting Guthrie's waist. She rushed.

Vasquez boiled up the steps at the distant end of the trench. The darkness of the shadowed pit seemed more like daylight to her. Parson heaved a stone toward the near archway, then wound up another before the first crashed. She didn't look for his target. Her arm snaked out atop the bridging slab of stone, caked with grave dust, and she fired. The giant's tan duster plumed at each shot. He staggered, spilling an oblong stone from his hand.

Morales darted from the archway with a pistol extended. Before the killer leaped from the walkway into the shadow-barred pit, Guthrie shot him with the air gun. The report sounded like a handclap. The Mexican twisted in midair, fired twice at the little detective, then fired a handful of shots at Parson as he stumbled to a halt. He staggered into one of the piers and brushed the tranquilizer dart away.

Rough laughter replaced the gunshots. Parson spun around the pier; Morales fired one shot into the giant's broad chest and then his pistol locked open. Vasquez dropped her soft-loaded. .40-caliber Special, and reloaded her .45, catfooting up the stairs as her hands worked.

"*Que lástima, mi muchacho,*" Parson said. He grinned and slid a pistol from his pocket. "Here's a trick I learned from Mother."

Resting against the earth wall of the pit, Guthrie hooked his elbow and shoulder over the edge for support. He propped his forehead on the frame of his revolver, but the air gun dropped from his dangling left hand. He wheezed blood.

The giant hammered Morales with shots. Blood spattered the flashlit sigils on the pier. Morales jerked and fell. The giant turned, vaulted onto the walkway, and lunged for the arched entryway. Guthrie leveled his revolver and fired twice. Parson roared, thudding on the stones of the hallway. A bark of laughter died quickly.

Vasquez rushed down the length of the pit to the little detective. He slid down onto the dirt and jumbled stones. Kneeling, she rolled him onto his back. A gasp slick with blood escaped him.

"I shot his knees out, Rachel," he hissed. "Damn rat won't get far."

She dropped her pistol and ripped his vest open. The white shirt was dark with blood. His eyes drifted onto nothingness. She ripped the shirt aside and listened to his chest, heard his heart, and rose again with one bloodied cheek. A dark hole bubbled in his chest. She pressed a fingertip to the wound, harder, and her finger slid inside his chest. He sighed softly.

She shook his chin with her free hand. "*Viejo!*"

The little detective's eyes lit. He sucked air like a swimmer.

"*Eres estúpido,*" she breathed. She drew her knife, flicked it open, and abandoned the dike in his chest. The dark hole bubbled in the long moments she needed to yank free her shirttail, cut a wad, and stuff the oozing hole. The little detective sucked air and grinned like a surfacing shark. She sliced his shirt free of his bleeding shoulder; a fingertip's pressure dammed the trickle. She dressed the hole and pocketed her bloody knife.

"Rat got Morales?" Guthrie breathed.

"Shut up, will you?" Vasquez said. "I got this."

"How about the girl? Check on her . . ."

The young Puerto Rican rose to her feet, stepped around Guthrie, and vaulted gently onto the walkway. The chamber was quiet enough to hear the old man's hoarse chanting. Olivares was crawling slowly from her dark corner toward the burning flare, but Morales was sprawled at the base of the heavy pier in the pit.

Vasquez felt like she was wrapped in flames. Flecks of Parson's blood pointed at the dark entryway. She paused at the corner, listened, and heard the giant gasping for breath in the darkness. She drew the Colt from her utility vest; once she gripped the pistol, she felt volcanic, burned away by rage. The black bullets would have pierced the giant's vest, but she had unthinkingly held on to her Special.

She strode forward. Beyond the archway, Parson had drawn himself up against a squared stack of rough limestone blocks, with his bloody legs outstretched in front of him. Seated, his size wasn't apparent. He was tightening some hasty bandages.

"Miss Vasquez," he said softly, "I could certainly use some help. A crutch of some sort—" He paused when she stretched out the pistol.

"I did *not* kill her—" His hands lurched up in supplication.

Vasquez fired three shots through his hands into his heavy, twisted face. The bullets jolted him, but didn't bounce him from the stones. He sagged. Blood poured like water from the wounds, drenching the front of his duster in seconds. She stepped closer and set the muzzle of the Colt on the crown of his shaggy head as gently as a kiss. Stillness and silence.

Trembling, Vasquez turned away. Blood flowed on the stones, stretching out like a satin sheet in the darkness. She hurried back toward the light in the other chamber. She felt relieved and safe, but riding beneath the rush of that warm surf was an undertow of cold fear.

Months before, while she hid in a hospital bed in the city, Tommy Johnson had visited her again and again. He was hokey but cute, a big dumb blond stereotype that insults and silence couldn't drive away. Vasquez wore bandages for a mask, fighting discharge with complaints about pain. She didn't want to see any more of the bright light of summer. The blinds stayed drawn in her hospital room.

"I should have killed him," Vasquez said bitterly, one time when Tommy stood at the window, sipping brief glimpses of First Avenue outside Bellevue.

"You mean Gagneau," he said.

"Yes!" she hissed. "Who else?"

Tommy nodded. Gagneau had hurt her, almost killed her.

"If I get that chance again, I'll kill him," she said.

"Gagneau's never leaving prison," Tommy said.

"Not him. Anyone like him."

Tommy nodded again.

"You're a prick," she said. She rolled over and faced away from the window. She watched the light rise on the wall as he peeled the curtain and took a quick look at the avenue.

"My grandfather shot himself in the head," Tommy said. "He was a drunk. He emptied a straight fifth of Maker's Mark every day before sundown. I suppose that could be a lie. He died a long time before I was born.

"My dad knew him, at least. He was born in 1968. He was seven when my grandfather died," he continued. "I thought about that a lot. My father fell from a bridge and drowned in 1987. I didn't draw my first breath until 1988 so I didn't ever see him. He was drunk. Or maybe he was a drunk. Maybe he jumped. I ain't decided if there's a difference. When I was fourteen, I had a man get drunk and say to me that my mother didn't want my dad."

Vasquez watched the light rise and fall on the wall.

"That man still had a few teeth when he woke up in the morning," he muttered. "I wanted a father so bad."

Vasquez closed her eyes, but she could still hear the curtain move.

"There can be a long gap between what you want for and what you get," he said. "That won't get it back once it's done."

The dark arch spit Vasquez back onto the walkway, looking down at Morales. His corpse lay in deep shadow behind the rotten pier. Vasquez uncocked the Colt, slid it back into her utility vest, and dropped into the pit. Guthrie waved his fingers.

"The woman's alive," she said, glancing back across at the walkway.

"I'm cold," he said softly.

She stripped off her jacket and utility vest and draped him. The radio blurted a hiss, then Walker said, "You all right down there, Clay? This Encinas ain't a bad shot. We're foursquare up top."

"Come down here and get me. I'm hurt."

The radio hissed. "Señor, some men and helicopters are coming from Chiapas. Thirty minutes more."

"I'm afraid they need a bag for Morales. The rat got him. Angel, will you save some breath? You're gonna need it to carry me."

"You little bastard."

"It's good to know you still care."

CHAPTER THIRTY-NINE

On Friday, nine days before Christmas, the city was completely decorated with lights and snow. Tommy Johnson's rusty red Challenger slid through downtown traffic that jerked and pulsed like flurries of snow. Tommy paused to let Vasquez out on Chambers Street, and she bolted up the steps of the Surrogate Court. Inside, the dark polished corridors led upward to a conference room.

"Thank you for coming so early," William Sinclair said as Vasquez settled at the conference table. He spread Ludlow's journals and some papers on the tabletop. "Your report is very good, but it can't answer questions."

Vasquez nodded. She placed her palmtop beside the red file she brought for the meeting. "I get it, Mr. Sinclair," she said. The final day for filing Stephanie Morgan's will would fall on the following Monday.

The silver-haired lawyer grilled her, taking notes to master the details of the report. He practiced unraveling the coded dates in the journals, and they reviewed the video of Amanda Troubiano, Ludlow's first wife from Bruin, Pennsylvania. Using the journals and visa records, Vasquez had uncovered their marriage in Malta during a summer holiday from college. At the interview, Troubiano had cried with relief when Vasquez told her that Ludlow was dead. The bigamy voided his marriage to Stephanie Morgan and erased his claim to her estate. After an hour, the details were fine hash.

"Miss Vasquez, you do remarkable work," Sinclair said.

Vasquez nodded. She drifted to the window, looked out, and smiled. Tommy was shadowboxing a marble pillar across the street to keep warm. His unbuttoned peacoat wagged like a tail as he snapped jabs and crosses.

"Our managing partner authorized a special fee for your services," Sinclair said. He pulled an envelope from his vest pocket.

Vasquez turned back from the window. "I hope he made it out to Clayton Guthrie Detective Agency," she said.

"I felt this should go specifically to you." Sinclair shrugged meaningfully. He opened the envelope and slid the check onto the tabletop.

She drifted back to the table and bent to examine the check. "That's a lot of zeroes," she said quietly.

"Our managing partner raised the question whether you might be interested in a specific arrangement."

Vasquez pushed the check back with a fingertip. "The old man pays pretty good," she said. "You better put his name on that." She floated back to the window and looked out. Behind her, William Sinclair looked faintly pleased as he pocketed the check.

She looked down, admiring Tommy's brisk stride and how he blew into his cupped fists. Her heart hit a quick drumroll when he paused for a flurry of punches. She smiled. He was becoming impatient. Sometimes he was more fun when he was impatient.

"Let's go through the journal again, Mr. Sinclair," she said as she turned back to the table. "I want to make sure you got it." She smiled, thinking about Tommy's patience. "That might be enough."

ACKNOWLEDGMENTS

I owe my best moments to God; I owe my good moments to others; the moments best unmentioned are all mine. Some of those others—

Toni Plummer and Sarah Weinman: Thanks for the encouragement, swift corrective kicks, and ice-cold buckets of honesty. That feels like sunshine to me.

Dr. Leung Teung, Richard Guerrera, and Richard Almogabar: Thank you for the courage it needed to teach the *quai loh*, for surviving the war with your determination unbroken, and for walking through the wire for me.

Jason Hunt and Dewayne Stafford: One is always there and the other is the only one who bothered. Thanks for brothers everywhere.

Janice Hill: Thank you for catching me when I fell. Good-bye for a while, Little Momma; I'll see you soon and very soon.